# THE DEAL

Henry steered Ellie through the château's living room, into the bedroom. In the soft glow of a night lamp, Raymond and Jill lay on the bed. Both were naked, their limbs entwined, faces buried in each other.

Ellie gasped.

Raymond looked up. "Thought you two would never get here. Come on, get naked."

"Damn you, Henry!" Ellie cried. She felt her self-control thinning out, fear of what she might be forced to do, what she might want to do, replacing her resolve. "I want to leave, Henry. Now!"

Henry leaned her way, speaking in a penetrating hiss. "You want this sale? He's willing to pay twice what the damn necklace is worth." His face loomed over her, grinning fearsomely, eyes shining. "Take your clothes off..."

*"Solid, stylish ... polish and skill!"*

—PUBLISHERS WEEKLY

# BURT HIRSCHFELD

# Flawless

A JOVE BOOK

FLAWLESS

A Jove Book / published by arrangement with
Freundlich Books

PRINTING HISTORY
Freundlich Books edition published 1984
Jove edition / June 1985

ISBN: 0-515-08246-5

Jove books are published by The Berkley Publishing Group,
200 Madison Avenue, New York, N.Y. 10016.
The words "A JOVE BOOK" and the "J" with sunburst
are trademarks belonging to Jove Publications, Inc.

PRINTED IN THE UNITED STATES OF AMERICA

*To Brenda Brody . . .*
*A true friend who truly helped*

# chapter
## 1

ON A BRIGHT, piercingly clear day, the drying harmattan wind blew in from the Sahara over the streets of Monrovia, capital city of Liberia. It was a day Robert Foxman had willed into being, created out of his imagination, his privately kept, unflagging drive. It was his personal independence day, a day of glory and of profit. It was going to be the best day of his life. It was going to be the last day of his life.

In his mind he went over each step already taken: the phone calls to Antwerp, to Lugano, to London, all made at odd hours from public phones in midtown Manhattan, the meetings held in sleazy bars and bad restaurants, the money advanced, the payments promised, the risks taken. He had examined each possibility, checked every commitment offered, weighed each commitment against his personal and professional security.

He showered and shaved, and chose his clothes carefully: a tan tropical worsted suit tailored expressly for his wide-shouldered frame in Savile Row, a blue oxford-cloth shirt, a soft green tie with small red and yellow figures, all adding to the look of casual elegance he was after. He looked out of the window of his Ducor Palace Hotel room at the Atlantic, pinpoints of morning brightness exploding off a calm sea. By nightfall, he would be on his way home. A brief stopover in

1

London to take care of some business for Maurice, then back to New York and the culmination of this new life.

He went to work. At the hotel travel desk, he confirmed his reservation aboard British Caledonia's flight to Heathrow that afternoon, arranged for a taxi to be at the hotel at the appropriate hour and went after his exit permit. Next, a leisurely hour at the National Cultural Centre, shopping for souvenirs. He bought a Loma tribal doll made of reeds for his sister and a polished camwood ancestor mask for Maurice, an orange-and-black batik cloth with a fish motif for his mother.

Carrying his purchases in his free hand, he set out on foot for his first appointment. Tall, handsome, with the easy arrogance of a man who expected to get his own way, Robert moved at a brisk pace, despite a pronounced limp and his dependence on a thick knobby wooden cane.

Monrovia was a good place to walk, a city of contrasts and surprises. Built originally on a reef of rocks, the city had spread out over sand, split by beach lagoons into islands, peninsulas and rugged headlands.

New office buildings abutted traditional African huts, which sported television antennas like tribal headdresses. Blocks of shining new homes were separated by tin-roofed shacks, and long American cars lined the streets. Robert went past porticoed houses constructed in the graceful colonial style of the American Deep South, a reminder that many of the nineteenth-century settlers of the country were former slaves, no longer required by the plantation economy of the Old South. What irony, Robert thought; those early black freedmen had imposed a colonialism on their new land not dissimilar to the white colonialism on other parts of Africa.

Just beyond a cookhouse redolent of Black Beauty and Ponkie rice, Robert came to a low, modern office building. A long colonnade brought him to an unmarked door. He went inside. A pretty receptionist in a starched white blouse greeted him with flashing smile.

"Mr. Foxman, how good it is to see you again! Mr. Khamoury is expecting you, sir."

Bakshir Khamoury, a wiry Lebanese with large shining eyes and the sharp features of a sly satyr, was waiting in his private office. He greeted Robert with a quick, soft handshake, head bobbing affirmatively.

"Ah, Robert, at last. At last, Robert. I had begun to ask myself. Has Robert forgotten our appointment? Were Robert and I destined not to do business after all? Allah's blessings, you are here." He clasped Robert's hand in both of his, gazing up into his face with obvious approval. "So very American you are. What an impressive race. So tall, so fair, so handsome. And your women—the most beautiful of any women anywhere. Ah, yes. I mean it, sincerely. You might say I have conducted a survey. A clinical study. Comparison shopping, if you will." He giggled at his own joke and released Robert's hand. "Be seated, my good friend. Please. Your uncle? Tell me how that distinguished gentleman is? How admirable he is. How clever. How handsome still and vital. How successful." An elaborate sigh issued from his mouth. "And that most heavenly creature, your sister—Ellie. What a superb specimen, a living tribute to your society, she is. If women were judged as diamonds are—certainly she would be D-flawless." Again the giggle, and a quick sibilant intake of air. "And who dares say they are not, men being the salacious sort of creatures we are."

"Bakshir, let's do business."

The Lebanese rubbed his hands together and sat back down behind his desk. "Ah, so American. Always direct. Always ready to get on with it, finish your work, advance to still another profitable enterprise. Is it that you Americans expect to run out of time? Take heart, my friend, time is abundant, enough to go around. We Arabs understand the uses of time, the endless flow of a great inexhaustible river. Allah, the merciful, provides time for everything. To take some pleasure, to turn a profit, to live a little while and to die in His own time. There is no reason to hurry so."

"Bakshir, I am terribly fond of your company but I did not come all this way to sit and gossip. I have other business, other meetings, other deals to make."

Bakshir's thick brows rose and his black eyes glinted with curiosity. "Permit me a guess—certainly you do not deal with the Russian in behalf of your uncle?"

"Privacy, my friend, is still a desirable element in the trade."

"Oh, indeed, yes. None of my business, exactly. It is simply that I have been told that Tarassuk is in town looking to sell. Stones without a provenance, I have been told. It is true, yes? Not that I would deal with such a one as he. Buy a little, sell a little, make a little profit. Sufficient enough for Bakshir. Why take chances?"

"The stones, Bakshir."

"Of course. Yes. I understand your reluctance to speak of certain matters. Everyone tries to supplement his supplies outside the usual sources. A little here, a little there. Enough to make it worthwhile but not so much as to attract unwanted attention, yes? No one objects to what he doesn't know, isn't that right, Robert? Trust me, my friend. I am among the most discreet of persons in this world. My lips are sealed. My memory is a blank. You have told me nothing."

"You're right. I've told you nothing."

"Exactly. Still, as you Americans might say, Monrovia is a small town. And certain Europeans visit here—well, secrets are seldom secrets for long in a town such as this. And our Georgy, he is definitely not a man to disappear in a crowd." He laughed out loud, a succession of breathy exhalations.

"The stones, Bakshir."

Khamoury sobered quickly and spread a square of dark green chamois cloth on top of his desk. From a drawer he brought forth two white envelopes and emptied one onto the cloth. There was a spill of colored stones.

"Emeralds," he said. "A few excellent rubies, some sapphires."

Robert examined the stones rapidly through his loupe. "Let me see the rest."

Khamoury emptied the second envelope. A dozen diamonds rolled onto the chamois. "The best I could do, Robert. I do diamonds, of course, but only in small amounts, as you know."

Robert appraised the diamonds, one by one. "These are fair, Bakshir. Disappointingly fair."

"Mostly colored stones, that's what I deal in mostly."

"My uncle's primary interest is diamonds."

"I know, I know. This is the best I could do. Perhaps next time..."

"You arranged an export license for this batch?"

"Done."

"No trouble?"

"Trouble! Why should there be trouble? These are mostly legitimate stones."

"Mostly?"

"A taint here and there, nothing to concern yourself with. Purchased directly in a mining camp in Central Africa, from a longtime friend whom I would trust with my life."

"Spare me, Bakshir. Your markup is outrageous. I will give you half of what you ask."

Khamoury clapped a hand to his brow. "Expenses rise. Overhead. Travel costs. Good help is hard to find. There is little margin in such a sale, merely an accommodation for an old friend. Your offer demeans me."

"Take it or leave it."

"Three-quarters. You are dealing with a businessman. Reliable. Honest. Living always by the law, obeying the rules."

"One-third."

"Robert. It shames me to refuse you. A man must live. I have wives, children, the fathers and mothers of my wives."

"One-third, a bill of sale and the export license." Robert pushed the stones toward the other man.

Khamoury pushed them back. "Seventy percent."

"Sixty-five."

"Sixty-seven and two-thirds."

Robert offered his hand. "Mazel und Brucha."

"Mazel und Brucha."

The Yiddish words for Luck and Blessing, the traditional way of sealing a bargain in the world of diamonds. Robert stood up and folded the stones into the chamois and dropped the packet into his jacket pocket.

"I will take you to lunch," Khamoury said. "We shall talk about America. About New York. What a magnificent city! The racket of life surrounds one. One is buried in sound and in energy. The press of people. The women. What a city to live in for a man with an appreciation of beautiful women."

"Remember your wives, Bakshir."

"Can one ever forget—two wives."

"A Muslim is permitted four. Why have you stopped at two?"

"Look at me, dear friend. Am I a man who can afford four wives? A poor trader of this and that."

"In my country, one wife is sufficient."

"One wife would be a fearsome burden. Put two wives in the house and one keeps the other unsure and so always intent on pleasing her husband. You Americans are a brilliant race in many ways, but when it comes to women you have much to learn. Now, about lunch, my friend?"

"Business, my friend. I have another engagement."

Khamoury laid a forefinger alongside his long nose, tapping thoughtfully, eyes agleam. "Let me see—you are on a buying trip for Foxman and Company. Could it be Sartarwi? I think not; he deals only in leftovers, the dregs. Perhaps the South African, McDonald? I am told he can lift a ten-carat stone out of a widow's lavaliere without the lady ever knowing. No, no. Mr. Maurice Foxman would never tolerate doing business with a thief. So, if not Sartarwi and not McDonald, who? Who that you keep so assiduously to yourself, my friend? Why, of course! We return to the Russian, the only new boy in town. So I must say to myself, would the nephew of the great Maurice Foxman transact business with a bent case such as Georgy Tarassuk, a man of uncertain ethics and unidentifiable connections? What would your uncle say, Robert?"

Robert laughed and shoved himself erect, leaning on the sturdy walking stick. "Is it gossip you're after, Bakshir, or information?"

"Is there a difference? If so, it is immeasurable, infinitesimal, invisible to the naked eye. Question, dear friend: is it the great Maurice you buy for or do you function in behalf of other patrons?"

Robert steadied himself on the cane, started out, Khamoury close behind. "I deny nothing, Bakshir. I admit nothing. I give credence to nothing you say by commission or omission."

Khamoury giggled. "What a clever man you are, Robert. Clever and so amusing."

On the street, they shook hands. "This business," Khamoury said with considerable satisfaction. "It is part deceit, part quickness of hand. Part created desires and part intelligence, or at least as much intelligence as one is able to muster. Take care of yourself, Robert. Do not injure yourself again."

"Again?"

"The cane, your leg."

"Oh, yes. My knee. I damaged the ligaments skiing, nothing serious."

"You Americans, such a physical race. It will be the death of you all one day."

From Khamoury's office, it was a twenty-minute walk to Gurley Street. Alongside a shattered discotheque was Annabella's, a modest restaurant with a nondescript façade. Inside, rough wooden tables were haphazardly scattered. On the walls, tribal masks, a pair of war shields, matched pairs of crossed spears and two lengths of brightly colored cloth edged with geometric designs. Hunched over a table near the entrance, a rumpled cotton jacket straining across his broad back and shoulders, was a bear of a man, black-haired and bearded, round gold-rimmed glasses perched low on a pug nose. With unabashed glee, he spooned food out of a wooden bowl into his mouth, giving Robert a quick glance of recognition. Still chewing, he spoke in a low, accented rumble.

"Excellent," he said. "Jolof rice. Have some."

"No, thanks."

"Fish this time instead of chicken and an occasional prawn."

"A Star beer," Robert said to the waiter.

"This mania of Americans for thinness, it can be fatal."

The waiter brought the beer and a tall glass. Robert waited until he was gone before speaking. "I'm booked on the afternoon flight, Georgy, so I don't have a great deal of time."

Tarassuk spoke around a mouthful of food. "You brought the money?"

"You brought the merchandise?"

Tarassuk dug into the side pocket of his jacket, and his hand emerged with a soft leather pouch. He tossed it on the table. "See for yourself."

Robert emptied the contents into his hand. Fifteen rough diamonds, each between five and ten carats. Even to the naked eye they were stones of promise. He fingered them, one at a time, finding great pleasure in the touch. "Impressive," he said.

Tarassuk slurped tea from a tall glass. "Better than that. Put your glass on them, you'll see. First-class merchandise."

Robert examined the diamonds. Satisfied, he looked up. "Russian goods?"

"Please." An alarmed expression came into Tarassuk's dark, patient eyes. He glanced around. "Discretion in these affairs is in order. Let us attract no trouble."

"Suit yourself. But I should know how you came by these stones."

The burly man was offended, and said so. "They are in my possession, that should be enough for you. From where? By what route? From whose hand? Of no consequence. None," he ended flatly.

Robert gave a long, slow wink. "Via a mysterious and clandestine route, a route populated by scoundrels and black-guards and other nefarious characters."

"I see no humor in this affair." Tarassuk's face closed up and he seemed to retreat behind an invisible but insurmountable protective barrier. "You are not a serious man, Robert, and so a substantial threat to us both. You play games, I do not. You find much to laugh at, I do not. Clearly, we are not destined to do business."

Robert slid a white envelope across the table. "American dollars in precisely the amount you asked for. The money's for you. I will take the stones."

Tarassuk stared at the envelope for a long time before making up his mind. In a swift, smooth move he swept it up and deposited it into the inside pocket of his jacket. "Mazel und Brucha," he said.

"Mazel und Brucha."

"On this one, there will be no export license."

"Not to worry, Georgy."

In his hotel room, Robert made final preparations to depart. The Khamoury stones went into his shoulder bag, along with the bill of sale and the forged export license. Next, he turned his attention to the Russian gems. He rolled them out on the table the way a crapshooter rolls dice. They far exceeded his expectations in both size and potential value. He fingered one and then another, rolled them around his hand, enjoying the rough look of them, the dull reflected light they gave off, the uneven edges biting into his palm. Each stone was an unsolved mystery with its own secret history, given up by the earth reluctantly, brought to his hand by dark and devious means. He, Robert Foxman, would unlock the mystery, cause all the trapped beauty in each stone to be brought forth, full of glitter and excitement, to provide joy and beauty. And a very substantial profit.

Working under the imprimatur of Foxman and Company, he anticipated making other such illicit buys. Perhaps as many as eight or ten a year. He would work through Tarassuk, and others like him, men willing to operate outside the strict monopolistic sanctions of the worldwide diamond cartel. Already, Robert's numbered account in the Bahamas contained a substantial sum. He anticipated a steep and steady growth in the future.

He took up the walking stick and applied pressure to the triangular knob nearest the rubber-capped tip; under his hand, it depressed slightly and he turned it to the left until he heard a faint clicking noise. He worked the carved handle counterclockwise and it came free in his hand. He deposited one diamond after another into the hollow shaft of the cane, fixing each in place with wads of absorbent cotton. The job done, he replaced the handle, put the cane aside and went on with his preparations.

He phoned the concierge. "This is Mr. Foxman. I have a taxi on call to take me to the airport at Robertsfield. Let me know when it arrives."

He packed without haste until a tentative knock brought him to the door. A man stood there, an inquiring expression on his sharp-featured face. He was small, with the kind of taut muscular body you saw around a racetrack; an exercise boy or a jockey, since retired.

"Mr. Foxman?"

"I'm Foxman," Robert said. "I thought you were the bellboy."

The small man reached under his jacket and brought out a stainless-steel target pistol, complete with noise suppressor.

"What is this?" Robert was surprised but not alarmed, annoyed at the interruption, the enforced delay. "Who the hell are you?"

The small man advanced into the room, forcing Robert backwards. He closed the door behind him.

The small man shot Robert Foxman three times in the chest, driving him to the floor, his back against the bed. After making sure that Robert was dead, the gunman put his weapon away and began to search the room. He came across the Khamoury stones and examined them briefly before returning them to their place.

He went on looking. Swift, neat, he worked with practiced efficiency. Only when he was convinced he had overlooked nothing did he leave, made uneasy by the failure of his mission. He had done his job properly, with a high degree of professional competence. If only others did as well. There had been a mistake somewhere along the line, a miscalculation, and such miscalculations, he knew from experience, led to unpredictable consequences. A straight line to trouble. And he was a man who preferred to avoid trouble.

## chapter

# 2

ON THE DAY BEFORE her brother was shot to death, Ellie Foxman discovered that the Chamblay was up for sale. A diamond choker created out of twenty-one carat pears, with a three-carat centerpiece, the Chamblay belonged to the Marquise Jeanette Manière, who, at eighty-five, it was rumored, supported two former husbands, each of whom visited her regularly, and one twenty-year-old lover. The lover was in attendance four days out of every week.

A phone call had brought the Marquise out of her apartment, not far from the Arc de Triomphe, to lunch at La Marée, that elegant and expensive fish restaurant in the Rue Daru. One of the many things Ellie had learned from her uncle was the inevitability of spending money in order to make it.

Both women dined on *belons au champagne,* the famous triple-zero oysters poached in their own juices and served on the half shell with a reduction of their essences, champagne and *crème fraîche*. The Marquise was a robust, fleshy woman under a wide-brimmed purple hat with a leopard band; her hair had been colored to the brightness of a ripe lemon and her hooded eyes were never still, hopscotching from table to table in search of a familiar face, or one to admire. She approached her food with the same energy and appetite she approached men, devouring whatever was set before her with zest and commentary.

Ellie, who had met the Marquise in New York five years earlier, waited for the older woman to shift the conversation around to her third obsession—money. Over a chocolate pastry heaped high with whipped cream and immature strawberries and coffee spiked with armagnac, the Marquise finally brought her attention to business.

"I am a great and lasting admirer of your uncle, my dear, a man of distinction, culture and great good looks."

Ellie braced herself, allowing nothing to show on her face. No matter who it was that spoke of him, Maurice was always described in the most laudatory terms. Wise. Courageous. Honorable. A man who had carved a diamond empire out of modest beginnings, a man of persistence and drive, all modified by his ever-present concern for the rights and feelings of other human beings. He was a man to be respected, admired, cherished. Was she, then, the only one to know the truth about Maurice Foxman? Could it be that only she could see that the emperor was wearing no clothes? She arranged her delicate features in a soft expression, giving nothing away.

"You and Maurice, madame, you've known each other for a long time?"

"For a very long time, longer than I care to remember. Compared to me, of course, dear Maurice is a mere child— no more than seventy, at a guess." She placed a thin brown cigarette in a long ivory holder and lit it with a bruised and scarred Zippo lighter. "A remembrance of the war against the Boche," she said, fondling the lighter. "A gift from one of your American GIs. A private, he was. In civilian life, a clerk in a fruit market. An ordinary man in every way but extraordinary in the one way that matters most, *n'est-ce pas!*" She closed her eyes and let her mind float back over the years. She smiled warmly and her eyes opened. "Ah, but Maurice. Nothing about dear Maurice was ever ordinary. *Mon Dieu,* no! A man of special gifts. So you follow in his footsteps, with the diamonds."

"In a way."

"In what way, my dear?"

"Maurice believes women should not deal in diamonds.

Wear them, yes. Sell them, no."

"Dear Maurice, always the man of tradition."

"He says the business is sordid, even dangerous. Too sordid for a mere female."

"And you do not agree?"

"The world is changing, madame. Our trade must change, too. Or be left behind."

"Sadly, too many of us are being left behind. Discarded. When you reach my stage of life, you ask yourself: How did it happen? Where has the time gone to? How did I become so old, so wrinkled, so near to the end? Within, there survives a young girl, planning her future, dreaming great dreams, charged with magnificent passions. What a sadness it is, my dear, to be forced to reconcile the two—a shock to the entire nervous system . . ."

"You're a vigorous and fascinating woman."

The Marquise permitted herself a wry smile. "But quite old." She summoned up a fresh supply of energy. The sparkle returned to her eyes and her cheeks seemed to become smoother under Ellie's gaze. "Your uncle is a wise man, a man of integrity. Trust his judgment."

Ellie wanted to argue, to defy this old woman as she had tried to defy Maurice. She had mocked him for the "bourgeois mind-set" that locked him into a lost era. She had accused him of clinging to old-world ideas, to outmoded and worthless concepts of morality in business and in life. Of being old-fashioned.

He had admitted as much. "When the new fashions are of value I shall adopt them. Otherwise, I hold on to what is proven. The old ways."

The Marquise said, "I think of dear Maurice in the fondest terms. We met during the war, you see. He had escaped the Boche, was making his way to England. He remained in Paris for a short period. Too short. Later he went back to fight the Nazis. He was a hero, that Maurice."

"A hero?"

"Truly. Is he as handsome as ever? His visits to Paris after the war were an event. A celebration. Women quivered at his glance. They besieged him with invitations to private dinner parties. Married women, single women, it made no difference. All done in very good taste, I assure you. Maurice could have enjoyed any of the beauties at the Folies and half the aristocrats in the city. Of course, he was too honorable to indulge in depravity of any kind. I myself could never perceive any sound reason to avoid such sensual pleasures when offered.

"Poor, poor Maurice. The joys he missed. *C'est la vie*, to each his taste." The Marquise fixed Ellie with the clear, encompassing glance of a woman who missed very little. She saw a young woman who was more than merely beautiful; healthy, vital, with a barely supressed supply of raw energy. In a suit by Saint Laurent and shoes by Ferragamo, Ellie was quietly chic, possessed of a confident, almost embattled style of her own. In subtle counterpoint, the Marquise noted, an undercurrent of uncertainty, a formlessness, as if Ellie had yet to locate and identify the center of her being, still searching for her proper place in the world. "You put me in mind of your uncle," the Marquise said. "The same sort of face—strong, *n'est-ce pas?* Yet delicate. Ah, but with you there is the look of a frightened fawn in your eyes, perhaps a touch of melancholy. Such excellent eyes they are, that shade of green that is not quite a true green. Unearthly, nearly golden at times. Hypnotic eyes, strange, but beautiful all the same. And the mouth is exceptional as well. Sensuous, inviting, a suggestion of petulance, yes? A hint of irony when you smile. And why should it be otherwise? The world is an amusing place, is it not so? Amusing. Well, not all the time but certainly, as Camus instructed us, absurd and very little understood. Still, we try. To strive, that is God's gift to us humans . . ."

"You are a believer, madame?"

"And you are not? To be young is to disbelieve in so many pieces of ancient wisdom. To be young is to be skeptical, impatient with the hypocrisies, the clumsy stupidities of an earlier generation. Well, once upon a time it was that way with me and my friends. I believe, you do not." She gave an eloquent roll of her shoulders, graceful and, at the same time, dismissive. "Makes little enough difference in the end. Soon enough I'll discover for myself all answers to all questions."

"Or perhaps not."

That elicited a cheerful response. "Or perhaps not. So, onward to less morbid and certainly more pragmatic matters, the question of the Chamblay . . ."

"It is for sale?"

The Marquise's chin rose and her eyes hardened. She assessed Ellie with a frank, cool stare, the look of a fighter measuring a potential enemy.

"You have excellent sources."

"I've been in the business for a long time."

"Still—I was thinking along other lines."

"An auction?"

"I have considered that. The Chamblay is much admired and competitive bidding would certainly bring a considerable price . . ."

Ellie's mind turned over rapidly. She said, "You must have many, many friends in Paris, madame. When they learn that you intend to divest yourself of a precious possession, when they learn that the Chamblay is to be made publicly available . . . the bidding will be brisk, I'm certain."

The Marquise held Ellie's gaze for a long beat before looking away. "You do business roughly, my dear. And why should it be otherwise? You desire a certain conclusion to this encounter and you are willing to fight to achieve it. Still, you are so young . . ."

"I'm thirty."

The Marquise laughed. "An ancient age to you, mere adolescence to me."

"Give me an idea of how much you want to clear on the Chamblay, I'll see that you get it." Ellie wished she was as confident as she made herself sound. She needed this commission, needed to make an important sale to prove to herself and to her uncle that she possessed the qualities necessary to become a force in the business equal to any. "I guarantee it, madame, to get the best possible price."

The Marquise shook her head, a stubborn set to her mouth. "I am not yet convinced. The only reason I agreed to this meeting was because you work for Maurice . . ."

"I'm associated with him."

"Which means precisely what?"

"I work out of his New York office, but I work for myself."

"An independent?"

"My uncle's interests and mine do not always coincide. Occasionally I do jobs for him. I buy, I sell, as the situation demands. When that happens, we share the profits. Otherwise, I am on my own."

"Maurice does not completely approve of you, I take it?"

Ellie swallowed her words, rethought her reply. "I choose to maintain my independence."

The Marquise's shining, ancient eyes were direct and dangerous, revealing nothing. "Maurice," she said in a low, slow voice, "has never entirely approved of me, either. Certainly he would not look favorably on the way I have lived these past ten years. Not that I have ever asked for approval, from Maurice or from anyone else. How well do you know diamonds, my dear?"

Ellie answered at once, more comfortable with trade talk. "My first passion. I began by sorting and grading for Maurice. I worked summers and school holidays. Once in a while he allowed me to sit in witness when he bought or sold. After college, I accompanied him occasionally on his trips abroad to Paris, to London, to Tel Aviv, as an assistant, a secretary, a companion. I know stones, madame, I have a talent for marking and deciding how to cut . . ."

"And yet Maurice does not employ you?"

Ellie commanded herself to give no response. The Marquise was on a fishing expedition; there was no need to answer.

"He uses you as a specialist, perhaps? A troubleshooter. Targets to specific assignments, *n'est-ce pas?*"

Ellie nodded once and the Marquise smiled.

"What to do," she mused, licking the residue of her pastry off her fork.

"Let me sell the Chamblay for you."

"What if you fail? What if the price you get is less than its true value? I am not sure, my dear."

"But, madame, I have the perfect client in mind, one who is primed to buy."

"I could not bear to have the Chamblay leave France. It is French and must remain so."

"I understand. Your patriotism is commendable. At the same time, you certainly would prefer not to see the Chamblay adorning the throat of another woman. And an auction would be so . . . public."

"You state the problem exactly. What am I to do?"

"My solution is this—the Chamblay should go to someone who loves France as you do, a Frenchman, naturally. But one who for reasons of his own no longer lives in France."

"Where will I find such a one?"

"I have just the customer for you, madame. A young aristocrat about to be married. He wishes a special gift for his bride, a lovely French girl. They plan to live in Quebec, where his family has business interests. So you see, a perfect solution."

"An aristocrat, you say?"

"With a long and honorable family history."

The Marquise was impressed with the way Ellie had identified the problem and arranged for its solution even before they had met. She was a clever young woman, determined and expressive, all qualities the Marquise admired. "The Chamblay must fetch a substantial price, dear child. Substantial . . ."

"Have you a figure in mind?"

The Marquise sighed and shook her head.

"Would one hundred and fifty thousand be satisfactory?"

"Dollars?"

"Yes, madame."

"Less your commission."

"I will be fair, madame. Certainly fair."

The old woman slumped, a concession to age and the weakness of her flesh. The light in her eyes dimmed. "The niece of my old friend, how could you not be? I owe so much to Maurice. Yes, yes, I shall allow you to sell the Chamblay for me. As a small repayment of the good memories your uncle has left me. Could I do otherwise? You will please let me know when the arrangement is concluded. I thank you for a lovely lunch, dear child. So few pleasures remain for a woman of my years, dining is surely one of the most important . . ."

Ellie had gotten what she came for. But why, she asked herself, did she feel as if she'd suffered another loss? Another setback at Maurice Foxman's meticulously groomed hands.

The two women parted outside the restaurant and Ellie went back to the rented apartment in the Sixth Arrondissement she shared with Henry Wilton. She undressed and donned a long white terry-cloth robe and, while running the water for a bath,.

put a call through to Lucien Duquette. Lucien was visiting his family's estate in Tarascon, a small city on the Rhone, south of Avignon. She told him that she represented the owner of the Chamblay choker and described it for him.

He grew excited. "I must see it!"

"I intend for you to."

"When, *chérie?* When?"

She laughed to herself. Lucien's impulsiveness was as well known as his inherited wealth. "This choker has a history, Lucien."

"Naturally, it is French."

"The stones are superb, with an intrinsic value. The setting is a work of art, unmatched in its rendering."

"I must have it. Cici will enhance its beauty."Cici, his fiancée, was the spoiled and somewhat sullen daughter of an equally aristocratic family with vineyards, a shipping company and timber interests in Canada. Neither Cici nor Lucien had ever inhibited a response or repressed a desire in their young lives. Neither of them intended to begin soon. "You must arrange for me to see it."

"It will be extremely expensive."

"No matter, *chérie.* What else have I to do but squander my father's fortune on pretty baubles? When?"

"Tomorrow. Perhaps."

"Perhaps?"

"Such matters are never simple." She wanted his lust for the Chamblay to intensify, his judgment to cloud, his desire to possess it to increase sharply. "An item such as this, it is always in considerable demand."

"You must not let anyone else have it, *chérie.* Give me your word."

"I'll get back to you."

"Tomorrow?"

"Or the day after."

"Do not torment me, *chérie.* I will meet any price you are offered."

*"Au'voir,* Lucien."

Satisfied with her efforts, she removed her robe and examined her reflection in the long mirror behind the bathroom door. The body she saw had been described by Henry Wilton as typically American, the legs long and tapered, the belly flat and firm, the hips flaring. Her breasts were gracefully contoured, neither too large nor too small, the nipples cushioned upwards by their fullness. She reminded herself that she had not exercised in nearly six weeks, had not run or done laps in a pool. That was Henry's doing, insisting on her constant attention, mocking her for what he termed "your New World compulsion for perfectibility." Yet without exercise, she felt sluggish, discomforted, some essential quality subtracted from her life. She climbed into the tub and lay back in the hot water, allowing her muscles to go slack, willing her mind to remain empty. Impossible.

It had been a good day for Ellie. She was a women propelled by a powerful urge to miss nothing life had to offer, to experience everything. An almost obsessive craving for accomplishment, for reward, for personal satisfaction, sometimes put her into personal and professional risk. Too often the risks seemed greater in retrospect than the odds justified. Her inexperience, her willingness to accept strangers at their word, caused her trouble and resulted in considerable personal anguish.

Maybe Maurice was right. Maybe she was too immature, too impulsive, unable to function efficiently within established guidelines. She envied men their ability to battle openly for what they wanted. No criticism was ever leveled at a man for being too combative or too competitive, willing to take chances.

As a woman, she had been cautioned repeatedly to conceal her ambitions, to mask her desire for adventure, excitement and success. This she refused to do. She wanted everything diamonds could bring: respect, acclaim, wealth. She intended to get them.

"Keep your strange ideas to yourself," her mother frequently said. "Don't take chances. Don't get people mad at you. Don't go too far."

But that was exactly what Ellie wanted to do. To go farther than any woman in the business had ever gone before. Or dared to go. To stretch the limits of her freedom. To open all aspects of the diamond world to women everywhere. Ellie wanted it all.

"Find a good man," her mother would say. "Settle down. Get married."

An acceptable idea. Many men, attracted by her maturing beauty, had proposed marriage. Attractive men, men of substance and status, men on the fast track. She had refused them. Marriage was not for her, not yet. However, her need for male companionship and attention was pervasive, and seemed to intensify with each experience.

These last four months with Henry Wilton, for example. An ever-changing adventure, a sexual and emotional roller coaster. Henry, sophisticated, with the quick wit of a three-card monte dealer, so daring, so very European in his tastes, was a man without a conscience. He was so unlike Maurice; at least unlike the proper image Maurice liked to present to outsiders. She knew better.

With each passing day, it had become easier for her to accept Henry's minor forays beyond the law, beyond accepted social behavior. Henry attracted danger with the insistence of a powerful magnet, willing to risk himself and those around him for profit and for the most transient of pleasures. When one of his escapades ended—always safely, always successfully—there was a sense of relief, a game well played and now gratefully over. But always there was the taste of imminent disaster that lingered in Ellie's mouth and she wondered what terrible disaster the next time would bring.

There was that about Henry, the ability to keep coming up with new games to play. Especially in the bedroom. He was an inventive, innovative lover, carrying them closer to the brink, daring her to go over the edge into the dark unknown. Always a new endeavor, a fresh adventure to savor, a new role to play.

Nothing was forbidden to Henry. Nothing was wrong. Nothing was reprehensible. There was only new experimentation, a more intense and frightening ascent to the apex of pleasure. To the unbearable climax. The ultimate come.

How far? she often asked herself. How far would Henry take her? How far would she dare to go? Sooner or later, she would have to find out.

After a light supper—three different cheeses, sausage, a baguette loaf from the *boulangerie pâtisserie* at the corner and a fine St. Emilion—Ellie brought out the Chamblay. It glittered in the soft light, shimmered as it sat on the coffee table, as if displaying itself for approval.

Henry admired it at a distance, never touching it. With traditional British reserve, he inspected the choker, too wordly to be outwardly impressed.

After a while, he sat back and lit a joint of North African hashish and drew deeply. When he offered it to Ellie, she waved it away.

"Isn't it fabulous?" she said of the choker.

"Wonderful setting," he offered blandly. "One doesn't see workmanship of that caliber much these days." He drew hard on the joint.

"I thought I'd give Lucien Duquette first look at it. He's getting married and is looking for a gift for Cici. I've already spoken to him."

Henry gazed off into space, his pale, slender face without expression. "Lucien's such a simp, don't you think?"

"He meets the Marquise's specifications. He's French, he's rich and he's going to live abroad."

"Still, he lacks the sensibility to appreciate such a fabulous piece. If it were my choice, I'd look elsewhere for a buyer. What are you asking for it?"

"One hundred and fifty."

"Pounds?"

The question startled her. Had she underestimated the worth of the Chamblay? Or merely her own ability to exploit the full value of the choker? She searched Henry's face for the answer and saw there only indifference.

"You think I'm asking too little?"

He sucked the joint and allowed his eyes to close. "You are the expert, of course. Still, you wouldn't want to sell for less than your best price, would you now? Your choice, of course."

"What would you say to two hundred thousand?"

He inspected the choker again. "Precisely how good is it?"

"A step below museum quality, though it does have a family history. But it's an outstanding piece of work, the stones displayed to advantage."

"I think," he said deliberately, "we could do much better than Lucien."

Ellie avoided his eyes. Increasingly their lives had melded together in ways that seemed to profit Henry more than herself. His experiences, his rewards, his joys; all were expressly singular. What she did, her accomplishments, belonged to *them*. Of mutual benefit. Us. Ours. We. All her life had been like that, slices of her individuality stolen away, nourishing others more than herself.

"Lucien wants to buy. A quick turnover..."

He dragged again on the joint, his eyes cloudy and out of focus. "Have you told your uncle about the deal?"

"That's the last thing I'd do! He'd be sure to find fault with something."

"Exactly. The estimable Maurice knows from experience that one goes where the money is, the *most* money."

"This is my deal, not his."

"As you like. But is it good business to sell to the first prospect? Shop the product, create some competition. Let the potential buyers work against each other."

"What would you have me do?"

He spoke lazily. "I have a friend with a great deal of money and an equal interest in acquiring such a pretty bauble."

"Who is it?"

"We can visit him in the morning. I'm certain he'll buy. We'll ask half a million and let him jew us down. Settle at a decent price, collect our money and fly off to the South. How does St. Tropez sound to you, my darling? I could certainly do with a couple of weeks. Sun and sand and all that. We'll put you out on the beach and get those exquisite boobies of yours tan all over." He reached for her thigh.

She made a face. "Not now, Henry...let's get back to the Chamblay. Who is this friend of yours?"

"Raymond Wentworth. He's rented a château outside the city. With some friends. We can go down for a few days..."

She poured more wine into her glass, buying time. "I don't like Raymond very much."

"Nonsense. He's a good fellow, lots of fun. Lots of laughs."

"Go without me, Henry."

He took her face between his hands, gazing relentlessly into her eyes. "We'll go together, my darling. If you wish, we'll stay only for lunch. You and me and the Chamblay."

"You know how Raymond is, he's always at me."

"You're a beautiful woman and Raymond appreciates beauty in all its forms. He's sure to appreciate the choker."

"He wants to sleep with me."

"As does every man fortunate enough to lay eyes on you, my darling. I'm told Raymond's an animal when it comes to women, biggest tool in Britain."

"Spare me the details."

"Tomorrow..." He squeezed her breast and she gasped. "We'll make the best deal we can. After all, Raymond has all that money, no reason we shouldn't get some modest share of it."

"No."

He reached under her skirt. "There," he said, watching her expression soften. "In the morning, then. We'll turn a tidy profit and have ourselves a few chuckles along the way."

"Don't force me, Henry."

"We must choose your wardrobe carefully. That flimsy white evening dress for starters. The see-through blouse. Let them all see what super boobies you have."

"I won't do it, Henry."

He pressed himself against her, nibbling at her ear, his breath warm and insistent. "Of course you will, my darling. You will. For a little while. I'll see to it, you can depend on me. Every time..."

The château was set back on a gentle slope at the end of a dirt road lined with massive plane trees. Built of a pale yellow stone, it was surrounded by gardens and silvery pools which shimmered in the morning light.

They drove down in Ellie's Peugeot, parking between a white Jaguar XJ-S and a bright red Alfa-Romeo GTV-6. Both cars belonged to Raymond Wentworth.

"He's fascinated by speed," Henry explained. "He loves cars, loves racing them."

A servant greeted them with the news that Monsieur Wentworth and his guests were still asleep, and would Mademoiselle and Monsieur care to inspect their room? The room turned out to be a generously proportioned apartment in the château. A spacious sitting room and bedroom to match. A huge tub on lion's claws had been put down in the center of the great round bathroom, complete with shower, the pipes disappearing into the ancient tiled floor.

By the time they changed clothes and descended to the cavernous main hall, it was time for lunch. Afterwards they strolled the gardens waiting for Raymond to appear. Late in the afternoon, he finally materialized.

He was an awkward lank of a man in a blazer and ascot, hair pasted slickly to a long head, his eyes bulging, his fleshy lips pursed. His long-fingered hands fluttered, stroked the air and washed each other nervously.

He leaned over Ellie, holding on to her hand. "What a prize package you are, my sweet. I'd forgotten. Top-of-the-line merchandise, Henry. I congratulate you. So prettily turned out." He aimed a kiss at her mouth which she skillfully avoided. His lips landed on her ear and his tongue probed deftly. She pulled away.

"Behave yourself, Raymond."

"Exactly so, luv. Lucky Henry, is she as good as she looks?"

"Even better."

"Care for a communal endeavor, would you? Always had the bit of the Red in me, y'know. Share the wealth and all that."

"One never knows."

"Stop it!" Ellie demanded.

"Fierce creature, isn't she?"

"One of those combative Jewesses," Henry said, laughing.

"It's the Israeli influence, you see. Making them march and train and carry Uzis, that sort of thing. Not armed to kill, is she?"

"Ellie's weapons deliver pleasure, dear boy. Never misses."

Ellie made a face. "Spare me the oh-so-clever Cambridge decadence, you two. I'm here to talk business, Raymond, and that's all."

"How sad."

"She means the choker, dear boy."

"Oh, yes, the Chamblay. Is it all it's said to be?"

"See for yourself." Henry nodded in Ellie's direction, a silent command.

Permission granted, she thought, resenting Henry's intrusion into her business. Resenting his assumption of authority. But this was no time to voice her objections, she had come to make a sale. On a refectory table along one wall, she spread a soft black velour cloth and arranged the Chamblay on it, graceful and sparkling, as alive as it was dormant. The stones, the skillfully wrought setting, the reflected light; a thing of beauty, a work of art.

"My God," Raymond said, clapping his hands soundlessly. "What a masterpiece it is! Oh, you were so right to bring it to me, Henry. I want it, I must have it. Jill will love it. We're getting married, y'know, Jill and I. Dear girl's done half the beds in London and I've done the other half. Met in the middle once or twice, I don't mind telling you. Point is, we're making it proper and legal, inviting all our friends to the first night's doings. Everybody's going to be up for the taking. Jill. Me. Do come, as many times as you can manage, my dears..." He leered at Ellie. "Jill will have to pass on it, you understand, the Chamblay, I mean."

"Of course."

"When?" Henry said.

"Soon as she delivers her little fanny down here. The dear thing's never on time. Part of her charm, I'd say. Frightfully expensive, is it?" He shivered with anticipation.

"Frightfully," Ellie said, wishing she hadn't permitted Henry to talk her into coming. Too often it had been what she did best, allowing men to convince her to do what she didn't really want to do.

"Say the numbers," Raymond said.

Before she could answer, Henry spoke in a cool, detached manner, apparently bored by the mere idea of doing business.

"Nine hundred thousand," he said.

Ellie cast an alarmed glance his way. Transactions of this magnitude had to be dealt with skillfully, sensitively, never pushing too hard or too long. This was no fish market, they weren't haggling over pennies. To set a price too high could destroy a sale before it got off the ground. Raymond Wentworth—whatever else he might be—certainly was not a fool.

As if reading her mind, Henry backed off. "Just a beginning price, Raymond, you understand."

"Never did enjoy bargaining."

"I'm sure we can strike a fair price."

"Suppose I make you a counter offer." Raymond looped his arm through Henry's. "Let's go off and chat a bit. Just the two of us." He grinned salaciously at Ellie as he steered Henry through the tall french doors into the gardens. She watched their retreating forms, heads close together, exchanging intimacies. She made up her mind; if this fell through, she'd contact Lucien in the morning, see if he was still interested. He too needed a wedding gift for his bride.

A shuffling sound brought her around. Coming her way, a lovely young woman with a vaguely surprised expression on her face. She wore a full skirt that came to the floor and a peasant blouse made of an almost transparent cotton that played over her breasts as she moved, nipples visible through the thin fabric. She offered her hand.

"Hello . . . you must be Ellie. I'm Jill."

"Hello, Jill."

"Raymond's told me all about you. You're as stunning as he said you were. What lovely hair you have, so soft, so luminous. Oh, my! Is that the Chamblay? Isn't it a beauty. Is it yours?"

"I represent the owner."

"And it's up for sale, Raymond said."

The men came up from behind them, Raymond's arms going around Jill's waist. She leaned back into him, swinging her perfectly round bottom in slow circles.

"Well, luv," Raymond said. "What do you think of it?"

"The choker, oh, it's lovely."

"Only lovely?"

"Fantastic."

"That's better. Would you like to have it?"

"Oh, yes, darling. May I have it? May I?"

"Henry and I have been trying to strike a deal."

"Raymond's made a good offer," Henry said.

"May I hear what it is?" Ellie said.

"All in good time, luv, in good time." He folded the Chamblay into the black velour and dropped it into his pocket.

"Much later," Raymond said. "For now, let's all have a sip of champagne, if you will."

"I just adore champagne," Jill cooed.

"Party time!"

By ten o'clock, everyone was high. With the exception of Ellie. Hers was a sober presence that infiltrated the château, waiting with rising impatience for Henry to close the deal with Raymond Wentworth.

"Have you spoken to him yet?" she asked for the third time.

"Get off my back, luv. Everything in its place."

He snorted cocaine provided by Raymond, as he'd been doing for most of the evening, becoming alternately euphoric and sullen, declaring his dislike of most of the people present, the French, the English lower classes, unnamed enemies and anyone who kept him from getting what he wanted when he wanted it.

Ellie searched out Raymond and Jill, huddled on a deep, soft sofa across the room, sharing a joint. They laughed a lot and talked almost not at all, pawing intermittently at each other. Finally, without announcing their departure, they withdrew to a room at the top of the stairs.

"Damn," Ellie said. "I wanted to finish up here tonight, get back to Paris."

"Exactly my thought, luv. We can clinch the deal right now." He took her hand. "Shall we go . . ."

She held back. "Where to?"

"Trust me," he said, drawing her to her feet. "I know what I'm doing." He led her into the center hall and the majestic staircase. They started up. "What did you think of Jill?"

"She's all right, I suppose."

"Terrific boobies, hasn't she?"

"And making sure everybody sees them."

"Raymond doesn't mind. You know how she got them?"

"Same way the rest of us did, I imagine." The turn of the conversation made her uneasy.

He laughed and reached for her bottom. She pulled away and he laughed again, mocking her this time. "All artificial," he said. "Shot full of silicone or whatever it is they do. Stand straight out, even when the dear girl's lying down. Hard as rocks."

"How would you know that?"

"Raymond insisted I give them a try."

"And you couldn't resist the opportunity."

"Tactile experiment was all. I prefer my boobies soft and pliant." He cupped her right breast and she slapped his hand away. "What a beautiful body you have, my darling, let's enjoy it to the fullest."

"In the right place, at the right time." She let him lead her up the long staircase.

"Learn to be freer, luv. More daring. There's so much pleasure to be had." At the top of the stairs he kissed her, his tongue working her lips apart. "Marvelous mouth," he murmured. "Best I've ever encountered."

"A handy tool to have around the house, is that it?"

"Oh, it is useful."

He opened the door nearest them and guided her inside.

"This is not our apartment," she protested.

He steered her through the living room, into the bedroom. In the soft pink glow of a night lamp, Raymond and Jill lay on the bed. Both were naked, their limbs entwined, faces buried in each other.

"What is this!" Ellie gasped.

Raymond looked up. "Thought you two would never get here. Come on, get naked, get down, get with it."

"Damn you, Henry!" Ellie cried. "You promised." She felt her self-control thinning out, fear of what she might be forced to do, what she might want to do, replacing her resolve.

"Come along, dearie," Jill cooed from her place under Raymond. "Be a good sort. We'll have fun, fun, fun..."

"Part of the bargain," Raymond said to her, and then to Henry: "Keep up your end, dear boy, and I'll keep mine."

"What is going on?" Ellie almost shouted. She was shot through with the pain of being. "I want to leave, Henry. Now."

"Take your clothes off," Henry said.

"Grow up. These communal gropes are not my scene, Henry." Her voice sounded strange in her ears, the voice of someone she used to be. A child's voice.

Henry leaned her way, spoke in a penetrating hiss. "You want this sale? He's willing to pay twice what the damn thing's worth. All for us, you and me. Pure profit. All that money and all this fun. Come on, take your things off."

"You bastard!" She swung an open hand and he moved swiftly to deflect the blow, jerking her around and tearing at her blouse. His face loomed large over her, grinning fearsomely, eyes shining. Without warning, he hit her. She staggered back against the wall and he followed, both hands swinging, rocking her head from side to side. She begged him to stop, began to weep.

"Get undressed!" he yelled.

"Bravo!" Raymond cried.

"Olé!" Jill was standing, maneuvering for a better view.

Henry pulled at her skirt and she fought him until, suddenly, it came away in his hands. With that, her will to struggle deserted her and she slumped back, unable to resist.

Jill began to applaud.

"What a beauty!" Raymond exulted, advancing her way. He squeezed her breasts and pain radiated into her chest. She begged him to stop, still in that feeble, child's voice. She made a futile effort to free herself.

Then Jill, face split in demonic joy, knelt alongside. Without thinking, Ellie kicked out hard. Her knee caught the blond girl on the nose and she fell back, screaming, blood beginning to run.

"My nose! She broke my nose!"

"Oh, shit!" Raymond said. "Cost a small fortune to make that nose."

Ellie struggled to her feet, searching for her clothes.

"Look what you did!" Raymond shouted.

"I'm bleeding!" Jill shrieked.

"You made her bleed!" Raymond cried. "Ruined the evening for us, you did!" His fist landed hard on Ellie's hip, sending her spinning around. He went after her, huge and spidery, a deadly threat.

She flung a vase at him and it shattered against his forehead and he went down on all fours, moaning, complaining about his fate.

"Damn!" Henry exploded. "You've spoiled it all. A fortune gone down the drain!" He punched her and she stumbled backwards, tripped and fell. She rolled and came up at once and ran for the door. From behind, she heard Raymond's long bleat,

"I want her! I want her! I want to hurt her bad . . ." And she knew they would be coming after her.

She made it to the Peugeot and burned rubber getting out of the cobblestone courtyard. Pain dug into her body and fear electrified her senses; escape was paramount. Naked and sobbing, she put her foot to the floor and the Peugeot leaped ahead. A succession of sharp turns on the unfamiliar road forced her to brake often. In the rearview mirror, headlights were catching up. Raymond and Henry in the white Jag XJ-S, the distance between them closing fast.

Within a mile, they had cut down the gap to less than a car's length. Now they began bumping her from behind. Playfully at first. Then harder, maintaining contact for as long as they could. Sending the Peugeot into wild, screeching skids. She fought the wheel and imagined she could hear them gloating at her terror, toying with her, extracting every last ounce of perverse pleasure from the situation.

The Jag swung to the left, as if to pass. She blocked his access. Raymond tried the other side and again she outmaneuvered him. They intended to bring her to a stop on the shoulder, take her back to the château by force, make her do as they wished. She vowed not to give in without a fight.

The Jag struck again as the Peugeot lurched, front wheels shimmying crazily. She had barely regained control of the car when they hit her again, harder this time. A blind corner loomed up ahead and she wrenched frantically at the wheel, fighting to make the turn. Simultaneously, the Jag made contact with her right rear, sending the Peugeot into a desperate spin. It tilted, rose up on its side, still spinning, still under power, and rolled deliberately onto its back.

She listened to the awful song of collapsing metal against rock and dirt, the shatter of glass. A thunderous crash brought the Peugeot to a sudden stop, bringing with it a startling, unbearable pain. Too much pain. And more fear than she had ever before encountered. She stopped caring. She turned loose of it all, and began the slow inexorable drift toward oblivion . . .

# *chapter* 3

DAVID FOXMAN LABORED DILIGENTLY on the slant board, doing tough sit-ups. Noisily breathing in and out, hands clasped behind his head, twisting toward his feet to intensify the effort. Sit-ups, push-ups, running laps, pumping iron, working the Nautilus. All designed to get himself into competitive condition. Strengthen the old heart. Improve his circulatory system. Increase stamina. In fact, David was in the finest physical condition of his life. He had never been much of an athlete, always lacking the physical skills, the eye-hand coordination, the reflexive nature to make his body react without thinking about it.

It was his body David was concerned about. The look of it. Coming up to thirty years of age, he yearned to sculpt it into a graceful, clearly defined mass of muscle and bone. The beau idea of female fantasies. A thing of beauty, responsive to the needs of his social and sexual activities. Both of which David longed to improve. Oh, there had always been women in his life; dates, lovers, even one or two of whom he'd contemplated marriage. But something was always wrong. Each of them flawed. Never quite smart enough. Or beautiful enough. Or chic enough. With an improved physique and a more pres-

31

tigious place in business, he anticipated all that changing for
the better. Better women would come his way, find him attractive, sexually stimulating, a more exciting man. He saw
himself transformed into a figure of glamour and mystery, a
shifting shadow out of an old Hollywood movie or a new
advertisement for Jockey shorts. David concentrated on his
body.

Until the Striped Leotard appeared. She was a serious dis-
traction. Three times in as many days, she had shown up at
the Body Shop, that fashionable health club located in the space
once occupied by a Chinese restaurant between Lexington and
Third avenues. The Body Shop shone with the instruments of
good health, strength and beauty. Polished steel equipment,
floor-to-ceiling mirrors, purified, dehumidified, carefully cooled
air. Handsome men and lithe, well-proportioned women, strong,
shapely and struggling hard to become more so.

In the Relaxation Room, a glass topped bar that served fruit
and vegetable drinks and pure spring water straight from Maine.
Unsalted nuts and dried fruit were served in blue Chinese serving bowls, left over from the previous tenant. You could get
unflavored yogurt and buy vitamins by the jar or by the tablet
and get a quick shot of wheat-germ oil if that was your style.

The Body Shop was designed to improve the human body
and mind, in health, in spirit, in vigor. It also, incidentally,
brought men and women together who often had designs on
each other. It was, David believed, much better than going to
a singles bar to meet women. Here mutual interest made conversation easier and removed the intrusive sexual onus of a bar.
Not that it helped David very much, he was too shy to approach
a woman he'd never been introduced to; words froze on his
tongue and he felt clumsy, plain, unable to measure up. Still,
he kept coming, kept working out, building himself up for
whatever lay ahead, mapping out strategies that would enable
him to deal with Miss Wonderful, whenever a benevolent destiny caused her to appear.

Striped Leotard did not quite measure up. It would have
been nice if she'd been a shade taller and slightly less robust;
but there was no denying her powerful allure. What a great
body; strong and determined in its articulation with aggressive

hips that flared into great muscular, round buttocks. Her breasts were equally round, the nipples large and prominent. Her mouth was wider than he would have liked but extremely sensuous, the lips parted to reveal small white perfect teeth.

He watched her get ready to work out. Superb stretches, engaging twists, provocative bends, impressive leg extensions. How supple she was, how strong, how flexible. What would it be like, he wondered, to caress that satiny skin, to experience the flex of those well-developed thigh muscles? She placed herself on a rowing machine, working steadily.

David rose up on the slant board and watched her openly. He silently applauded every move she made, every thrust and pull, straining to visualize her without the striped leotard, naked and sleek and marvelously enticing. He fell back on the slant board with a low moan of despair; why did he never get to go out with a woman like that?

"Nice action," a mellow male voice said for David's ears only.

David answered without turning. "The best."

"A friend of yours?"

David swung off the slant board. The man who had spoken sat on a nearby bench. He was tall, athletic, muscular in a gray T-shirt and white shorts. His features had been carefully assembled, designed by a master sculptor. A noble brow, an inviting mouth, a strong round chin, a steady gaze out of large lambent eyes. He might have been a movie star or an aristocrat, bred to type over the generations. David was almost as impressed with him as he was with the Striped Leotard.

"I don't have that kind of luck. Never knew anyone who looked that good."

That amused the tall man and when he laughed David was compelled to join in. David felt the urge to explain himself to this stranger.

"I'm not much good at it, picking up women. I freeze. My brain turns to mush, lockjaw sets in. I want to hide and feel sorry for myself."

"You shouldn't have that problem with Cindy. She's friendly and easy to get along with. A really nice lady."

"Cindy! Her name is Cindy."

"A lovely person."

"You actually know her?"

"We've talked once or twice, over a carrot juice cocktail." He gestured toward the Relaxation Room. "You'd like her..."

"You bet I would." David's mind tipped and tilted as he tried to assimilate the opportunity that had presented itself. He thrust out his hand. "I'm David Foxman."

"Peter Downes here."

Downes's grip was strong and firm, the handclasp of a man you could trust. Though they were almost of a height, David felt slight next to Peter, insignificant.

"You called her Cindy," he prodded.

Downes nodded once. "I never did find out her last name."

David was reassured. Despite Downes's incredible good looks, Cindy had not succumbed to him. What a woman she was! Certainly had they become intimate, she would have told him her last name.

"Someday," David said hesitantly, "maybe we can have lunch, the three of us..."

"Better than that..." Downes looped an arm across David's shoulders. "Let's talk to her now." They moved toward the rowing machine, both of them smiling.


"A regular Yankee Doodle Dandy."

"What's that supposed to mean?"

The little man who faced him across the table in the coffee shop of the Americana Hotel had an unsettling effect on Peter Downes. The contrast was marked; Harry Geis was slight, round of shoulder, with the sidelong feral eyes of a scavenger, eyes that often saw more than other men saw. He reminded Downes of a ferret, quick, daring, ready to fight or flee.

"It means," Geis said between bites of his sandwich, "how far back your family goes. That's what it means, a hundred years? Two? Whataya say?"

Downes fiddled with his salad. The lettuce was soggy, the blue cheese dressing bland and runny.

"What's your family background, Harry?"

Long ago Downes had taught himself to confront unwanted questions obliquely, to divert curiosity about his personal history, to use his easy charm and steady intelligence to protect his privacy.

"Tell me about you, Harry."

"Me! You wanna know about me, just a pushy little kike is all." Downes frowned and Geis grinned in gleeful response. "Bother you, huh? You never heard a Jew call himself a kike before? Tell you what, that's what me and most of them on Forty-seventh Street is. You seen 'em, those momsers in their black coats and beards. Hasidim, they call themselves. Hustlers is what they are. No different than you or me. Only they practically spit on the rest of us. Stay to themselves like the rest of us is dreck. You know dreck—shit, garbage. To them we're not Jews, only they are. Like they've got a person-to-person call in to God's ear, y'know. Fuck 'em is what I say. Okay, so I'm not a Yankee Doodle sweetheart like you, but I'm a hundred and ten percent American all the same. What the hell, ain't this my country, too?" he ended in a petulant whine.

Downes, with all the sincerity he could muster, said, "I agree with you completely."

"Thanks a lot. The way some people act, I might've just as well got off the boat yesterday, you know what I'm saying?"

"Your parents come from Europe?"

"Grandparents," Geis snapped. "I told you, I ain't no green-horn. One set from Poland, the other from Austria. Part of the big wave of Jewish immigrants after the pogroms. My folks, hell, they might as well've been old-country, the way they were. My old man, going nowhere. Dumb and useless. Scratching in the land of plenty and coming up empty." He shot a quick glance at Downes. The permanently tanned cheeks were smooth, without lines or furrows, the brows carefully arched, the nose short, strong and straight. "Bet you never go without."

"Without?"

"Dames, dummy. What with that punim, bet they're all over you."

Downes answered with restraint. "There's plenty to go around, Harry."

"Sure, after guys like you lap up the cream. What's left is curdle. What I get is dogs. Dogs and hookers. Which brings us back to yesterday. You made contact, you got it going?"

"No trouble at all. You should have seen the expression on David's face when I introduced him to Cindy. I made a friend for life."

"That was the idea. Believe me, he's necessary."

"Cindy seemed to go for him, too."

Geis snorted. "Course she did, dummy, I own her. Cost me five hundred."

"You hired her?"

"Whataya think? She's a hooker."

"I had no idea."

"Course you didn't. Went down better that way. Boy meets girl, boy fixes boy up with girl. Like it was all natural and very friendly. Cindy was at my shop at ten o'clock this morning with her hand out. Five hundred bucks for an all-night stand and the sucker made another date with her. I told her I'd spring for a couple of more shots is all. After that, she's on her own."

"What if David finds out?"

"Who's gonna tell him? You? Me? Cindy? Smarten up, putz, it's me Cindy does business with. I use her regular to service big customers. She costs a lot but it pays off." Geis examined Downes directly. A little puffed up with his own self, straining to make himself out to be what he wasn't, and doing a pretty good job of it. The act was good enough to fool the suckers, but not someone with real smarts, someone who's been there before, not Harry Geis. "Now you want to be paid off. Right?"

Downes felt a twinge of apprehension. He'd been hired to do a job, no different than Cindy. He wanted his money, wanted to be on his way.

"We made a deal."

"Bet your sweet ass, we did, only all of a sudden you ain't so sure." Geis's laugh was tinny, abrupt, laced with mockery. "Lemme tell you, pal. With what you got, you oughta be traveling first-class all a the time. The best dames, the best restaurants, the best of everything. Only you go mainly tourist, strictly small-time, and it ain't likely to get any better soon. Not the way you're going."

The big muscles in Downes's thighs contracted and his hands balled up into fists. People seldom attacked him directly; he was too intimidating a presence, too big and too muscular. Seldom was he even criticized to his face; men and women alike tried to ingratiate themselves, to win his favor. It was, he knew, the result of his laidback style, the cultivated charm and the great good looks that had served him so well all of his life.

Nevertheless, this sleazy little man had managed to get under his skin. To doubt him. To insult him. To call his so very carefully constructed persona into question. He dipped a slice of fatty ham into the salad dressing and chewed with enthusiasm.

"I don't know what you're talking about," he said, with more assurance than he felt.

Harry's grin, thin, humorless and challenging, came and went. "You know, awright. Gelt, money. Cunt. You're after all of it. Okay, only you ain't getting quality merchandise. And why? I'll tell you why. Because you ain't got your act together is why. You just ain't good enough. Eats at you, don't it? No matter how hard you put on, nothing drops into place for you."

Downes patted the corners of his mouth with his napkin. He sipped some water. He raised his head without urgency.

A mocking expression flashed onto Geis's face. "Oh, that's smooth, Peter. Very smooth. Every move figured in advance, rehearsed, down pat. Okay, so you bought yourself some time to think, okay. So what've you come up with?"

Downes felt sick. Weak. He wanted to get away from Harry Geis forever. What an offensive little monster he was. How irritating. How unattractive. But an overwhelming curiosity kept him in place; Geis wanted something from *him* and he had to know what it was.

"You barely know me, Harry."

"Here's what I know, hot shot—you got the credentials, all right. The family history and like that. Only not half the brains you need or the balls you should have."

Downes couldn't let it pass. He leaned, one hand coming up in a big, lumpy fist. "There are limits, little man. Don't push me too far."

"Hey, that's okay! I like it. There's some moxie in you yet. Only I don't want to fight, I want to talk. Okay?"

Downes unclenched his fist. "About what?"

"Tell me, what brought you to New York in the first place?"

All logic told Downes to collect his money and get out, cut Harry Geis out of his life. The little man was a weasel, a sneak, and in some way Downes could not yet understand, dangerous. At the same time, some instinct informed him that through Geis lay the road to wealth and status, although Harry appeared to be the last man on earth to know the techniques required. Downes made up his mind; he would go along until he found out what Harry was after. If matters got too sticky, he could always back out.

"I've been a dealer for a long time," Downes said.

"A lousy liar is what you are."

Downes started up again. "I told you—"

"Sit down, schmuck. You were never a dealer. Last gig you worked was the phones in a boiler room operation in Chicago."

Downes sat back down. "How—?"

"Never mind how. I got contacts is how. Before that you peddled chazerei to pensioners looking for investments, shit stones."

"This is—"

"Listen for a change, maybe you'll learn something. Couple of years ago you ran a mail-order house in L.A. in cheap jewelry. You pulled off a couple of scams that went nowhere and you fleeced one or two lonely old dames for some cash. Big fucking deal. You got out of L.A. one step ahead of the cops."

"I'm not going to listen to this vileness."

"Better listen. A schmuck gets to be a schmuck by not listening, by telling himself he knows it all already. Lemme tell you, you don't know nothing about what I'm talking about. Anyway, you're getting a free lunch out of it. Which doesn't mean next time you don't pay."

"There isn't going to be a next time."

"We'll see. You came to New York to play the big time. To make a big score."

"Instead I came up with you, Harry."

"Your big break."

"A debatable point."

Geis stopped eating. He wiped his lips. He drank some beer. "I'm gonna make you rich."

"Harry, you own a small shop in Forty-seventh Street. Like a lot of people in the diamond district, you deal in artificial stones, cheap jewelry, maybe even fence stolen goods when you get the chance. You employ a part-time mechanic to fix watches and a girl to watch the store when you're out. Strictly small-time, Harry. You're not about to make either one of us rich."

"Hey, I like it!" Geis enthused. "You did some homework. Could be you're smarter'n I figured. Proves I made the right choice."

"Choice?"

"You figured it was an accident, us meeting the way we did. I spotted you for what you are, for what you can become, decided you were the kind of character I needed. Sure I did a little detective work, I'm no dummy. You heard the saying— better safe than sorry. I'm telling you straight, Peter, I'm the stuff your dreams are made of."

Downes doubted it very much. A gaping void separated him from Harry Geis, the small man was a bit player in a secret game to which only he knew the rules. Downes knew better than to trust him. What was Geis after? Where did his loyalties lie? What were his goals?

"Nightmares," he corrected.

"I'm on my way up, pal. I got a plan, the number one diamond sting ever invented . . ."

"Your idea, Harry?"

"Ain't nobody else here, is there? It's gonna make me rich, it could make you rich, too."

"Assuming I believe any of this, why'd you pick me?"

"Because you got the right natural equipment, for starters. The way you look, the way you talk. The right style, the right background. And you're as crooked as a snake behind it all. You're just what I need, the perfect front man."

"A big sting, you said?"

"The biggest."

"That takes money."

"It's all set. When I'm ready to move, the money will be

there. Whataya say, you in or you out?"

Refuse the offer, Downes commanded himself silently. No matter the prize, it was bound to turn out badly with Harry Geis. But Downes could not turn away from the big shiny carrot being offered. Geis was right; he'd come to the big city looking to crash the big time. The big score, it was what he'd always longed for. Maybe this was it. He filled his lungs with air and slowly exhaled.

"In," he said.

## chapter
# 4

THE BELLMAN TURNED THE KEY in the lock, opened the door and stood to one side. Keller went past him into the room and looked around. Not much different from a thousand other such rooms he had seen. Fancier maybe, the furniture more expensive than most, the bathroom larger, the towels thicker and softer. Otherwise, just another impersonal space for transients to sleep in, to do business in, to do bought sex in.

"You're the one found the body." Keller made in a statement, rough in the accents of an American city. A voice out of place in Monrovia, where English was spoken by soft black voices in melodious rhythms.

Keller stood with the forward lean of a schoolyard handball player, alertly poised on the balls of his feet. He held his head at a high angle, as if thinking out of the side of his mouth. His eyes, pale blue and sardonic behind strong cheekbones, were steady. His nose was a short twist, broken more than once. His mouth was wide, the lips sensuous, at once mobile and restrained. He had lived more than half his life and whatever time remained to him was more than he chose to think about. He had learned to do what was expected of him, expected by

**41**

himself and whoever paid for the privilege. That alone was
reason enough for Keller to go on.

"Yes, sir," the bellman said in a deferential voice. "I found
Mr. Foxman."

"Where?"

The bellman entered the room reluctantly. He found the
American disturbing, a man in whom violence seemed alarm-
ingly close to the surface. His fear caused him to be responsive.
"Here, sir. On the floor, his back pressed up against the bed.
As if he were resting, sir. His legs spread. His arms loose. His
eyes were open."

"What else?"

"There was blood, lots of blood."

Always the blood, Keller thought. Not like in the movies
where bullet holes were aesthetically symmetrical and blood
trickled in neat patterns. Lots of blood, mostly. Blood pumping
wildly out of severed arteries, taking life along with it. Broken
chests and jagged holes in the skull, bellies ripped open, legs
dangling by a thread of flesh. That's how men died from gun-
shot wounds. At least in war they did. In the wars Keller had
fought in, they did. For him the worst part was the stench. The
stink of rotting flesh, of voided bowels, and the pervasive smell
of fear. It filled the cavities of his skull at a time like this, the
remembered odors of men who had wanted very much to live
even as they were dying in strange, cruel places.

"Anything in his hands?"

"His hands, no, sir. Just resting there, that's all. I told the
police. The room was a bit of a mess, things scattered about."

"The killer searched the room?"

"I would say so, sir. At least, it looked that way."

"He was checking out, I understand?"

"He had called for someone to help with his bags."

"And you were the one who was sent?"

"The door was closed when I arrived. Closed but not locked.
The latch hadn't caught, you see. I knocked and the door
opened up and there he was."

"Did you see the man who shot Foxman?"

The question alarmed the bellman and he looked away. "I
passed a man in the corridor, sir. But I couldn't know for sure
that he—"

"Describe him for me."

"I wasn't paying much attention, sir. You see—"

"Describe him."

"A small man."

"Short?"

"Yes, sir, and slender."

"I'm six feet," Keller said. "I weigh a hundred and eighty pounds. How'd he compare?"

"Oh, much smaller than you are, sir."

"You're shorter than I am . . ."

"He came to about here on me . . ." The bellman placed his outstretched fingers to his chin. "Yes, about to here."

"Five feet high?"

"A bit more, I'd say. An inch or so more than that and built accordingly. Rather tightly put together, I'd say."

Keller grunted softly. "White or black?"

"Oh, a white man, sir. Definitely not an African, sir."

"Was he carrying anything?"

"Not that I remember, sir."

"What else can you tell me?"

"Nothing, really, sir. I don't know anything."

"What about Foxman? Anybody visit him? Women?"

"I wouldn't know, sir."

"Dope? Was he a user? Did he try to buy?"

"I have no knowledge of drugs, sir."

"What kind of people did he associate with?"

"I wouldn't know, sir. Mr. Foxman, he went out mornings and came back to change his clothes and sometimes he'd go out again."

"He was in the diamond business, you knew that?"

"It may have been mentioned, sir. Lots of people come to Liberia for the diamonds, sir."

Detective Sergeant Middleton was a large black man in a conservative suit. He shook hands without enthusiasm and read the inscription on Keller's business card.

"Joseph Patrick Keller. International Minerals and Mines, Limited." He dropped the card into his desk drawer. "What's IMM's interest in this, Keller?"

Uninvited, Keller sat down. "Foxman and Company is a

diamond merchant of substance, Sergeant. The dead man worked for Foxman, nephew of the president."

"If it happens with diamonds, IMM sticks its nose in, that it?"

"That's it exactly."

"And you're the nose?"

"This time, yes."

"You wasted no time getting here, less than twenty-four hours since Foxman was murdered."

"My company doesn't approve of its people being killed."

"It doesn't look like a diamond job to me."

"What makes you say so?"

The policeman indicated a cardboard box on his desk. "The dead man's belongings. A wallet full of cash, credit cards, that sort of thing. A package of colored stones and diamonds. If the gunman was after diamonds—well, he left them behind."

Keller inspected the stones, then read the bill of sale. "Have you contacted this Khamoury?"

"He confirmed the sale, identified the stones and the dead man. Robert Foxman, age twenty-four, lived in New York City."

"Nothing else?"

"His clothes, two suits and a sports coat, slacks, shirts, the usual. One piece of expensive luggage with a Mark Cross label. Oh, yes, the walking stick. According to Khamoury, Foxman damaged a knee skiing." He brought forth the knobby cane.

Keller hefted it, shook it, and shook it again.

Middleton nodded sagely. "Solid as a rock."

"Nature of the trade, to be suspicious."

"Exactly."

"Okay, it wasn't robbery. What was the motive?"

"Grudge. Maybe."

"Maybe." Keller stood up.

"Any reason for me to hold the body and the belongings? I imagine the family would like the young man buried in the States."

"Have you contacted them?"

"Any reason not to?"

"Seems okay to me," Keller said on his way out.

At the local office of IMM, Keller put a call through to the

New York office of Foxman and Company. It took nearly an hour for the connection to be made.

"Let me speak to Mr. Foxman," he said, identifying himself.

"Mr. Foxman isn't here, sir."

"Where can I reach him?"

"At the Connaught Hotel, in London."

Keller hung up and made another call, booking passage for himself on the next flight out of Robertsfield for England.

## *chapter*
# 5

MAURICE FOXMAN WAS, he had long ago acknowledged, a man of the city. New York and London were his favorites, an urban tandem connected by language, heritage, a similar tone and tempo; in either place, the people he dealt with in the course of his day had much in common. The long personal history attached to each city gave him comfort and confidence, made him feel at home. Other cities continued to play important roles in his existence; Paris, Amsterdam, Brussels, Tel Aviv, others. All of them were secondary, however; yet all of them were vital to his economic well-being.

He was a familiar figure in the long city streets, a tall, white-haired man, erect and alert, striding along at a pace that belied his years. For him nothing compared with the changing façade of city life: the multitude of shops, the incredible variety of faces, the individual ways people conducted their affairs, the way they dressed. He enjoyed it all.

Foxman had devoted himself to assembling the social fragments that constituted the fabric that was his life. For him, it was a never-completed painting, constantly enlarged, deepened, offering up fresh and richer details to be explored. There was never time enough to discover all that he wanted to discover. Never time enough to study everything that caught his eye or piqued his curiosity. Never time enough to assimilate all of it, to make sense of the puzzles, to answer all the questions and enter what he learned into the larger scheme into which all men fit.

The night before, Foxman had attended a concert, dined late with friends at a private club in Curzon Street and read Henry James for an hour before turning off the light. He lay in the darkness, unable to sleep, aware of his rapid heartbeat, of the pulsing in his wrists. A spreading awareness of his own mortality took hold; the body that had served him well for so many years in pleasure and in pain had begun to send out signals that it was succumbing at last to the stresses and strains of time. It wearied, it was running down. How sad, he mused without regret, that all a man's accomplishments altered nothing; each breath brought each being inevitably closer to his demise. The thought depressed him and he put it aside. He caused his mind to go blank and drifted gradually into a deep sleep.

He woke at six-thirty, instantly alert and functioning fully. By the time he had shaved and showered, room service had delivered breakfast: hot croissants with plenty of fresh butter and a pot of strong coffee. He dined without haste, reading *The Times*, in no rush to get on with the demands of the day.

At eight o'clock, a manicurist arrived to do his nails. They discussed the weather (not bad for London this time of year), the lure of Alaska (the manicurist longed to visit; Foxman suggested she read Jack London instead) and the woman's conviction that Jewish men made the best husbands.

"Do you have a Jewish husband?" Foxman inquired solicitously.

"Oh, dear me, no. But a friend of mine once did and he was splendid, says my friend."

"They're still married?"

"Not so's you could notice. Left her after a year, he did. For a French lady. They say French women are different than the rest of us, if you get my meaning, Mr. Foxman. You ever known a Frenchie, Mr. Foxman?" She cast a sly glance his way.

He considered his answer. "A long time ago I made friends with a beautiful, very proud, very courageous French woman. She helped save my life. A unique human being, by any standards."

"There you are, then. Jewish husbands and French mistresses, there's the combination for you!" Delighted with herself, she cackled contentedly and began to hum a tune while she buffed Foxman's nails.

When she was gone, Foxman inserted a cigarette into an ivory holder and smoked, contemplating the day that lay ahead. He allowed himself three cigarettes a day, one after each meal. No cigarettes, Dr. Altbaum had cautioned. No caffeine. No alcohol. "We don't want to overstimulate your heart," the doctor had explained. "Exercise restraint, do everything with restraint, and that heart of yours will last for another twenty years."

Neither of them believed that and so Foxman established his own rules. A single cup of coffee in the morning, one glass of wine with the evening meal. He had never led a spartan existence and didn't intend to begin now; for him, the quality of life took precedence over a less than satisfying longevity.

The chauffeured Rolls-Royce was waiting in front of the Connaught when he appeared. The driver greeted him by name, saw him settled in the soft leather back seat, and only then did he close the door. Once behind the wheel, he glanced back at his passenger.

"The City, Mr. Foxman?"

"The City, as usual, Mr. Dugan."

Ten times each year Foxman visited London for his regularly scheduled "sight" at the impressive Georgian mansion that housed the London Sales Office (LSO) of International Minerals and Mines, Ltd. These sights produced the largest portion of his stock; here he was supplied with the best diamonds at a price that allowed his operation to function smoothly and profitably. Any other purchases he made were insignificant by comparison, often at much higher markups.

Foxman and Company functioned in three different areas. Primarily, it sold rough stones to manufacturers in the trade, moving as many diamonds as the company could afford to obtain at wholesale. For the most part, Foxman's customers depended on him for their supplies even as he depended upon IMM, assured of a steady source of first-rate stones.

Foxman also produced cut diamonds in his own factories. In New York, a small operation produced selected stones, only those larger than three carats. The factory outside of San Juan, Puerto Rico, manufactured a substantial number of finished diamonds, smaller in size and of lesser quality; these were shipped out to jewelry manufacturers around the world. In Bombay, in a loose partnership with an Indian merchant, three cutting shops worked on product that was too small or too impure to be profitably cut in the United States or in Europe.

Lastly, Foxman operated a chain of elegant shops, each one strategically located in an exclusive hotel in a major city, in countries around the world. The jewelry sold had been made up from the debris of each sight by gifted designers located in New York and Amsterdam.

Foxman and Company, despite its considerable size, was ranked just below the Big Three of the diamond world. But Maurice Foxman, by reason of his character and integrity, had taken on the force of a moral leader in the industry. His rectitude was a foundation of the industry's reliability. His name was familiar to everyone, he was widely respected and frequently turned to for advice in times of difficulty. To be approved by Maurice Foxman opened financial and marketing doors which without him would have remained tightly shut.

But like the other 250 major dealers, Foxman looked to IMM for product, the main source of rough stones. Without them, his business was impossible.

Through it mines, its selling monopoly and its control of the marketplace, IMM dominated the diamond world. Through some five hundred corporations and businesses—wholly owned or controlled by IMM—diamonds were mined, shipped, bought and sold.

IMM dealt with nations as it did with dealers, treating them at best as equals and often as inferiors on the social and financial scale. Through its subsidiaries, IMM sought to buy up every new diamond that appeared on the scene, allowing only a prescribed number to be put up for public consumption. Through the application of sophisticated advertising techniques, the public's love for diamonds long ago had been created and continued to be nourished. Through its market researchers, IMM was able to predict with considerable accuracy how many stones would sell in a given twelve-month span and that number of diamonds was released into the market. Never more, never less. Thus was the highest possible price level maintained. Thus was IMM's profit margin kept healthy and stable. Thus was its political and economic power extended and made stronger.

Occasionally an individual or a company dared to function outside of IMM's rules. When word of such heretical behavior reached the upper echelons of IMM, the transgressor soon came under severe and sustained attack. Its sources of supply were terminated, its customers discovered they could make more profitable arrangements elsewhere, its inventory was decimated, lost or stolen. IMM's work? No one was ever certain; few people dared question or challenge the Syndicate, as it was commonly called, or its distant and imperious chairman, Sir John Messinger.

To Maurice Foxman, Sir John represented the dark side of the diamond industry. He ran the Syndicate with a strong hand and an inflexible will. He was capable of lifting a man up to the apex of material good fortune and of breaking him just as quickly. Industry gossip had it that Sir John had destroyed the businesses of men who offended him and had ordered some who had opposed him killed.

It was rumored that he worked closely with members of organized crime, when necessary, and collaborated with the most unsavory governments around the world in order to enhance the wealth and power of International Minerals and Mines. Foxman, who had dealt directly with Sir John only two or three times over two decades, loathed what the Chairman represented and the way he operated. But Foxman, as did all diamond merchants, needed Sir John's good will in order to do business.

Sir John, like IMM itself, was, it seemed to Foxman, omnipotent and apparently omniscient. It was widely held that the Syndicate was fed information by a global Security and Intelligence Division that had been favorably compared with the CIA, the KGB and Mossad (with, it was rumored, tight connections to each of these organizations). A whisper in the cutting rooms of Tel Aviv, the accepted wisdom went, a rumor in the jewelry exchanges of Amsterdam, a hint of rebellion in Ghana, and the news registered a day later in London or Rome or Johannesburg. Wherever Sir John happened to be.

The Rolls pulled up in front of the Georgian mansion and Foxman wondered, as he always wondered, what sort of a reception he was going to receive. All dealers approached these sights with the same kind of apprehension an actor felt before curtain on opening night on Broadway. A sight could make or break a dealer, even one as well established as Maurice Foxman. The stones offered might have substantial value or be worth next to nothing. The buyer had the right to accept an offering or reject it, at a price previously agreed upon. But to refuse meant to risk never again being invited back.

One poor sight might indicate a dealer's business practices had come under IMM surveillance and were frowned upon. It would be a wise dealer who searched his professional methods and ethics and swiftly changed his ways. Another merchant might have let slip some unflattering reference to the Syndicate, or to Sir John himself. A second such utterance could mean the end of his days in the trade. The crimes against IMM were too many to list and there were stories of dealers separated from the major source of product who never discovered what their transgression had been; they simply disappeared from the scene.

The stately Keeper of the Door admitted Foxman, greeted him by name and led him across the thickly carpeted floor to a small elevator which took him to the fourth level below the street. A plump pink man waited there to greet him with a limp handshake.

"Mr. Foxman."

"Mr. Severn."

Severn was one of three sales managers, one of whom was always present at a sight. For the last ten years, Severn had been Foxman's only contact with the Syndicate. The man to whom his orders were addressed, the man who, as far as Foxman knew, selected the contents of each sight, the man who accepted payment. Yet he was, in the overall scheme of things, of no more importance to IMM than the uniformed Keeper of the Door.

Severn took Foxman past armed guards into a morgue-like room with a marble floor, the walls lined with stainless-steel vault boxes. Foxman seated himself at a long table covered with a soft black cloth.

"Foxman and Company," Severn said, his voice commanding and sonorous.

A guard unlocked the appropriate vault box and set a carton about the size of a shoe box in front of them. He took up a protective position at one end of the table, Severn at the other.

Foxman opened the box to reveal a number of envelopes, each one containing diamonds of different quality and size. He emptied the contents of each envelope onto the black cloth, examining them quickly and expertly. His heartbeat went faster and the nighttime throbbing in his ears returned; his hands began to tingle. When he spoke, it was to Severn, though he never looked up.

"These stones are not nearly as valuable as they should be."

"Are you making a formal complaint, Mr. Foxman?"

"They are hardly worth the two and one half million cost of this sight."

"A matter of judgment."

"If I accept the offering, I will lose a great deal of money."

"You're rejecting the sight?"

Foxman lifted his head and pulled air into his lungs. Lifeless air; the shining walls appeared to be closing in. He wondered if Severn ever saw the light of day. Did the man have a family, a home, a human existence beyond these secure and sterile confines?

"Just by looking at the rough, the flaws are visible to the naked eye. See for yourself."

"If you care to make a written complaint, I'll see that it reaches Sir John's desk."

"This stone, for example. The location of the inclusions are such that it is impossible to obtain substantial final cuts. In order to eliminate the flaws, I'll be forced to cut to undesirable sizes."

"A complaint form," Severn demanded of the guard.

Foxman struggled to control his emotions. "This has to be a mistake."

"No, I don't believe so. Sir John detests mistakes."

"Perhaps the box was intended for someone else. I've always been treated correctly. Over the years—respect, courtesy, with—"

"Precisely, Mr. Foxman. Your box, your offering, your diamonds, sir. Are you refusing?"

"I'd like to discuss it, negotiate . . ."

Severn's plump little mouth twitched and grew still, drawn down as if in shame at the near display of amusement. "We don't discuss, Mr. Foxman. We don't negotiate. We don't change our minds. You know that."

Foxman stared at the stones glittering under the special overhead lamps that reproduced the purity of daylight. Aware of the unsteadiness of his hands, he placed them in his lap. Rage spread through him, the urge to strike out was almost overwhelming. He knew who his enemy was, had always known. Sir John. Always Sir John. Exercising his power behind the scenes in ways acceptable only to him, for reasons known only to him. Sir John was his tormentor, the threat to his present and future well-being. Sir John was the man he longed to battle. He braced himself against the intense anger he felt.

"I must talk to Sir John."

Severn met his gaze with no change of expression. "Impossible, sir."

His control breaking, Foxman shoved himself erect. "There are reasons not known to you people!" he said, voice uncharacteristically loud. "Explanations for the business steps I've been forced to take. When I talk to Sir John, he'll understand. He'll have to understand. Tell him I wish to speak to him. At once."

"I can't do that, Mr. Foxman."

"When we talk, Sir John will put things right again. He's a businessman and can sympathize with the drives and needs of another businessman. This sight—it is an insult. A humiliation! I will not permit you to humiliate me this way. I will not!" He broke off, swallowing his words, struggling to contain the rage that had been building in him over the years against Sir John. He shook his finger at Severn. "I do not have to tolerate such cavalier treatment."

"Mr. Foxman," Severn said with elaborate patience of voice and manner. "I am simply a salesperson, nothing more. That is Sir John's business, selling diamonds. One need not buy if one is dissatisfied, that is the rule and it always has been. Are you dissatisfied, Mr. Foxman?"

Foxman started to protest further, to make one last attempt to break through the wall of indifference, when the answer to his questions came rushing back to him. Some months before, he, and a handful of other dealers, had tried to gain a government concession for the development of a new mine in Venezuela. It would have meant a substantial alternate source of product at much lower prices, enabling them to step up production in all areas, at the same time circumnavigating IMM restrictions. Foxman, and the others, had convinced themselves that their new endeavor would be only a small pebble in the Syndicate's huge pond, not large enough to cause any alarm. They had been wrong. Foxman understood; it was a gross error of judgment to believe that IMM would tolerate even such a miniscule source of competition.

Through one of his South American subsidiaries, Sir John had tried to buy them out. When that had failed, political pressure was brought. Next, there were attacks on the mine itself. Some workmen were killed and much of the heavy machinery was destroyed. Eventually operations ground to a halt and the government licenses ran out and were never renewed. This then was Sir John's final message, a warning to Foxman, and the others, not to step out of line again. He looked over at Severn. The bland face was implacable, disinterested, immovable, an uninvolved element in Sir John's massive money-making machine. To argue with the man was futile, to be angry with him a waste of energy. Sir John had issued his orders and they were being carried out. Nothing remained but to suffer this poor sight as graciously as possible, to accept his punishment and go on: the next offering would be better and business would return to normal. Foxman replaced the diamonds in the envelopes and returned the envelopes to the shoe box. He straightened his shoulders, his emotions back under control, the aristocratic face lined with weariness but unyielding.

"I accept the sight," he said in a firm voice.

Severn allowed himself a brief smile. He watched Foxman leave without saying another word.

Back at the Connaught, the dealer found a message waiting; Mattie had telephoned from New York. Manager of his New York office, the widow of his brother had worked for him for a very long time. She was a low-key administrator who kept the day-to-day operations of his business running efficiently. The message said Mattie would call again when she arrived in Paris. Why Paris? What business did she have there?

Not given to brooding about what he couldn't change, he put the matter out of his mind. Eventually Mattie would explain her travels, her reasons for leaving the New York office in lesser hands, would explain it all succinctly and completely. Still cradling the box of diamonds in one arm, he headed for the elevators when his path was blocked by a tightly knit man in a sports coat, a blue shirt and a knit tie. How long since he had seen a knit tie? And this one, twisted and faded, knotted casually, a concession to fashion and to the general social order; at the same time, a clear signal that the wearer certainly did not give a damn about such things.

"Mr. Foxman."

Foxman looked the man over: the compact body, the bony hands, strong and large, the face marked by time and bouts of violence, the pale eyes that seemed to miss nothing. The eyes of a scoundrel, Foxman assured himself, or of a policeman.

"I don't know you," he said.

"I'm Keller, IMM Security Systems."

Foxman had heard about the Syndicate's security operatives, mostly tall tales of extreme behavior; here was the first such he'd ever encountered. Keller looked fully capable of carrying out Sir John's most dramatic commands, a man intelligent and rough, his skills for hire.

Foxman tapped the box of diamonds once. "My affairs of the day with IMM are completed, sir."

Keller made an almost imperceptible shift of weight from one foot to the other. And cut off Foxman's path to the elevators.

"This is important, sir."

"IMM's business. At the moment, I am very little concerned with any of it."

"IMM's business and your own, sir. Personal and professional."

Foxman braced himself. "Exactly what are you trying to say to me?"

"It's about your family, Mr. Foxman. May we talk in private?"

Foxman could read no threat in those still eyes. "Very well, come with me." He headed for the elevator, Keller a stride behind.

Once settled in the sitting room of Foxman's suite, the two men examined each other with frank interest. To Foxman, Keller represented the worst aspects of the diamond world: a pervasive greed that went far beyond the bounds of a proper and decent profit, an increasing disregard for standards, for the traditional ways of doing business, for rudimentary good manners, for the elimination of men of culture and education and sensibility in the trade; and always the imminent threat of violence.

Foxman was known to Keller by reputation. A man widely respected and admired, a gentle man, a man of taste and refinement. He was taller than Keller, straight and proud, the clean lines of his face framed by white hair that ran long over his ears and his collar. He possessed an Old World quality that Keller appreciated, as if he clung tightly to some essential element of his European youth. When he spoke it was in a voice faintly accented, prophetic and reproachful.

"You have had your breakfast?" he said.

"Nothing for me, thanks."

"Some coffee?"

"Nothing."

"You're an American."

"Born in New York. I travel a lot."

"Doing Sir John's work."

"Security's my work. I'm good at it."

"I'm sure you are. I've heard stories about IMM security people."

"There are always stories. They don't necessarily apply to me."

"Very well, if you say so."

Another man might have reacted to Foxman's wariness, to his suspicions. A shrug of dismissal. A word of contempt. Not

Keller. He never apologized, he never explained. To do either, he had long ago decided, would do lethal damage to his opinion of himself.

"Why are you here, Keller?"

"You have a nephew name of Robert Foxman?"

Foxman brought his hands together prayerfully. "What about Robert?"

"He was in Monrovia?"

"On company business. Why should that concern you?"

"Buying diamonds?"

"Exactly why are you asking, Keller? Yes, Robert was making a brief business trip. Buying for Foxman and Company. Colored stones mostly for the line of jewelry we produce and sell in our own boutiques. A few diamonds, yes. But nothing substantial. There are no secrets here. Why this concern about Robert?"

Keller never flinched. "The news I have is bad."

Nothing showed on Foxman's face but his heart began to race and a weakness came into his knees. He sat down.

"Tell me . . ."

"It's Robert, he's dead. He was shot at the Ducor Palace Hotel two days ago."

All blood drained out of Foxman's face and suddenly he seemed much older. His eyes fluttered shut and he swayed in place. His lips began to move and Keller strained to hear the words.

"Yisgadoel, yisgadasch . . ."

Rocking back and forth, Foxman softly intoned the prayer for the dead in Yiddish. Keller waited for him to be through.

Finally Foxman's eyes opened and skittered about as if unable to locate the other man. "No question, it was Robert?"

"No question."

"How could such a thing happen? Was it a robbery?"

"His money, credit cards, his watch, the stones. Nothing of value was taken."

"Then why?"

"I hoped you could provide a reason."

Foxman's caution returned. Keller was a member of the Syndicate, one of Sir John's hirelings, not a man to be trusted.

"The business takes a man to many places," he said.

"For example?"

"What does it matter now?"

"When diamonds are involved, when diamond people are involved, it's my job to investigate. Robert worked for you, he was on a buying trip when he was killed. Yet the stones were left behind. Curious business."

Weariness spread through Foxman's body. He longed to withdraw, to take himself away from the onslaughts of the day. First the bad sight and now this. How would he tell Mattie about the death of her only son? Or did she already know? Was this why she had called? If so, what had taken her to Paris? He raised his eyes to Keller.

"If they weren't after the diamonds, why did they shoot Robert?"

"They? Who are you talking about?"

"The people who murdered my nephew. Your people."

"You think IMM people killed him?" Keller was unable to keep his astonishment out of his voice.

"Who else? Sir John has been trying to squeeze me out of the business. Me and my friends, those of us who have dealt in diamonds for so long." He indicated the box of diamonds. "Two and a half million dollars' worth of junk. Garbage. My punishment, Keller, and for what? For daring to try to improve the nature of my business. For that IMM would destroy us, if it can."

"Sir, I have no connection with the selling office. Security, out of New York, that's my job. If IMM had your nephew killed, would I be on the case? It makes no sense."

"Or it makes a great deal of sense. Part of the cover-up, an effective way to pretend innocence. You belong to Sir John and his terrorists. I accept nothing you tell me."

Looking at Maurice Foxman, Keller wondered if the old man had gone bad. Maybe he had been in league with Robert in some kind of shady transaction. A great deal about the affair struck a sour note, roused Keller's suspicions, and he vowed to pursue the mystery wherever it led. Foxman might have begun a campaign to acquire stones in the shadowy fringes of the business where stolen and smuggled diamonds were bought and sold. It would not have been the first time a respected dealer was bent by circumstances. Was Foxman's antagonism a camouflage for his own subversive activities? It was Keller's job to answer such questions satisfactorily.

"Robert was in Monrovia only to make a buy from a man named Bakshir Khamoury? Is that right?"

"Obviously you know the answer to that question."

"Yes, I do. I tried to question Khamoury but he had already left the country."

"A trader is constantly on the move."

Keller nodded once and spoke without emphasis. "Too bad Robert didn't have time to defend himself, to fight back. He was an athletic young man..."

Foxman stared. "Athletic! Yes, I suppose he was. A bit of a tennis player, I believe. He liked to swim, laps at the Ninety-second Street YMHA."

"He skied a great deal?"

"I don't really know. Robert worked for me but away from the office we seldom saw each other. Except holidays. Mattie—his mother—made a Seder—you know what a Seder is, Keller?"

"The Passover meal, yes."

"Jesus' Last Supper was a Seder. Did you know that?"

"I never heard it before."

"Too many Christians ignore His Jewishness, I'm afraid. No, Robert and I were not close. He might have been an avid skier and I would not necessarily know about it. I never cared much for cold weather myself, though I did some skiing many years ago. Why do you ask?"

"He was using a cane."

"Robert, a cane?"

"Hurt his knee skiing, I was told."

"That's odd. I have no memory of him with a cane. Still—at my stage of life, you don't always notice a lot of things. Is it important?"

"Probably not." Keller rose and handed Foxman his card. "A policeman's mind, cluttered with details. If you think of anything that might help..."

"Yes, of course. You'll let me know if you solve the mystery."

"Depend on it, sir. I'll be in touch."

\* \* \*

Mattie Foxman owned the quiet competence of a born manager, an arranger, created by a perceptive Maker to attack the red tape and incompetence that inhibits so much of human activity and so get things done. She listened patiently to the arguments of the French police inspector who insisted that he had many questions to put to her daughter, that the hospital was the best place for that interrogation to take place, that departmental policy recommended she remain where she was. Mattie agreed with everything he said in a gentle, helpless manner, she conceded, she suggested, she flirted, and in the end she got her way.

"You may take Mademoiselle from the hospital, madame, but only to your Paris hotel."

"Absolutely, Inspector."

At the hospital, she had to confront the physician in charge, a pinched little man with rimless glasses and an equally officious manner. "Madame, your daughter was most fortunate. An accident of that magnitude, her injuries might have been terminal. Even so, her flesh has been badly treated and her system is profoundly shocked. I would advise . . ."

Mattie listened. She nodded, she smiled helplessly, and an hour later had Ellie in the spacious back seat of a rented limousine, on their way back to Paris. Only when they were comfortably settled in a suite at the Plaza Athénée, only when a waiter had brought a large pot of hot tea, only when they were finally alone, did Mattie sit at the foot of Ellie's bed and gaze with considerable disapproval at her daughter.

"How do you manage it?" she said, trying to understand this so very unladylike child of hers. "Is this how I raised you? To be racing naked around the French countryside and wrecking cars?"

"I told you—they drove me off the road. Damn Henry Wilton!"

"But naked! It is hardly the way you were brought up. I have always considered myself a sophisticated, worldly woman. But driving a car with no clothes on. I must say it, Ellie—I simply cannot approve of such bizarre behavior."

Ellie laughed and the effort sent pain stabbing through her battered rib cage. She gasped and shook her head, regaining her composure. "There was no time to dress."

"Crazy Englishman," her mother said. "They are certifiably insane, those aristocrats. I have always avoided that sort."

"And I will, too, from now on."

Mattie was not mollified. "There was definitely some genetic confusion in our family. You should have been the boy and Robert the girl. When you were children—you fought his fights for him. You were the more aggressive, the most stubborn and single-minded of children."

"Someone had to protect Robert."

"Girls are not supposed to fight."

"Where is it written? If I didn't fight, both of us would have been beaten on."

"Was it necessary that you play football, too?"

That drew a small laugh and another grimace at the pain in her jaw. "I promise you, Mother, no more football."

"One good thing, you have my sense of humor."

"And good looks."

"Flattery won't work. Anyway, maybe that's the problem— you're much too good-looking. If plain would make your life easier, I'd opt for plain. Being beautiful certainly hasn't brought a good man into your life."

"I'm still young, Mother."

"And still without a husband," Mattie said dryly.

"I made one mistake. That should be enough." It was said facetiously, meant to elicit a small smile; Mattie failed to react.

"It's time you grew up, my dear, found yourself a good, solid man, someone like your uncle."

"Not another Maurice, please," Ellie replied with thinly veiled sarcasm.

"You won't do better and you've already done a lot worse."

"Many times," Ellie said, with a thin, humorless smile.

Mattie persisted. "Isn't it time you raised a family of your own?"

"Ah, wife, mother, gal Friday. Is that what the Fates have in store for me, Mother? No, thanks, not my scene."

"You're such a smart one, Ellie. Those up-to-date ideas of yours. Look where they've got you—a lot of men who treated you badly and a French hospital bed. That you weren't killed is a miracle."

Ellie grinned good-naturedly and changed her position. Again the pain, digging deep. "There isn't a part of me that doesn't hurt."

At once Mattie was compassionate, clucking sympathetically over her daughter, straightening the sheets, pouring another cup of tea. "According to the doctor, there's going to be pain for at least a week, maybe more."

"It's a little embarrassing, to total a car and end up without even a broken bone."

"Thank God."

"Clean living and good luck."

"If I didn't know better, I'd believe you were somebody else's child."

"Why, Mother! Are you telling me you were fooling around while you and Daddy were married?"

"Bite your tongue." Mattie laughed behind her hand. "You rest for a while. We're flying back to New York in the morning. I won't be satisfied until Dr. Hammaker examines you."

"He's not the only doctor in the world."

"I've known him a long time, I trust him. Now get some rest."

"I'm all right, stop worrying."

"You're not all right and I'll never stop worrying. It's the nature of the beast. But with God's help maybe I can keep you from killing yourself."

Ellie tried to make her response dismissively satiric, but her fear made her smile a mask. "With men like Henry, killing myself would be redundant. And, Mother, while I barely got away with my life, Henry got away with 'The Chamblay.' That slimy bastard has probably peddled it by now. How am I going to make good on it? The Chamblay is certainly worth a couple of hundred thousand."

"Your uncle will think of a way. You seem to think of ways only to fail. To humiliate me and yourself."

Ellie turned away. "I don't need Maurice's interference."

"I'm talking about help and you call it interference. This accident must have destroyed some of your few remaining good brain cells. I refuse to help someone bent on defeat and humiliation."

"This is my problem, I'll find a way to solve it."

"Stubbornness, that's your main problem. Maurice is your

father's brother, why not let him help, if he can."

"I said I'll do it myself."

"Maurice has always been there, whenever anybody in the family needed help."

"Mother, let's not argue. Your opinion of Maurice is considerably higher than my own."

"I've noticed. More than once you've treated him rudely. If nothing else, your brother and you were brought up to have good manners. What happened to you? Your uncle has cared for you and Robert and me ever since Emil passed away. How many other men would be so generous?"

"Too generous."

"Maurice is a good man. An exceptional man. A man with love and regard for his family. Even his rambunctious niece."

"Is it love or is it just a way for him to assuage his guilt, another way for him to exercise his power over us?"

Mattie frowned. "Guilt? What has Maurice ever done to feel guilty about?"

Ellie clamped her mouth shut. Her mother refused to acknowledge her own history, the history of their family. Had Mattie conveniently forgotten all the differences between Emil and Maurice, the profound moral and ethical divisions that had made conflict between them inevitable, a bitter enmity that had kept them apart for so many years? Was she able now to forget how Maurice had demeaned and humiliated her husband? No, not forgotten; Mattie had simply chosen to stand with Maurice against the man she had married.

"Let's just say that I don't trust Maurice."

Mattie shook her head. "I don't understand."

Ellie supplied no answer.

"He is a man of honor."

"Our definitions differ. Perhaps the family does owe him a great deal. Still..."

Still; a nagging thought persisted. To think well of Maurice was to betray the memory of her father. Another reason to free herself completely and for all time from dependence on Maurice. To separate herself from the rewards and the strictures of Foxman and Company. To turn away from his free-flowing largesse.

The phone rang and Mattie picked it up. "I put a call in to

Maurice." She spoke into the instrument. "Hello, Maurice. . . . Yes, I'm all right but Ellie was in a car accident. . . . No, not seriously. Banged up a little but nothing broken. . . . Yes, to-morrow. . . . What?" She listened intently and Ellie saw the blood drain out of her mother's face. "No," Mattie whimpered. "No, no, no! My God, no!" she screamed, and crumpled to the floor in a dead faint.

## chapter
# 6

KELLER ARRIVED IN NEW YORK on the night before Robert Foxman was to be buried. The case had captured his imagination; maybe Foxman himself was at the root of his interest. The man was full of shadowed corners, complicated, yet very much what he appeared to be. Direct, intelligent, proud. Keller wondered: What did it mean to a strong man to know he was on the down side of his life, still active and powerful, virile, yet slipping inexorably down the dark and distant slope. Traces of the young man Foxman had been were still in evidence; his straight stance, his clear challenging glance, his agile mind. Keller wanted to know more about Maurice Foxman, know him better, discover how he had created the man he was now, a man other men looked up to, a pillar of his world.

He doubted that anyone at IMM headquarters was as involved in this case as he was. Certainly not Sir John, definitely not Koenigsburg, who insisted that all mysteries be solved before the results were brought to him. Details bored Koenigsburg. Problems and dead ends irritated him. He demanded quick solutions to all investigations. Neat endings.

New York revived Keller. The familiar sounds and smells of the city intensified his awareness, they sharpened his instincts and aroused the old blood kinship to all the beasts in this particular jungle.

The city was always the same. And acutely different. Streets once crowded with ancient tenements and the ebb and flow of human existence, lived out under the shadow and the rattle of the El, were now lined with glass-and-steel skyscrapers that reflected nothing except each other. The El had been torn down, the tenements blasted away, the old brownstones destroyed, the city improved; why then wasn't life on the sidewalks of New York better?

Below the streets, the subway was filthy, overcrowded, neglected by generations of self-serving politicians, managers and workers alike until the system had begun to break down. Graffiti scarred the sides of the cars; Art of the Common Man, some famous and pretentious writer had characterized it. The writer, of course, could afford to stay out of the subway, out of the dirt, the rancid smells, the constant threat of robbery, violence and death that faced the ordinary citizen.

Once it had been different. A dime would take you from the upper reaches of the Bronx, where Keller had been born and raised, to the far edge of Brooklyn. Biggest travel bargain in the world.

Pinky was the girl's name and she had lived near Coney Island; Pinky had been blond and buxom and generous in ways Keller had never before experienced. Every Friday night he made the long ride to see her. And after a full night of warm pleasures, he made the return trip to the Bronx. He'd sleep most of the way, secure in the knowledge that no one would bother him, and no one ever had. Later, when he met Doris, who would become his first wife, he stopped making the trip. Doris lived only a short walk away; Pinky became geographically undesirable.

From Kennedy Airport, Keller went directly to the apartment building Robert Foxman had lived in. In the East Sixties, studios and one-bedroom flats piled one on top of another, occupied by stylish young men and beautiful young women paying exorbitant rents for a prime location. New York drew them by the thousands every year, the best and the brightest, scrambling for the Holy Grail. Few of them ever attained their goals. The city ground them down, exposed their flaws, made them aware of their ordinariness. Twenty years later, they woke as if from a nightmare, confused, bitter, lost, no longer young or hopeful, no longer in touch with the best part of themselves.

Keller located the manager of the building. He wore a pencil-thin moustache, an expensive toupee and a cologne that lingered on the still air like a poisonous mist. Keller flashed his ID and said that Robert Foxman had been murdered.

"So I heard," the manager said.

"Don't break up, mister."

"Look, was he my brother or something? No matter, there's people waiting for every vacant space. It's only fair, all those people in need of housing. A building like this, there's hardly any turnover at all. I better make some calls. Have to start showing it at once."

"The body is still above ground, pal."

"Yes, yes. The belongings will have to be stored. The place should be painted. Do me a favor, don't let on. About his being murdered, I mean. Tends to make people uneasy."

"Maybe we can work something out."

The manager frowned. "What's that supposed to mean?"

"I want to look at Foxman's apartment."

"Oh, no. I mean, I can't. It's impossible. Respect for the dear departed and all that . . ." The pencil moustache lifted in what passed for an insinuating smile.

Keller folded up a twenty-dollar bill and shoved it into the pocket of the black silk jacket the manager wore. "Now," he said.

"If you'll follow me, sir."

The apartment was neatly ordered. Recently dusted and vacuumed. Everything in its place, a place for everything. A quality view of the East River and the UN to the south. Balcony drenched in the morning sun. Beautiful.

Keller worked swiftly. The bedroom closet revealed some expensive suits, half a dozen sports coats, some slacks and more shoes than Keller had owned in his life. The drawers of Foxman's chest were stacked with made-to-order shirts and high-count cotton underwear. The bathroom contained nothing to catch the eye.

"Who cleaned?" Keller said.

"A cousin. Name of David Foxman."

"Did he take anything?"

"No, nothing. He dropped into my office before he left. No, he didn't take a thing."

"What happened to the skis, the boots, that stuff?"

The manager shrugged. "I never saw anything like that. Maybe he rented his equipment."

"Maybe. What did the cousin have to say?"

"Not much. Only that they're burying him today. Jews are like that, can't wait to plant their dead. Too bad you didn't find anything."

"I found out a lot."

"Like what?"

"That you're a coldhearted son of a bitch."

Services were held at a chapel on Madison Avenue. Nondenominational. Robert, it appeared, had made it clear that he was a nonbeliever, an atheist, and desired a funeral in accord with those beliefs.

"He was a Jew," Maurice insisted.

"We have to respect his wishes," Ellie argued, with more vehemence than she felt.

Mattie remained neutral and they arrived at a compromise; a service without theology, a burial with the Jewish prayer for the dead and a eulogy delivered by Maurice. Everyone seemed satisfied; Robert, if he had strong feelings one way or the other, failed to let them be known.

The director of the chapel informed Keller that he was late. The procession had departed for the cemetery only minutes before.

"Any personal effects? Who claimed them?"

"Normally such items remain at the deceased's home. We receive the remains only. Odd transaction this one. The poor man expired in Africa, alone in an alien land. How very sad! Sent home by airfreight, as it were. We took delivery at Kennedy, effects and all."

"Where are they now?"

"Oh, right here, with me. I'm to send them on to his mother. I have the address somewhere."

"What about the stick?"

"The stick?"

"The walking stick."

"Oh, yes, the cane. That goes, too." He pointed; in one corner of the office, the knobby walking stick was propped against the wall.

"I'll take that," Keller said.

"Oh, I couldn't, sir. It just isn't done."

Keller placed a twenty flat on the desk. When the director hesitated, Keller matched it. "Sentimental value," Keller said flatly.

"Ah. You were acquainted with the deceased. In that case, I suppose there's no harm..."

"No harm at all."

"Yisgadoel, yisgadasch..."

More than one hundred mourners pressed in on the gravesite. Friends, business associates, family. Many had come out of respect and affection for Maurice Foxman, and when he began to speak in a voice low with melancholy, everyone listened attentively.

"Robert, not yet in the prime of his life, is gone from us. Murdered in a foreign land by an unknown killer for motives that elude us all. But I have no difficulty in naming the motive for this cruel and wanton killing—greed.

"Most of our people are righteous and honest. Honest folk making an honest living. And when one stumbles, we have our own arbiters of justice and fairness. We seldom require police intervention. We seldom look to the courts to dispense justice. We are our own best judges and most of us adhere to the rules and rulings passed on from generation to generation.

"But always there are the few who persist in functioning outside those rules. Men concerned only with their own welfare, no matter who gets hurt in the process. More is what they are after. More profits. More wealth. More power over the rest of us. This lust for riches and power is the true reason my nephew was killed.

"Diamonds have been a part of my life since I was a boy. During the war against the Nazis, when Jews were slaughtered simply because they were Jews, diamonds saved my life, the life of my beloved brother, Emil, may he rest in peace..."

His eyes sought out Ellie and she met his gaze briefly. Then she shifted around in her wheelchair, looked away.

Foxman resumed speaking. "We Jews have dealt in diamonds since the Middle Ages. For even then we were a people scorned and persecuted and we recognized that those small sparkling stones were a perfect instrument for those who must always be able to conceal the means of their livelihood from the bandits who would otherwise rob them. We have always been a people who might, at a moment's notice, be forced to flee for our lives. Diamonds—easily concealed, easily transported—were therefore ideal wares.

"Mazel und Brucha. Luck and Blessing. And a handshake. No man required more of another to bind a deal. A man's word was sufficient. Honor was the glue of every transaction. Self-respect counted for something, the true currency of life.

"No longer, sad to say. Changes for the worse have set in. There is a diminution of our value system. Selfishness, cruelty and violence seem to dominate our lives.

"Unsavory elements have infiltrated our ranks. Irresponsible and uncaring people who are not bound by our traditions and our codes have caused widespread grief and damage. Swindles abound. Lies and deceptions are passed for the truth. Men are robbed and murdered in cold blood.

"We are under attack. Our profession is in jeopardy, our futures, the well-being of our businesses and our families are in mortal danger. Some of us know from personal experience what it means to be subject to the dictates of a vicious and uncontrolled power. A number of us barely escaped the Holocaust. And now the Syndicate, Sir John Messinger's Syndicate, International Minerals and Mines, has the economic strength to crush every one of us again. He possesses outrageous wealth and political influence and armies of hard men willing to do anything he commands. Sir John's heavy hand weighs down each of us. When it suits him, he will surely bring us to our knees, one after the other."

Foxman's eyes ranged out over the mourners to where Keller stood, alone and still. He raised his chin and spoke directly to Keller.

"Syndicate terrorists are everywhere, ready to strike should we dare to follow the dictates of our consciences. Let a man act in his own self-interest and Sir John will punish him. Make him weak and inadequate. Force him to surrender his business, perhaps even his life. Every one of us, every one of you, recognizes our vulnerability.

"I cry out for freedom from this oppression, an end to dictatorship, to ruthless attacks on old and honorable families. Let us go back to the old ways. The old values. Let us honor again the traditions of those who preceded us.

"Those who care must band together. Oppose the common enemy. Make it safe for fine young men like Robert to work as we have worked, to create a life for themselves. This awful crime must be avenged. In one way or another. And so it will be. Amen..."

"Mazel und Brucha," someone said.

"Mazel und Brucha."

Alone in the living room of Mattie's apartment, they sipped hot tea and lemon and for a very long time neither of them was able to speak. Outside the long shadows of the tall buildings brought a premature dusk to the city, to fit the gloom of their day. It was Maurice who finally broke the silence. "You didn't cry," he said compassionately. "Not at all during the funeral."

"Oh," she said, not meeting his eyes, "I cried. Inside, I have been crying since the moment I heard. Grieving is so painful, Maurice. Does it ever stop?"

"He was a fine boy." Foxman wanted to comfort her, ease her anguish, and understood what an impossible task that was. "A fine boy," he repeated lamely.

"The way he looked when he was a baby. Never wrinkled and red the way so many babies are. Always beautiful. How handsome he was! I miss him so much."

"We all do. Everyone who knew him will miss him."

"So young to die. Why him, Maurice? So very young."

"There are no reasons, no logic. Remember how it was before the war in Europe with the Nazis? My family, your family, all of those others who disappeared into the camps forever. To give logic to such affairs is to dignify them, to give them humanity and meaning."

"Life can be cruel."

"Life is what life is—random, illogical, an interlude that means only what you cause it to mean. Robert—he was a good boy, a good man. One day he might have taken over the company when I stepped down."

She raised her cup and lowered it without drinking. "That a boy like Robert should be taken away so soon. It isn't right. It isn't fair. He meant so much to me."

"You still have Ellie."

"Yes, Ellie. But he was my only son. It isn't right, I know, but it was always different for me with Robert. Different from the way I loved Ellie. Different from Emil."

"Different," Maurice said, as if not wanting to hear any more.

"Different," she said again. "More. I loved Robert more. Oh, yes, it's true. More than Ellie from the start. More even than Emil. Somehow Robert filled a void in me Emil never touched. With Robert, I felt fulfilled and it didn't matter that between Emil and me there was less than there might be between a man and a wife."

"Emil was your husband," he felt compelled to say. "He cared for you, he did his best. He was Robert's father, Ellie's father. And my brother."

She raised her eyes to his. "I mourn for Robert as I never mourned for Emil. Nothing can change that, Maurice. I will always mourn for him. Inside me the tears will never stop. I weep for him all the time."

"Time, Mattie. Time will make it easier."

She almost smiled. "Easier, maybe. But never better. Accustomed to the pain, yes. Accustomed to never seeing him again. But the emptiness, that will never pass. Not ever." And then, finally, the tears began to flow.

*chapter*
# 7

IT WAS ONE OF THOSE early-spring days in New York, bright and clear, with a lingering bite in the air. People walked more swiftly than usual, as if to warm themselves against the chill, keeping to the sunny side of the street. Along Forty-seventh Street—the single block reaching from Fifth Avenue to the Avenue of the Americas (no New Yorker called it anything but Sixth Avenue)—the usual babble of sights and sounds, of deals offered and made in a variety of languages with gestures and nuances to match.

Bearded Hasidim in long black coats aggressively transacted their business in Yiddish. Black Africans sold to agitated Italians. Britishers bargained with Hollanders, and Israelis sold to Arabs in Hebrew or Arabic or French. Caste-marked Indians offered their wares to any passerby willing to listen. All of them were intense, minds clicking away, ready to give a little, take a little, whatever was necessary to close a deal.

"Mazel und Brucha..."

In his shop on the street, Harry Geis was doing a deal. The woman was in her forties, overweight, with bleached-blond hair. She was examining the tray of diamonds Geis had set on the counter. She isolated the three largest stones and hefted each one in her hand, asking about their weight. Geis responded with an economy of words unusual for him. "Let them sell themselves," was his philosophy of business. Give only as much as you have to give.

"I want a perfect stone," she said, as if invoking some higher power in her behalf.

"D-flawless," Geis said. "Every one of these." He offered her his loupe. "See for yourself."

She looked; he was ready to bet she didn't know what to look for. He was familiar with her kind; loaded up with their husbands' money, hunting for bargains, something for nothing. You should live so long, he intoned to himself.

"If you're after a stone for a ring," he said, "or a brooch. One or two of the smaller ones should be just as good."

She answered without looking up. "No, no, I want an investment stone. Something guaranteed to go up in value."

"You know what they say—'A diamond is forever.'"

"I don't want to take chances."

"You won't do better than these three."

"Which one is the best?"

Hooked, Geis gloated. He delivered what was meant to be a reassuring smile. "You've got a good eye. Any of these, you can't go wrong."

"Which would you choose, were you in my position?"

He considered. He pointed. He spoke intimately, letting her in on a secret. "Here, this is the pick of the litter. Look at that sparkle..."

"I noticed..."

"The truly artistic cut."

"I spotted it right away."

"Of course, a gem of that quality..."

"Expensive, huh?"

"Bound to be."

"How much?"

His mind was already made up. "In this market, you're lucky. The right time to buy. Since it's been a slow morning and I'm ready to make my first sale. For you, nine thousand flat. I'll absorb the tax myself." At that price, he reckoned his profit at seven thousand dollars.

She hesitated. "Shouldn't I have it appraised?"

"You bet. No way I'd let you have it without you first getting it appraised. Diamonds is my business, right, not yours. Lemme tell you, take the stone you want, whichever fits your needs. Take it and go to any dealer on the street. Get a price. If it costs more than nine thousand, I'll take the loss. If he tells you less, I'll let you have it for that. How can you lose?"

"That seems fair enough."

"That's the kind of operation I run. Fair. Honest. Every item guaranteed. Go ahead, take it. When you're satisfied, come back. If we can do business, fine. If not, also fine."

The blond woman picked up the stone, fingers closing around it possessively. "You want some kind of a deposit?"

"Gimme your check. I'll hold it right here till you get back. Whatever price you come back with, you can tear it up and write me a new check. Fair? You bet it is."

She giggled and leaned his way. "Would you believe I brought cash?"

Dummy, he thought, and gave her his best grin. "I take real money, too. I'll write you a receipt."

They completed the transaction. "I appreciate this," she said. "I really do. I'll just get another opinion and I'll be right back."

"Take your time." Geis busied himself returning the rest of the stones to the display case. As soon as the woman was gone, he called to the back room.

"Hetty!"

Hetty appeared in the doorway, still holding the Patricia Matthews romance she'd been reading. "What is it, Harry?"

"You get a good look at her?"

"Yeah."

"Go after her and get back to me soonest."

"Okay." On her way out of the shop, she passed Peter Downes coming in. She gave him a long, approving glance, wondering why it was she never got guys who looked like him. Then she went about her business.

"How's it going?" Geis said to Downes. "You and David Foxman getting thick?"

"I've seen him four times. We meet at the Body Shop and work out, have a bite to eat, a few drinks."

"He's costing me with that damned Cindy. I figured one or two shots and he'd dump her. Only the horny momser can't get enough and that bitch won't give me a break on the price."

Peter laughed. "Cut him off."

Geis snarled his answer. "I would if I could."

"I think David's falling in love."

"With a hooker! Some schmuck that is. In a world where dames can't wait to give it away, he gets a hard-on for a hustler. He ain't nothing like his old man."

"That was a fine talk Foxman gave at the funeral."

"You were there?"

"I figured it would sit well with David. He introduced me to his father."

"That's using your head."

"We just shook hands."

"Yeah, okay. Play it cool, let it grow."

"You still think Foxman is the best place for us?"

"Hey, listen. I gave this a lot of thought, I know what I'm talking about. Foxman and Company, it's just right. Big, but not too big. Respected, you know what I mean. A man with a reputation. His main business is buying and selling rough. IMM is his primary supplier, only he had the nephew out making smaller buys wherever he could. Looks like the old man is out of touch with sources. Also, he's got three factories and about ten years ago he started up some small shops. Boutiques in classy hotels only. That's the way he is, everything he touches, Foxman goes in style. Just the kind of situation to be connected with."

His small face clenched up in sudden anger. "Tell you what, I'm cutting that David off from Cindy. He wants to get laid, let 'im get his own. She wants to keep humping him, let 'er do it for free. The connection's made, what do I need her for?" The phone interrupted and Geis answered and listened.

"Awright," he said. "Come on back." He hung up.

"What if David goes into a funk? What if he wants my help with Cindy? What then?"

"Explain him the facts of life, is what. Everybody gets dumped by dames, even a first-class stud like you. Tell him that. Let him cry in his beer, it'll make you guys real tight. I got to make a call."

He dialed. "Irwin, Harry Geis talking. Don't say my name. You got a hefty blonde in there wants to appraise one of my stones. One point one carat white. Give her a price of seven thousand five, okay. There's a thousand in it for you, Irwin." He hung up and grinned at Downes. "Business is business. My customer will be back in a couple of minutes, so you get on your horse. Follow through with David, offer him the proposition we worked out. The way I got it figured, it ain't gonna make him mad. Okay, what're you waiting for?"

When the blond woman returned, Geis greeted her affably. "What I tell you, worth every cent, right?"

She placed the diamond on the counter. "Walberg and Sons said it was worth no more than seven thousand," she said without flinching.

Bitch, Geis thought. Hell with it, let her think she was getting away with something. "Seven thousand!" he said, with contrived alarm. "At that price I can barely break even. All right, all right, I said it, I meant it. You want the diamond, it's yours. For seven thousand even. Let me tell you, lady, you got yourself a steal." He handed over the nine thousand dollars and watched her count out the correct amount. He wrote her a new receipt,

"I like doing business with you," she said, gloating over her triumph.

"Anytime," he answered with as much sincerity as he could muster up. "Anytime at all..."

*chapter*
## 8

MAURICE FOXMAN'S OFFICE was dominated by a Georgian walnut partners' desk, the surface inlaid with worn dark green leather. Behind the desk, three large windows overlooking Forty-seventh Street, ten floors below. Foxman was seated in a tall swivel chair, waiting for them to get settled, studying each face as if he'd never seen it before.

A secretary poured coffee and passed around a tray of small Viennese cakes before departing.

"This is not a happy occasion," he said, drawing attention to himself, allowing them time to shift their focus from the refreshments to him. "And what I am about to say is not designed to elevate anyone's spirits. Robert's death brings home to us all the lengths to which certain parties in our business will go in order to achieve their ends..."

David, performing isometric exercises as he sat in place, said, "Do you really believe Sir John would resort to murder?"

Foxman appraised his son. Older by five years than Robert, David was a competent man, but no more than that. Give him an assignment within his limited capabilities, his limited ambition and imagination, and he would get it done. He managed the showroom at Foxman and Company, greeted customers with a barrage of harmless pleasantries, fulfilled their professional needs, offended no one. But he lacked the determination and drive to move even an extra carat a month. Once Maurice had looked forward to the day when David would take over the company. No more; that dream had died slowly until finally it had been laid to rest.

"I believe," Maurice said quietly, "that the Syndicate kills when it suits its purpose to kill. It will go to any lengths to achieve its ends. Steal. Cheat. Libel an honest man. Do whatever is in its self-interest to do, concerned only with greater profits, greater power."

"It's hard to believe they would murder," Mattie said. She had refused to go through a period of mourning for her son. Had refused to take even a single day off from work, tried mightily to bury her grief in the mountain of paperwork on the job, to think only of what had to be done next. She arranged an apologetic smile on her face. "Sir John is a man who has lunch with the Queen and dinner with the President. Is it possible that such a man could be so evil?"

Maurice swung his chair her way. His cool presence infiltrated the room, dominating each of them. "Sir John is a man without human warmth. He has affection for no one. He is capable of any act, no matter how cruel."

"Still," Mattie persisted. "He is a diamond man."

"And also a Jew," David put in.

Maurice tried to supress his astonishment at their naïveté. "He and I are nothing alike," he said firmly. "He is not a Jew, he has become a heathen, neither a Christian nor a Jew." It was said more in sadness than in anger, a sense of loss in his voice.

Ellie, still in the wheelchair, smiled. "That's carrying assimilation to its ultimate end, isn't it?"

"There is no humor in this, Ellie. Historical imperatives have shaped Sir John, placed him in another world, a world hostile to us. He has become the enemy."

Ellie reminded herself that she was present by sufferance, a member of the family, not the firm. She was an outsider, rejected by her uncle in that area of his life he deemed so vital, so important, his business. But she was unable to remain quiet.

"In my opinion there are more immediate enemies for Foxman and Company to be concerned with."

"And who are they?"

"Indians with cheap goods, for one." When no one interrupted, she went on. "The rising involvement of organized crime in the industry, using the industry to launder dirty money. Those gangsters from Israel who care nothing about human life, they kill whenever it suits them."

"All these are legitimate problems," Maurice conceded.

"And the Arabs, all that oil money. Diamonds provide them with a hedge against inflation, portability of wealth and . . ."

"And another weapon to be used against the Jews in Israel," Foxman broke in.

"What about the pipes in Australia?" David said. "They say there are hundreds of them not yet discovered. If that's true, the market will be severely damaged."

"See how we are!" Foxman said. "Without cohesion, out of focus. Each one perceiving different dangers, different threats to our collective welfare, so that in the end we overlook the very real threat—Sir John and the Syndicate."

"I don't understand," Mattie said. "Why would Sir John want to hurt you, Maurice? Or the other dealers?"

"Let me tell you this—this last sight, it was a disaster."

"Why?" Ellie said, her interest piqued.

"Ask Sir John. Perhaps it was the Venezuelan proposition, perhaps not. The box was full of flawed stones, the color bad, the sizes wrong. Not worth half of what I paid. Not a single first-rate stone in the bunch. Another sight like this and the business is in serious jeopardy. The clients, they want product, not excuses. If they can't fulfill their needs with Foxman, they will go elsewhere."

"But you've done business with the same people for years," Mattie protested.

"And they have their own problems. Families to feed. Employees who depend on them. Loans to pay off. If the Syndicate decides to break a dealer, it's the end. This is the time for us to put aside personal differences, to stand firm and pursue a united course."

"Tell me what I can do, Father," David said. He did some weightless curls with his right arm, visualizing his biceps swelling and growing hard.

Foxman stared at his son. The face was pale and heavily boned, the face of an athlete, but with an emptiness in the eyes he couldn't fathom, had never been able to accommodate. One more time, he told himself. He would make one more attempt.

"Good, David. This is what I want you to do. You will take over Robert's responsibilities. I want you to go into the market, establish new sources at favorable prices. For too long I have depended on IMM. Now other connections must be made. Get to know the dealers, David, the cutters, everybody in the industry. Visit Australia, see what they can offer us. Go to Nigeria. Zaire. Angola. The South American producers. Begin at once."

David gripped his thick thighs with his fingers. He prided himself on his physical strength and yet he had understood for a very long time that he was not a man of strength, not in the vital way his father was strong. Or the way Robert had been strong. Whenever he had been faced with a challenge, David had failed: at work, playing football in high school, with women. Always he fell short. Always he failed to fulfill expectations. Those of the people closest to him. And of himself. He yearned to become the man his father wanted him to be but whenever the chance presented itself David backed down. Even as he retreated now.

"I'd rather not, Father."

Foxman fought back an angry response. Once again his son refused to be what Maurice wanted him to be. Once again he surrendered his manhood without a struggle, without an attempt, unwilling to risk either defeat or victory.

"Why is that, David?" he said in a deceptively tranquil voice. "Why would you rather not?"

A tentative smile curled David's mouth. "I prefer to remain in New York," he offered lamely. When Maurice said nothing, he went on, the words coming rapidly now. "My life is here. My friends. My interests. I don't want to travel, constantly on the go. I'm no Gypsy. All my needs are satisfied in the city."

"And the needs of the company—what about that?"

David's eyes flitted to Ellie, to Mattie, as if seeking an ally, but found no help in either face. "My job is here, Father. I've worked hard to establish my contacts and it's unreasonable to ask me to give them up like this. People come into the showroom, they expect to see me. I do a good job. My value is here. My future is in the office, it's what I do best. The road is not for me," he ended weakly.

Foxman spoke coldly. "If not you, who?"

Ellie stiffened in place. She wanted to protest, to cry out against this blatant insult, this indignity, to say everything that was on her mind. But that would only work against her and so she said nothing.

Foxman sat back in his chair. A tiredness flowed down into his legs, a tightness in his chest as he agonized over his plight. "Exactly," he said. "So there is only one path open to me." He stared in Ellie's direction, yet seemed not to see her. "I will have to look outside the company to find a good man, get the help I need."

That evening Mattie visited Ellie at her apartment on the twenty-second floor of a new building on Third Avenue. Everything was sleek and new, polished steel, glass and leather. It made Mattie feel as if she were in the waiting room of a doctor's office. She preferred deep, soft chairs and sofas, natural woods, the look of furnishings lovingly used and slightly worn. They dined on a pasta salad and herbal tea and avoided any mention of Robert, striving for a tranquil evening.

But Ellie was unable to hold up her end of the unspoken bargain, unloosing a tirade against her uncle. "Don't you see how little regard he has for me?" she exploded finally. "He needs someone to replace Robert and he asks David. David, who doesn't want the job, is incapable of doing it and always will be."

"Don't be too hard on him."

"David's a little boy who's never grown up. All he wants is to hide out in the showroom and puff up his muscles."

"Some people develop more slowly."

"It doesn't matter, Mother. It isn't David I'm angry at, it's Maurice. With me sitting right in front of him, the only solution he can see to his problem is to go outside the company for help. To find a *man*."

"What else can he do, my darling?"

Ellie fought back her rage. "Why does it have to be a man?"

"I don't understand."

"Why can't it be a woman?"

Mattie found the idea startling. "Oh, I can't imagine any woman would enjoy all that traveling, never being home with her family. What would her children do without her? What would her husband feel?"

"I don't have children. I don't have a husband. And I'm much more qualified to do the job than anyone he's likely to find."

Her mother said nothing.

"He never considered me, not for a second. My God, it's frustrating!"

"Maurice is an old-fashioned man with old-fashioned ideas. His standards . . ."

"I measure up to his professional standards. He taught me himself. Everything he knows, I know."

"My darling, you haven't had the experience."

"I've been in the business since high school. There isn't a job I can't do, or haven't done. If I were a man, he'd hire me in a minute."

"I'm not so sure."

"To Maurice, women are good only to keep house, to bear children, to give dinner parties. Man's work, the truly important things, that can't be left to a mere female."

"It's not that simple."

"Mother, you make me so angry. You always defend him."

"And you always attack him."

"With good cause."

"Give Maurice a little bit of credit. He must have reasons for not offering you the job."

"For example!" Ellie challenged.

Mattie sighed. "Your record is not the best."

There had been a succession of professional and personal disasters for Ellie over the years since she had been graduated from Barnard. Love affairs with one unsuitable man after another. Two of them had been married and another proved to be a transvestite. And then there had been Henry Wilton and the Chamblay.

"You're valuable to me," Maurice had once told her, "as

family. I cherish you dearly. But when it comes to business you are unreliable and I can't afford repeated errors of judgment."

"My record!" The words exploded out of Ellie, targeting her mother. "You can't expect better from someone too incompetent, too unworthy to be allowed a fair share of responsibility! Isn't that the way it's always been? Protect Ellie, shield Ellie, prevent Ellie from becoming a strong, independent human being. And when I've tried to break out I've been rapped across the knuckles, treated by Maurice—and by you, Mother—as if I was a misbehaving child.

"Well, I'm neither an incompetent nor a fool. I understand that you and Maurice both believe I'm not good enough to take on adult responsibilities, so you shouldn't be shocked when I act in a manner that confirms that belief.

"What have I been prepared for, Mother? To wear clothes well, to look good, to be a satellite to some man, generally a man not as smart or as strong or as courageous as I am. Never have I been encouraged to spread my own wings, to fly free, to be my own woman, a full human being, never have I been allowed to make my own place in the world."

"Why are you so angry?" Mattie answered softly. "Robert wasn't so angry."

"Robert was one of the boys, allowed to try things, to explore, to experiment, to work towards becoming his own person. I wasn't."

"I wish you were more tranquil, Ellie. More accepting of life. More like me."

All rage whooshed out of Ellie. She felt deflated, repentant. "Whatever's happened, Mother, it's all over now. I've learned from my mistakes and I intend to make up for them. As for the choker, I'll find a way to make up for that, too. Mother, I'm smarter than anyone Maurice is going to find. I'm more aggressive, stronger inside. Sometimes it takes me a little while, but I do learn. I can change. My instincts are good. Couple that together with my experience and I can do the job better than any man Maurice is likely to find." She was furious, the more so because her rashness, her own carelessness, were too recent for Maurice to dismiss as youthful improvidence.

Mattie wanted to believe Ellie had changed, had matured,

but she couldn't be sure. She, too, knew her daughter's history, recognized Ellie's shortcomings. "Have you spoken to Maurice?"

"His mind's made up."

Mattie longed to help her only remaining child, wanted to shield her from the dangers of the world as she had been unable to shield Robert. At the same time, she had come to admire Ellie's drive and ambition, her desire to better herself.

"You'll find a way to reach Maurice."

"He's made up his mind and you know how stubborn he can be."

"And are you that much different? Find your own way, create your own destiny. You have to convince Maurice that you are the person for the job."

"And if I can't manage that?"

"We both know the answer to that. You'll keep trying until you make him change his mind."

Keller lived on the third floor of a brownstone on West Sixty-ninth Street, just off Central Park. Fifteen-foot pressed-metal ceilings, paneled walls, a fireplace that worked and shutters on the tall windows. Scuffed leather chairs surrounded a cut-down country trestle table.

Keller slumped in his favorite chair, feet up on the table, and glared at Robert Foxman's walking stick as if commanding it to give up its secret. It was a carefully carved length of rugged wood, made from a single limb of a tree. Each of its knobs represented another branch, cut close to the stem and skillfully shaped and burnished. A solid stick able to support the full weight of a man as large as Robert Foxman.

A knee damaged while skiing. A common accident, happened all the time. Where? Here in the East? All snow had long since melted. Vail, perhaps. Or Aspen. In the mountains of Utah. In which case, it would have been a recent occurrence. Yet Maurice Foxman had known nothing about it. Wouldn't he have noticed Robert hobbling about the office, exchanged a few sympathetic words about the injury? Hardly cause for alarm and yet . . .

Keller lifted the stick. It had the solid feeling it deserved, the bulk. Or was it a shade less substantial than it should have been? He shook it from side to side, up and down. Nothing. His work had begun to make him more than a little paranoid, seeing puzzles and problems where there were none. Sometimes a cane was only a cane.

He circled the spacious room using the stick for support. Someday he might require the use of such assistance. His right knee was a latticework of stitchery, thanks to an old football injury. He carried the scars of old wounds on his torso and on damp days there were aches to remind him of past adventures.

And there were invisible scars and aches as well. Remembrances of failed efforts to change his life, of failed marriages, of failed loves. There was that about Maurice Foxman, he thought with grudging admiration. The man was in charge of his own existence, confronting the future bravely. Keller wondered if that straight old man had ever really known real fear, the kind of fear Keller battled against every day of his life.

He examined the bottom of the walking stick. A rubber cap was in place to provide better purchase. He worked the cap off; the tip of the cane was solid, ungiving. He tried to turn the handle of the cane; it resisted firmly. He put the stick aside and went back to his chair and glared at it some more.

Why?

Why had Robert been shot? Clearly robbery had not been the motive, nothing was missing. Revenge? An irate lover? People killed for a variety of reasons. Keller felt his irritation spread, dissatisfied with his inability to penetrate the mystery. Too many diamond killings in the last few years. Couriers went down, messengers, some cutters, two dealers. Where would the next victim come from? Who would it be?

A question floated up into his consciousness. A question he should have asked before. He reached for the telephone and placed an overseas call. So much about this affair was out of sync, didn't quite fit. Once the question was asked and answered, things might begin to fall in place.

Maybe.


Again he was struck by the commanding physical presence of the tall man. Even more, by Peter's confidence and easy manner in every situation they encountered together.

Now they sat over drinks at the Algonquin, amidst the small

oak serving tables, the tall-backed chairs, the ancient call bells
to summon a waiter. David had never felt at home in these
surroundings, steeped as they were in literary tradition. Wooll-
cott, Parker and all the others who had peopled this lounge,
sat at the Round Table in the Rose Room, loomed intimidatingly
over him, made him feel inept and insignificant. Once David
had dreamed of becoming a writer and had started two novels,
finishing neither; and a play which he had completed but allowed no one to read; and a dozen short stories never submitted
for publication. Oh, yes, an hour spent in the Algonquin certainly kept him in touch with the world to which he aspired;
but he remained always a transient visitor, never a part of
things.

Peter, however, looked as if he belonged. Here or any other
place he chose. Those startling good looks that caused women
to stare and men to steal envious, sidelong glances. His tapered
physique, his musculature smooth and supple, the deep-seated
confidence of a man who could be depended on in any cir-
cumstance.

Peter had clutched his arm when they met. Had held firmly
to David's biceps, an insistent reminder of his growing friendship, of his sincerity.

"It's good to see you again, David."

The words evoked a joyous response in David, happy to
have made this good, new friend.

"There's something I've been meaning to discuss with you,"
Peter said, once they were seated, drinks in hand.

"What is it? Is there something I can do for you?"

"Matter of fact there is." He hesitated. "I may not have the
right to ask . . ."

"We're friends, aren't we? What is it?"

Peter fixed David with a long, penetrating stare. "I want us
to be, David. I really do."

"What's on your mind?"

"If you want to say no, I'll understand. No beating about
the bush."

David was enjoying this. That Peter Downes was able to
come to him for help was flattering, made him feel important,
vital. "Let's have it, Peter."

"I've got a client. Potential client, that is. He wants to give his wife a special gift on their twenty-fifth anniversary."

"Diamonds, of course."

"Of course."

"And you're looking for the right stones?"

"Not exactly, David."

David felt something shrivel inside of him. As if he'd been rebuked, shamed in front of a company of friends, as if he were still a child.

"My client is after a pair of round brilliants, up to three carats. Loupe clean, no internal blemishes or inclusions."

"No problem so far."

"Here's the hooker—he insists the stones be newly cut. Nothing old, nothing used. In his words, something virginal."

"The man is a romantic."

"That's it exactly, David, a romantic. The man is very much in love with his wife."

"You want me to come up with the stones?"

"I've already got them."

"Oh. Well, where do I come in?"

"The client insists on doing business with an established outfit. A company of reputation, to use his phrase. He's wary of anyone without a strong base . . ." Peter gazed questioningly at David. "Will you help?"

"What do you want me to do?"

"Foxman and Company is known around the world. You are a legitimate member of the company, you bear the family name. If my client believed the stones were being sold to him by your father's firm . . . well, that would certainly close the deal."

"Consider it done."

"Maybe you'd rather not be involved."

"I want to do it, Peter. You're my friend."

"I appreciate this. It's an act of true friendship."

"My pleasure."

"But on one condition only."

"What's that?"

"That you accept a substantial commission."

"I can't do that."

"Then it's no deal."

"But we're friends."

"Business is business."

"Okay. If you insist."

"I do insist. After all, it's only right." He offered David his hand. "Who knows? Maybe we can do business again sometime."

"Sort of a partnership. I'd like that, Peter."

"So would I, David. So would I."

*chapter*
# 9

ELLIE WAS ABLE TO WALK into her uncle's office unaided. She had been out of the wheelchair for more than twenty-four hours and her legs were still unsteady, pain stabbing intermittently along her nervous system. But she was determined to reveal no weakness to Maurice, to appear normal, graceful, her full mouth arranged in a pleasant smile. He greeted her affably, asking about her health, seeing to her comfort in a cinnamon-colored chair at one side of the partners' desk.

Only then did he seat himself, gazing benevolently at her with hands clasped prayerfully. Maurice was not a pious man, as he sometimes confessed with some regret. He loved the traditions of Judaism, admitted to a sentimental attachment to the God of Abraham and David and Moses, but often without prayer or ritual.

He carried a profound debt to all who had preceded him, to that anonymous company of biblical ancestors, to those who had lived—no matter the suffering, no matter the indignities—and died as Jews.

For Ellie, born and bred in America, it was different. She had been influenced by traditions peculiarly American; the frontier history, the myth of equality, of justice under the law, the tantalizing dream of wealth and a good life for all. Like the nation itself, Ellie was strong, though still incomplete, full of the promise that one day she would surpass the efforts of those who had come before her.

What a lovely woman she had become. Resembling no one in her family. Separated from her mother and her father by genes long dormant. The open visage, the bright, shining eyes, the unruly auburn hair. She was, he had long ago concluded, the most beautiful woman he had ever known.

"You're feeling better," he said. "I can see it in your face."

"The doctor says I'll soon be back to normal."

"You were very fortunate." He had watched her grow up, had loved her when she was a child as he would have loved a daughter of his own. But gradually they grew apart, some private dislike of him revealing itself in her attitudes and her actions, though never in words. There was resentment, as if he'd damaged her, at times raw hatred, none of it comprehensible to him.

He watched her struggle to grow up too fast, helped pick her up whenever she stumbled and fell. How hard she had tried to stand alone on legs that were not fully developed, a child fighting desperately to be without the need of another human being. As if that were a desirable condition.

"This must have been extremely difficult," he said. "First Robert's death and the accident..."

"It was hard for everyone." She didn't want to discuss the accident with him. She had been found by the police at the crash site, naked and bleeding, unconscious; no mention was made of a white Jaguar, no mention of Henry Wilton. He had left her at the side of a French road to die, taking off with the Chamblay. Someday she'd repay him for the pain she'd endured, the emotional anguish, and for stealing the Chamblay. How would she ever repay the Marquise?

As if reading her thoughts, Maurice said, "My people located the choker. It showed up around the throat of Raymond Wentworth's lady. My agents, with the assistance of the gendarmes, reclaimed it for its rightful owner. It has been returned, in your name, to the Marquise."

Her eyes went round. "I didn't want you involved. I—"

He went on. "The police, Interpol, are looking for your friend Wilton. As are investigators from the insurance carrier.

Insurance people take a dim view of such behavior."

"I would have taken care of it myself."

He assessed her gravely. "How?"

"I'd've found a way."

"I think not. Such affairs require training, manpower and money."

She understood that she was being rebuffed, made to see how helpless and useless she was when it came to doing anything important. While she had been recuperating, and feeling sorry for herself, Maurice had accomplished what she only dreamed about doing. Resentment, and a scorching glob of rage, lodged in her chest.

She forced herself to speak in a mild manner. "And Henry?"

"Word is, he is living in Colombia with an aging movie actress who owns coffee plantations. He is out of your life. For good, I hope."

"I wanted to do it..."

"It's taken care of, that's all that counts."

"Doing it myself mattered, it mattered a lot."

He shrugged. "It's done, over, let's put it behind us."

"I thank you," she said without emotion. "It will never happen again, nothing like it."

"I'm always here to help. I'm your father's brother, what more can I say?"

She set herself against the impact of those words, forced herself to remember why she had come.

"I want to talk to you, Maurice."

"Of course, my dear. What is it?"

"About Robert's place in the company."

"A tragedy, that boy's death."

"I can do the job, Maurice."

He frowned. "You're still young, there's time. You need more time."

"I'm a woman," she retorted, with more force than she'd intended. "I admit it, I've made mistakes. But who hasn't? I can do the job."

Even as she pleaded with him, her anger mounted; directed now at herself. She was begging to be allowed to follow in Robert's footsteps when what she really yearned for was a place of her own.

Maurice said, "Diamonds are for women to wear. They enhance a diamond's beauty and are made lovelier by them. Women don't belong in the trade, it is a man's world."

"That's absurd!" She struggled to get her temper under control. "That's an old-fashioned attitude."

"I am an old-fashioned man, then, in an old-fashioned business."

"Women are doing everything these days. Women are cops, firefighters, they do construction work. Isn't it time the diamond business joined the twentieth century?"

He longed to grant her wishes but a catalogue of prior restraints held him in check. "What are you after, Ellie? More money? Let's do this—you've been working on an assignment basis, filling in here and there. Why don't I put you on a retainer plus commission. I'll increase the number of jobs you get and that will increase the amount of your annual income. Would that satisfy you?"

"Look at me, Maurice," she replied with searing intensity. "Am I someone to be satisfied with halfway measures? One of the things I love about this business is its possibilities. All it takes is imagination and energy and drive. You can go as far as you want, be as big as you want. The sky's the limit."

"People who reach for the sky very often crash. Work for me and you'll always do well enough, you'll be safe."

"The way things are, I'm just another employee."

"What is it you're after?"

She filled her lungs with air. "What you've got, Maurice. My own company. I've got ideas, plans, new ways of doing things." She spoke more slowly. "I want to be the first woman to be granted a sight by International Minerals and Mines."

"Ah, a trailblazer, is that it?"

"Damn!" She was on her feet, moving toward the door. "I should've known you'd react this way. You don't respect me. You don't take me seriously. Asking was a mistake."

"Gently, gently. I mean no harm. Come back, sit down. What if you did take over for Robert—still an employee and it would not win recognition from the Syndicate."

"A long step closer. A chance to do good work, to make myself noticed."

"You underestimate Sir John's prejudices. He has a wife,

daughters, and has kept them all away from the business. I have heard him say . . ." He broke off.

"Say what, Uncle? 'Women don't belong in the business.' Is that what you're telling me?"

"There are dangers."

"I'm not afraid. I can take care of myself."

"That is what Robert used to say. 'I can handle myself.' Unhappily he was wrong. There are times in this life when no one can take care of himself by himself."

"I'm stronger than Robert was and smarter."

"What good is it to be smart if somebody shoots you? Or hits you over the head with a club and takes away your merchandise? Three days ago, two men shoved Charlie Wilson, one of my salesmen, into a doorway and helped themselves to his goods, at knife point. Charlie is strong, Charlie is smart. A quarter of a million dollars."

"The Kennedy sale?"

Maurice nodded. "Brave is not enough. Strong is not enough. What happened to you in France, to Robert in Africa . . . it isn't even a freak happening anymore. This business of ours has become too dangerous. Not only for women, for heaven's sake. There is no regard for honor any longer. No regard for property or for human life. Thugs, criminals, murderers are everywhere. Sir John himself rules by open intimidation and terror."

He was breathing rapidly, conscious now of the irregular flutter of his heart. "I will tell you why Robert was killed. As a warning. A warning intended to keep me in line. To shut my mouth. To keep me from speaking out against the Syndicate's bully tactics. The bad sight was also a warning. 'See,' Sir John is telling me, 'see what I can do if pushed too far.' And for emphasis my nephew is killed.

"No, Ellie. I cannot expose you further to the corrosive elements of this business. If something happened to you, your mother would never forgive me. I will not allow you to be destroyed."

"You can't stop me! No one can. I intend to succeed. Before I'm through, Sir John will have to recognize me."

"And give you a sight?"

"Yes."

"You sound exactly like someone I used to know," he said in a small, reflective voice.

"Never anyone like me," she said haughtily on her way out of his office. "No one."

"Oh, yes," he said softly. "There was one . . . and it was me."

*chapter*
# *10*

KELLER PHONED, said who he was and why he wanted to talk to her, and she agreed to see him. "But not in my uncle's office," she added quickly.

He suggested lunch and they settled on the Ginger Man, across from Lincoln Center. He was at the table when she arrived, standing to greet her. She examined him with interest and shook his hand. One of the beast's tentacles, to hear Maurice tell it. One of the evil extensions of the Syndicate's dark eminence, Sir John Messinger. A conniver, this Keller, a man of violence, a killer for hire.

There was an air of impermanence about him. The pale, still eyes, the broken nose that gave his face a diffident, almost blurred look, the regretful expression of a man whose connections had been effectively severed and for whom no new ones had yet taken their place. He struck her as someone able to take care of himself.

"I'm Keller," he said, holding her hand longer than was necessary.

"How do I know you are what you say you are?" She withdrew her hand and sat down.

He hauled out his ID and presented her with it. "That satisfy you, Miss Foxman?"

She barely glanced at it. "You said you wanted to talk about my brother?"

A waiter appeared. "A drink?" Keller said.

"White wine will do."

"White wine for the lady, Michelob for me." Keller watched the waiter leave.

"Why?" she said.

"My job is to follow up on this kind of thing. Get to the bottom of it."

"My brother was murdered. I doubt that you want to get to the bottom of that."

"What makes you think so?"

"It might lead straight back to your boss." When he offered no response, she felt compelled to rush ahead, the silence amidst the lunchtime babble around them intolerable suddenly. Something about Keller made her uneasy, made her wish she hadn't come. As if he had thrown out some indefinable challenge, daring her to come up to his standards. Daring her to measure up, to be something he wanted her to be. No, that wasn't it. Daring her to be whatever it was *she* wanted to be . . . A shudder wrenched its way along her spine and she sat up straighter. He was unlike any man she'd ever met. She braced herself, determined to hold her own against him. "Ask your questions, Keller. This investigation of yours, both of us know it's a formality, an empty gesture. Nothing will ever come of it."

Keller refused to respond to her hostility. He would not defend what he did. Nor make excuses for Sir John. Nor offer explanations. Ask a question, listen to the answer, match it against what he learned elsewhere. Follow leads, locate people, ask some more questions. Put it all together and try to make sense of the results.

Once in a while it got rough. Rough and dirty. Keller knew how to deal with that, too. All part of the job. Cleaning up the mess other people left behind, all for the greater good of IMM. She was right about that, at least. Sir John was his ultimate boss, his master, a master he seldom saw or spoke with. Ultimately the man to be satisfied.

He inspected Ellie, watched her sip her wine. Every gesture was graceful, her wrist delicate, her fingers tapered. She man-

aged to convey glamour and a simmering sexuality without
effort. The sea-green eyes were cool, steady, seeing a great
deal, her features exquisitely molded; the electric shock of hair,
shimmering each time she moved her head. She was the most
beautiful women he'd ever met and it was clear that she disliked
him on sight. Too bad. But not necessary that she like him. Or
him her. That wasn't part of the job description.

"Your brother ever mention any enemies? That he feared
for his life?"

"Of course not."

She had altered her game. No more open hostility. In its
place, a casual dismissal, a refusal to take him seriously. Made
no difference to Keller. The questions would be the same, the
answers revealing something, by omission or commission. Some
obscure morsel of information that might open things up for
him.

"He ever let on that he felt threatened?"

"You didn't know Robert. He had it all, looks, personality,
intelligence. He was easy to get along with, everybody liked
him."

Not everybody, he wanted to remind her, but swallowed the
words. "He enjoyed his work?"

"He had a great future ahead of him."

A hard note had crept into her voice, softened by a quick-
silver smile that almost made him smile back. Was it envy he
heard? Bitterness? Perhaps her admiration for her brother was
not as unqualified as she pretended.

"He got along with your uncle."

"Two of a kind," she said. "My uncle the king, my brother
the jack. Of diamonds, of course." She laughed to take the
edge off her words.

"Mr. Foxman is highly thought of along Forty-seventh
Street."

"And elsewhere. With the possible exception of the IMM."

That was the second reference she'd made to London, to
the Syndicate, to Sir John. Why such strong animosity? He
made a mental note to check it out.

The waiter presented himself and they ordered lunch. Sole
amandine for Ellie, a small steak for Keller. The waiter thanked
them and left.

"Robert ever mention anything about smuggling to you?"

His manner was so casual, his inflection so mild, that the impact of the question escaped her at first. When it hit, her eyes glistened and her voice flattened out. "Are you accusing my brother of smuggling diamonds?"

He shrugged. "Monrovia is a good place to make an illicit buy. There are no mines in Liberia, but plenty of stones. They come in from Sierra Leone, from all over West Africa. The so-called Liberian diamond always comes from someplace else."

"My brother was scrupulously honest."

"And is your uncle?"

That drew a short laugh out of her. "Check around. Maurice is a paragon among paragons. Honesty, honor, self-respect; the keystones of his business. And of his life."

He swallowed some beer; it had lost its chill. He had no taste for warm beer. "An untarnished reputation," he said, hoping to provoke her into some indiscretion. "Few men can claim that."

She made no answer. She was good, Keller decided. Quick to learn, tougher than he'd believed at first, able to control her impulsiveness. Beauty and brains, a deadly combination.

"You ski, Miss Foxman?"

Her brows rose slightly. "A change of pace, Keller?" She was mocking him. "Yes, Keller, I ski. I'm an excellent skier. Do you ski, Keller?"

"I never learned."

"I'm also an outstanding tennis player. Tournament caliber when I was in college. Do you play tennis, Keller?"

"In my neighborhood, it was basketball, football, handball. Tennis, that was for the rich kids."

"I've always been a rich kid, I guess. Thanks to Maurice's business sense. Rich and somewhat spoiled, I've been told. Nobody ever spoiled you, did they, Keller?"

"Not so you could notice. Did Robert ski well?"

"Robert ski? He hated it. Scared of heights. When we were both very young my father took us to the Statue of Liberty, we climbed all the way up. Robert froze and my father had to carry him down. No, Robert would never even ride the lift to the top of a slope."

"I thought he hurt his knee skiing."

The waiter brought their food. When he was gone, Ellie looked quizzically at Keller.

"There was nothing wrong with Robert's knee."

"My mistake. Robert was doing business with a Lebanese trader."

"Bakshir Khamoury."

"You know him?"

"My brother made small buys on behalf of the company. Bakshir was a source, mostly colored stones."

"What other buys did he make in Monrovia?"

"None that I know of. You still believe my brother was into some kind of dirty work?" She felt her pulse racing; what was it about Keller that provoked her so? He was not the sort of man she was ordinarily drawn to. Older by twenty years and not nearly pretty enough. Certainly not sophisticated or cultured enough. She blinked and found herself avoiding his gaze and that troubled her even more. She stood up. "I've had enough of this..."

"Finish your lunch," he said evenly.

"Instead of throwing mud, Keller, find out who murdered my brother."

"I intend to."

"What you're doing is protecting Sir John's profits and I am not going to help you do it."

She marched away from the table, with the easy stride of a natural athlete, drawing a great deal of attention as she went. She was, Keller told himself, a very special piece of work.

A matched pair of marquises, certificate stones. Perfect rounds, each weighing in at 1.2 carats. Each one D-flawless. Harry Geis admired them lovingly before turning them over to Peter Downes.

"Nice," Downes said. "They must have set you back plenty."

"Money is no problem when you've got a connection."

"Shouldn't I meet this connection? I mean, if I'm going to be part of this scam..."

"Trust me."

Downes laughed with real pleasure. "No, Harry, nobody in his right mind is going to trust you. But that's all right since we need each other. Now about the money man?"

"Smartass," Geis said; he thought it over. "Okay, no reason you shouldn't know. Ralph Browning's the money."

"You mean Browning, Inc.? The private bank? I hear he's mob-connected, Harry. If that's true then I'm out. I don't like to be around guys who grunt and eat with their fingers. They tear arms off people like you and me."

It was Geis's turn to laugh. "Browning is legit, believe me. He deals with some of the biggest people in the business. A very correct guy, very well financed, a really conservative operation."

"You guarantee that he's not Mafia?"

"Don't listen to that crap. Even if he was connected, where would a small-time operator like me go for cash? Chase Manhattan? Lehman Brothers? Let me take care of the dough and the thinking. You look after David Foxman."

"Fàir enough. What do you expect to get for these stones? They should make exceptional earrings."

"Ask for seventy, settle for sixty-five. Only be sure you make it look good. You got it straight?"

"Yes."

"All right, let's do it then. The bait's out and we are gonna catch us one big fish."

## *chapter* **11**

ON THE NIGHT before she left, Ellie visited her mother.

"I don't like it," Mattie said. "I don't want you to be hurt again."

"I'm doing what I believe is right."

"Is having your own business that important?"

"It isn't that simple, Mother. I want to utilize what gifts I have, the skills I've developed, all the experience I've accumulated. Maurice is not sympathetic to that."

"What is it you want—to be the best diamond dealer in the world?"

Ellie shook her head, golden highlights shimmering in the mass of auburn hair. "I want to be the best Ellie Foxman I can be. That means finding out what I'm capable of being, what I'm capable of doing. For myself."

"You'll be all alone. With Robert gone, I don't think I could stand it if something else happened to you."

"Nothing's going to happen. Not this time."

"You really expect IMM to give you your own sight?"

"I'll make it happen."

"Maurice is convinced Sir John will never permit it."

"I've spent most of my life around diamonds. When I was

a kid, I worked for Maurice on weekends, during summer holidays. I've been around cutters, salesmen, the office, all these years. Even Maurice admits that my instincts about stones are good. I'm better equipped for the business than Robert was, with one exception . . . I'm not a man."

"Spare me the sexual politics."

Ellie laughed and embraced Mattie. "The point is, I have the ability to make a sound judgment about a stone's potential for fire and life and not many people can do that. Let Maurice come up with an exceptional stone and he calls on me for my opinion."

"An opinion is not a final judgment."

"I can determine the direction of the grain in a diamond better than most men my senior. I can pinpoint the inclusions, plot a cut for maximum value. I know all there is to know about color, clarity, cut and carat. And I can mark a stone with the best of them.

"I've studied the market. I've learned to buy and sell and my time to break through has come. I intend to give it my best shot, to find some way to put what I've learned to work. Mother, is it wrong to fight for my career?"

Mattie grew thoughtful. "Your judgment about stones may be all you say it is but you still have a lot to learn about people. Be careful, Ellie, it's dangerous out there. Remember Robert." Mattie's eyes filled with tears.

Ellie spoke rapidly. "This isn't just for me, Mother. It's for Robert and you and Daddy, too."

"No!" Mattie said, with unaccustomed vigor in her voice. "Your father is gone, Robert is gone. Let me live my life and you do the same."

"Yes, I'm going to do that no matter what it takes. Thank you for understanding and for your support."

The two women went to each other in a long, silent embrace.

"I love you, Mother."

"Mazel und Brucha," Mattie said.


Pieter Van Vooren was a huge man with a great round hairless head and a stomach to match. As a child, Ellie had met Van Vooren in her uncle's office and now he greeted her in his own office behind his factory in Amsterdam. He listened while she described her plans and said nothing until she was finished.

"So, you have come to me to be a supplier for this new enterprise of yours." He spoke English with a Dutch accent that matched his bulk, pound for pound.

"What I'm after is a steady supply of quality goods."

"My operation is not nearly as substantial as your uncle's."

"I'm trying to open up a number of different sources."

"You will launch your own company, I presume?"

"I've been looking for appropriate space on Forty-seventh Street. My lawyer's drawing up the papers."

"Maurice, he approves of this?"

"Maurice takes a jaundiced view of the business. Everywhere he sees wild beasts about to pounce on his helpless and innocent niece."

"I think you are neither innocent nor helpless."

"Maurice wouldn't agree."

"Blood ties often blur the vision. So, not innocent, not helpless. Their absence will not be missed if you are to become an entrepreneur. Still, Maurice is not entirely mistaken. We do function in a jungle and the beasts are indeed wild and voracious. What is it you wish from me?"

"Gem-quality stones on a regular basis. The Syndicate is your primary supplier and you operate within IMM's parameters. But you're free to sell to whomever you wish."

Van Vooren rolled his head. "Last week I attended my regular sight. The box was filled with stones worth half of what I requested. When I pointed this out, it was suggested that I might choose to look elsewhere for supplies."

"Maurice is convinced Sir John is out to rid the industry of the old-timers."

"Your uncle is perceptive and wise. His opinions are not to be taken lightly. I have heard rumors about other dealers, other poor sights. If Sir John has declared war on us . . ." He spread his hands helplessly.

"How is this going to affect our business, Pieter?"

"We are not going to do business, I'm afraid. I do not have stones enough in stock for my regular clients. The quality you want, the quantity, I will not be able to help you. Odd lots occasionally, perhaps. But nothing near the level you are seeking after."

She tried to hold Van Vooren's eyes but he looked away and a fugitive thought surfaced. Had Maurice anticipated her moves and contacted Pieter, as well as the other dealers she intended to do business with? Had he told them not to sell to her? It was not the Syndicate she had to fear but her own family instead.

She continued her travels and at each stop her dreams of glory were further chipped away. In the Beurs voor Diamanthandel, the most important of Antwerp's four diamond exchanges, she was welcomed graciously, listened to and presented with reasons why no diamonds were available for her; in Idar-Oberstein, in Germany, the same results. From there she made the long flight to Tel Aviv and the Ramat Gan exchange. Again she came up empty.

Occasionally she was able to make a small buy but when the time came to consummate the deal, it would be canceled, some feeble excuse offered. Delivery dates were postponed, prices earlier agreed upon were doubled or tripled, and when she at last got to examine the merchandise it was never what she had been promised. Vowing not to return empty-handed, Ellie booked a flight to Freetown, capital city of Sierra Leone.

Diamonds were first discovered in Sierra Leone in 1930 on the banks of the Ghobora, a tributary of the Bafi River in the Yengema-Kodu region. Over the next forty years, those deposits gave up more than fifty million carats, about half of them gemstones of the finest quality. Those first fields were essentially alluvial. Later a group of diamond-bearing dikes were found and still later the first kimberlite pipes were located.

The diamondiferous landscape consisted of rounded hills and valleys with many streams and rivers. Heavy annual rainfall eventually swept away so much soil and vegetation that the underlying rock was exposed in many places. In time the kimberlite dikes were deeply eroded along the surrounding rocks until the diamonds were gradually freed to feed the alluvial deposits of the Sewa River.

After World War II, British soldiers who had been stationed in Sierra Leone returned to take advantage of the great wealth lying along the riverbanks, free for the taking. A diamond rush was underway. Not even the presence of the police deterred the searchers, neither side anxious for a confrontation.

When the situation became intolerable, the government stepped in. Laws were passed and a system of licensing put into force giving the central government control of mining operations and the export of diamonds. Diamond regions were declared "forbidden areas" and foreigners were denied entry to them. Despite all the precautions taken, however, the illegal traffic persisted and diamonds were smuggled without much trouble into Monrovia, only 120 miles away, for easy sale to visiting buyers.

Kenema, in Sierra Leone, was a typical African village, marked by the main street and a large market. On the flatlands around Kenema, the landscape was alternately green and black, signifying the traditional slash-and-burn method of farming. Surrounding the village, people lived in huts made by the wattle-and-daub construction peculiar to the region. Within Kenema itself, buildings had been erected with more durable materials, some of them two stories high.

It was to Kenema that Ellie Foxman came in a last desperate bid to locate a supplier on whom she could depend. It was in Kenema that she found Bakshir Khamoury. Or, more precisely, where Khamoury found her.

Under a scorching sun on a dusty street outside a fairly large African hut, complete with thick mud walls, a bony black man in a red fez and Bermuda shorts was doing business. To this informal buying office, a group of searchers had made their way to peddle their illegal wares. Leaning against the wall of the hut beneath the overhang of the thatched roof was a handsome native girl in a long, brightly colored batik skirt, bare breasts gleaming.

All transactions were suspended when Ellie approached, eyes watching her warily. One or two of the men hurried away. Others straightened up, eyeing her as if expecting an attack. The man in the red fez remained in his crouch, a fixed smile curling his mouth. The girl in the long skirt faded into the shadowed interior of the hut and seconds later Khamoury appeared, shading his eyes against the glare of the sun. When finally he recognized Ellie, his sly face broke open and he clapped his hands enthusiastically.

"Miss Foxman, indeed! It is you! What a spectacular surprise it is! How splendid to see you once again."

"Bakshir!" This was a sign, her luck was changing. Her luck and her fortune. "What are you doing here?"

"I am here, oh, yes. Bakshir Khamoury. In the flesh, as you Americans like to say. Khamoury, very good friend to Miss Foxman, to all Foxmans. How sad I am to learn of your brother's passing. What a fine young man he was. But please, please, not to stand in the midday sun. Much too hot. Come inside where there are chairs and a cool liquid. What are you doing in this place that Allah, blessed be His memory, forgot?"

He led her to a rickety rush chair and dusted it off with his handkerchief, saw her seated. A gesture sent the native girl away, to return almost at once with a cool drink in a tall plastic glass.

"Fruit drink," Khamoury assured her. "Excellent lubrication for the organs, all of the body, if I may say so. Flushes out the poisons, oh, yes. Be comfortable, Miss Foxman. Tell me, how may I be of service to the beautiful niece of the illustrious Maurice Foxman? I am honored by your presence."

Around the hut, silently observing, a dozen men and half as many women. They had taken up positions along the wall, moving on silent feet, careful not to give offense.

"To look at you is a heavenly moment in their miserable lives," Khamoury said cheerfully. "They are impressed that such a one as you should appear without warning. They see very few white people, even fewer white women. Certainly they have never encountered anyone who looks like you do, Miss Foxman. But then neither have I, neither have I."

She threw back her head and laughed. Relieved that at last she had met a friend, someone who didn't suspect her of shadowy connections or dual purposes.

"Seeing you is such a very great pleasure, Miss Foxman, and also a surprise. Why, why are you in Kenema?"

She told him. Tracing her search from one European diamond center to another, detailing the obstacles that had been put in her path, voicing her suspicions, outlining her desire to go into business for herself.

"Ah," he said, when she finished. He spoke in a sober, confidential manner. "To come to Kenema was not a good thing. Indeed, I am pleased to feast my eyes upon your beauty once again. But not here. In this place, foreigners are forbidden to do diamond business. It is against the law. Beyond that, there are several immediate dangers. Even for a person with such friends and influence as I possess. Especially for a beautiful young woman alone—dangers, disasters lie lurking. May I suggest, Miss Foxman, dear, a quick return to the world beyond. Conduct your enterprise from safer locations. In New York or London or Paris. In such sedate and correct cities."

"I can't do that, Bakshir. I must open up a clean source."

He threw up his hands. "This way is impossible! I will tell you, I shall arrange transportation to Monrovia..."

"Not unless..."

"Please. Please, listen, Miss Foxman. I will join you tomorrow. For lunch. At Julia's. Perhaps you are familiar with Julia's? First class all the way. Three times each week the highest-quality foodstuffs are brought in directly from France. Excellent French cuisine. Excellent service. French owned, naturally, and operated. Shall we say one o'clock?"

"One," Ellie replied gravely, "will be just fine."

Bakshir Khamoury ordered a chilled rosé from Tavel and toasted the good fortune that had brought Ellie back into his life.

"I would put it the other way," she said. "You can help me."

"Oh, indeed. Though business is nothing. What passes between a man and a woman is everything. I told your brother— may he discover contentment and glory in the presence of Allah—I told him that you were a diamond, truly a gemstone. D-flawless, of course." He giggled and drained his glass.

She smiled. "I thought Muslims never used alcohol."

"I thought Jews never ate pork. Truth lies somewhere in between, is it not the case?"

"It is indeed the case, Bakshir."

He reached into his pocket and brought out a rose-pink pear-shaped diamond stickpin and placed it on the table between them.

"How lovely, Bakshir."

"No lovelier than the lovely Miss Foxman is. Wear it as a reminder of an ardent admirer."

"Oh, no, I can't accept that. It's too valuable."

"The only value it possesses is to enhance your beauty, dear

Miss Foxman, an expression of my affection and my admiration."

"Bakshir, you are wicked. A married man giving gifts to another woman."

"Oh, yes, married. Twice over. But that has no bearing on the matter."

"I try to avoid married men, Bakshir. Especially those twice over. It gets too complicated."

He took her hand. "This bauble is for you, a gift without attachments, except of the heart. So is my affection, which exists whether to your liking or not. Never fear that I would do something to embarrass you or damage you, Miss Foxman. I am your friend for always, no matter how it becomes otherwise between us. There. It is settled. Let us proceed to crasser affairs—commerce, yes. What is it I can do for you?"

She explained the reason she had come to Africa, what she was trying to accomplish. Khamoury listened intently, chin resting on his hand. When she finished, he cleared his throat.

"You will not obtain the stones you require."

"Why?" Resentment clouded her vision and slowed her reflexes. No matter where she turned, ambition and diligence were not enough to gain her ends. "Is it because I'm a . . ."

He waved her silent, sweeping away her words and her logic and her dreams with a gesture. Arrogance and acquired superiority; he was a man and naturally wiser, better equipped by nature and experience to deal with the vicissitudes of this world. A man with two wives and the freedom and authority to take on two more, should he so wish. To come and go without hindrance or condemnation.

"Word has drifted out of London, out of Johannesburg, it is on the air—Maurice Foxman no longer has the good will of Sir John Messinger. Other names are mentioned also, other dealers once respected. The word is that traders—even such lowly individuals as this person—are to do no more business with Foxman. With any Foxman."

"You're saying I'm being cut off from supplies because of my name."

"Indeed, yes, dear lady. You, your uncle, all of you."

"Does that mean I'm to be murdered, the way they murdered Robert?"

He blanched and his brown eyes grew sad. "I sincerely hope not, Miss Foxman. What a monumental loss that would be. Certainly no man in his right mind would harm such a lovely and gracious person as yourself. On the other hand, wisdom dictates that one should give no provocation, no cause for displeasure. Besides, it is only talk of business dealings with Foxmans that I have heard about."

"And you're turning your back on me, too?"

"Never. Absolutely never. However—to trade openly with a Foxman puts one at risk, a fact of life I am attempting to convey to you in my poor way. As you know, I deal mostly in colored stones. But diamonds become available to me on occasion. Neither the quantity nor the quality you might choose, of course. Enough, however, to permit you to make a deal with this one or that one. If you wish to go beyond such feeble efforts, you will have to look elsewhere."

"Where do you suggest?"

"Australia, perhaps."

She felt it all slipping away. All the dreams and hopes that for so long she had been told were beyond her. Her mother had conveyed that damning message. Her uncle. And the entire diamond community had boomed it out, loud and clear. "No," she murmured. "Not Australia. Prior commitments, they told me. Firm contracts. Moral obligations. To other U.S. sales offices and elsewhere. Elsewhere," she went on grimly, "is a euphemism for the Syndicate, you see. Seems that I've run into one dead end after another."

"I understand dead ends. Even my flow of product is irregular recently and often nonexistent. Shipments are incomplete or do not arrive at all. My primary sources have been closed down."

"Who is doing this?"

He raised his hands to heaven. "It is incumbent upon me to seek other ways to make a living."

"Is that what you were doing in Kenema? Making a living?"

"Attempting, dear lady. Scratching at soil in which very little grows. In my modest opinion, you might do well to continue your relationship with Foxman and Company."

She gazed at him steadily. By no stretch of the imagination

a big operator, Khamoury knew his way around the back roads of the industry. Men like him found product where others came up dry. "What other ways have you discovered to make a living, Bakshir?"

"Oh, yes. Well. In this world, there are always items to buy, items to sell."

"For example?"

"I have always done well in colored stones."

Emeralds, rubies, sapphires. Profitable enough, but not what she was after. Diamonds were what she craved. They were an irresistible lure, in the glitter of each stone an unsolvable mystery, a lingering magic, a never-ending appeal.

"Also gold," Khamoury was saying.

"Gold?" she said automatically.

"In substantial amounts, if the funds are available."

He was offering her an opportunity. If not diamonds, if not diamonds *now*, then perhaps later. She needed to buy time in order to plan and organize her next strategy. Colored stones could buy that time. Gold could buy it.

"Where does the gold come from?"

"One makes many contacts in my work. Purchases can be arranged. Risks must be..."

"Risks commensurate with profits, Bakshir?"

"Precisely, dear Miss Foxman."

"I must think about this."

"Naturally. Nothing is certain. Circumstances change."

"Next time you are in New York, I will buy you lunch."

"And we will talk some more about colored stones."

"Colored stones, yes."

"And gold?"

"Colored stones, gold and diamonds, Bakshir."

He sighed. "Such a meeting would give me great joy. The rest—it will remain in Allah's hands. Now, lovely lady, shall we order our lunch? I am famished and in all of this irrational and unpredictable world nothing can take the place of French cuisine..."

The Marquise greeted Ellie in the breakfast room of her apartment on a side street off the Champs-Elysées. A bright, sunny room containing a glass-topped table, some chairs and an abundance of green plants along the walls and hanging in pots from the ceiling.

The Marquise served tea and assessed the younger woman stoically. "You have recovered from your accident, I am glad to see."

"I owe you an apology for the trouble I've caused. I handled the affair badly."

The Marquise looked into her cup. "Bad men are the curse of every good woman. I have known my share."

"I should have not mixed business with pleasure, though there was little pleasure involved. I allowed matters to get out of hand."

"In the end, all is well. The Chamblay has been returned, and only time has been lost to me, although I can ill afford to spend that recklessly. This time I shall engage an established house to auction the Chamblay for me."

Ellie found it difficult to meet the Marquise's eye. "The drawbacks of an auction still exist, madame. The publicity, the gossip."

"I must get money, dear girl. My funds are depleted and I cannot wait any longer."

"I understand. But the advantages of a private sale are still many. My client—I spoke to him this morning and his craving for the choker has increased. So too has the price he's willing to pay. A deal could be made almost immediately..." She let the words hang on the still air.

The Marquise fitted a long brown cigarette into her holder, lit it from the old Zippo and smoked thoughtfully. "I admire your perseverance, my dear, but..."

"But you no longer trust me?"

"In the light of what has gone before, am I to blame?"

"I came here to ask for a second chance. Not for the money—I'll forgo the usual commission—but to prove my reliability. Let me finish what I started. Let me sell the Chamblay and place the money in your hands."

"I compliment you on your drive, my dear, on your conviction and confidence. You remind me so much of myself when I was your age. I cannot afford the risk..."

"There is no risk this time. The client is waiting for my

call. As I told you, a French aristocrat about to embark for Quebec. The circumstances are ideal for you and for him. Put the Chamblay in my charge and I'll be back in Paris by sundown with your money."

"Oh, it is all so difficult! The Chamblay means more to me than any piece of jewelry I've ever owned. I want to do the right thing. And the money, always the money..."

"It's equally important to me. I want to prove myself to Maurice."

"Maurice! What has he got to do with this?"

"It was my uncle who tracked it down, retrieved it and got it back to you."

"I should have known. It came in your name, my dear, with regrets and good wishes. No mention that Maurice was involved in any way. How like Maurice."

Yes, Ellie thought with considerable resentment. Playing God with other people's belongings, with their lives, and remaining always in the background, pulling the strings.

"All the more reason for me to sell it for you," she said quickly. "Let me have it, madame, let me get the price you're entitled to while keeping your name out of the public eye."

"And also to send a not so subtle message to your uncle. To make him know that you are capable of doing the job. To rub his nose in it, as you Americans like to say. Precisely what I would do in your place. The taste of revenge can be sweet indeed. I do like you, my dear. Truly I do. But if I turn the Chamblay over to you again after what has happened, would I not be a fool? Oh, yes, that is exactly what I would be. A doddering old fool seeking to squeeze a bit more excitement for herself out of the lives of others. And that is what I am— an old fool. Very well, the Chamblay is yours to sell. If you are not back by the time of the evening meal, I shall assume you are not coming and I shall forget about you and the Chamblay. I am not prepared to endure another such ordeal."

"You won't be sorry, madame."

"We shall see, won't we?"

*chapter*
## 12

KELLER FIXED HIS EYES on the African walking stick as if mesmerized. He told himself that an ancient wood-carver deep in the African bush had labored meticulously over the branch of a mahogany tree with a razor-sharp blade, eventually bringing forth this magnificent stick, strong and dependable, designed to last forever.

Or was it?

Keller reached for the stick. It felt good in his hand, substantial, the same brutish sensation a nightstick possessed. He raised the stick and brought it down with controlled force into the palm of his left hand, the impact shivering along his forearm.

Was it a work of art? he asked himself. Did it have some special value? He chose to view it as a singular creation, utilitarian and aesthetic at the same time. In New York were art galleries specializing in African artifacts; would such a gallery display this stick?

Or was it just one of many? Mass-produced by underpaid hand labor especially for the tourist trade.

He placed a hand at either end, raising it to shoulder height. He braced himself and then, in one strong, swift movement, brought it down across his knee. Acute pain shot up and down his leg and he wondered if he'd done himself permanent injury.

He swore and waited for the leg to feel better.

He addressed the walking stick aloud: "Give it up," he demanded. "Give it up."

He carried the stick into the hallway outside his apartment and smashed it against the metal banister alongside the stairwell. He struck again and again with no apparent effect on the stick.

"Nice piece of work," Keller said, and went back inside the apartment.

Was he wrong about the stick? Wrong also about Robert Foxman? Was his murder a robbery gone wrong? Or the result of a private feud? Keller had to know.

In the hall closet, an elaborate tool chest. Above it, hanging from pegs on the wall, a series of saws and power tools. Carrying a coping saw, Keller went back to the walking stick, resting on his round coffee table. He tightened the stick in place with one foot. He sawed carefully at a point three inches from the tip of the stick. He cut all the way through and examined the result: solid wood. He went to work on the other end and with the same result. He moved the blade to a point three inches down the shaft of the stick and began another cut, sawing very slowly. He was a third of the way through when white threads appeared on the blade. Cotton! He began to work faster. When the cut was finished, he examined the hollow center of the stick. Keller upended the cane, and nothing fell out. Furious with frustration, he pulled a pencil-sized flashlight from his tool kit, and shined it into the dismembered cane. The beam focused on something white. Keller straightened out a wire hanger and fished out a ball of absorbent cotton. Beneath it was an incredibly beautiful diamond. It was one of fifteen. Keller, eyes fixed on the glittering stones, wondered glumly what part Maurice Foxman had played in all this.

Keller placed a call to IMM headquarters in Johannesburg, asked to speak to Koenigsburg. Seconds later the big man was on the phone.

"What do you want, Keller?"

A typical greeting from Keller's boss; brusque, to the point, a man who never permitted himself to waste time. Keller almost smiled; there was something reassuring about Koenigsburg's consistent rudeness.

"I found out why Robert Foxman was killed."

Koenigsburg was unimpressed. "So?"

Another expected reaction. Koenigsburg functioned without emotion, without praise. An investigator was hired to answer questions, to acquire information, to solve cases. Anything less was unsatisfactory.

"He had some stones hidden away. In a hollow walking stick, can you believe it?" Koenigsburg offered no response; he was a man seldom surprised, never shocked, always anticipating the unexpected. "If I were betting, I'd say they're Russian product."

Koenigsburg cleared his throat this time.

"You think young Foxman was smuggling, then?"

"It would seem that way."

"It would," Koenigsburg said dryly, "wouldn't it? For the uncle, naturally."

"I'm not so sure of that."

"Seems to me you're not so sure of very much today, Keller. Is that what I'm to tell Sir John, that you're not so sure? Sir John is a man with a preference for certainty."

"I intend to confront Foxman the elder with the stones."

"Good. I'd be interested in his reaction."

"He's in Europe now, on his way to Rome. I thought I'd catch up with him there, ask a few more questions along the way."

"What has this to do with me, Keller? You're wasting my time."

"The stones. I want to take them along but I'd rather not be picked up for smuggling. Arrange it for me, will you?"

A soft grunt before Koenigsburg answered. "Very well. Contact Nick Arno in the New York office. By the time you call, he'll have authorization. Is there anything else, Keller?"

"Nothing, Mr. Koenigsburg. Thank you."

Koenigsburg hung up without another word.

The call woke Keller. The red numbers on his digital clock told him it was ten minutes after four, the middle of the night. A functionary in IMM's Paris office, a man assigned to the security section, an officious bureaucrat, the same round the world. Bored, convinced of his natural superiority, existing only for his pension.

"This man you made inquiry about, investigator," came a supercilious voice in heavily accented English, "this Arab, this Khamoury. He arrived in St. Tropez this morning. He is at the Hotel Byblos, don't suppose you know it?"

Keller held back the angry remark that came onto his tongue. "I know it," he said flatly. The Byblos was on the Avenue Paul Signac, where one could always find the Rolls-Royces gathered like covered wagons lined up against attacking Indians. And inside the famous and wealthy matched wit and reputation with each other.

"For how long?"

"The booking is for three days."

"I'll be on the first plane out of Kennedy. I would be unhappy if Khamoury is gone before I arrive."

"I can assure you . . ."

"Good. Who have you got in place?"

"The Irishman . . ."

"McLoughlin, he's a good man."

"The best I have."

"Check me into La Mandarine. Tell McLoughlin to contact me there."

"As you wish."

Keller broke the connection and put a call through to Pan American, giving his priority status, assuring himself a seat on the next flight to Paris, with a connection to St. Tropez. Within the hour he was packed and on his way to the airport. He checked in, managed a light breakfast and made three telephone calls before boarding. He slept most of the way across the Atlantic.

By the time he arrived in St. Tropez, it was night. The tiny Mediterranean fishing village made famous by painters, writers and movie stars vibrated with movement and anticipation. The streets and bars and cafés were alive with people searching for a glimpse of the licentious activities of the very wealthy, the very gifted, the very famous. Most were unlikely to even snatch a glimpse of Brigitte Bardot's chauffeur.

Keller checked into La Mandarine and found a message

waiting for him. He ordered a pot of black coffee sent to his room and shaved and showered. By then the coffee had arrived and he drank some and made a call.

"McLoughlin?"

"Is that you, Keller? When did you get in?"

Keller was in no mood for small talk. "I want to see Khamoury."

"When?"

"Right now."

"Let me tell you, this Khamoury, after four a.m., he buys some *pain au chocolat* at the bakery behind Sénéquier's and settles in to hold court at Le Gorille."

"I don't know it."

"An all-night bistro. Khamoury has a taste for the high life. Young women, that sort of thing. He seems to have a sufficiency of money to spend. Anyway, that's where you'll find him. Shall I pick you up?"

"Meet me there."

"You'll know me." McLoughlin chuckled softly. "I'll be alone and wearing an expectant smile."

McLoughlin was easy to spot. He was tall with a quizzical expression on his long face and the angular body of a tennis player whose legs had gone bad. His handshake was firm and he wasted no time getting to the point.

"Khamoury," he said, pointing with his long chin.

Keller looked around. Everywhere beautiful young people dressed in white. Women in sheer blouses that displayed their breasts, the men bored and seeking other forms of diversion. Here and there an older man, tanned and eager, hovering over a woman thirty years his junior. An air of expectancy permeated the place, all of them waiting for social lightning to stike and change their luck.

"The one with the three pretties?" Keller said.

"That's him."

Khamoury was at a round table, a cup of hot chocolate in front of him, holding hands with one girl, talking to a second, examining the third. All were blondes, all were young, all were slender and self-consciously casual.

"An ambitious man," Keller commented.

"Energetic. Different cast of characters every night."

"Pros?"

"Around here, in one way or another, everyone is."

"I'll talk to him now," Keller said.

"Need my help?"

"You wait and watch. It shouldn't take long."

As Keller approached the round table, he caught Khamoury's attention. Something about the compact man troubled the Lebanese and he frowned, releasing the hand he was fondling, and sat up straighter in his chair. A cop, he decided at once.

"I came a long way to talk to you," Keller began.

Khamoury waved a hand in dismissal. "As you can see, sir, I am thoroughly occupied. Another time."

"This is business."

"Business. Oh, business. I do business only during the daylight hours. Contact me at my hotel."

"Syndicate business," Keller said. He pulled up a chair and straddled it.

Khamoury recognized Keller as a man to be treated with care, lest he be offended, a man to be feared. All the world over, he reminded himself, policemen were the same.

"Business," he said in regret.

"Private business."

Khamoury rolled his eyes and spoke to his companions in excellent French. Alternately pouting and smiling in Keller's direction, they departed. Khamoury watched them go, Keller watched Khamoury.

"IMM, you said?"

"Security."

"For a moment, I believed the worst."

"And that was what?"

"Who can say until it occurs? What does the Syndicate possibly wish with me, sir?"

"My name is Keller."

"Ah, yes, Mr. Keller."

"Just Keller will do. Tell me what you know about Robert Foxman."

"Ah, poor Robert. A lovely young man. I will miss doing

business with him. What a shame, his passing. Allah's ways are beyond the understanding of us mere mortals, is it not so, Mr. Keller?"

"What business did you have with Foxman?"

"Stones."

"Diamonds?"

"A few poor samples. Mostly colored stones."

Keller shifted gears. "Why would anyone murder Foxman?"

"For the stones, of course."

"Keep on going."

"What more can I say? Robert was buying, I was but one of his suppliers. Buyers are always vulnerable to thieves. Unfortunately this one was violent, lethal. Poor Robert."

"Tell me this, Khamoury, why did the killer leave behind the stones you sold to Robert?"

"Is it true?" Khamoury grew alarmed, seemed to shrink inside himself, a small man becoming smaller, hoping to conceal himself behind an invisible shell.

"It's true."

Khamoury hugged himself. "Clearly, there is no way I can be of assistance to you, sir."

Keller ignored the remark. "What did you and Robert talk about?"

"Talk? Business of course."

"What else?"

"I inquired about the health of his uncle, the estimable Maurice Foxman. I inquired about his sister. His sister is the loveliest of women. Nothing more."

"Did he mention other deals, other suppliers, other buys?"

"No." Khamoury's eyes shifted nervously.

"Tell me," Keller insisted.

Khamoury read an implicit threat in Keller's rasping voice, in the hard brightness of those pale eyes. The Syndicate's man was not to be trifled with, not to incite to anger, not to have as an enemy.

"Go on," Keller said, playing on the obvious fear in the other man.

Khamoury raised his hands to frame his narrow face, a gesture of supplication and of regret. "There was another person he intended to see. An appointment he spoke about."

"Give me a name?"

Khamoury inspected the room as if seeking his former companions. Or an available escape route. He knew there was no way out. "Robert mentioned no names . . ." His voice drifted away.

"Go on."

"Please, you must believe me. This is conjecture only. I had heard he had come to Monrovia . . ."

"Who?"

"The Russian."

A spark flickered deep in Keller's brain. The old familiar signal that he was about to be drawn into something complex and convoluted; something of massive proportions, bigger than the death of one man or the theft of a handful of diamonds. He felt himself leaning toward Khamoury in order to receive his answers a millisecond earlier, perhaps.

"This Russian, does he have a name?"

Khamoury became agitated, face pinched, eyes darting from side to side. "A name, yes. All men have names. But is it the name with which he was born? Who can say about such a man!"

"By what name do you know him?"

Khamoury exhaled and his shoulders gave way. "Tarassuk. Georgy Tarassuk."

"Where will I find this Tarassuk?"

"With such a man, who knows? He surfaces at his own pleasure at the time and the place he desires."

"A dealer?"

"He sells only."

"Outside the Syndicate's jurisdiction?"

"Outside IMM. Outside De Beers. Always outside, far from rules and regulations. A man like Tarassuk, it is not fair. I ask you, is it fair? He appears with a pocketful of stones, excellent stones. Expensive stones. Where do they come from? you are about to ask. I shall answer honestly—I do not know."

"Stolen?"

Khamoury lowered his eyes. "Was I present when a theft took place? I was not. Could I place the Russian at the scene of a crime? I could not. But always he has stones in abundance. Or so I am told."

"And Robert Foxman met with Tarassuk after his business with you?"

"I guessed as much."

"He didn't actually say so?"

"I would be less than honest if I told you that he did."

"What else can you remember?"

"Robert claimed the right of privacy when I pressed him. A man is entitled to privacy."

"So you don't actually know where Robert was bound for? Who he was going to see?"

"Call it a presentiment. What you Americans call a hunch." Keller handed the Arab his card and stood up.

"Stay," Khamoury urged with little enthusiasm. "Have a *café au lait*. The ladies will return and you may take your choice. So much pleasure to be had . . ."

"You hear anything, you call me at the nearest IMM office. Leave your name, I'll get back to you."

"I doubt that I . . ."

"Sir John would be grateful. I would be grateful."

Again that cold cloud of danger cast its shadow over Khamoury and he set himself against the chill. "For a friend, I shall keep my ear to the ground, as it were." A feeble smile creased his face. "That is the correct figure of speech, is it not?"

"On the nose," Keller said, before he left.

"On the nose," Khamoury repeated. He scribbled the words on a napkin; every experience broadened one, he believed. Every encounter provided knowledge, knowledge and experience eventually brought wisdom.

The three French girls returned to the table. "Are you ready for us again, Bakshir?" one of them said cutely.

"On the nose," he said, grinning slyly.

Keller and McLoughlin ambled through the old fortified city. During the daylight hours the chic and expensive botiques that lined the narrow cobbled streets would be crowded with shoppers. Now only the sound of their own slow footsteps broke the nighttime stillness.

"Was the Arab worth the trip?" McLoughlin asked.

"He gave me Tarassuk. Georgy Tarassuk, a Russian."

"Never heard of him."

"Neither did I. A sometime seller of good merchandise, as Khamoury tells it."

"Where does he get his stuff?"

"Khamoury didn't know."

They walked on without speaking. "What are you working on?" Keller said.

"The usual sort of things down here. Quick young men lifting expensive jewelry from rich old women. Nothing exciting."

"Any talk of smuggling?"

"Just a small item now and again. Comes in off the boats. Rich people get their jollies beating the system when they can."

"It's epidemic," Keller said. They were in the port area, walking along the harbor front crowded with shining white yachts.

"Lots of money in the world."

"Seems that way."

"Some guys got the knack for getting their hands on the stuff. Not me."

"It's a big club and I'm a charter member."

McLoughlin grunted softly. "You think the Foxman killing is connected to something big?"

"Nothing definite yet. All the questions turn into more questions."

McLoughlin stopped and gestured. "Unless you need me, I've been up for twenty-four hours. I need some sleep. My digs are that way."

They shook hands. "Take care of yourself," Keller said.

"You too."

Keller was halfway back to La Mandarine before he became aware that someone was following him. He increased his pace by half and the footsteps kept up, an echo slightly out of sync. He turned into a narrow street, climbing from the port area. Around a short block and down again, walking faster, seeking an escape route, or a refuge from which to observe the man behind him. A glance back revealed a shadowy figure, no longer concerned with concealment or subterfuge, closing fast. Keller examined his choices; flee or fight. He made a run for it.

He avoided the open areas around the harbor, heading back

up toward high ground. The footsteps never faltered, getting closer. He ran faster, hoping for a well-lit bistro or a disco where he might find sanctuary among the dancers. No luck. Only the deserted street lay ahead. Around a corner, past a pale pink building looming ghostlike in the pre-dawn darkness. A tall iron gate stood ajar and he went through and found himself in a garden; he closed the gate behind him. A high stone wall separated him from the street. He listened to his pursuer charge past.

Keller pulled himself up to the top of the wall, where glass shards were embedded in cement, intended to keep burglars at bay. He felt the skin on his palms tear and he set himself against the pain. Once atop the wall, he gathered his legs under him in a cat-like crouch. He waited.

Down the street came a small man, slender and strong, a man born to be a jockey, he thought. In the jockey's right hand, a pistol, complete with a noise suppressor.

A professional, Keller warned himself, and crouched lower. The jockey moved slowly, searching the darkness for his prey. When he was directly underneath, Keller launched himself in a headfirst dive.

The jockey sensed Keller's presence before they came together. Already twisting away, rolling, jerking the pistol in a short, swift arc. Pain flashed across Keller's brow and he tumbled off to one side. He came up fast, legs pumping hard. The gunman turned and ran, Keller at his heels.

The speed of the little man was amazing. He opened up a lead of five lengths, then fifteen, still pulling away. Fifty feet separated the two men when the jockey turned back, coming to rest in a shooter's stance, steadying his gun hand, taking aim. Keller dived for cover. A slug whizzed overhead and then another. Keller stayed down. The jockey, having made his point, pocketed his weapon and walked away.

Keller climbed to his feet and brushed himself off. Enough excitement for one night, he told himself. It was time to get some sleep.

## *chapter*
# 13

LATE IN THE AFTERNOON of the day after she returned to New York, David presented himself to Ellie in her small office.

"Got a minute?"

"More time than I need," she answered.

"How was the trip?"

She almost told him about the sale of the Chamblay to Lucien Duquette, but thought better of it. Not even the positive ending to that affair mollified her; what a fool she had been, allowing Henry Wilton to use and abuse her that way. Never again.

"Not very good," she said aloud. "Oh, there's one or two things cooking, but I don't hold out much hope. The Foxman name doesn't open up many doors these days. And being a woman certainly doesn't help."

"The old man doesn't have any more faith in me that he does in you. Neither one of us fits his image of a diamond person."

"Maybe we'll both prove him wrong one day."

"That's why I'm here. What do you think of these?" He showed her the two diamonds Peter Downes had passed on to him. "Nice, aren't they?"

She put a glass to them. "Very nice. What do they weigh?"

"One point two carats each."

"You're selling them for Maurice?"

"That's just it, no. A friend of mine. Well, we're really partners in the deal..." He broke off.

"I see." She watched him with renewed interest. By nature, David was forthright, easy to read, seldom holding back anything. This time his behavior was uncharacteristically secretive and it stirred her curiosity.

He retrieved the stones and dropped them into his jacket pocket. "Will these bring seventy thousand, Ellie?"

"Maybe. They look good under the loupe."

"They're perfect, Ellie, D-flawless. You saw for yourself. I'm going to try for seventy-five." He ducked his head sheepishly. "What would you say if I told you I was thinking about opening up my own outfit?"

"Leave Maurice? I don't believe it."

"Not exactly."

"What then?"

"What would you say to a subsidiary? P & D, Inc. How does that sound to you? Do some buying, selling, open up some new sources."

She saw David in a new light suddenly, a competitor, a threat to her own ambitions. "P & D. D for David. Who is Mr. P?"

"A friend of mine. Do you think I can pull it off, Ellie?"

"That's going to take some money."

"Yes, I know. I thought Maurice might be the guarantor. With him behind us..."

David could go that way. It was consistent with the way he had lived his life, leaning on his father, unable and unwilling to stray too far from home. For Ellie it was different; her time had come and she would continue to work for Maurice only in a position of authority, with a liberal dose of autonomy. David wanted to work for someone else; she yearned to be free.

"That might work," she said. "Tell me about this friend of yours, your partner."

"Peter Downes. A really terrific fellow, Ellie. You'd like him. With a great deal of experience."

"Have you mentioned your plan to Maurice?"

"After I make this sale. I want to see how it goes."

"Good thinking, David."

"It was Peter's idea. He's the kind of partner I need. He sees the whole picture, thinks things through. I want you to meet him. I'd appreciate your opinion. You're good at that, Ellie, judging people."

What irony, Ellie thought, after Henry Wilton and all the others. Did David really believe that? If so, it was a reflection on the quality of *his* judgment.

"You'll like Peter," David went on. "Everybody does. Why don't I arrange something."

She thought it over. "Have you introduced Peter to Maurice yet?"

"Frankly, I'm scared to, Ellie. I have visions of bringing Peter into Maurice's office and Maurice going into that disapproving act of his. You know how he can be, so proper, so courtly and so dismissive. If that happens, the partnership is out the window before it begins."

"Do it another way."

"Have you got an idea?"

"Make it a family affair, all of us meet Peter at the same time. You, me and Maurice."

"That might work. What about Mattie?"

"No, leave Mother out of it. And nobody puts a move on Maurice for backing. Any talk of a partnership is left for another time."

"What would you say to dinner at the Four Seasons?" David said, his enthusiasm rising.

"A little less than that. A quiet lunch, where we can talk. A leisurely lunch, after which we can all go our own way. Nothing forced, nothing pressured."

"Sounds good to me. I'll set it up. You always see things so clearly, Ellie. I'm sure this is going to work. Maurice is going to like Peter. And so will you, Ellie. I'm sure of it."

She smiled benignly. "We'll see about that . . ."

Tom Horn looked the part. A West Texas cowboy with what he described as "an itty-bitty little ole spread, runnin' jes' a handful of cows. Weren't fer the water we brought in a few

years back, we'd be scratchin' n' hackin'. Course, it is a true
fact that some good ole boys found a mite of oil in them parts
and that set me to diggin' agin."

"And?" David said, fascinated to come in contact with a
real-life cowboy and rancher.

"An' we hit the Big Casino, friend. Got us a dozen or so
pumps goin', night 'n' day."

"Made you rich," David said cheerfully.

"Not Texas-rich, but rich enough to send Rachel and Thomas
Lee to college, when the time comes around. Sure ain't com-
plainin', though. Better'n pickin' at dirt jes' to get somethin'
to feed your own self with, ain't it, though."

David agreed that it was.

Horn, slender with far-seeing eyes and regular features,
turned a pleased expression from David to Peter Downes and
back again. In black tooled-leather high-heeled boots, jeans
and a western-style jacket, there was no mistaking his origins.

"Mind if I eyeball them two purty things one more time?"
Horn bent over the diamonds on David's desk. "D-flawless,
you said?"

"That's right."

"What exactly does that mean, Mr. Foxman?"

"A diamond's purity is determined by the visibility of flaws
when magnified ten times and exposed to normalized light.
Corrections are made for chromatic and spherical aberration.
Flawless rating tells a buyer he's getting a stone which is absolutely transparent. There are no inclusions or external blemishes."

"Sounds mighty good."

"It is mighty good," David said. "Color is rated by letter,
the highest being the letter D. A D-flawless stone is virtually
perfect."

"They sure are the cutest little ole things, ain't they? What
d'you say, Mr. Downes?" Horn said. "Reckon my Madeline's
gonna cozy up to these two?"

"No doubt about it, Tom. What we have here is top-rated
merchandise. These stones have certificates from GIA, the
Gemological Institute of America, and they're backed by a
first-class operation. Foxman and Company is nationally recognized with international connections. Check on Maurice Fox-

man and you'll hear only good things."

"Take the stones anywhere you like for an appraisal, Mr. Horn," David said. "Our prices stand the test."

"Well, now," Horn drawled. "Let's us talk about price. Jes' how solid is your askin' price? Eighty thousand seems a mite on the steep side to me."

Horn was no fool, David decided. He might know very little about diamonds, but he knew a great deal about money. A rancher with oil and water was no financial innocent.

David said, "You won't find better stones than these brilliants, Mr. Horn. I want to give you the best deal I can." Out of the corner of his eye, he saw Peter nod once, a slight, clear signal. "My margin is not all that substantial . . ."

"Well, sure. A man's entitled to a fair profit. Don't mean to cheat you, Mr. Foxman. Jes' ain't lookin' to have my pocket picked, in a manner of speakin'."

"Why don't we say seventy-five and you've got a good deal."

"I was more'n mind of about seventy."

David reached for the stones in a slow, considered movement; Horn covered his hand with his own. "You want to deal and so do I. Let's split the difference—seventy-two five."

David didn't hesitate. "They're yours, Mr. Horn."

"My check do you boys okay?"

"Your check will be just fine," David answered.

They watched Horn write out a check. "Pleasure doin' business with you, David," Horn said. He dropped the diamonds in his pocket and rose to leave.

"I'll walk outside with you," Downes said.

"You'll be back?" David said.

"Just as soon as I get Tom here settled in a taxi and on his way back to White Deer and his Madeline."

"That Madeline, for sure the Yellow Rose of Texas, and that's no lie!" Laughing, Tom Horn departed, Peter Downes trailing him outside.

On the sidewalk, the two men shook hands and the diamonds went from Horn's hand to Downes's and very quickly into his pocket.

"Did my performance suit you, Mr. Downes?" Horn said, no hint of a drawl in his voice.

"Perfect, pal. You did a hell of a job on the accent, sounded real."

"I'm an actor, it's what I do."

"Fair enough. Okay, you've got your dough, so on your way."

"Ever need me again, just call my service."

"Depend on it."

Downes went back to David's office, very pleased with himself. Matters were proceeding according to plan, right on schedule.

They met for lunch at a small French restaurant on East Fifty-first Street. David, Ellie, Maurice and Peter Downes. To anyone watching, they seemed an extraordinarily attractive and congenial group. Ellie, whose auburn hair danced and sparkled with every movement, every gesture, her finely sculpted features drawing the admiration of every man in the place. On either side of her, David and Peter, both handsome and charming, quick to respond to her every word. Across the table, Maurice Foxman, white-haired, distinguished, listening attentively, his alert eyes missing nothing, a king with his court.

Ellie made a concerted effort to distribute her attention evenly, to laugh at David's witticisms, to favor Maurice when he spoke; but it was Peter Downes to whom she responded most. And with an intensity she had seldom before felt on first meeting a man.

A deceptive vulnerability made it seem as if he welcomed her into his life without reservation. Holding back nothing. Ask a question and he responded without hesitation, without guile, his manner frank to the point of being naïve. Add to that his startling good looks, a face that might have belonged to a movie star; the deeply tanned skin, the eyes warm and richly brown, the luxurious hair to match, growing thick and long over his ears, skillfully barbered. A perfect smile appeared on command, just the right display of perfectly matched teeth, shining white. Ellie felt herself succumbing too quickly, too completely, and grew uneasy, vaguely fearful, suspicious of her reaction. Keller had been disquieting. This man was different, even disturbing. He reminded her of somebody she had once known but she could attach no name to the memory.

Since Henry Wilton had left her lying in her car nearly two months ago, she hadn't had the slightest desire to be near a man. She'd met no one of interest—unless Keller counted, and he wasn't at all her type, chipped and scarred as he was, an unfinished man with none of the natural beauty that she found so exciting.

She stole a look at Peter, at that classic profile, the graceful throat, and a shiver of anticipation stepped down her spine, the distinctly icy touch of danger.

Whenever Peter talked directly to her it was as if they were alone. The others at the table were excluded from her mind, out of sight, and she clung to his gaze, turning away only when he broke contact. If he smiled, she smiled in return. If he spoke, she listened. She scolded herself for acting like a schoolgirl. Be cool, she commanded herself. Cool...

Abruptly, and to her surprise, Peter put an end to the interval. He spoke to Maurice, his voice firm, without apology.

"It's been a pleasure meeting you, sir. But business intrudes."

"I understand, Peter." Ellie reacted; seldom did Maurice address anyone he'd just met by his first name. He was much too formal for that. "Good manners," he liked to say, "is what keeps us from each other's throats."

"I have a client waiting."

"Business comes first."

"Too many stones, too few customers."

Maurice was surprised. "I've said the same thing myself..."

"At the Diamond Club banquet a month ago. Your speech made a great impression on me. My professional Bible ever since."

"You're very kind, Peter."

Downes was on his feet, shaking hands all around. "I made a recent acquisition of considerable substance that I hope to transform into a rather profitable..." He broke off, embarrassed. "Sorry. No reason to spoil a lovely lunch with trade talk." He stepped back from the table.

"Bernstein is conducting the Philharmonic on Tuesday," he said to Ellie. "I have tickets, if you'd care to go?"

She hesitated.

"I understand," he said smoothly. "You have other plans."

"No. No plans. Tuesday will be fine."

He nodded once as though to seal the bargain and was gone. A waiter brought more coffee.

"Quite a guy, isn't he?" David said.

"An impressive young man," was Maurice's comment. "You liked him, Ellie?"

"Very straight arrow," she said.

David rose to the defense. "He's very unusual, better than most you'll meet."

"You saw something you did not approve of?" Maurice said, thinking that David was right, Peter Downes was in some ways unique, the sort of young man he had always appreciated.

"I barely know him," Ellie replied.

"You'll get to know him better on Tuesday." Said by David with a smirk the others chose to ignore.

"How well do you know him?" Maurice said to David.

"We've become friends. We work out together. We dine together two or three times a week. We play a little chess."

Maurice approved; a good chess player developed foresight, anticipation, mental agility, patience.

". . . And we do a little business."

"Perhaps Peter will favor me with a match one day," Maurice said. "What sort of business?"

"Nothing important."

"All business is important, I have found. Fail small and you will eventually fail big. The same laws apply always. Was it a profitable arrangement, David?"

"Yes, Father, it was. As a matter of fact, Peter and I have been discussing the possibility of getting up a more permanent arrangement."

"Interesting. You must tell me about it, when you and that young man are ready." Maurice called for the check.

"This is my treat," David protested.

If he heard, Maurice gave no sign. He was always the host, he always paid, it was his way of doing things.

*chapter*
# 14

HARRY GEIS LIVED in a tenement apartment on West Fourteenth Street. By any measure, it was ordinary, without architectural distinction. Downes made the furniture out to be early Salvation Army, hand-me-downs found in secondhand shops or picked off the streets. No pictures on the walls, no books, no rugs on the floor; but along one wall was an expensive television set, a VCR, two audio tape decks and a high-powered multi-band radio. Neither the electronic equipment nor Ralph Browning belonged in these surroundings.

Like the equipment, Browning had the look of money to him. Big money. The suit was tailor-made, the shoes were English, the watch on Browning's wrist was Baume et Mercier. He was a man of style and wealth, a man out of an old British film. The kind of man Peter had always longed to be.

Browning, relaxed and in charge, spoke in a voice cultivated and resonant, his speech without the slightest impediment.

"Harry informs me you are planning to go into business together?"

"We've talked about it," Downes said. He wondered how much Geis had told Browning. Why would a man of Browning's position and accomplishment be interested in this kind of a deal, no matter how impressive the numbers were?

"Talked," Browning said, clearly rankled. He shifted his attention to Geis. "You gave me to understand, Harry, that you and Downes had reached an agreement."

"We have."

"Peter's in, aren't you, Peter?"

Downes hesitated, then nodded.

"That's better," Browning said, settling back. "How far have matters gone?"

"We've zeroed in on Foxman and Company. Project Flawless, I call it. Peter's made contact with the old man, his niece and David."

"David's Maurice Foxman's son," Downes felt compelled to say. "We've already done a deal."

"Peter and David are really tight..."

Browning stared at Downes. "You understand how complicated this job is?" Downes turned it over in his mind; Browning *did* know, was aware of the dimensions of the project, had been told the amount of money involved. "It will take drive and courage and intelligence, Downes. Are you up to it?"

"I think so."

"I'm sure of it, Mr. Browning," Geis said, playing along. Good cop, bad cop; it was intended to keep Peter Downes from stepping out of line.

"I'm not so sure. Let's face it, Downes, your track record isn't precisely impeccable."

"Don't worry about me." Downes felt like a small boy boasting to bolster his courage. Intimidated by Ralph Browning, he kept wondering how Geis had managed such an impressive connection.

"A man in my position must worry, Downes. About matters large and small. One mistake and—" He threw up his hands. "We'll take a bath."

"I like Peter," Geis said quickly. "I trust him."

Downes set himself against the fear that gripped him. "I didn't ask for this. Harry came to me with the job. I don't need this crap..."

"Without Peter, Mr. Browning, we haven't got anything going for us. No contact at Foxman, nothing..." Geis grinned at Downes. "Tell him about the girl, Peter. Tell him."

"I'm seeing her Tuesday night."

"She's crazy about Peter already, Mr. Browning. With David as his pal and Ellie begging to get schtupped... well, what the hell, we're almost all the way home."

Downes spoke with a confidence he didn't feel. "I'm not here to beg for handouts. You don't want me in, okay, I'm out. Get yourself another boy."

"Just a minute!" Geis cried.

"Well," Browning said. "There's some fire in you, after all. Good, very good. As I understand Harry's proposal, the job is going to take some time from beginning to end. Perseverance, Downes. Can you stay the course?"

"I can cut it."

Browning kept his eyes fixed on Downes. "Understand my position, gentlemen. If I put up the seed money, my bank's funds are on the line. My personal reputation. The greatest risk is mine."

"I can cut it," Downes said again, more forcefully this time.

"Lines of credit have to be established."

"I'll do it."

Browning turned thoughtful. "That old man, he's smart. Been around a long time. He knows every trick in the game."

"Foxman likes Peter," Geis insisted. "We got the word from the son."

Browning crossed his legs, straightened the creases in his trousers. "What we have here is no wall-to-wall hustle. We are talking about a great deal of money—*twenty million dollars*. No matter how easy it looks, it won't be easy to pull off. It will take brains and guts and staying power."

"I'll deliver Foxman," Downes said.

"How?"

"David and I are planning a joint venture, a partnership of our own—P & D, Inc. A trading subsidiary of Foxman and Company itself."

"Credit?"

"David is convinced we can get Maurice to stand behind the operation. Once this is launched . . ."

"How much will you need from me?" Browning said.

"A quarter million for starters. Once the credit lines are set up and if Foxman will be our guarantor, we can't miss."

"Can't miss!" Geis exulted.

"How long will it take to get it done?" Browning said.

"Three months, start to finish," Downes said.

"It mustn't be allowed to simmer for too long. Deals burn out, lose their momentum."

"Three months."

"You're satisfied, Harry?" Browning said.

"Yes, sir."

"If I'm to come in, there must be certain stipulations. Any money I put up will be in the form of an interest-bearing loan, is that understood?"

"No problem."

"After credit is established, and Foxman is clearly behind you and the initial buys are made, I will direct you to certain dealers."

"We're going to need to buy in quantity," Downes said, trying not to let his nervousness surface.

"There'll be no trouble about that. But no papers will be drawn up. No signatures required. Just a verbal agreement, binding on each of us. Am I making myself clear, Mr. Downes?"

"Clear."

"Above and beyond that, I shall be a silent partner. *Silent*. With no visible connection between us, Downes. And no one is to learn of my participation. Is that clear?"

"Clear."

"Any and all profits will be equally divided among us. There it is. Any question? Any objections?"

"Then we've got a deal," Geis said eagerly. "Peter?"

"Okay," Downes said. "Okay."

"Okay!" Geis echoed exuberantly. "Okay! Okay!" He sobered quickly. "What about the dame?"

"Ellie? That's my business," Downes said.

"Nothing about this is your business," Browning said, his eyes flat and opaque, his mouth lacking all softness. "All aspects of this are of mutual concern."

"Mixing business and pleasure," Geis said. "Not so good."

"I don't agree," Browning said. "Cement your relationship with Miss Foxman and with the old man. But always remember where your true interests lie and who your partners are."

"Partners," Geis said, with obvious relief.

"Partners," Downes said, still not sure he was making a good move. Not sure at all.

\* \* \*

They sat next to each other without touching yet he was a palpable presence caressing her skin, shattering her concentration. The concert was impeccable, the music washing over her in great satisfying waves, yet she was conscious only of Peter. The warm, manly scent of him filled the cavities of her skull and she could almost hear the powerful pulse of his heart in counterpoint to the music.

She longed to reach out to him, but didn't dare, afraid she would spoil it. He made her feel like a schoolgirl again, full of vague cravings, of unnamed needs, stealing looks at the best-looking man on campus. All the boys she had known, all the men, were stunning physical creatures aware of their own masculine beauty, too busy preening to pay any attention to the people around them.

Her track record with men was poor, a flawed intuition at work, a perverted taste. All those beautiful young men, all that promise and all the emptiness they displayed. So often she had been left wanting more, too often wanting something, anything. At twenty she had married: Craig Bergson had been the most beautiful of men, sleek and smooth, an athlete, a scholar, the most desirable young man she'd ever met. Two years later she divorced him, unable to defer any longer to his megalomania, to his selfishness, to his inability to consider any other human being, least of all his wife.

Since then her choice of lovers had been equally poor. Empty suits, she called them. Beautiful men with finely muscled bodies; clever, seductive men who promised so much and delivered so little. Men who saw their looks as talent and used them accordingly.

Always there was frustration. And bitterness and anger. And always she had left, unable to tolerate the disintegrating relationship any longer.

Peter was different, she assured herself. Handsome, yes, but friendly and gentle, concerned with her welfare. All that and a penetrating sensuality that provoked and excited her. What sort of a lover would he be? Demanding, she imagined, but providing a great deal of satisfaction. She longed for the concert to be over.

When it was, they picked their way down to Fifty-seventh Street.

"The Russian Tea Room," he suggested, less a question than a declaration of his choice.

She agreed, being careful not to look at him, afraid of what he would see in her face.

He watched her devour blinis and strawberries and sour cream, all with an excellent Pouilly-Fumé.

He drank coffee and barely tasted his pastry.

"You're not eating," she said at last.

"But you are. I like to see a woman enjoy her food."

"I'm starving."

"Most women pick at food as if it's a mortal sin to be hungry. It's this national mania for thinness, coast-to-coast anorexia."

"Men are the cause of it."

She expected him to respond, to make some sexually provocative remark, to tell her she needn't concern herself about putting on weight, to tell her what a stunning figure she had. Instead he remained silent and, in that, he was so unlike other men she'd known. She was further intrigued.

"Tomorrow," she said, "it's starve Ellie Foxman day, and a three-mile swim at the Y."

"I run in the park four or five days a week. And work out at the Body Shop."

"That's where you and David met, isn't it?" She giggled. "Maurice claims exercise ruins the human body. Says that he spends all his spare time going to the funerals of his friends who exercise."

Downes produced a soft laugh. "I admire your uncle a great deal."

"Most people do," she said dryly.

"But not you?"

"No comment."

He raised his brows. All was not what it appeared to be between niece and uncle; he would pursue the subject with David, discover what the problem was. Any rift in the family Foxman might be exploitable, make his job easier. He directed the conversation elsewhere.

"You happy operating on your own?"

"I won't be happy until I'm entirely on my own. Isn't that the way you work?"

"I go where the chance is."

"An opportunist," she said without criticism.

He flashed a devastating smile her way. "I'd be a fool to deny it. I do what the business offers to get along. But if a top job came my way, I'd jump at it. As it is, I manage to keep myself in spending money. Not rich, but happy."

"I'm glad somebody is."

"You aren't?"

"Define your terms."

"I'm not sure I can do that."

"Neither can I. I just know that I want more, much more. I always have."

"Such as what?"

"A company of my own. A sight from IMM. Recognition from my peers. Success, however you define it. Everything Maurice has, everything that came so easily to him."

"Was it really that easy for him?"

"You can bet on it. He came here from Europe with a pocketful of stones and the next thing you know he was in business for himself. He hasn't looked back since. All *his* luck was good."

"Maybe it's not luck. Maybe he's smarter than everyone else. Maybe he's better."

"Better? I doubt it, Peter. My father—well, he was the best man I've ever known. Honest, compassionate, understanding of other people's problems. He was raised in a traditionalist environment in Europe, but he came to understand that life in the New World demanded a change in attitudes, a rejection of the old ways for what was creative and right in America.

"That was a moral commitment for Daddy, but it hurt him in business and even in his personal life. My uncle stood fast in his belief in the male-dominated world of the family and the diamond business. Women to the rear—bookkeepers and typists, dishwashers and mothers, good for little else. Maurice viewed my father as a weak man and ultimately incompetent because of his ideals. In the end, Maurice won out. His business succeeded, Daddy's failed. If not God's will, it was surely proof positive of Maurice's natural superiority over his brother. Even my mother thought so.

"My father was forced to go to work for Maurice, the ultimate defeat, the ultimate humiliation. Did all that mean that

Maurice was the better man? Believe it, if you wish. I don't.
I never shall."

Again that hostility toward Maurice Foxman. And again he
chose not to explore it. He wanted to do nothing to antagonize
her, everything to keep her on his side. He turned the conversation back to the music they had listened to earlier.

When they left the Russian Tea Room, they walked up to
Central Park South and hired a horse-drawn carriage for a ride
through the park. His closeness was intimidating in the cramped
confines of the cab, charged with promise and with threat.
Used to men's advances, she waited for him to move. An arm
circling her shoulders, a flirtatious word, a hand on her thigh.
He did nothing, maintaining a sedate separation, and that irritated her even more, yearning for his immediate attention.

From the hansom to a taxi that carried them to her apartment
house. He saw her to the door of her apartment. Now, she told
herself. Now he's going to reach for me, kiss me, invite himself
inside. How to respond? To give in to the cravings of her flesh
and the wild imaginings of her mind? Or hold him off until
another time? She had no good answer.

He provided one, offering his hand in a cool handshake,
saying, "I enjoyed the evening. You must be tired. Good night."
And he left without so much as a perfunctory kiss on the cheek.

She was relieved. And furious with him at the same time.
Grateful that he hadn't tried to make love to her and resentful
that while she was so responsive to him he seemed uninterested
in her.

She went inside and tried to remember who it was he reminded her of. Those refined features, that fine physique, the
same casual confidence that bordered on arrogance. Of course!
Henry Wilton. They were two of a kind, at least in appearance,
in manner. Though their style was opposite: Henry demanding
and harsh, almost cruel in the way he treated a woman; Peter
soft and considerate, concerned with her well-being. Or so it
seemed.

She loathed Henry Wilton; she couldn't wait to see Peter
Downes again.

## chapter
# *15*

LA RIVE GAUCHE, that traditional student section, the center of French radical thought and political ferment. The quarter, Keller observed without judgment, had managed somehow to retain its exuberance, its surging youthfulness, its often infantile outrageousness.

Keller circled the Place St. Michel, that broad, traffic-crowded square along the Seine, opposite the old Royal Palace, moving past clusters of young people, lovers and tourists. *"T' as pas cent balles?"* a young man with long hair and an outstretched hand called; the French equivalent of "Buddy, can you spare a dime?"

How many were actually students? Keller asked himself, trying to weed them out as he went. Some were clearly in their thirties, hanging tough to their scruffiness, hanging out and waiting for the action to commence.

He strode past cafés in which black coffee and beer were consumed endlessly, all to the clicks and the bells and the electronic squawks of the pinball machines. French youth, it seemed, were dedicated to pinball, Jerry Lewis movies and American blue jeans with the same fervor they spent on insulting foreigners or on demonstrating against whatever government happened to be in power.

On a side street, Keller stopped in front of a brick building adorned with carved stone lizards and gamines. Inside, a curved marble staircase took him to the second floor and a tall paneled door. At his knock the door was opened by a thick-necked man with the powerful shoulders of a wrestler and the dour expression of a professional bodyguard. The bodyguard looked him over with disapproval.

"I'm Keller, he's expecting me."

The bodyguard made a sound that reminded Keller of a rutting hog and admitted him, turning him over to a second man, shorter, thicker, with no neck at all and equally powerful shoulders. He led Keller down a long hallway. The apartment was a sprawl of chambers of varying shapes and corridors that went off in three different directions, the floors dark and polished to a blinding gleam, the ceilings high. At the end of the hallway, double wooden doors. No Neck knocked and opened the door. With a single jerk of his heavy hand, he gave Keller to understand he was to enter.

The room was nearly forty feet long with fireplaces in each of the short walls, neither lit on this warm day. Floor-to-ceiling windows that needed cleaning admitted rectangles of light from the street and antique Moroccan rugs were scattered on the floor, diagonal patterns of pale yellow and orange and red, accented with blue and green. At the far end of the room, to one side of the fireplace, a long, narrow table on which stood a battery of telephones, each a different color. Behind the table, a chair that resembled a throne that had once belonged to an out-of-work king.

On the throne was Vadim Lukas, looking more like a Mongol warrior running to fat than Keller remembered. A blue workman's jacket cloaked his massive bulk and he wore a beret to mask his great bald pate. Lukas, a man of dubious ancestry and untraceable roots, owned unadmitted connections to men of dubious character throughout the Western world. He squinted at Keller out of tiny, nervous eyes and his fat hands beat an impatient tattoo on the tabletop. When he spoke it was in an impeccable Oxford accent, though he had never attended that university—or any other. Rumor had it Lukas had been born in eastern Poland, raised in Hungary and survived a number of years in Liverpool. It was further rumored that he had been a hairdresser during his young manhood in Istanbul, a pimp in Paris and later the proprietor of a sandwich shop in Soho. All that changed when he discovered diamonds.

He scowled at Keller. "What in hell do you want of me, Keller?"

"Good to see you again, too, Vadim." The bony face, lined and drawn down, was tipped to one side. "Been a long time."

Lukas hawked his throat clear and peered past Keller to the cold fireplace at the far end of the long room. "Have I got business with International Minerals and Mines? I have not. Do I own Sir John great sums of money? I do not. In fact, I have no use for the Syndicate nor it for me. Go away, Keller."

"Does that mean we're not friends anymore, Vadim?"

"You appear and there is always trouble for me. You stir still waters, Keller. You kick up dirt. You make me nervous. Always trouble, always. Perhaps not enemies, you and I, but certainly never friends."

"That pains me."

"From time to time I have been forced to deal with you, but the experience is never enjoyable. Many of the others are unsavory characters. Unethical. Crooks, some of them. Even sadists. You, you are better than they, Keller. In your own strange way, you are a person, with a certain roughhewn charm, don't you know. But always one of them. Forgive me for saying so, dear fellow, but Sir John's legionnaires are not to my taste, don't you know. What are you here for this time?"

"Tarassuk."

Lukas raised and lowered his plump hands. "What is a Tarassuk?"

"Spare me the humor. Georgy Tarassuk, a Russian who deals. He surfaced recently in Liberia and did business with an American named Robert Foxman. That same day Foxman was shot to death."

"I may have heard some talk of the killing. Every day there are such occurrences—murders, robberies, terrorism. Seems it is easier for our species to kill than to live in peace. The human tragedy. This Tarassuk, he did the killing?"

"I doubt it. What do you know about Tarassuk?"

"Perhaps I heard the name mentioned somewhere."

"Don't double-talk me, Vadim. Just give."

The tiny eyes fluttered shut and remained so for a long time. His pink lips pursed and trembled. "Something comes to me. Georgy Tarassuk, you said. A Russian butterfly who flits around the market. Not an important figure at all, in my estimation."

"Where do I find him?"

"It is as I told you, he flits. Finds a consignment and sells. Discovers an opportunity and settles down for only so long as it takes to consummate an exchange. Not my sort at all."

"I want him."

"Keller. It is time for the midday meal. There is a small taverna nearby. You appreciate Greek food, Keller? They make a superb moussaka. Almost as good as it is done on the islands, almost. And a salad with feta cheese, Greek olives. A tasty baklava, equal to any anywhere, and who would know if not I? All washed down with some retsina. We shall discuss the history of the Greeks, the work of Plato and Aristotle, and talk about women. A delightful way to spend two or three hours . . . someday I shall transport myself body and soul to the Aegean . . ."

"Tell me about Tarassuk."

"Why trouble yourself about that one? He is a cipher. A trader in trash. A person of little value. If you wish to buy, Vadim shall be honored to fulfill your needs, no matter how complex."

Keller brought out the walking-stick stones, let them spill out onto the long table.

Lukas, sucking air noisily, shifted his immense bulk forward. "Lovely," he husked out finally. "Beautiful. You are looking to sell, then? Very well. I shall make you an offer. Equitable, an honest transaction. You will walk out of here with your pockets stuffed with currency."

Keller swept up the diamonds with the practiced snatch-and-grab of a crapshooter going for the dice. "Tell me about them."

"Excellent, some of them. I would want to examine them under a glass. These came from Tarassuk?"

"That's my guess."

Lukas sat back, one thick forefinger tapping the edge of the table. "You bought for yourself or for Sir John?"

"From Tarassuk to Robert Foxman to me. I believe the killer was after these."

"But he didn't find them?"

"I did."

"Violence," Lukas said. Enjoying the sound of the word, he decided to expound on the theme. "Duplicity. Mendaciousness. What a revolting animal man is. I long for a gentler time, a time when men lived as brothers, dealt openly and fairly with each other."

"When was that?"

"Always the realist, Keller. Have you no dreams, no yearnings for the impossible? You are right, of course. I dream of what never really existed and never will be. How depressing. Was Tarassuk the shooter?"

"Is he rough trade?"

"Not to my knowledge. A man of many interests, a man hungry for wealth, a man with a great love of life and its pleasures. But not a murderer, Keller."

"What else do you know?"

"About Tarassuk? I told you all."

"Try harder."

Lukas rolled his massive head under the beret. "He is a Russian, émigré. Perhaps a Jew, perhaps not. Not a political, certainly. Even in the Soviet Union he wheeled and dealed, or so I have been told. Black market stuff. Forbidden books. Japanese cameras. American blue jeans. He made his first diamond deal in Moscow, an insignificant transaction designed to get a dissident family out from behind the Curtain. Diamonds bought their way and showed Tarassuk the future and he went along for the ride."

Keller displayed the stones once more. "I'd say these came out of Russia, too."

"None of them bears the Hammer and Sickle."

Keller showed his teeth in his most awful grin. The pale eyes gleamed, his voice serrated and chilling. "The Russians are the third-largest producers in the world. Only South Africa and Zaire are ahead . . ."

"Moscow publishes no production figures."

"But solid estimates can be made. Two million carats a year is what I hear, plus more than eight million industrial."

The huge round head rolled. "The numbers are not unreasonable."

"For a long time, IMM bought the entire Soviet production. Very hush-hush. The Kremlin didn't want it known it dealt with racist South Africa's prestigious producer of capitalist wealth."

"The Russians don't care what they do, actually, as long as they get their money."

"In 1972, that agreement was modified. Russ Almaz was created to sell a certain number of stones to the West through other conduits."

"The men in Moscow are nothing if not pragmatic."

"We all know Russ Almaz held back a number of selected stones from IMM and they were released through three independent distributors, Vadim."

"A minor operation, hardly worth mentioning."

"Borokin in Bombay. Yuraki in Istanbul. And you in Paris."

Lukas squirmed on his throne. "Of no consequence, none of it. Small dealings. A pittance, a dribble, equal shares of next to nothing."

"Some equals are more equal than others. You keep the lion's share, Vadim, we both know that. And that share is substantial."

Lukas looked grieved. His mouth turned down. He rubbed one hand against the other. "Diamonds are the prototypical capitalist activity, my friend. Socialism frowns on such ostentatious displays by individuals."

Keller's laugh was mirthless, metallic, a reminder that his patience was running short. "You are no more a socialist than I am. You are in it for the money, as is Russ Almaz. When it comes to hard currency, the Kremlin never stands on principle. Moscow would deal with the devil, if there's profit to be had. The number of quality stones moving from East to West is increasing. You know it and I know it, Vadim. I also know you handle a very large number of them."

"A man must feed his family."

"What family? No wife, no children, nobody but yourself. A greedy man, Vadim, nothing more. Did you supply these diamonds to Tarrasuk?"

"No, no. I never saw them before, I swear it."

"Where are they from? The Mirnyi field? Or the Mir pipe in the little Batuobiya field, the one in the upper basin of the Marka?"

"You have studied the subject," Lukas said with considerable admiration.

"Maybe the new strike in the Urals?"

"You know about that!"

"The richest strike yet, I hear."

"Your sources may be better than mine, Keller."

"I doubt it."

"You give me too much credit. Working with these people, it is not such a good time, I tell you. They are rude, demanding, and the money is not as good as it should be."

"It never is."

"They never pay on time. Definitely an unprofessional way to do business. I buy, I transmit funds, I have responsibilities, debts that must be met. If I am late paying my bills I get complaints and once or twice thugs have been sent to expedite matters. Can I reciprocate? Can I send thugs to Moscow? Am I permitted even to complain? Not with impunity, I swear it. Let me so much as remind them that they owe—they threaten to stop the flow of product. Ah, Keller, it is time for me to give it all up."

"Why?" Keller said brusquely.

"Why? What are you asking me?"

"What is going on, Vadim? A rich strike in Russia. Increased production, we know that. Yet in the last few months all sources report that shipments west have decreased. Why, Vadim?"

Lukas grew agitated, moving around heavily in the big chair. The tapping of his fingers became louder, went faster. "Is it true? I thought that only I, that I alone had been singled out. One begins to see shadows..."

"What are the Russians up to?"

"Who can say! They are all madmen, every one of them. Always have been. All through their history, each of their governments. Czars, commissars, dictators, makes no difference. Distrustful of foreigners, of everything foreign. Afraid of attack, of loss of control, of the dilution of their purity. What a bad joke! Most of them are not Russians at all. Ukrainians, Georgians, Mongols, a potpourri of ethnic strains. The Russians are a minority and determined to retain power over the others.

"For centuries they kept the world outside. Visitors, businessmen, even books. Only the priesthood could read or write. They came late to culture, to literature, fashion, to what the rest of the world was up to."

"Back to diamonds, Vadim. Given: the Kremlin wants hard currency to buy grain and technology on the open market. If so, why cut back on diamond transfers? What's the answer, Vadim?"

"What do I know of such things?" He jerked a thumb toward the closed double doors. "Those beasts of burden out there, you believe they are mine? They belong to Russ Almaz. Russ Almaz pays them. Commands them. Speak to them, if you like. Certainly they know more than I do. But be careful. Some of their answers can be dangerous to your health. Terminal, you might say." He laughed without humor, a sound that ended in a racking gasp, a sob.

"Why?" Keller said again.

Lukas turned back to the diamonds. He used a loupe to study them, fingered them with the dexterity of an expert. "Cut properly these should bring as much as two million American."

"A large enough sum to kill for."

"According to you, Keller, the killer didn't get them."

"Unless I am the killer." Again that awful grin; Lukas shuddered. "Try this on for size, Vadim. The stones were stolen from Russ Almaz while in transit or lifted in Russia proper and smuggled out. Either way, the killer was sent to retrieve the stones and punish the transgressors."

"Punish the Foxman boy?"

"He had the stones, that was his mistake."

"And Tarassuk? If your theory holds, he also is a target."

"Yes, and he knows it by now, is on the run."

"They'll find him, they always do."

"If you were Tarassuk, and the Russians were on your trail, where would you go?"

"Who can say? Even now he may be alive and thriving somewhere behind the Curtain; he would dare it. Or maybe he is already dead in an alley somewhere. Maybe chained to a wall in Lubyanka. Maybe sleeping with mulattoes in Brazil. Who can say? Certainly I cannot. Nor for that matter do I give a damn . . ."

## chapter
# *16*

DAVID FOXMAN WAS WITH HIS FATHER when Ellie appeared. Both men rose to greet her. When they were all seated, Maurice spoke. "David has been telling me how much he has come to admire Peter Downes." A protective scrim shielded Maurice's eyes. He was not a man to reveal his thoughts too easily, always holding something in reserve.

"I've done a couple of deals with Peter," David said.

The stones he had shown her, Ellie assumed. That accounted for one deal; what was the second? Not that it mattered.

She had seen Peter three times since their first dinner date. Each meeting had been carefully spaced from the one preceding, each minutely planned as if Peter were deliberately revealing different aspects of his personality in different surroundings, different conditions. Or was it the reverse and he was assessing her? Weighing her behavior, her personality, her intelligence, the way he might weigh a diamond?

"I, also," Foxman said, "have come to value that young man. We played chess on two different occasions—" Ellie felt a pang of irritation; or was it envy? Why hadn't Peter mentioned his meetings with Maurice? "Peter is a good player. Conservative, which is in my opinion a plus factor, quick to take advantage when opportunity presents itself, able to look ahead, never out of control . . ."

"Is he as good as you are, Maurice?"

"Not yet. But he's had considerably less experience. I understand you two have been seeing quite a bit of each other."

"Not so much." Always hold something in reserve.

"And you've formed an opinion of him?"

She was reluctant to respond. "Personal or professional?"

"Whichever you care to offer."

If only she were capable of ignoring his question, of closing him out of her life as he had closed her out of his company. But she wasn't prepared to defy him openly, still attached to him in a hundred different ways she couldn't name, connections that diminished and in part defeated her.

"Peter's an unusual man," she offered.

Maurice continued to speak. "I find I have much in common with that young man. His approach to his life, his attitude about work, the diamond business, this is what I appreciate. Peter is willing to work within the established parameters, not so quick to rebel against the proven ways, as are some young people.

"My impression is that he respects tradition, that he comprehends that traditions have grown out of the varied experiences of those who have gone before him. He values that experience as a proven path, he respects its meaning as I do. Yes, indeed, Peter Downes is an outstanding young man."

Ellie fought to contain her rising resentment, aware that every good word spoken about Peter was implicit criticism of her. Yet at the same time she was glad that Maurice's reaction to Peter matched her own and somehow that made him even more attractive to her, more exciting and desirable.

It was David who brought her back to the present, saying, "Peter's a good person, a good friend, a good partner."

"Yes," Foxman said, "he is a good diamond man. I find him intellectually subtle, modest about his accomplishments, serious about his future. He has a surprising amount of knowledge about the history of the business, a genuine sympathy for the way it developed. He understands all areas of the work, not only his own, and that is a quality I can appreciate."

Ellie struggled to keep from bursting out: "I, too, am knowledgeable, experienced, and deeply attached to the business. I, too, am ambitious and subtle, sophisticated in the way I deal with clients, charged with a profound respect for diamonds and diamond people. None of which means that we function in a perfect world; changes are in order, modernization, recognition that talent and drive and energy are not exclusively male qualities." Instead she kept her counsel; her time would come, she would make it come.

The word drilled straight into Ellie's heart. David and Peter partners. She remembered David mentioning something much earlier, something to which she had paid little attention. Why hadn't Peter spoken about it to her?

"What do you think of that, Ellie?" Maurice said cheerfully. "My son, the light of my life, the joy of my heart, has at last decided to go into business on his own."

"Not exactly on my own, Father," David said, with a deferential nod in Ellie's direction. "Peter & David, P & D. I told you about it about a month ago, Ellie. Things moved so fast."

"I'm impressed," she said.

"No big deal. We couldn't do it without Father's support."

"Merely the guarantor, nothing more," Maurice said. "You two young men will have to develop your own supply lines, sell your product, become self-sufficient. David will continue to manage my showroom, of course. And he and Peter will work out of this office under the Foxman umbrella."

Envy and resentment flooded Ellie with a rush. In accepting Peter this way, in backing him and David, Maurice had again rejected her. Again found her lacking in ways she was unable to comprehend. He had never offered to back her play. He had never offered to guarantee her buys. Not that she had ever asked. Not that she ever would. And Peter, that *bastard*, never said a word.

"Congratulations," she said, without inflection.

"Do you see this as a good move, Ellie?" Maurice said, observing her as if from a distance.

"It's your company, Uncle, do with it as you wish."

"Uncle!" He smiled a small sad smile and massaged his left wrist. "Whenever you call me Uncle I suspect disapproval on your part. Yes, my company. Someday it will pass along to your generation."

But not to *me*, she thought furiously. Never to me.

He continued talking. "I value your opinion, my dear. Consider, Peter will be the first non-Jew to work at Foxman. Not that it was planned that way. Now, Peter—"

David broke in. "But we control our own operation," he said, a note of rising panic in his voice. "Even when we buy for Foxman."

"Of course."

"P & D is an independent company, remember."

"A technicality," Maurice said, eyes fixed on Ellie. "Well, niece, have you something to offer?"

Perhaps it was just as well, she reminded herself. Around Maurice, there could be only one boss. Only one person with real power. In theory, Peter and David might be free of his authority. In fact, they would be beholden to him in all matters, expected to jump on command, never truly on their own. Ellie could never tolerate that, not now, not ever.

"Certainly Peter will be a valuable addition to the firm," she said.

"Certainly," Maurice answered dryly. "My opinion exactly."

Ellie and Peter dined on steak and salad and an excellent Beaujolais at a restaurant on First Avenue. With her wild cloud of auburn hair rising around her head, in a short black dress held up by shoestring straps, she drew a great deal of attention from the other diners. Peter, if he noticed, made no remark.

She did nothing to bridge the silence, her emotions roiled, divided in her reactions to him, unsure suddenly of how she felt or what it was that she wanted of him. She should have stayed at home, alone.

He had yet to mention his arrangement with David. Or with Maurice.

*Why?*

Low-level suspicions formed, unpleasant perceptions of Peter, hints of concealed flaws. Suddenly he seemed too perfect, too good to be true. The gentle care and concern for her welfare in matters small and large, his willingness to tolerate her swift changes of mood, to accept her darker side without complaint. He was attentive, took what she had to offer and allowed her always to be herself, never insisting she change to conform to his needs or his perception of what a woman should be. He never tried to maneuver her into a subordinate position, as so many men had done before. Had she fallen, again, for a façade instead of the man himself? For the first time Ellie had second thoughts about a man before allowing her hormones to control her judgment.

"You're too far away," he said, summoning her back.

How to respond? Should she voice the resentment she felt? Should she strike out, revealing her bitterness toward Maurice and his cavalier treatment, his disregard of her in favor of a stranger? This stranger, this Peter Downes. She examined his face openly; superbly fashioned features, a nose straight and strong, a mouth sensual and inviting, guileless eyes; the handsomest man she'd ever known, the nicest, the most understanding and patient. Why couldn't she be as accepting as he was, trusting and free, accessible to him? Always she held back, never permitting him to see her true feelings. And she did resent his great good fortune.

*It's not enough that you succeed, your friends must fail.*

Was she really that petty? That mean and vengeful? She shook off the emotional barnacles that clung to her and forced herself to smile openly at him.

"Not so far."

He took her hand. "You're tired. Why don't I take you home?"

"My uncle is convinced you're a very special person."

"And you?"

The question surprised her. Did he need a glib compliment, a touch of flattery to feed his ego? Certainly women had been flattering him all his life, fawning over him, offering themselves. Or was it something deeper? Tell him how you feel, she ordered herself. Make him a part of your life and you a part of his. Instead, she forced her gaze elsewhere, spoke diffidently.

"And so does David."

"I like David, I want to be his friend."

*I want to be his friend* . . . Another man would have spoken to the friendship *he* craved, voicing his needs for companionship and support. Not Peter Downes.

"If I just met both of you—you and David—I'd never put you together. The differences . . ."

"The differences are what make it interesting. Fun. Our differences complement each other, we fit."

Fit! The word nibbled at the edges of her psyche. Had she ever fit comfortably with anyone? All her relationships had existed in a deathly stillness—she and her lovers separated by invisible barriers, artificially created voids—a sense of time wasted. Even her brother, Robert, whom she had loved so dearly, had kept his distance from her, as if she were a stranger. Or a threat to him.

And her father; she missed his easy smile, those casual expressions of affection. A kind and gentle man. They too had lived at a distance, unable to admit each other to the private, darker parts of themselves.

All the men she had known; passing fancies, decorations in time, drifting dimly out of her past. Fugitive shadows who had left no firm trace of their comings and goings, nothing to cling to, nothing of value, just transient moments of pleasure. She longed for more.

She squeezed Peter's hand and said, "You and David, a contradictory pairing. Maybe you do fit, but you certainly don't match."

"Maybe that's the key to friendship, to all relationships. Mismated parts coming together in a friendly arrangement."

"I need time to think about that one. Maurice is especially fond of you . . ."

"He's an impressive man."

"You're the son he always hoped David would become. You're smart, Peter, aggressive and subtle. And you love the diamond business as much as he does."

"You're the best of us all." He kissed her fingertips, one by one.

She shivered, remembering something her father had once said. "You are the star of the younger Foxman generation. If you were a man, nothing would stand in your way. But Robert is the male and Maurice favors him, therefore, shouldering you aside. As for David, even Maurice concedes that he is neither smart enough nor capable enough.

"Unfortunately, my brother is gripped by an obstinacy born in the old country and he uses it against the best interests of the family. It saddens me to say that your mother sides with Maurice. She, like him, believes a woman's place is not beside a man but in his shadow. She has come to believe that I am

some sort of revolutionary who will destroy the safe harbor
that exists for her under Maurice's protective wing. I encourage
her to take her rightful place in the Foxman hierarchy, to insist
on her rightful rewards, and that serves only to threaten her
even more.

"Interesting, yes! I try to help and in some distorted fashion
I am transformed into an evil presence. My views are too
radical, when all they are is just, truthful, fair, in the American
fashion. I am too much the contemporary man, too liberal, too
committed to change for change's sake, or so I am told. Not
only are my views the cause of my difficulties with Maurice,
but they are at the root of the tensions that exist between your
mother and myself."

He had smiled a rueful smile then, amused at his own seriousness. "But you, Ellie, are the light of my life, the most
gifted of us, the most intelligent, and you will prove it to them
all one day. I am convinced of it."

She retrieved her hand from Downes and turned away.
"Maurice," she said evenly, "doesn't agree."

"Don't be too sure. He's shrewd and hardheaded, he recognizes the quality in you. When he's ready, he'll make it
clear."

"He sees me still as an adolescent girl, always into trouble
of one kind or another. Making mistakes. Mixed up with the
wrong kind of people. The wrong men."

"Am I one of those men? A wrong man?"

She barely heard his question. I'm an intelligent woman,
she reminded herself. Perceptive. Sensitive. And perpetually
self-deprecating.

"Maurice needs someone to fill Robert's shoes," she said.
"Someone he can groom to take over for him one day. He sees
you as that someone, Peter."

"You give me too much credit," he answered. But the idea
excited him, unloosed visions of the future he had seldom dared
to entertain.

"I'm a loner," he told her.

"Maurice will give you lots of room to operate. It's the way
he works. You make it or you don't. If you don't, he writes
you off, as he has written me off."

"That's not true, Ellie. You're still young, you're still—"

She put an index finger to his lips. "Hush. I'm able to deal with the truth, no matter how much I dislike it. I can handle whatever comes along, which Maurice has yet to discover about me. Now, enough trade talk. Let's get out of here. I can use a walk, a long dose of polluted New York air . . ."

Back at her apartment, she turned the key in the lock, opened the door and entered first, drawing Peter in behind her. In the darkened foyer she turned, lifting her face to him.

"A nightcap?" she offered. "Anything at all . . ."

"It's late," he answered evenly. "An early meeting in the morning." He kissed her lightly on the cheek and left.

What, she kept asking herself for much of the night, was wrong? What was wrong with her?

The next morning, Bakshir Khamoury materialized. A phone call informed her that the Lebanese trader was in New York and would be honored to lunch with Miss Foxman, dear, that very day.

"On one condition," she said.

"Anything, dear Miss Foxman."

"That you take me someplace where I've never been, a place no diamond person would be caught dead in."

"I know exactly the place."

The Arab Delight was on lower Lexington Avenue, decorated to look like an American's idea of a Middle Eastern harem. It was complete with exotic music piped in from overhead speakers. A plump woman in a dancing girl's costume led Ellie to Khamoury's table. He embraced her, he kissed one cheek and then another, he went to work on the knuckles of her hands.

"For God's sake, Bakshir, enough kissing. Sit down and let's have a drink."

The little Lebanese had a way of undressing her with his eyes, stripping away her inner defenses at the same time. Arab men, went accepted wisdom, were super lovers, demanding, strong, passionate beyond description. But so, according to the same purveyors of popular social knowledge, were Italians, Greeks, blacks and Spaniards; Frenchmen had gone out of

vogue. All of them, by their own lights, certainly, were great
lovers; a more modest opinion of their sexual talents might be
forthcoming from their women.

"You are more beautiful than ever. Oh, what grief it causes
me not to have you as my wife."

"Two is more than enough for any man."

"You would assume an honored position, preferred always
in my eyes. Marry me and I shall cloak your marvelous body
in the most sensational garments. Rings for every finger—
gold, silver, the most incredible gems. A lavish way of life
shall be yours as my number one wife."

"What happens to numbers two and three?"

"They are good Muslim women and will accept whatever
it is that Allah, blessed be His name, decrees. You, of course,
will have to become a Muslim. Shall we set our wedding date,
my love?"

"First, tell me why you are in New York."

"Out of a raging desire to feast my eyes on you, dear Miss
Foxman. Your beauty inflames my spirit, it infests my blood,
it shatters the nervous system. My brain boils with thoughts of
you. My..."

"Enough!" she cried, in mock terror. "Too much of a good
thing."

"I do not understand, oh, delicious one."

"An American saying, it doesn't matter."

"Am I to understand the wedding must be postponed?"

"There is going to be no wedding."

"Ah. The ways of Allah are impenetrable to the feeble minds
of mere men. My time will come, I am sure of it." His eyes
lit up and he clapped his hands. "What an excellent idea I have!
Until the day of our marriage, I shall keep you in high style.
I have been most fortunate financially. A deal or two proved
profitable. Let me bury you in emeralds, in gold, in furs..."

"Diamonds," she said.

"You shall live in a penthouse in the most fashionable section
of the city."

"I already have an apartment."

"An expensive automobile. A Mercedes, perhaps."

"In New York a car is a nuisance."

"You prefer a domestic vehicle? A Cadillac, then?"

"No car, Bakshir."

"Let me prove to you the depth of my love, the heights of my passion. What noble deed may I perform in your behalf?"

"Diamonds," she repeated. A sense of time and purpose fused in her; Bakshir had connections, sources she could never reach without his help.

"How persistent you are. If you are to be a proper Muslim wife you must practice humility, surrender to your husband's wishes, obey his commands." He examined the tips of his fingers. "My connections are limited."

"Those deals you mentioned?"

"I prefer not to involve a woman in my trading operations."

"You're beginning to sound like my uncle."

"A giant of a man, the honorable Mr. Foxman. Without equal. Everywhere he is respected, everywhere honored."

"Let's get back to my business, Bakshir."

"You work for him, is it not so? Your brother worked for him and your mother. He cannot be a bad man."

"I work for myself. But without a regular supply of product..." She shrugged.

His sly satyr's face closed, the dark eyes troubled. "The men I trade with, they often appear in the night with shipments. Sometimes there are no bills of sale. No export licenses. No provenance of any kind. One takes what is offered or one does not. Always making payment in cash. Sad to say, men I have bought from have turned up dead days later. Myself, I have been three times attacked, twice cut with knives and once shot with a bullet. These are not pleasant details to report."

"Why do you keep on, then?"

The question made him think. "What else is a man such as I am to do? Without wealth or family position to call upon. Without education. Without friends in government or in business. In the beginning I dreamed of one day owning a fine shop catering to fine people. In Paris, it would have been nice. But Bakshir is not the man for such lofty endeavors. I am consigned by destiny to the back roads, the shadows and the alleys, to acquire what I can, where I can, to sell for whatever I can."

"You did business with Robert, I know that."

"Your lamented brother dealt squarely with me and I with

him. Always on top of the table, as you Americans say."

"Aboveboard," she corrected.

"I had a great appreciation for Robert, I think of him often, I miss him."

"Why was he killed, Bakshir?"

"Who can say why such things happen? The blind fate of a man under Allah's mysterious guidance. It is not for us to question. If you wish, I shall try to get diamonds for you."

A brief moment of inner conflict sent her brain tipping and tilting. Was this what she wanted, after all? Was this the chance she'd been searching for?

"You be careful, Bakshir. Don't take chances on my account."

"Chances are fundamental to my existence. Do you have the necessary sums available, my dear? My sources will demand payment on delivery, no exceptions made. They are men who do not believe in credit."

"I'll see what I can arrange."

"There are difficulties. The Syndicate will not be happy with our bargain, should it become general knowledge what we are up to. Yes, dangers. And money must be distributed along the line. I will do what I can but I cannot guarantee the results."

"We will both try."

"Our very best," he said sadly.

She took his hand. "Thank you, Bakshir."

He held on staunchly, as if afraid to let go, afraid he'd made the very worst deal of his very uncertain life.

"Mazel und Brucha."

## chapter
# 17

THAT EVENING ELLIE PRESENTED HERSELF at Mattie's apartment, to her mother's surprise.

"Am I interrupting?"

"At my age, there's very little that can't be interrupted."

"Oh, Mother, you're still a beautiful and vigorous woman."

"Ellie, this is your mother you're talking to. And, my dear, with a little bit of luck and some cooperation on your part, I'll be a grandmother one day soon."

"Maybe. Someday."

"Maybe," Mattie said. "I'll make some coffee."

Listening to her mother bustle around in the kitchen reminded Ellie that Mattie had always been a sheltering presence, protective, nourishing in all the ways mothers are supposed to be nourishing; yet her freely given support was easily translated into a challenge and a threat.

Compared to Mattie, Ellie had always come out second best. Less a woman, somehow, less a human being. Mattie the beautiful, the wise, the generous. Always on call when needed. An ordered life, properly designed and executed, admirable. Mattie had never been too tall or too plump, never too shy or too intrusive, never anything but exactly right. Mattie Foxman, welcome anywhere.

Unlike her mother, Ellie had seldom felt at home in her skin. Not as a girl, not as a woman. She had attained her full growth long before she was emotionally prepared, taller than her friends, taller than most of the boys in her class, with full, heavy breasts by the time she was fourteen. Whenever she went out in public, she hunched her shoulders in an attempt to conceal the unconcealable, to diminish what could not be made smaller. Alone, she sometimes stood naked in front of the mirror on the back of her bedroom door and contemplated her body, less in admiration that in wonder at the changes taking place. For every visible alteration, dozen invisible changes were taking place in her heart, in her mind and in her soul.

When boys began to court her, Ellie could not believe they truly wanted her, truly found her beautiful. In her existed a dull and homely girl and a changing reality did nothing to alleviate the awkwardness and anguish and shame she experienced each day.

Her life had been a succession of errors, tactical mistakes, one false start after another. Nothing the way it should be. Her working life had repeatedly fallen short of her aims. Her personal life was filled with relationships ephemeral and in retrospect distasteful, not worth the effort it took.

Yet she remained full of hope, her dreams still alive, if unrequited. She smiled when Mattie appeared carrying coffee and brownies and sandwiches on a tray.

"Are you hungry?"

"Not really."

Mattie set the tray down. "Eat something anyway. It'll make you feel better."

"I feel fine."

"You don't look fine, you look pale and tired. What's bothering you?"

Ellie helped herself to a tuna and cucumber sandwich, nibbling without enthusiasm around the edges. Mattie could be persistent to the point of stubbornness, seldom giving in before getting what she wanted. All done gently, with the soothing rustle of a mother hen.

"It's just business," Ellie said. "Things are not going well."

"Have you discussed it with Maurice?"

"He isn't interested in helping me."

"He's a caring man, go to him. If anybody can help, he can."

"Those are your biases talking."

Mattie conceded as much. "Yes, when it comes to Maurice, I am biased. I admit it. He's been exceedingly generous to us all. He's full of love toward his family, his friends . . ."

"We see him differently."

"So I've noticed. Maurice has been good to you, Ellie. He brought you into the business, taught you everything you know, provided opportunities."

"And made sure I didn't get what I wanted."

"When he thinks you're ready . . ."

"*I* think I'm ready. I am ready."

"You're still very young."

"I'm a woman."

"If you don't mind my saying so—the trouble you can get into . . ."

"I've forgotten about Henry Wilton, why can't you?"

"It isn't only that. One problem after another. What about the Abarbanel affair? You don't keep the appointment and Abarbanel sells his collection to Kornbluth in San Francisco."

"I explained that. The airports were closed in all over Europe, the fog. What was I supposed to do?"

"It just wasn't professional. Maurice would have found a way to get to Barcelona. Boat, train, car, something. He would have jogged if he had to. That cost him almost a hundred thousand dollars. The man has a business to run. A lot of people depend on him for their livelihoods. Don't blame Maurice. He's been more than good to you and to all of us. He's taken care of us since your father passed away."

"That," Ellie, knowing her mother was right and wanting to hurt her for being right, said, "is because he's always had his eye on you. Even when Daddy was alive."

Mattie gasped. "You can't believe that!"

"It's true. I'm not a child, Mother. I've known for a long time."

"You know nothing. Nothing at all."

"I know that Maurice has always been after you, always wanted what Daddy had."

Mattie spoke softly. "It was never like that. Never."

Ellie was unable to stop. "He owes us, every one of us, for what he did to Daddy."

"What are you talking about? When Emil's business went bad, it was Maurice who took him into his company."

"As a worker, a subordinate, never as an equal. Daddy knew as much about diamonds as anybody did. He had every right to be a partner."

"Is this your idea of logic? Maurice built his company, he was the heart and soul of it. Why should he take in a partner, even his own brother? Besides, there's nothing wrong with working for another man."

Ellie answered in a low, slow way, letting the words cut one by one. "You love him, don't you? You always have. You and Maurice, I know all about it and Daddy did, too."

"What are you talking about?"

"For a very long time, ever since I was a child, I could tell. The way you looked at him, the way you looked after him."

Mattie's hand went to her heart. She stared at the beautiful young woman facing her. How difficult to believe this was the flesh of her flesh, her daughter; they were so unlike each other. Yet her love for Ellie had grown and intensified since Robert's death.

"Don't hate your uncle, he doesn't deserve it."

Ellie shuddered. "It's just that I love Daddy so much and he had such a difficult time of it."

"He wasn't the only one. All of us human beings—we're all so vulnerable. Maybe I should tell you..."

"About you and Maurice?"

"If you're sure you want to hear."

Ellie, her fears swelling, jerked her head in assent. Perhaps it would be better to go on with her own version of the past, to live without doubts, without questions, all her beliefs unshaken. But it was too late; Mattie was speaking.

"In Vienna. I was young, much younger than you are now. Maurice was a grown man, nearly twenty-five. How young that seems to me now. Handsome, tall and slender. Straight as an arrow. His hair, it was thick and wavy and very black, as black as a raven's wings. He was so gentle a man."

"You became lovers?"

"Of course not! I was raised in a proper Jewish home and

would never go to bed with a man I wasn't married to. Maurice respected me, and whenever he was in Vienna we would spend time together. Oh, how happy those meetings made me. I loved Maurice with every fiber of my being. He was in my dreams at night and in my thoughts during the day. There was never enough time to be with him . . ."

"But you married Daddy."

"Later, much later. In America, in New York. The war had come and gone, the Nazis had been defeated, our lives—the lives of everyone we knew and cared about—had been changed forever. My mother, my father, my little brother, Kurt, poor little boy, all were killed by the Nazis."

"You met Daddy in New York?"

"We both believed Maurice was dead. He disappeared during the fighting. After a while, Emil and I were married."

"But you still felt the same way about Maurice?"

"No. The love had dimmed. When he showed up in America, when he found Emil and me, it was like seeing an old friend again after a very long time."

"How did he feel? About you being married to his brother?"

"He told us he was happy for us."

"And you believed him?"

"If Maurice tells you something, you believe it. Anyway, to know Maurice is to know that he is an easy man to love but an impossible man to be married to. He is hard on himself and too demanding of others. Soon after his marriage to Paula—she was a good woman—she told me how difficult he could be, so precise, so organized, so perfect. The qualities that make a good businessman don't necessarily make a good husband. That was why Paula left him, you see, she could not continue to live according to his strict rules."

"He never speaks about her."

"Not from the day she left. She was gone, the marriage was over. Not till David came looking for a job, years later, did he see either one of them again. I was there when David walked into Maurice's office—he asked me to be there—and Maurice embraced David and said, 'You look very well, my boy.' Then he went back to his chair and said, 'Is your mother well?' David said she was and that was that. He never mentioned her again. Paula hurt Maurice very much, but he will never admit it. No, Maurice is not a man to be married to. But neither is he a man who could deliberately hurt a member of his own family, certainly not his brother." Mattie took her daughter's hand. "It's odd, always being a displaced person, without a culture, always an outsider. Wandering Jews, that's what we are. I am a woman without a place of my own, without a man, an outsider wherever I go."

"I didn't know you felt that way, Mother." Ellie clung to her mother's hand. "I thought it was just me, that I was the only one with those feelings, those fears, as if I never belonged."

"That's why the family matters so much, what's left of it. Including Maurice."

Ellie sat back. "All this—makes me feel like a child. Is that what I am, Mother, a child? A crybaby?"

"I think you're just a woman still searching for herself."

Ellie said presently, "That special way you felt about Maurice. How can you tell when it's there?"

"You'll know when the time comes. Unless it's come already. Is it Peter Downes you're thinking about?"

"You don't miss very much. Yes, it's Peter."

"You love him?"

"I think so."

"You think so! When that special feeling takes hold, you are sure. Absolutely convinced. Is he in love with you?"

"He hasn't even kissed me. Well, just on the cheek."

"I talk about love and you talk about kissing. It's not a generation gap, it's a regular Grand Canyon."

Ellie smiled ruefully. "He's the most attractive man I've ever known."

"Seems to me I've heard that song before." Mattie sang the lyric in a sweet, pure voice. "The old songs were best," she said. "All of them were about love, the way a song should be. Attractive men are the most dangerous, of course, the hardest to resist."

"I don't want to resist."

"Just be careful, please."

"I never have before."

Mattie allowed herself a small, indulgent smile. "Then start now. Personally and professionally. Prove to Maurice how wrong he's been about you—and prove to yourself you're in control of yourself, of your life."

Ellie hugged her mother and said, "I hope I can, Mother, it's time."

Mattie held her daughter and crooned wordlessly against her hair a melody out of her own childhood, a melody sung by her own mother. She couldn't remember the words, but there was no need for words.

# *chapter*
## *18*

KELLER WAS ON THE MOVE. From New York to London, where he made a brief, incomplete and unsatisfying report to his immediate superior.

"You're putting in an inordinate amount of time on this affair, Keller," he was informed with lofty disapproval.

"It runs deep, Mr. McClintock."

McClintock was a pudgy man with pink skin and eyes to match. Following his retirement from the British Army, he'd joined IMM security as Chief of Operations, Western Europe and North America. An administrative job, it suited McClintock's mild and basically passive personality. "I've seen enough action for a lifetime," he liked to say, giving no hint of what that action had been or where it had taken place. Keller didn't care what McClintock's military experience had been, as long as he was left alone to pursue his job in his own way; and this McClintock was generally inclined to do.

"Can you tell me a bit about it, old boy?"

"No, I can't. I keep turning onto cold trails, to hints and suspicions, rumors. I'm trying to piece it together."

"We are not fiction writers, Keller. Remember that. Leave the mysteries to Dick Francis and his ilk. Close it up, will you, and get on to something else. There's a monstrous backlog of cases building."

"As soon as I can."

"Where are you off to now?"

"Vadim Lukas. I've got a few more questions for him."

The tall carved doors to the sprawling Paris apartment were solidly locked and when Keller rang the bell no one answered. The bodyguards were nowhere in evidence. Down the curved marble staircase, to the cramped office of the concierge. Keller addressed him in faulty French. "Monsieur Lukas, he is not at home?"

The concierge, his fragile French ear bruised by Keller's coarse accent, buried his face deeper into the newspaper he was reading. He shook his head.

"When will he return?"

A massive roll of his Gallic shoulders gave full expression to the concierge's huge contempt for foreigners, especially rich Americans. He turned the page.

Keller waved a large bill in front of the concierge. The man hardly noticed. Keller doubled the offering. The screen of Parisian indifference was lowered and the two bills disappeared inside his workman's tunic.

"What is it you wish of me, monsieur?"

"Vadim Lukas, when will he be back?"

"He did not say."

"Where is he?"

"He did not say when he departed."

"Are you saying he's gone? For good?"

"In the small hours of the night, I heard him depart. A noisy person, inconsiderate of the sleeping habits of others. He woke me and my wife."

"He was talking to someone?"

"No, monsieur. Slamming the door of his car, loading the bags."

"What kind of a car?"

"He drove an Opel, monsieur. A bilious green in color. Not even a word of farewell, not so much as a sou in gratitude for the many favors I bestowed upon him. And two months owed on the apartment. No more honor among people."

"The bodyguards?"

"They left the morning after. When I protested the failure to pay, they insulted me."

"When did all this happen?"

The concierge consulted the calendar on the wall of the tiny office. "Tuesday."

"Three days ago. What else can you tell me?"

"Nothing, monsieur."

"Anyone else asking for Lukas?"

"Only the small man."

"Small?"

"With the face of a rodent."

"Looked like a jockey?"

"Perhaps. But too old. The eyes were almost Oriental, but neither Chinese nor Japanese, I am certain. He asked his questions and went away."

"And you gave answers?"

"There was nothing to give. Besides, Russians are not nearly as generous as Americans are. It is something in the blood."

Keller felt his anticipation quicken. "Why do you say that, that he was Russian?"

"The same bad accent as the bodyguards. They are not a graceful people, the Russians, in movement or in language."

The IMM security office in Paris was housed on the top floor of a nondescript apartment building at the crest of the steep hill of Montmartre, looking over a forest of television antennas to the city below. In a modest office containing only a desk and a phone, Keller began making calls, supplying information, providing guidance, making suggestions. He had a pretty good notion as to Lukas's eventual destination. The diamond dealer was a man of strongly defined tastes in food and women, a man with a clear preference for a warm climate, for surroundings easy to deal with, someplace near the sea. A resort area would be best, Keller decided, replete with sunshine and an abundance of nubile young women.

Wherever he did go, Lukas would be at home. He had plenty of money, spoke seven languages fluently and had a face and figure that would fit many environments. It was Keller's hunch that Lukas was headed for Greece; a good guess would be the Peloponnesus, certainly a beach with good restaurants and easy access, definitely someplace away from the big urban centers.

Keller put out the word: descriptions and photographs were

distributed, IMM agents worked overtime. Hotel registries were checked. Informants were queried. At airports, harbors and railroad stations, off-duty policemen in plain clothes were engaged for special duty. Ticket clerks were alerted and porters and flight attendants were given telephone numbers to call should they see the big man.

Late at the end of the third day, Keller learned that Lukas had flown out of Orly for Rome on the morning of the night he had fled his apartment. From Rome, a hired car had taken him to Pescara, on Italy's east coast, where he disappeared into the port area.

"Lukas disappeared into the port area," Keller's Italian contact reported. "The trail is cold, no one has seen him since."

Keller swore under his breath. "I want that man. I must know where he went, where he is now."

"And if he's dead?"

"I want to know that, too."

Keller arrived in Rome on Monday night. He slept in an IMM-owned apartment on a narrow cobblestoned way used by those of its representatives who, like Keller, preferred more privacy than a hotel could offer. Awakened by the clanging of church bells and sunlight streaming through the tall windows, Keller breakfasted in a street café near the Piazza del Popolo. When he was finished, he made a phone call.

"I have been trying to reach you for an hour," the voice on the other end of the line complained in Italian.

"What have you got for me?" Keller's Italian was a clear improvement on his French. In the Bronx streets, where he'd been raised, lived a mix of Italians, Germans and Jews. As a result, Keller had picked up a smattering of each language, later refining his ability in language school.

'Your man went to Yugoslavia by boat. But we lost him there. This time for good, I'm afraid."

Keller swore under his breath. "If you had to guess, where would you say he's heading?"

"If I had to guess, Hungary, maybe. Or Rumania. Maybe even into the arms of Mother Russia."

Keller weighed the possibilities and matched them against the risks Lukas was taking, slowly mixing what he knew of the fat man's personal habits into the stew. The Soviet Union was an unlikely destination for Lukas. First, he was not a Russian, had no links there. No cushy job waited for him in Moscow, no retirement fund, no hero's welcome. And Lukas was a man who enjoyed the good life, a life that only money could buy, a life filled with good food and luxurious apartments and beautiful young girls. Nor would any other Eastern Bloc nation provide a safe haven. Especially if the Jockey was after Lukas. Did Vadim know he was being pursued by a professional hit man? That would surely lend wings to his heels or send him deeper to ground, perhaps too deep for even Keller to dig him out. He had to be found soon, in a matter of days, in order for both of them to benefit.

Where to begin? Lukas had gone east, a clear signal to Keller that eventually he intended to circle around, head back west. In the West, Lukas would have money hidden away, a cache of diamonds, whatever it took to lead the sweet life he treasured so. Sooner or later he had to wind up where a fat foreigner would be made welcome without attracting too much attention.

"No," Keller said into the phone, "not behind the Curtain."

"You want me to keep looking?"

"I'll take care of it myself," Keller said, and hung up.

He reached back, reviewing every conversation he ever had with Lukas, proceeding methodically back through the years. He plucked words and phrases out of context, passing references that might have spiced a conversation, lighthearted references to women, to food, to beaches . . . Keller straightened up and almost laughed out loud. He reached for the phone to book passage on the next flight out.

As soon as the plane began unloading at the airport, Keller was on his way through the green lane, a carry-on bag in hand. He passed through the customs station without being stopped and made his way to the taxi stand, to the left of the small airport building. The blinding sun beat down sentiently and sweat broke across his shoulders, trickled into the hollow of his spine.

The taxi took him to the Grand Bretagne Hotel on Syntagma Square, diagonally across from the Parliament building. A reservation had secured a suite for him on an upper floor providing an unobstructed view of the Acropolis, floating like an ancient white dream in the blue-gray smog that blanketed modern Athens.

Keller wasted no time making it to the Street of Shoes before the start of the long Greek lunch break. Sandals hung on the walls outside the shops and worry beads for sale to tourists and natives alike; coffee grinders made by Gypsies were prominently displayed and those classic wool shoulder bags, the *tagarias*.

Inside Vardis's shop, the air was cool and dark, the pulsating hum of an air conditioner closing out the noise of the street. Vardis, stocky and dark-skinned, with a graying moustache that drooped around the corners of his mouth, was attending a customer when Keller appeared. A flicker of recognition and then his eyes returned to his customer. Keller spent the time studying artistically wrought gold chains in a display case until the transaction was completed. Vardis began stacking trays of rings into the safe at the back of his store. Without looking up, he spoke in English.

"It does not put joy in my heart to have you visit my shop, Keller."

"*Kaliméra,* Tassos," Keller said.

"*Kaliméra.* Sophia is expecting me for lunch."

"Your wife is in good health, I hope."

"Excellent health. Expanding her horizons, as you Americans say, also her hips. So it is, so it should be. I am good to her. I provide a fine house, stylish clothing, holidays abroad. No other Greek wife has a husband as generous and considerate as I am, Keller. I swear it. My wife is spoiled. Also my daughters. Not one of whom is married yet and may never be with their unreasonable demands for perfection in men. Who is perfect? None of them surely. Not you, Keller. Not even I. And Elena, you would think with a wart in the middle of her forehead she would learn modesty, but no. She refuses to have it removed. What man in his right mind desires a girl who has a wart between her eyes? I tell you, Keller, it is no easy thing to be a Greek. Your health is good?"

"No complaints. And you?"

"The same. So, maybe now you will say why you are here, causing me increased concern and worry?"

"Vadim Lukas, I want to find him."

"He left Athens more than ten years ago. For London, I was told."

"Paris," Keller corrected.

"No matter. Now, if you will excuse me, my lunch is waiting. Sophia does not like it when I am late."

"Lukas is on the run."

"A sensible man. That is what I should do. Flee. Hide. Put all unsatisfactory things behind me. Find one of those yellow-haired Norwegian girls with firm thighs and an insatiable lust for my body. There are islands where nobody ever goes. Well, almost nobody. Islands where I would never be found, unless I wanted to be. I could conceal myself forever."

"And leave Sophia behind? I do not believe you, Tassos."

"That Sophia, she would seek me out. That woman gives me no rest, allows me no peace. Why come to me about Lukas?"

"You two did considerable business in the past."

"In the past. A small exchange of goods and services once in a while. Not worth mentioning. The man is gone, I know nothing of him."

"You were friends."

"Hah! A man like me has no friends, only Sophia's relatives, of whom there are many and each one of whom believes it is my destiny to support him beyond the grave. If Lukas is gone, good riddance."

"For nearly five years, he has been handling Soviet stones. He has been one of their outlets for product they sell directly to the market."

"Such things are beyond me."

"Suddenly it ends, Tassos. Lukas closes up shop and runs for it. I want to know why. I want answers to other questions."

"I can't help you, Keller."

Keller said, "This is Syndicate business. Serious business." The rough voice shifted down, the sardonic eyes fixing the other man where he stood. "I want Lukas, I will find him. My friends will offer help, my enemies will obstruct the search. I shall reward my friends and punish my enemies."

Vardis shuddered and began fingering his blue worry beads. "Keller, tell me—what manner of man are you?"

"A fair one."

"Yes," Vardis said grudgingly. "You are fair."

"I want information, Tassos."

"I have not seen him."

"Since when?"

Vardis hesitated before answering. "A year or two after he left Athens . . . he was talking about setting up a pipeline through Morocco to West Africa."

"Stolen goods?"

"He didn't say, I didn't ask."

"But you dealt with him?"

"The price was right."

"You and Lukas, transporting illegal diamonds."

Vardis's fingers moved rapidly over the beads.

"A conduit was all I was. A brief stopover in a long chain. Never let them believe in London that it was other than I say it was. A courier would appear with a package, I would place it in my safe. Another courier would claim the package, I gave it up. Nothing more. I never knew what the packages contained."

"For how long did this go on?"

"A few months. Three, maybe. Certainly no more than eight or nine. Then it stopped. An innocent man helping out a friend, that's all it was, Keller. I swear to you."

"Where is Lukas now?"

"We were partners for a long time. Friends. We danced in the tavernas together. We ate *spanakopita* and drank ouzo together. We visited the houses together. Don't ask me to harm my friend."

"Talk to me, Tassos. Tell me where he is. Someone else wants him, a Soviet killer."

"What a fool, that one. Fat and foolish. Still, it is true, I have not seen him."

"You spoke to him?" Keller said on a hunch.

Vardis lowered his gaze. "He called me."

"And?"

"Said he was going to disappear for a while."

"Here in Athens?"

"The man is insane. You know how he is about the sun, about beaches, about young girls . . ."

"Mykonos," Keller said. "He might be able to lose himself on Mykonos, among all those tourists."

"Too obvious."

"Where then?"

"Skiathos."

Skiathos lay off the coast of Pelion in central Greece, a short flight from Athens. Keller booked himself into the Xenia Hotel at Koukounaries Beach. After a walk on the narrow beach and a swim in the calm, cool sea, he lunched at the taverna on a platter of *mezés* and cold Greek beer. He napped until late afternoon, took care of some paperwork and went for another swim. After a long shower, he dressed for the evening, a thin white shirt and white trousers, a pair of sandals. A taxi took him the ten kilometers to the harbor town and he began his search for Lukas. By nightfall, with no sign of the big man, Keller took a table at the Taverna Anemos and dined on the fish-kebob and beer and watched the tourists, sunbrowned men and women all lean and hipless, with bony shoulders and flat chests.

When he finished his meal, he made his way down the hill to a café facing the lines of yachts drawn up in the old harbor. He ordered coffee and strawberries, patiently scanning the passersby, convinced that sooner or later Lukas would appear. A few minutes before midnight, his patience was rewarded; Lukas came upon the scene, a magnificently outsized figure in loose-fitting black trousers and a shirt to match, grinning happily under a wide-brimmed straw hat clamped firmly down on his great round head. On each arm, a young girl, each blond, beautiful and tan, each lean and laughing, gazing up into Lukas's face adoringly.

They were almost past Keller, on their way to the miniature Venetian fortress at the end of the harbor which served as a disco, when he called out.

"Vadim . . ."

Lukas stopped in his tracks and reluctantly turned, shedding the girls, smoothing the loose black shirt.

"I should have known," he said without expression.

"Have a coffee," Keller said.

"How did you find me?"

"Sit down."

"Was it easy? I thought I was very clever, covered my tracks."

"Easy for me, easy for anyone else."

Lukas got himself settled onto a chair much too small for him. The blond girls took up positions at either shoulder.

"Go," he said, with a wave of his hand.

"What about the dancing?" one of them said, pouting.

"We love to dance," the other chimed in.

"I thought here I would be safe," Lukas said to Keller. "At least for a little while. Go," he said again to the girls. "I'll see you both in a few minutes. Won't I?" he ended plaintively to Keller.

"That's up to you."

"Go," Lukas said again. The girls drifted away. "Beautiful," he said nostalgically. "Sisters. German sisters. Have you ever had sisters, Keller? It fires the imagination. What artists they are! Wasn't it even a little bit difficult to find me?"

"A little bit."

"But you managed it?"

"You're too big to hide, Vadim. Too smart to be left alone. Too dangerous to ignore."

"I want to live out my time in quiet. In peace. With occasional pleasures."

"On a small island in Greece. Not a wise move, Vadim. With a pair of nymphs on your arm. Not good. If I found you, he will."

"He! Who do you mean? Is someone after me?"

"I call him the Jockey. A small man. He tried to take me out in St. Tropez."

Lukas sagged and the chair groaned under him. "Leonid," he muttered.

"Tell me about Leonid."

"You were right, he'll find me here. Leonid is a pro. He works for Russ Almaz or maybe KGB. It makes no difference. He moves around, is very good at his work. He's been waved in my face before but never seriously till now."

"He was at the Paris apartment less than a week ago, asking about you."

"That's serious." He fell silent, chin on his great heaving

chest. "What if he trailed you here?"

"Nobody trailed me."

Lukas measured Keller. "I suppose not, not without you knowing. Why are you here, Keller?"

"I want Tarassuk."

"Last I heard of him he was in Budapest."

"He surfaced in Antwerp ten days ago. Lugano four days later. And now out of sight again. What's going on, Vadim?"

"Russ Almaz is stepping up the pressure. I began to feel it. More stones to pass at higher prices. Not top quality, you understand. Some good, yes. But many second-rate or worse. I was being pushed too hard. More sales, bigger profits, faster remittances."

"And Tarassuk?"

"Is Leonid after him, too?"

"Tarassuk picks up Russian stones where and when he can. Stolen, smuggled, a man on the make. What do you think?"

"If they want him, they'll get him."

"My thought exactly. Where do you think he would go?"

"I don't know. I can't help you."

"Damn."

"Thank you for coming, Keller, for warning me. What am I to do? If Leonid wants me, he will certainly track me down."

"Go somewhere else."

"Where?"

"Anywhere but that disco, Vadim. Stay away from beaches. Stay away from diamonds. Stay away from young girls."

"That's easy for you to say."

"And another thing," Keller said, getting ready to leave.

"Yes?" Lukas said eagerly.

"Lose weight. It's bad for your health."

## chapter
# *19*

WHEN MAURICE PRESENTED HIMSELF without notice in Peter Downes's office, the younger man became apprehensive. In the weeks since P & D, Inc., had been created, had begun doing business, his only contacts with Maurice had been at the weekly company meetings. Still not assured in his new position, Downes was nervous, looking everywhere for flaws in the plan.

"Mr. Foxman. How may I help you?"

"A few minutes of your time, Peter."

He advanced into the office, placing his feet gingerly as if afraid of damaging the fine Persian rug. When he had purchased this old granite-faced town house just off Fifth Avenue to serve as his showroom and headquarters, he had the inside of the building gutted, rebuilt and completely redecorated. The old fireplaces with their black marble mantels were preserved and brought back to working order. The walls were stripped of layers of paint, revealing the original walnut paneling, which was restained and burnished to a rich patina. The old crystal chandeliers were dismantled, each piece polished by hand and skillfully reconstructed. Gradually, the old Victorian mansion was summoned back to life.

Maurice had selected the antique furnishings by himself, as

well as the old rugs and the graceful drapes that framed the windows. Eighteenth-century portraits by Peale, Stuart—even a Copley—hung on the walls. A Tiffany wisteria lamp graced his desk.

"May I sit, please?" He placed himself into a tall wing chair covered in a blue-and-beige eagle pattern on rough linen. His hands came to rest in his lap, fingers clasped tightly. He appeared tense and unusually anxious to Peter.

"Is something wrong, sir?"

"No. Just a friendly little chat is all. Whenever I've been away, I always enjoy spending a bit of time with the people who work for me. Catch up on what's been happening in my absence. And always, to my despair and regret, I discover that life proceeds apace without me. What a blow to an old man's ego! What a blow." He chuckled softly at his little joke.

Downes produced a complimentary laugh, not entirely natural. He was still in awe of Foxman, secretly afraid of him, of his vast background, his lofty intelligence, the undertone of toughness in the old man. What would happen if Maurice discovered that he had already put the scam into operation, moving more quickly and more ambitiously than he felt was prudent? All at Harry Geis's insistence.

"Foxman is shrewd," he'd warned Geis. "What if he finds out?"

"He won't."

"But if he does?"

"We'll handle it. Don't be a schmuck. Sniff the air, man. What you smell is money. Twenty million shekels on a can't-miss proposition. Hell, boychick, you are a member of the company and legit. You couldn't be more legit if you tried." Geis had been amused at the thought.

Peter followed instructions. Cautiously at first. Geis had supplied him with a list of sellers, men anxious to get rid of their diamonds, he was told. His first purchase was for fifty thousand dollars, made by phone to a number in Tel Aviv. The stones were to be delivered at once by courier, payment due within thirty days. When the diamonds arrived, Downes wasted no time moving them, selling them to dealers around the country at prices substantially lower than Syndicate product would sell for. A safe, quick transaction at both ends, a positive note in the ledger. And over the next few weeks, he bought and sold with similar restraint.

His courage bolstered, and at Geis's impatient urging, he stepped up his activities. His buys ranged upwards of seventy-five thousand dollars, only now no sales were made. Instead, he turned each shipment over to Harry Geis for safekeeping. P & D, Inc., its credit rating solidly established, its purchases guaranteed, began to create an ever-expanding debt, as well as a private inventory of outstanding product.

"I hope things went according to plan," Downes said to Foxman.

"Ah, yes. But whose plan?" Again that small laugh, self-deprecating, wry, but without humor. "This latest sight was another disappointment. Two in a row, the stones provided were not worth what I had to pay for them. I admit to considerable concern, my boy. Considerable. A company such as mine cannot continue to function with such inferior product."

"Why is this happening?"

"I have my theories, of course. What it amounts to is the Syndicate is out to punish me. To damage me. Nor am I alone, there are others. I added a few more cities to my trip—Antwerp, Amsterdam, Zurich. The dealers I spoke to, men not much different than I, reorted similar sights. Poor offerings, rudeness, as if in some way we had offended the Syndicate, or outlived our usefulness to it."

"What explanation do they give?"

"Explanation! On the day you attend a sight of your own, you will discover Sir John offers no explanations. No soft blows. A virtual monopoly, IMM offers the best stones at prices one can live with. What they do not produce, they buy; what they cannot buy, they suppress. The Syndicate is a dictatorship. Sir John is another Hitler, unconcerned with the welfare of other men, cold, distant. He dispenses largesse when and where he chooses, dishing out punishment as he sees fit."

"Is there nothing you can do?"

"That accounts for my visits to the other dealers. To gather information, to listen to their ideas. We find ourselves in a dim and unattractive position."

"It's all temporary, of course. Things will get back to normal and in the meantime—"

"In the meantime, Foxman and Company has already suffered. Our sales are off and continue to falter. The factory in Bombay—well, that's gone."

"Gone! How can that be? You owned it."

"In partnership with a local merchant. He pulled out when I no longer could provide quality gems in substantial amounts."

"There's such a thing as loyalty."

Foxman nodded approvingly. "There are a few of us left who think that way. Matters are bad, Peter, and getting worse. My overhead, here and in Puerto Rico, is high and monthly receipts are down. As much as I hate to do it, I may have to start laying people off. I can't go on forever losing money every month."

"What can I do to help?"

"I've tried to come up with new sources, but with no luck. This operation is geared to Syndicate diamonds. Syndicate prices. Many sources are closed to me, their supplies committed to their regular customers. What little I've been able to find is at a price so high that when I add my regular markup my goods will be priced out of the market."

"You make it sound pretty grim."

"It is grim. Stones are out there, available, but not necessarily to me. For example, you've been able to buy steadily . . ."

Downes felt his muscles grow tense. "Thanks to your backing, Mr. Foxman. Without your guarantees, P & D doesn't amount to very much."

"That will all come in time, my boy. Meanwhile, Foxman and Company needs product, a great deal of it . . ."

"What I'm buying is inferior to your regular line."

"I understand. But we'll have to take whatever the market throws up. Keep making your purchases, from whatever sources are available. Keep selling, we need all the income we can generate. And in your day-to-day transactions, keep your eyes open for a dealer with a substantial quantity of good stones to sell. I will buy all you can lay your hands on."

Downes turned it over in his mind. This opportunity might never present itself again. If Foxman went under, it would help none of them; he and Harry would have to begin all over again.

"Maybe I can come up with something," he said. "What

amount are you talking about?" He could feel his confidence ballooning.

"I'll guarantee up to five million on a single buy, Peter. It's much more than I usually spend but I have to make up for those poor sights. Shall we give it a try?"

"Yes, sir."

"Good. New supplies. New blood. New life. Reliable, safe sources. Do this for me, Peter, and I'll always be in your debt. I'm planning another trip, to see if it is possible to build a defense against Sir John and his totalitarian policies so that this sort of situation cannot be possible again."

"Can that happen, for a single dealer to oppose the Syndicate?"

"We'll see. During my absence, there's David and Mattie to call on, should you need assistance."

But not Ellie, Downes remarked to himself. By omission, she had taken up a prominent position in the room. Yet neither of them referred to her. Maurice stood up. "Thank you for sparing me the time."

"Thank you, sir."

When he was left alone, Downes went over their conversation again and again. In the end, there could be no doubt, he had won Foxman's confidence and his trust. The old man depended on him more and more each day. His old fears of failure were groundless and there was no reason not to push the scam along. But first the five million . . .

He called Harry Geis, ran down the meeting with Foxman.

"Shall I stall?" he said, winding down his excitement. "Tell him I'm working on the five million?"

"Whataya wanna do that for?" There was a snarl in Geis's voice.

"You make the buy, give Foxman his cushion. At the same time, build up your own position. Meanwhile, keep racking it up for P & D. Nobody's gonna so much as give you a look on your own buys, get it?"

Peter got it. "But where do I go for the five million?"

"I'll talk to Browning. He's got the contacts, he'll come up with the stuff. I'll get back to you. The way things are going, we've got the twenty million nailed."

* * *

Back in her apartment, they found their way into her bed with the calm inevitability of old lovers treading a familiar path. Afterwards, they lay quietly for a long time, dozing, talking, drinking cool white wine from oversized goblets, careful not to touch each other. She didn't want to be touched, caressed, told the loving things that lovers told each other.

"I want to be good for you," he said.

Staring at the ceiling, she tried to summon up his face. Those startling good looks, the handsome, molded physique, the resonant voice empty of concern or caring. Distance separated them and she wondered what it would take to bridge the void.

"It was fine," she managed to answer.

"Are you all right?" he said.

Men were compelled to ask the question. As if a solitary sexual encounter inevitably left a woman depleted, deprived, damaged forever in body and soul.

"I'm fine," she said automatically. Neither fine nor all right, she amended to herself. Rather the common emptiness, a suspicion of something precious wasted, spent without a reasonable return.

He changed his position; still no contact. "Do you want me to go?"

Go! The word exploded against the back of her brain. Go and never come back. Go because what you have to give and what I want and need are on divergent paths. Go and leave me hollow and fearful.

"Of course not," she said instead.

Something about him stirred her deeply. A warm, encompassing reaction. Unlike the electrified sexuality of Henry Wilton that had left her always craving more while at the same time loathing herself for being cowardly and submissive. Peter was different, she assured herself. He was a softer man, gentler, genuinely concerned about her welfare, about her feelings. She believed that, she had to believe that.

"Can we talk?" he said.

Was he mocking her? She checked out that idealized profile, each feature precisely made. Too good to be true.

"Of course."

"I've been meaning to tell you, what you're doing is admirable."

"Admirable Ellie Foxman, that's me."

"I'm serious."

"So am I."

"I'd like to help."

"Ah," she said, making no effort to disguise the irony.

He came up on one elbow, gazing down at her. "You possess a rare gift for the business. The way you judge rough, your talent for seeing a cut before it's made."

"Flattery will get you everywhere."

His earnestness washed over her. "Even Maurice thinks so."

"My loving uncle."

"He's wrong, to keep you out of the company, I mean. You could take over for him when he's ready to step down. You're the best of us all."

There it was again, the same words. Everybody ranking her high, highest. But nobody permitting her to get where she wanted to go. Was it unnatural to have this much ambition? Was there something perverted and obsessive about her? Some genetic mishappening that made her eternally dissatisfied with her existence, with her accomplishments? She looked Downes over as if seeing him for the first time. He seemed to mean it; sincerity was his strong point. "He's got his eye on you, Peter. You are what David can never be."

"But you're a blood relative."

"And you're a man."

"That doesn't matter."

"It does to Maurice, it does to most diamond people. One of the last bastions of male superiority."

"I'm an outsider. I'm not even Jewish."

She touched him then, letting her fingers step across his thigh in delicate inspection. "I never noticed."

He laughed, his ego stroked. Events proceeding according to plan, he reminded himself. "You have a dirty mind."

"Only when necessary."

"Maybe I can help you."

"Cleanse my dirty mind, you mean?"

"Help you with the work."

A glob of resentment lodged in her throat and her joints locked in place. "How do you propose to do that?"

Her mood swings were swift, dramatic, coming without warning. The most unpredictable woman he'd ever known, always close to the flashpoint. "Money," he said. "That's the answer."

She stared at him. "I don't get it."

"I can help you get the money you need."

She willed him to leave business behind and trying to help. What she was after had to be achieved on her own. For herself, by herself. Everything Maurice Foxman had, she would get for herself. She wanted to *become* Maurice Foxman: successful, important, honored. To beat him at his game. To outstrip him in every way. The ultimate triumph for herself. And revenge for her father and brother.

"The usual sources are all closed to me," she said, unable to let it go. "I've tried everywhere."

"Not everywhere." When she said nothing, he went on. "Have you tried the Browning Bank?"

"You know him?"

"We've met."

"And done business?"

He froze at the precise way the words came out of her mouth. The tone, the tempo, the voice itself belonged to Maurice Foxman, scored with disapproval, raising up the specter of sudden failure and defeat.

"Maybe it's not such a good idea," he said, making a cautious withdrawal.

She focused on a spot on the ceiling. "Browning's reputation is not good."

"I found him to be a charming man. But if you'd rather not—"

"They say he's mob-connected."

"I don't believe that."

"But you've heard the talk?"

"There are always rumors."

"Are they true?"

"He's a distinguished man, educated, worldly, sophisticated. Ralph Browning is no gangster."

"What if I decided I'd like to meet him?"

"Maybe it's not such a good idea," he said again. "If that's the popular perception of Browning—"

"Can you arrange an introduction?"

"Your uncle might not approve." Why hadn't he considered that before raising the question? Geis was right, getting involved with Ellie was a bad move, fraught with negative possibilities. "Let's forget about it."

"My uncle has nothing to do with this."

Maurice was only one concern; what about Geis, about Browning himself? How would they react? It was too late to worry about that, too late to back down; Ellie lay next to him and he had to follow through.

"Okay. You want Browning, you get Browning."

She looked into those dark, opaque eyes, and saw nothing. She stored away the words he had spoken and those he had left unsaid. There was more going on than she understood, more to this man than he was willing to reveal; given time, she assured herself, all questions would be answered. But for now, she took him as is.

"I want Browning," she said firmly.

"And there's something I want," he said, touching one finger to her lips. She opened up to him, drawing his finger into her mouth, lips working wetly, eyes never leaving his.

## chapter
## 20

THEY SAT AT ONE of the more strategic tables at "21" as Ralph Browning's guests. Ellie and Peter Downes. Browning controlled the proceedings with the subtle skill of an experienced stage manager. He avoided direct references to business while they were eating, avoided mention of the word "money" as if it were a contagious disease, all the time holding forth on a variety of subjects from the mild winter that had recently passed to the musical genius of Haydn and Mozart and John Cage, to the benefits of a summer spent at East Hampton.

"One weekend," Browning said, "you will have to be my guests. Both of you."

"You're very generous," Downes murmured.

"You're one of the more attractive men I've met, Peter. And now, Ellie. It's very easy to say the same about you, my dear. You are a stunning woman."

"Thank you, kind sir."

He made a small nod and called for coffee and brandy. "Peter informs me you're about to branch out on your own."

Finally, she thought. She matched his nod with one of her own. "It's all very complicated."

"I'm surprised to hear you say that. With your uncle's backing, all doors should open easily to you."

Her eyes flickered over to Peter and back again. How much had he told Browning? How much had been left unsaid? Just how well did these men know each other?

"This project does not include my uncle. Not in any way."

"Is that a fact?"

Ellie braced herself against Browning's charm, coming at her in waves. The honeyed speech, tinged faintly by alien inflections that tantalized and disappeared before she could identify them. He used his hands for emphasis, the graceful moves of a musical conductor, hands that were pale and soft, the nails expertly manicured to a high gloss. Hardly the sort of man she'd come to associate with those who worked with organized crime. Yet he remained threatening in a quiet, almost exotic way, and she wished she had not come. But if he would help—

"It's true, I am looking for backing. If the price is right." She smiled and he smiled back, as if to say he understood her ploy, understood she had just about run out of loan possibilities, that he was her last, desperate chance. "I will require credits of up to one million a month. Can the Browning Bank handle that?"

"The amount is no problem. It's all up to the loan committee."

"Peter tells me you *are* the bank."

"If only it were so. One always has associates to consider. Each application presents different problems, makes different demands. Your situation will be professionally analyzed and considered, Miss Foxman."

"When can I expect an answer?"

"After you make formal application, in a matter of days. We're quite good when it comes to making a decision and at expediting funds."

"Then I'll hear from you?"

"One way or another."

At first, she wasn't interested. Not physically, not emotionally. But he kept at her, kissing her eyes, her mouth, her ears, working his way down her throat. His lips were soft and skillful, his tongue a warm, wet reminder of the pleasures he was offering.

"I want to talk about Browning."

"Later."

"This is important."

"So is this."

"Please wait."

"I love the way you feel." He licked the hollow at the base of her throat. "The way you taste. You're the only real thing in my life."

"Diamonds are real," she said without thinking.

He released her and considered his reply. "Pure decoration, a calculated and contrived object. Everything about diamonds is a lie, that they are indestructible, that their worth is constant. All lies."

"Why, Peter, you're turning into a cynic."

"But it's true. People buy high, they usually are forced to sell low."

"You're biting the hand that feeds you."

"Like you, I'm hooked. I want it all, the glamour, the glitter, the excitement of a big deal, to be rich."

"You'll make it, I'm sure."

"You're better at this than I am. You've got the power and the push, Ellie. You can go as far as you like. Just don't let ethics get in the way of your ambition."

"Meaning what?"

"Meaning Ralph Browning."

"I told you, there's something there I don't like. I get the feeling that under all the refinement and the polish, he's pure slime."

"Money isn't good or bad. Here's your chance to set up for yourself, take it."

"We'll see. I still don't have the supplies I need."

"Have you tried Bobby Santorini? I hear he's tied solidly into South America."

"He won't do. He deals in cut stones and the markup is exorbitant. I'm after rough at first-source prices."

"Have you hit some of the large manufacturers?"

"That means wholesale prices. And payoffs down the line."

"There are always payoffs in this business."

"No good. Unless I can buy lower than market price."

"There must be a way. Life isn't perfect, neither is this business. Diamonds exist and people buy them. Let's face it, nobody *needs* diamonds. Hell, the Japanese hardly knew they existed until De Beers hired some high-pressure ad agency to make them *think* they needed them, and turned Japan into the second-biggest market in the world. That's good business, smart, the reason some men are rich and powerful and others just work for a living."

"Leaders and followers."

"Exactly. The way it always was, the way it is, the way it's going to be."

She wasn't sure she agreed. Always, when it came down to some fundamental moral issue, she failed to find a satisfactory answer. She felt like one of those diamonds she so admired; shining with reflected light but essentially useless and without practical value. She shrugged away such gloomy thoughts for fear they would deter her from achieving her goals.

"I haven't reached a decision," she said, in a conciliatory voice.

"About Browning? That's good."

"There's a man named Zimmerman."

"The attorney, Herbert Zimmerman?"

"That's the one. He represents a number of leading people in the industry. I've set up a meeting with him."

"You'll still need backing and that means Browning."

"Why do you keep pushing Browning so hard?"

A muscle leaped in his thigh, a nervous warning. He was going too fast, too anxious to sew up the entire package: Ellie, David, Foxman and Company. Jesus! What was he trying to do? Their entire plan was delicately structured; one wrong move and it would all come tumbling down. With or without Browning, he had her hooked. She needed him, she loved him. It was all right there for the taking; just close his fingers and Bingo! He was about to walk away with one-third of twenty million bucks in his pocket. This was no time to muddy the waters.

"It's your business," he said, mustering up all the sympathy he was capable of. "One way or another, it means nothing to me. If you're satisfied, I am."

She sat up, her naked back smooth and strong. He traced the curved line of her spine.

"Don't go," he said, loading his voice up with sensual promise.

"I want to shower, get dressed."

"Not yet." He nibbled at one smooth, round buttock.

"Don't," she said, her conviction fragmenting under his touch. "I'm not sure I want to."

"I'll convince you."

"There are times I wonder about you, Peter." He eased her onto her back, his lips and tongue moving expertly along the length of her body. "But not now," she breathed. "Not now."

Herbert Zimmerman was not what Ellie expected. He greeted her in his shirt sleeves, the cuffs turned back, his collar open. He owned the muscular bulge of a dedicated weight lifter, with square hands and blunt fingers. His fading yellow hair was trimmed close to a bullethead and he had small, spiteful eyes that missed very little.

"I'm an admirer of your uncle," he started out, in a thin, penetrating voice, brooking no interruption, inviting no comment. "You're much younger than I expected, Miss Foxman. Even lovelier than I'd been led to believe. I am at your service. How may I help you?"

"As I told your secretary, I'm looking to buy."

Zimmerman cracked the knuckles of his right hand. "We're discussing diamonds, I assume."

*Crack!*

"You assume correctly."

"I'm a lawyer, not a merchant."

"With clients in the trade."

"Yes, but merely as a legal adviser." All said with a finely styled irony.

"I've been in the trade since high school and the name Zimmerman was always spoken of with awe, one of the most influential men around."

"People exaggerate."

"I need stones, Mr. Zimmerman."

"International Minerals and Mines would seem to be your best bet."

"I'm not an established dealer, IMM won't give me a sight."

"Then via one of the larger houses."

"That's out of my league. In order for this to work, I must get supplies at a price lower than market. Preferably from a producer."

"That makes a great deal of sense." Zimmerman was giving nothing away, not information, not help.

She pressed ahead. "I've been told you have access to a number of countries that are into heavy production. That you have entry at the highest levels, to heads of state."

"You are after first-source price?"

"Yes."

"From what I hear, the business is complex, in some instances tricky. Is it true that anyone introducing a would-be buyer to a source often is paid a commission?"

"I'm willing to pay."

"Also the middleman in the country involved."

"I'll take care of anybody who is helpful, if I can deal at the top."

"You set yourself a lofty target."

"It can be done."

"You're a woman of determination, Miss Foxman. Are we talking about a national leader?"

"Presidents or kings."

"Determined and ambitious. A woman alone, however, hardly seems like the one to bring all this about."

"With the right connections."

"Exactly what manner of merchandise are we talking about?"

"Rough only."

"My understanding is that small parcel sales are of little interest when one buys directly."

"Up to a million a month."

"A modest amount. But it might elicit interest somewhere. Let's talk about quality. Size. In the Caroni River basin in Venezuela, one normally finds small, flawed, yellowish stones. During the last two or three years, with cheaper goods having a certain vogue, such items were able to find a considerable market. In South Africa, on the other hand, a range of stones are mined, most of them of gem quality. Australia—mostly industrial stuff, up to now. The Soviet Union—the Russians are digging industrial in large amounts in addition to gems of various sizes. Many of them, I am told, slip into the West by devious routes." He cracked another knuckle. "Take the Kimberly. What a special mine that is! Disgorging all those blue-white beauties. From Ghana, we get roughs of high quality, some large pieces among them. Of course, you know all this, don't you, Miss Foxman?"

The muscles across her stomach grew rigid and she held tightly to the arms of her chair. "As a matter of fact, I do."

"Of course. Your uncle's niece, you're privy to all such information. To accomplish your goals you need someone of stature, from Sierra Leone, let's say. Or may be Zaire, Tanzania or Angola. Ambassador level would be an advantageous entry, I'd say. Or a minister in charge of a major governmental agency. A million a month, you said. Are the funds presently at hand?"

"I can get them, I believe."

"I detect a note of uncertainty. Face it, Miss Foxman, money talks." His voice hardened, used now to prod and to punish.

"I can get the money."

"But only if you can first guarantee sources. Is that not the case?"

It was true; no one would advance her money unless she could promise an established supply.

He went on. "Rough, you said?"

"Gem quality," she said, as if by reflex. "That I can cut down to half a carat to ten carats."

"Grades?"

"From flawless to nothing less than a commercial $VVS_1$."

He lifted his eyes to the ceiling. "Uncut stones, there is no way to be positive that when cut they will come out the way you want them."

She rose and confronted him directly. "Has this been an amusing interlude for you, Mr. Zimmerman? Is this how you get your kicks, puncturing the dreams of ambitious little girls? Whose dirty work do you do here? Which of your clients is so intent on throwing roadblocks in my path?"

"Business is business."

"Dirty business."

"I'm going to give you some free advice. No one named Foxman is going to be able to make any substantial buys. Not through ordinary channels, for damned sure."

"You're the Syndicate's man," she said flatly.

"Sir John is displeased with your uncle. You bear his name, you work out of his office, under his protection..."

"I'm an independent."

"Sir John is an old-fashioned man. He believes a woman should wear diamonds, not deal them."

"Bastard," she said on her way out.

"Me?" he replied, with an ingenuous smile.

"You and Sir John both..."

## chapter
## 21

"SPEAK TO ME," legend has it Michelangelo commanded the statue he had wrought of Moses. And so it was, Maurice Foxman came to believe, that the magnificent works of art of Rome came to speak to all of humanity, to bring beauty and belief to a world trapped in disorder, in terror, in grief and disappointment. But for now the precious antiquities, the treasured art, the ancient history of the Eternal City provided him with no message of value. Empty of ideas, save one; devoid of hope, yet committed to one more attempt; without optimism, he departed the Hassler-Villa Medicis at the top of the Spanish Steps for his meeting.

Rome was Maurice's favorite city. The mixture of the old and the new, the beautiful and the profane, the works of the Old Masters existing cheek by jowl with the dregs of a society that lacked a true center. A city in which the rich and the poor cleaved to each other like opposite sides of a Roman coin.

Had it been winter, Maurice would have arranged a visit to the Opera, perhaps a Bellini; in summer, an open-air performance of *Aida* at the Baths of Caracalla. Not this trip, this time he was all business.

A high springtime sun had warmed the streets by the time Maurice reached Mastrostefano, that superb restaurant in the

Piazza Navona. His guests were waiting at an outdoor table, with an unobstructed view of Bernini's Four River Fountain.

"*Bentornato,*" they greeted each other, with embraces and handclasps. "Welcome back."

They examined each other with concern and the affection of men who had been friends for a very long time. Meier Halevi, a stubby man with a long nose and wattles that trembled when he spoke. Once a German nationàl, he was now an Israeli citizen. Jonas Greenfield, native of Berlin, currently a resident of Florence, citizen of the world, bright and learned, one of the most cultured men Maurice had ever encountered. Jacques Steinberg, cadaverous and pessimistic, checking everywhere for impending calamity and often finding it, and equally often fighting it off.

"A long time," Maurice said in English. They agreed; men of experience, they had each lived in many different ways. Each had adapted to the changing conditions of his existence, moving on when forced to, hiding when necessary. Fighting when that was in order. If they shared a single trait, it was their refusal to do less than live fully until the instant death appeared to claim them.

Along with a full-bodied Chianti, they dined on tender beefsteaks and freshly made pasta, and observed the fire-eaters performing in the piazza. They inquired about old friends and relatives separated by time and distance and recalled the good times they had had together. The Nazis had introduced them; in the cattle cars, in a basement in Cracow, in the mud of a death camp. They existed with awful memories, and if they chose not to talk of them, neither did they forget so much as the smallest details of those times. Not the pain, not the fear, not the degradation, nor the death of their friends.

"Choose life!" was the biblical injunction, and each of them had done so.

"So?" Jonas Greenfield said, pushing his half-empty plate away. "What brings us all to this place at this time?"

That drew a round of amused approval.

Halevi, his jowls shaking with delight, said, "Always it is Jonas who gets first to the point. No time to waste."

"Jonas," Jacques Steinberg said, "when God calls, will you also be in so much of a hurry?"

"Naturally," Halevi put in. "'Let's get on with it,' our friend will say to God. 'Stop wasting time.'"

As the laughter faded, all eyes swung toward Maurice. Like him, they were diamond merchants, men to whom a sight from IMM was as vital as life's blood. A bad sight would damage each man, a succession of such sights could ruin any one of them. They did not know the specifics of Maurice's difficulties, but word of his troubles had reached them: rumors, half-truths, informed guesses. When he asked for this meeting, they had responded without hesitation.

"The Syndicate has given me two unacceptable sights in a row," he said.

They busied themselves with their steaks. Slicing, chewing, trimming away the fat.

"My last sight," Halevi said finally, "twenty-five percent less good than it should have been."

Steinberg dabbed at the corners of his mouth with his napkin. "My last was subpar. Not enough to complain about, but enough to make me wonder."

"And you, Jonas?"

"Not good, not bad. The one before, that was a horror."

"You accepted it?"

"Of course he accepted it," Halevi said, voice rising. Of them all, his was the temper with the shortest fuse. "What choice does that momser give us?"

"Exactly my point," Maurice said. He attended to his steak; a shake of pepper, a dollop of Dijon, a small taste and a swift nod of appreciation.

"What is your point?" Steinberg wanted to know. "You, Maurice, you did not invite us here to complain or to discuss old times. Nor to gaze at our aging faces."

"*Momento!*" Halevi growled in mock indignation. "You others have aged, it is true. But not I."

There was the obligatory ripple of laughter before they turned back to Maurice. "I believe he's after us. He wishes us out of his hair, so to speak. To him, we have outlived our usefulness and now he casts us aside."

"Sir John!" Halevi exploded. "Certainly you are right."

Steinberg said, "You are sure of this?"

"Gently," Greenfield said. "Let's not run before we walk."

"Are we to be made prisoners again?" Halevi said, voice climbing. "After so many years, destroyed in another way? This time by the vagaries of a single man, by the oppression of the Syndicate?"

"Have you spoken to Sir John?" Greenfield asked.

"He refuses my calls. My letters go unanswered. My questions to those lapdogs of his, they give nothing back. Sir John is guarded more closely than the President."

"Why?"

"Why?"

"Yes, Maurice, why is he after you? Why is he after all of us? Why at this particular time?"

"You know me, all of you. Men like us, men who have come close to dying many times and have lived through it, we have learned to be careful, cautious, to eliminate risks where possible."

Greenfield said it for them all. "What you have done, Maurice, we have done. What you have felt, we have felt. Explanations are not required, not from any man here."

Maurice put down his knife and fork. He sipped some wine. He looked around. "Sir John means to crowd us out, us old-timers. We who have done well, whose operations share a substantial portion of the market. I have seen it coming and tried to prepare my business against the impact, tried to brace myself for the shock. I have branched out into colored stones, a small cushion against total disaster. I have thought about expanding my jewelry operations, add to the shops we have. But none of that will take the place of diamonds."

He sighed. "My nephew, Robert. He was in Liberia buying colored stones when he was murdered. A terrible warning to me."

"Are you sure it was Syndicate work?"

"Who else? I tell you, I have gone as far as I can go. No longer am I willing to be in the control of one man and that man a tyrant."

"What does he want?"

"To replace us with men more malleable, more sympathetic to his way of doing things . . ."

"Sir John is a businessman. Profit is what he wants, it is what all businessmen want."

"Yes, but not at the expense of personal dignity. Or self-respect. Yes, he is after more money and he sees his way clear to extracting it from younger men with less independence than we. Everywhere I go it is the same. Sights diminish in value and our profits go down accordingly. Complain, protest, argue, refuse the sights and we stand to be cut off forever from Syndicate supplies."

"Does it make sense?" Steinberg asked. "IMM is a monstrous cartel, all those companies, all that power. I'm told there are more than sixty tons of diamonds stored in IMM vaults. That is the foundation on which the entire industry stands. Release those stones to the public and prices will come crashing down."

"Agreed, Meier. But does that mean we must become his lackeys? Must we bow to his financial whims, no matter how unreasonable?"

"There must be something more to this," Greenfield said, in that cool, reasoned manner of his.

"I believe there is."

"So," Steinberg said. "Tell us what it is."

"First, Sir John converts. Then he marries the shiksa. Then the remarks about Jews begin. Too many Jews are in the trade. Jews are too independent, too rambunctious. Too this and too that. He has transformed himself into an enemy of the Jews."

"Sir John, an anti-Semite?" Meier said.

"You will have to convince me," Greenfield said. "What could impel a man whose father was a Jew, whose grandfather was a Jew, a man whose people were always Jews, what could make such a man turn on his own people? What makes such a man become an anti-Semite?"

Maurice managed a single nod. "In my view, Sir John has become a Christian the way the Germans were Christians. The way the priests and bishops were Christians during the Inquisition. The way the Poles were Christians while they made the pogroms. He has become an anti-Semite whose aim is to rid the business of Jews, to eliminate everybody who reminds him of what he once was. What his father was and his grandfather. He is a man intent on wiping out his past."

"A personal version of the Final Solution."

"I believe so."

"True or not true, what is to be done about it? The man has the power. The flow of stones, the price levels, it all emanates from the Syndicate."

"If I am right, Sir John will finish me off. Then it will be the turn of others. Perhaps you, Meier. Or you, Jonas. You, Jacques. And all the others like us, the last of a breed..."

"Stubborn old men," Halevi said without humor.

"Independents."

"Each going his own way."

"And seldom is it Sir John's way—not anymore. We know what it is to be constricted by outside forces, threatened, our property confiscated, our lives destroyed in one way or another."

"We are the lucky ones, Maurice. We survived."

"Yes, but to what purpose? Certainly not to permit Sir John to drive us to the wall. We must think about our futures."

Halevi thought that was funny and said so. "At my age, what future do I have? Am I supposed to begin a new business over again? Move to another place? I have children, grand-children, great-grandchildren, nephews, nieces, one sister."

"Spare us a listing of your progeny. We know you have populated half of Israel by yourself, Meier. It is not for nothing you are known as the Rabbit."

When the laughter died away, Maurice spoke again. "We must stand together."

"How?" Steinberg said. "I am not a big operator. Not as big as you, Maurice, nor you, Jonas. Even you cannot expect to oppose Sir John successfully on your own."

"Exactly. What we must do is to join forces."

"Maurice, have you become senile? What are you talking about?"

"About supporting each other in this affair. All the dealers and the cutters, all the big merchants. In Italy, in America and Israel, France, everywhere. A federation capable of standing up to the power of the Syndicate."

"Fight Sir John, you are saying?"

"Fight him and beat him."

"A union?" Greenfield said.

"A federation. An alliance that can close like a fist when any of its members are attacked. Power to meet power, strength to oppose strength, the collective will to survive and to win."

Halevi shook his head. "I don't like it, Maurice."

"Who likes it? Is it better to remain passive, paralyzed, while he picks us off, one by one? We are like people trapped in a marriage we never wanted and are too lazy and too afraid to break out of. We are like people who discover their idealized notions of the world don't match the real world. We practice self-deception in return for security and even wealth. Well— it is over and at last we are forced to confront the truth."

"It won't work," Halevi said.

"Tell me why not."

"I know you, Maurice," Halevi answered. "This is not your first stop nor your first meeting. You have spoken to others in the Netherlands, in Belgium, in—"

"So! Get on with it."

"By now word of your battle plan has gotten back to IMM. Sir John, with his British title, with his castle and his estates, you think he will sit still for this? I tell you, he will not. He will strike hard at you, at everyone connected with you."

Greenfield interrupted. "Is Sir John supposed to wait for us t form this federation, Maurice, for it to gain strength and influence? He will not, you know. He will close down our sources of supply. He will disrupt our operations. Our couriers will come under attack, our goods will be stolen. It's been done before, it will be done again."

Maurice felt it slipping away from him. "Do you deny it, Jonas, that Sir John is behind our troubles? When times were good we learned to live with his brutish behavior. But the killing of my nephew, that is not acceptable. Who will be next? Your sons, Meier? Yours, Jonas? Your brother, Jacques? He intends to drive us all out of the business."

Steinberg wasn't convinced. "There are always hard times, Maurice. Always troubles. Life is filled with problems."

"Life is an unsolvable problem," Greenfield added.

"Your answer then is no?"

"To a federation," Greenfield said. "Yes, my answer is no."

"You, Meier?"

"I'm sorry, Maurice."

"Jacques?"

"Also no."

Maurice pushed himself erect. "Very well, if I must I shall fight him alone for as long as I can. At least I have not grown fat and comfortable in my old age, and afraid."

"Maurice!" Halevi called as the tall man walked away. Foxman's stride was long and firm, his shoulders as straight as ever, and he never looked back.

*chapter*

# 22

SEEING MAURICE FOXMAN cross the Piazza Navona, Keller moved quickly to intercept him. He fell into step alongside the older man, spoke his name in polite greeting. His mind ranging ahead, seeking alternate ways of dealing with Sir John, Foxman barely noticed Keller.

"Mr. Foxman!" Keller said it again, this time louder.

Foxman lifted his eyes and for a moment appeared not to recognize the investigator. When he spoke, it was with neither warmth nor his usual graciousness.

"What is it? What is it you wish of me?"

Keller was impressed. These aging lions of Forty-seventh Street repeatedly surprised with their hidden strength, their staying power, their refusal to knuckle under to hostile forces. Foxman offered no polite chitchat. No indication that he was surprised to see Keller so far from home in a Roman plaza. No curiosity as to how Keller had located him amidst his wanderings.

"A few minutes of your time."

"You're Sir John's man. I have nothing to say to you."

Keller pointed. "Tre Scalini," he said. "Have you ever tasted

204

one of their *tartufi*? The sine qua non of ice creams. My treat, of course."

"Keller, you're a man of surprises. A connoisseur of ice cream along with a working knowledge of Latin. I accept your invitation, but with limited enthusiasm, I must add."

"Fair enough. Before we're through, we may yet become good friends."

"You're a romantic, Keller. I'm a pragmatist. Which shouldn't keep us from trying the *tartufo*."

An astonishing arrangement of chocolate-coated ice cream, decorated with brandied cherries. Foxman inspected the mixture with a wary eye. "Keller, there is no way possible for a sane man to devour and digest this monstrous creation."

"Nibble," Keller suggested.

"Nibble," Foxman said absently. "My mother used to say that to me when I was a boy. Nibble, it will last longer. Nibble, it will taste better. Nibble, and enjoy it more." Foxman looked at Keller across his *tartufo*. "Tell me, the work you do, is it something you enjoy? Always on the go. Always searching. What is it you hope to find? Mostly trouble, I'm sure."

"It's the nature of the job."

"And you find pleasure in this? You should have been a policeman."

"I was."

"Ah," Foxman said, as if that answered some unspoken question, and spooned some of the ice cream into his mouth. "Excellent. Very nice. Good." He put the spoon aside. "What made you become a policeman?"

"My father was a cop. Growing up, that's all I heard, about the cops. How there was right and there was wrong, about the law, which was all that separated a man from the beasts."

"So you joined up."

"A dirty job, the old man used to say. Somebody's got to do it."

"Put things right?"

"Make a better world."

"Yet you gave it up to work for Sir John?"

Keller shifted around in place, as if turning away from a bad memory. "Things happen. A man changes."

Foxman let that simmer in his mind. "Not you, I think. You were formed a long time ago, whatever you are. Men like you, you are always the same, only more so. Better and stronger, I think."

An unreasoning resentment took hold of Keller; Foxman was intruding, coming too close to that exclusively private place that he defended so effectively. "You don't know anything about me."

"Nor do you want me to know, isn't that so? No, you are not a man to reveal himself readily to others."

Keller stared at the older man, his eyes glazed and steady, his face hard. "A man was killed," he said after a moment. "My partner, my friend. I made a mistake, it was my fault."

"Accidents happen. Mistakes are part of the human condition."

"Ned Creer, my partner, he was too old for that kind of work. It was up to me to take care of him."

"Ah," Foxman said again, in that knowing way. "What kind of work was it?"

"There was a big jewelry heist. Metropolitan Gems, about ten years ago."

"I remember it."

"We were cruising midtown when the call came and we arrived first on the scene. Ned wanted to wait for some backup but I was so damned gung ho, so macho. I said I was going in."

"And?"

"And he was my partner. He came after me, looking out for my back. There were four of them inside, ready to split when we showed up. Maybe I made too much noise, I don't know. They were waiting for us and started shooting as soon as we went through the door. I hit the floor and returned their fire." He broke off.

"And?"

"I shot two of them, the other two got away with the jewels."

"You were a hero."

"Oh, yes. My picture was in the papers, the Commissioner pinned a medal to my chest, I was promoted. I was a hero all right."

"And Ned?"

"Ned took three slugs in the chest, dead before he knew it."

"I'm sorry."

"So was I. So was his wife and his kids. It didn't help."

Foxman filled his lungs with air. "Is that when you quit the force?"

"They let me go after the other two men for about two weeks. Then they told me to forget it, it was a dead item. There were more important things to work on. A man's partner is killed on the job, nothing's more important than to find the people who did it to him. The Department put roadblocks in my way. Too many restrictions, too many rules to obey, too many laws to uphold."

"So you quit and went after them yourself."

"IMM offered me a job. A year to find those guys. All the help I needed, all the money I needed. It took me seven months, but I got them. Both of them."

"They were brought to trial?"

Keller's expression was cold. "They refused to surrender. I shot them both."

Foxman shuddered. "Is that to be my fate, Keller? A bullet through the head, courtesy of Sir John?"

Keller's manner softened, his voice lost its edge. "I only want to talk to you, Mr. Foxman."

"Let me tell you, young man. If Sir John sent you to harass me, it will do no good. Threats will not work either. I concede your toughness, Keller. Yours and Sir John's. But I am not intimidated and you may tell him I said so."

"No harassment. No threat. No message of any kind from Sir John. I'm here on my own. I go where my nose leads."

"And your nose brought you to me in Piazza Navona?"

"News of your travels went through the trade like wind in the streets. I was in Dubrovnik when I heard and I caught a plane on the chance that I could find you. I picked you up when you left your hotel."

"I wasn't aware. You're very good."

"Part of the job."

"I used to be more alert. Maybe I am getting old. I see

personal attacks from all sides, against my company, my family, against me. Is that it, Keller? Have I grown paranoid and alienated in my dotage? An old man frightened of unseen enemies, fighting to cling to a faded vigor, a diminished authority? Have I slipped into senility, Keller, without knowing it?"

"No way. You've still got it all, more than most of us."

"I thank you for that." He eased the dish of ice cream toward the center of the table. "I never developed a fondness for sweets. Tell me, why are you here?"

"To talk about Robert."

"Is Robert also Sir John's enemy? The boy is dead, let him be."

Keller braced himself. "Robert was smuggling." Regret tinged his words, regret and shame that he was forced to give new life to old pain for Maurice Foxman.

Outrage swelled up in the white-haired man. Outrage and a remembered ferocity, a quick hard impulse to strike out against those who would harm him and his. Not this time would he and his family go easily to their ends. Not this time. Struggle had become the sole constant of his existence, the only thing that had saved him and Emil. Too many others had gone quietly and anonymously to their graves. To hell with that!

"Robert was a good boy. Honest, hardworking. He earned an important place for himself in my company, a young man on the move. He had no reason for dishonesty. No motive to cheat or lie or steal."

"Nevertheless, he was smuggling."

All energy seeped out of Foxman. The aristocratic face went gray. His eyes flattened out and his features sagged. Suddenly he looked old. His finely tapered fingers fluttered, not able to locate a suitable resting place.

Keller said, "Robert used a hollow cane to transport diamonds."

Foxman shook his head.

Keller brought a soft leather pouch out of his pocket and opened it, poured the diamonds into Foxman's trembling hand.

Maurice stared at the gems for a long time. His free hand rose to his temple, as if in pain, and he shuddered. "Why?" he said finally.

Keller offered the only answer that had satisfied him so far. "Robert had gone into business for himself, telling no one. Using Foxman and Company as a cover."

"Where did these come from?"

"From a man named Tarassuk."

"Who is he? Oh, what difference does it make?"

"A week before the transfer took place, there was a theft in Antwerp."

"You are telling me Robert stole these stones?"

"No. But Tarassuk probably did. These came from Russia. They were in transit to an outlet in Paris, a man named Lukas. I have reason to believe that Russ Almaz suspects Lukas was part of this conspiracy. They want him, they want Tarassuk, they took Robert out for his part in all this."

"I don't understand," Foxman said. "In the last few years IMM has bought up the entire Soviet output. Through London Gem Trading, Ltd. An open secret in the trade. Through World Diamonds International in Beirut. Through Mineral Traders, S.S., in Mexico City. All of them are fronts for the Syndicate."

"Quality stones, this lot."

"Maybe they are Russian, maybe not." He gave them back to Keller. "One thing is certain, Foxman and Company had nothing to do with them."

"Robert did and somebody killed him for them." One by one, Keller returned the stones to the pouch. "A million at least, to buy these."

"Closer to a million point five, at a guess."

"Worth four or five times that amount in the market. Worth killing to get them back."

"Think what you wish," Foxman said, all strength gone out of his joints. His temple began to throb and his fingers to tingle. He averted his glance and Keller understood that the interview was about to be terminated.

Keller stood up. "Thank you for your time, sir." Foxman gave no indication that he'd heard. "Are you all right, Mr. Foxman? Is there something I can do?"

"Leave me, leave me alone."

Keller had taken two or three steps when Foxman called out. A lonely, lost expression had settled onto his face, the terrors of a lifetime flickered like grotesque shadows in his eyes; it was the look of a man haunted and afraid of what he no longer understood.

"When you return to New York, Keller," he said, "come and see me, if you wish."

"I would like that very much, sir."

"Next time the ice cream is on me."

## chapter
## *23*

HARRY GEIS RECOGNIZED HER AT ONCE. He was standing in front of his shop warming himself in the afternoon sunlight when he spotted her, picking her way through the shifting mass of street traffic. She appeared from between two strolling Hasidim, was cut off from view as she walked for a few yards behind a giant black man listening to a Walkman, until he suddenly had an unimpeded sight line. He'd seen her only once before; a salesman had pointed her out to him the day after Downes began schtupping her.

Top-quality merchandise, he conceded. A face like a madonna, creamy skin, large almond-shaped eyes set under an intelligent forehead and the kind of mouth he knew what to do with. And her body, *madrone!* Tits performing under a plum-colored blouse, hips swinging smoothly in response to the reach of her long legs. Outstanding stuff.

She went past without a glance his way and he grinned in appreciation; a lady like that wouldn't have eyes for a weasel named Harry Geis. So be it! Only he'd end up screwing her in ways she couldn't dream about, the pleasure all his. Still— that was world-class goods, the kind only momsers like Peter Downes got to work on. Lucky bastard.

Ellie had opened her own office on the fourth floor of a

building close to Fifth Avenue. A showroom up front and two small offices, neither one facing the street. She rented the appropriate furniture, hung some paintings on the walls and had phones installed. A thousand embossed business cards and stationery to match; more expensive than she could afford, fancier than she needed, but vital to her emotional well-being, she assured herself. All that remained was to acquire an inventory and dispose of it at a substantial profit.

For that, she was dependent on Bakshir Khamoury. They had been in frequent communication by telephone and she knew he had been in New York the last two days; at the appointed hour, he presented himself at her office. He kissed her on each cheek, he complimented her in a seductive Arab voice, he clutched her hands for longer than she liked. But he remained circumspect; his body never made contact with hers, his words were flowery, suggestive, yet never vulgar, never direct. Too many American men, given the same opportunity, would have groped her by now.

"News, my lovely! Good news!"

"You can get the stones I need."

"Yes, yes. Not in the numbers you desire, I'm afraid. Nor in the quality you wish. But still..."

She sat back down. "All right, Bakshir. Give it to me straight."

"It grieves me. A million dollars a month is beyond my reach."

"Why? If I can get my hands on the money..."

"You do not understand. People respect and honor the Foxman name. Of course, your uncle is known to them."

"But I am not," she said bitterly.

"It has been pointed out to me that you are a woman alone, young, without an established firm at your back."

"A woman," she bit off.

"Alas, yes. From a personal viewpoint I consider that to be an asset, a magical advantage. But some of my colleagues take a somewhat more conservative outlook. To me you are a pure delight, my beautiful one. To see you again is to renew my passion for you. Have you considered carefully my offer of marriage? It is made with the utmost seriousness, with respect and courtesy. I will speak to your family, of course, make the suitable declarations of intent toward you and toward them. A marriage to Khamoury will guarantee your position in society in my country. That is, if ever again there is a society in my country. The fighting, the killing. The Israelis, the Syrians, the Palestinians, let them do as they wish with each other on their own lands, leave Lebanon to the Lebanese. Go home, I say to them, and leave us to conduct our lives, which is good business for everybody."

"Speaking of business." She placed her elbows on the desk, chin in her hands, looking solemnly at him. "Bakshir, how would your suppliers react if I said I intend to create my own bourse?"

His dark eyes went round and his lips pursed. "No woman has ever run a bourse!"

"It's about time one did, this one. If the Syndicate and its friends won't permit me to have the diamonds I need, okay. If I am to be limited to the open market for my purchases, again okay. All because I'm a woman. But there are others in the same position, and not all of them are women. Outsiders, operators too small to deal with the important suppliers, scratching for product, squeezing out a living. Too weak individually to fight the system. But what if we banded together? Our own exchange, sharing expenses, information, even sources of supply—the Foxman Diamond Mart. I like the sound of it."

"It won't work."

"I believe it will. It must. Collectively we will be stronger. Under one roof, we can absorb a considerable part of the overhead, cushion the impact of bad times or bad deals, buy the time we need to grow and attract others to join us. An independent exchange."

"Where would you put such a bourse?"

"I've been giving that some thought. My contacts in Paris are good, I speak the language fluently, I know the city as well as I know New York. Easy access to the other major diamond centers, to the African mines. Yes, Paris it's going to be."

"Where?" he began.

She cut him off, her excitement rising. "Naturally I don't have a specific location yet. However..."

He raised one hand to silence her. "The primary problem will not go away, my dear one. Where, I wish to know, are you going to obtain supplies sufficient for such an undertaking?"

"From you, of course. We are friends, Bakshir. I owe you the opportunity."

"Cancel the debt."

She managed to laugh, aware that he wasn't trying to be funny. "You are afraid, Bakshir?"

"Indeed, yes, very much afraid."

"Does that mean you're going to desert me in my hour of need?"

He matched that beautiful face against the results of a negative answer, perhaps the end of their friendship. He was not prepared to go that far so soon. "What's a poor man to do!" he wailed. He washed his hands, one against the other. "What is it you want of me?"

"Here's my plan: a commodity exchange selling only diamonds which can be categorized on the basis of Gemological Institute of America certificates."

"You would handle only on GIA categories?"

"Half carat, one carat, D-flawless. Only cut stones."

"An interesting idea."

"With your help, I'll make it work."

He went over it in his mind, the possibilities, the drawbacks, the dangers. He would have preferred to withdraw at once; but that magnificent face held him against his better judgment. He exhaled and threw up his hands. "Very well, my precious, we will do it your way. Do your part and I shall certainly do mine."

"It's a bad idea," Downes said without thinking. "You should've talked to me first."

"Talked to you! Why? It's my idea, my decision, my life. Why is it, Peter, that every man I've ever known automatically assumes a superior position, as if whatever I want, whatever I do, is the product of a lesser intelligence. I won't let you squash my initiative, I won't let anybody cripple my freedom of action."

"Is that what you think I'm trying to do? Well, you're wrong."

"I hope so. Who did you consult when you and David decided to go into business? Certainly not me. Who advised you to come to New York?"

"I'm not trying to hold you back."

"My experience tells me that is exactly what you're trying to do."

She was right, he acknowledged to himself. In some nameless, formless way he feared any action she took would endanger his plans, threaten what he and Harry were trying to do. Ellie was too visible, repeatedly drawing attention to herself, to Foxman and Company; that could bring unwanted scrutiny to his activities. He would not allow anything to get between him and his share of the twenty million. Nothing. No one.

"You're right." He spread his arms. He ducked his head. He produced a sheepish grin, making him look younger than his years, disarmingly attractive, boyishly appealing, so very innocent. "I don't want to control you, Ellie, only to love you."

She flung her arms around his neck, pressing against him. "I'm going to do it, darling. I really am. With Browning's backing and Khamoury as my primary supplier—oh, it will be slow in the beginning, difficult, and a lot smaller situation than I'd like, but it will come together in time. I'm sure of it. A dozen dealers, maybe twenty, if I'm lucky. Each renting space from me. A good deal for them and no overhead for me. I'll be in business for myself, a two-pronged operation. Biff! Bam!" She threw back her head and laughed. "Take that, Sir John!"

"I hate to disillusion you, but Sir John isn't going to get hot over a small bourse in New York."

"Not in New York, darling. Paris. A Paris address can only help matters when it comes to diamonds and jewelry."

"I thought you were talking stones only."

"Why limit myself? I contacted some of the top designers, famous names. What would you say to earrings by Saint Laurent? A collection of Halston rings and bracelets. Necklaces by Cardin? We'll be the first to combine high fashion and good stones—not costume jewelry. There's a market out there for designer items, top-ticket items."

The idea was sound, so sound that it frightened him. Without knowing how, he became convinced that Ellie's bourse was going to hinder his plans. "I'm genuinely glad for you," he heard himself say. And to his surprise he realized that he meant it, in part. Her excitement stirred him too and he wanted her to succeed, to become the first woman ever to be granted a sight. And yet . . .

"I know you are," she answered. "Sometimes . . . oh, hell, Peter, this business is so *intense,* we're all so desperate, everybody out for himself. Nothing is ever what it appears to be. Not the people, sometimes not even the stones. Hustlers, swindlers, thieves. I want to get past all that, make it to the top. But according to the rules. I want to be like . . ." She broke off and looked away.

He brought her face around. "Like Maurice?"

"Yes, damnit! Why not Maurice? He's done it all, he has it all. I want to do it too."

"And you will."

"You really believe that?"

"You can do anything you want to do."

She kissed him on the mouth, a lingering kiss that left her soft and vulnerable. And when he tightened his arms around her, folded her up against his hard body, she felt herself grow weak and her desire spread.

"I love you, Ellie," he whispered.

"I love you, Peter." The words sounded strange in her ears, a surprise, both the words and their meaning.

Downes felt proud that a woman like Ellie Foxman could love him, want him above all the other men she could have. And for the first time he was able to perceive the possibilities of a straight life for himself, a life without scams and stings, a life without deceptions and swindles. He saw himself as Ellie's husband, partner; Downes and Foxman, Fine Jewelry and Diamonds. They would have shops in the most fashionable quarters of the capital cities of the world. He envisioned a life of wealth and status, of power and pride.

And almost immediately, he was struck by the notion of it all slipping away. No millions, no solid business, no beautiful wife. A sense of loss set in and he was assaulted by visions of defeat and eternal despair. Only the void was left.

"Ellie," he said in a small voice that she took as a sign of his profound emotion. "Will you marry me?"

She was shocked, made afraid by the prospect. Marriage was always something to be put aside, something that lay far ahead in the dim future. "Hush, lover," she murmured. "Hush."

"I mean it," he pleaded.

She believed him and that troubled her even more. She wasn't ready for this, not ready for him. Something about him—about their relationship—something vague and unsettling eluded her, made her inwardly recoil as if in self-defense, made her want to retreat. Peter was perfect, she reminded herself. Was that it? she wondered. Was he too perfectly formed in body and in spirit, did she need flaws in a man to please her, forbidden areas to stimulate her senses, a twisted psyche to make her feel she was getting what she deserved?

"Later," she said, choosing not to think, not to see too much. "Later," she said again, and drew him toward the bed, where no thought was required, where she had only to surrender to sensation. "Much later..."

*chapter*
# 24

AT FIRST GEIS DIDN'T RECOGNIZE Georgy
Tarassuk. In a shapeless cotton jacket and baggy trousers, the
Russian looked more rumpled, more unsavory than ever. A
moustache, vaguely Oriental in design, had sprouted along his
plump upper lip and dark glasses concealed his eyes.

"May I help you, sir?" Geis began.

A booming joyful laugh broke out of Tarassuk, pleased that
his deception was working. "Harry, it's me, Tarassuk. Georgy
Tarassuk. Have you forgotten? It's been a long time, but not
that long, my dear friend."

Geis glared. He had hoped never to see the fat Russian
again, certainly not here on Forty-seventh Street, and definitely
not in his own shop. "Look at you," he complained. "What a
mess! You give the business a bad name."

Tarassuk arranged an apology on his round face. "Harry,
Harry, always making jokes. Tell me, you still pretending to
be a yid?"

The darting eyes narrowed and the tight mouth flattened
out. "Whatsa matter with you, talking that way? The mechanic's in the back, you wanna gimme away? Jesus H. Christ, no
wonder you're on the run, that big mouth of yours."

A snarl lifted one side of Tarassuk's mouth. "Where'd you
get that idea, that I'm running?"

"Word gets around, putz. I hear things."

Tarassuk leaned forward, speaking intimately. "Tell me the truth, Harry. What was it like? A grown man having his cock chopped that way? I'll bet it hurt the first time you got it up. A little guy like you, Harry, probably so small between your legs it doesn't matter."

"Go on, get out of here. I don't take shit from your kind."

"Always a great sense of humor, that's you, Harry. I say to people, you're in New York, look up my pal Harry Geis, great sense of humor."

"What's on your mind, Georgy?"

The Russian rolled two rough diamonds on the counter that separated him from Geis. "Make me an offer, Harry."

A small inner voice warned Harry to move with caution, to treat the moment with care. He looked at the stones through a loupe. "They're okay," he said.

"Oh, Harry, please. What am I, a virgin? You want to hondle somebody, find yourself a sucker. They're better than okay, they're excellent. The best. Cut properly, they'll bring seven, maybe eight times their cost. You're good with the glass, Harry, you know."

"They're okay, I said."

"For eighty cents on the dollar they're a bargain."

Geis pulled back as if the stones were contaminated. "No way. You're a hot number, Georgy. Your goods are hot. I don't touch you with a ten-foot pole."

"This is a legitimate acquisition. Fine stones like these..."

"You think I don't know where they came from?"

"Wrong. Wrong, Harry, wrong. Such quality seldom comes nowadays."

"Never kid a kidder, Georgy."

"Okay. But not these. These are from the Kimberley pipe. How did I get my hands on them? What's it matter? In Madrid, I picked them up just before I left for the United States. I'm going to do you a favor, Harry."

"Don't do me any favors."

"Sixty cents on the dollar. Is that a bargain? What do you say?"

"What do I say? I'll tell you what I say. I say show me a bill of sale. Show me an export license. What am I, a dummy?

I don't know how you operate, Georgy?"

"And don't I know you, Harry? For years you been a fence. Oh, yes, I know you, too."

"Take off, you goniff."

"Okay," Tarassuk said. "I admit it. I got to have some money."

"Go to somebody else on the street."

"I trust you, Harry. You can trust me. Fifty cents, cash on the line."

"You are in trouble."

Tarassuk snuffled wetly. "They're after me, Harry. They think I pulled a job or two I shouldn't have pulled. But you know me, Harry, I don't go in for heavy action. No garbage work. I function with my head, not my hands. What they think, well, they're wrong. Believe me, Harry, they're wrong."

"I don't want your stones."

"They put Leonid on me. Can you imagine, Leonid, after me? That's not right."

"That Leonid, he's crazy."

"You think I don't know? I know. That's why I came to see you, Harry. I have faith you'll do right by me. What I need is some money and I'm gone, someplace where nobody can find me. Not even Leonid."

"Last time, it was Arkadi put you up."

"I tried the old number. Out of service. Arkadi's gone, I don't know where. Harry, you got to help me."

Geis jiggled the stones.

"It's a good buy," Tarassuk said. "Fifty cents on the dollar."

"I ain't got that kind of dough on hand. Might take me a day or two to get my hands on it."

"What do I do until then?"

"Maybe I can help you there, too. I can let you have a couple of hundred now and an address. A woman I know. She's also from Odessa, Georgy. Tatiana is her name and she knows how to take care of a man on the run."

"You trust her, Harry?"

"Like my own sister."

"Okay, if you say so. Where do I find this Tatiana?"

"I'll write down the address. It's in Brighton Beach."

*  *  *

As soon as Tarassuk left, Geis got on the phone. Ralph Browning answered on the private phone he kept in the bottom drawer of his office desk.

"I gotta see you right away, Ralph. There's a couple of items that bother me."

"In an hour, the Oak Room at the Plaza."

"I'll be there."

Browning was already seated at a table against the back wall when Geis arrived. He hurried to join him.

"Well?" Browning began. His cheeks glowed with good health, his eyes were clear and steady, a man who existed in a world that offered him no threat.

"Guess who came to visit today."

"No games, please, it isn't my style."

"Georgy Tarassuk."

Browning frowned and that surprised Geis. The banker was usually among the least flappable of men. "I didn't know he was in New York."

"Just dropped in."

"What does he want?"

"He tried to sell me a couple of pieces. A three-carat and a five-carat. Nice stuff."

"And you bought?"

"I advanced him a couple of hundred, that's all."

"He's on the run, you know that."

"Sure I know, he told me. He said he thinks Leonid is on his case."

"And you let him walk away?"

Geis decided not to go too fast. "What's he done so bad?"

"Damnit, man," Browning said with unaccustomed vigor. "You know as well as I do how he operates."

"Smuggled stones, a little here, a little there. Nobody's ever cared before."

"Well, somebody cares now. Tarassuk jumped a courier in Antwerp, a *Soviet* courier. A few days later, he showed up in Monrovia and sold the stones."

"To Robert Foxman?"

"Tarassuk arranged the transfer. Leonid was a step behind. He found Foxman but Tarassuk was gone. Now you helped him get away again."

Geis grinned, showing his small, sharp teeth. "Never bet against me, Ralph. I put Georgy in touch with Tatiana, she'll keep him occupied for a while. All it takes is a phone call." He rose to go.

"Wait, there are other matters. How is our friend Downes doing?"

"Coming on strong. He's in thick with Foxman's niece."

"Not so thick that he puts his primary responsibility aside, I hope."

"Not to worry. He's making regular buys, his credit line is getting stronger all the time."

"Speaking of credit, he brought the niece to me. She's after a million a month."

"You gonna let her have it?"

"The girl is ambitious. She wants to open her own bourse. Downes called me to say he thinks she could damage our efforts. He's afraid it might attract too much attention to her, and so to Foxman and eventually to him."

"Sounds right to me."

"Yes. Peter's thinking ahead, that's good. I may follow his advice, turn the girl's application down. Why take chances? Now, about Downes, how are his buys going?"

"Very good. He's into the market for about a million five. That's a goyische kup on his shoulders, as the saying goes, but he's learning."

"As long as she does what he's told."

"He will."

Satisfied, Browning turned his attention to another matter. "I've been considering, Harry. What would you say if, rather than twenty million, we went after a full fifty million?"

"You kidding me?"

"Give me an answer."

"It's too risky. It will take longer, force us into bigger purchases. Somebody's liable to catch on, put Downes under the gun. We can't afford that."

"I don't agree. Downes is buying for Foxman fundamentally. The stock he's accumulating is company property. Foxman is the guarantor, the debt is his. The risk may jump proportionately but not geometrically and I think it's worth taking. Let's go for the fifty. We must be in a position to control the company."

"What if Downes refuses?"

"That's a droll idea. Have you ever given him reason to believe he's in a position to refuse any order he's given?"

"No."

"Then give him his orders. Make sure he obeys. Don't tell me this cushy capitalistic existence has made you forget how to deal with a man like Downes."

"Me! I forget nothing," Geis answered testily. Then, remembering his position in the pecking order, with some deference: "You ever miss the way it used to be?"

"The good old days, you mean? Nothing remains static in this world, nothing. But you are still a young man, Harry, not yet forty. Make peace with your destiny. You have a talent for this work and that talent is your future, for the good of us all."

"And you, what about your future? Tell you what—let's switch future and present. I'll take charge of the bank and park it in a large leather chair all day and eat in expensive restaurants and live in a Park Avenue apartment. You, you go down to Forty-seventh Street and hassle them Jews all the time, scratching for enough dough to live off. Believe me, it isn't easy."

"Your reward will come later."

"I know all about that kind of a reward. A medal and a cramped flat outside Moscow when I'm old. Not even a car, maybe not even a TV. Some reward. Big fucking deal."

"That kind of talk makes me nervous, Harry. It would make our people in Moscow nervous, too."

Geis screwed himself tighter into his seat. "Nothing serious, comrade. Just a little antsiness is all. A touch of discontent, not to be seriously considered, I promise you."

"I understand, my friend. I too have developed an appreciation for certain aspects of this new life. Its ways are seductive . . . and therefore extremely dangerous. The easy living, the beautiful women, the quick and tangible rewards . . . capitalism is . . ."

Geis spoke quickly. "You need have no concern about me, about my loyalties."

"Never doubted you for a minute. It's a dying system, this

vaunted democracy of theirs. It's flabby, confused, it appeals to the weakness in men. But you and I—we are prepared by training and experience to resist. We'll withstand all the blandishments and enticements. You know, my part in our endeavor is going to end soon enough and I shall be ordered home."

"What then?"

"I shall go, of course. One must be attentive to the needs of the Motherland always, even as one is concerned about the development of one's career—no?" He found this amusing. "First things first, our present assignment. If—no, *when*—when we are successful we shall both be heroes. Acclaimed and rewarded for our efforts. Won't that be nice, Harry?"

"Sure," he said vigorously, thinking: Nice for a little while, at least.


On his way back to the bank, Browning stepped into an empty phone booth. He dialed the number he had committed to memory and was surprised when someone picked up the phone.

Browning spoke first. "I wish to talk to Leonid."

"Why?" came the hard, flat voice.

"My name is Ralph."

"Many men are called Ralph."

"Some people refer to me as Ralph the Banker."

There was a momentary silence at the other end. "This is Leonid."

"Good. Are you still looking for someone named Georgy Tarassuk?"

"You know where he is?"

"Tatiana Petrov, who lives in Brighton Beach, in Brooklyn, she will know where he is."

"Anything else you have to tell me?"

"No, nothing else."

The phone went dead in Browning's hand; had he made a mistake? No matter, it was too late to alter the course of events. He continued on his way back to the bank, in no hurry any longer to get there. He had a great deal to think about, so much to consider.


Sir John's club was located on Pall Mall, one of many exclusive private clubs lining that handsome street. Spotless granite steps led Norman Kinard into a sober reception hall, up to a glass-enclosed porter's box. The porter looked inquiringly his way.

"I'm Norman Kinard . . ."

"Oh, yes, sir. Sir John is waiting, sir." The porter came out of the box and escorted Kinard down a long paneled corridor with high ceilings. The porter knocked deferentially at the last door, opened it and waited until Kinard had passed through before departing.

Sir John Messinger sat in an ancient leather wing chair, reading a newspaper. He folded the paper and put it aside. He rose and offered his hand.

"How good of you to come, Mr. Kinard. May I offer you some breakfast?"

"Nothing, thank you. I've eaten."

"Then to business. Please, sit down. I appreciate your giving me so much of your valuable time, Mr. Kinard."

Kinard managed a small smile. A well-padded man in his middle years, he possessed the confident set only success in one's chosen field can bring. Nevertheless, he remained in awe of the man opposite; one didn't come face to face with a living legend very often.

"A personal invitation from you, Sir John. A private jet bringing me from New York to London. A chauffeured Bentley and a luxurious apartment for my use. I confess, I've been wondering why the 'A' treatment? After all, what can I do for you?"

"A great deal. Without wasting words, Mr. Kinard, I summoned you here to talk about Maurice Foxman. You are his primary banker, are you not?"

Put as a question, Kinard understood Sir John already knew the answer. "I am," he said.

Sir John made an assenting sound back in his throat. "Foxman and Company has thoroughly distressed me, sir. Thoroughly. Through its subsidiary, P & D, Inc., Foxman is in your debt to some considerable amount, rising into the millions of dollars. And going higher, isn't that right?"

Kinard made it a practice never to discuss the bank's affairs outside the bank, though it was clear that Sir John's research was effective. He opened his mouth to protest but Sir John went on.

"Never mind, sir. I *know* what the numbers are. I know what the debt is."

"I've been doing business with Maurice Foxman for twenty years. He's a good man, trustworthy, reliable."

"If you say so."

"Am I to understand you have doubts about Mr. Foxman? I would certainly find that hard to reconcile with my experience with the man."

"There is something you can do for me, Mr. Kinard."

"If it's within my power."

"It is, sir. It is. I wish you to call in Foxman's line."

Kinard's ordinarily bland face twisted up in surprise and dismay. "Demand immediate payment?"

"And terminate any further credit."

Kinard hesitated, trying to think. "May I ask why, Sir John?"

"Not pertinent, not at all. However, it is supremely important to the continued good health of our industry. And that, Mr. Kinard, should be of vital interest to you, since ninety percent of your business is done within the diamond trade."

Kinard realized that he had just been warned, perhaps even threatened. It would take only a word or two from this man to send a considerable portion of his client list flowing to some other bank. He wanted to do nothing to offend Sir John and yet felt a powerful obligation to his view of himself as a man and as a banker.

"If I did call in the credit line, it would cause Foxman to go under, put him out of business, almost at once."

Sir John peered at Kinard from under hooded brows. "I had you brought here, sir, in order to convey my wishes to you personally. Explanations are not in order."

Kinard shook his head. "I don't mean to be argumentative, but it seems to me that should Foxman fail it would in fact damage the industry."

"We differ on that point. Foxman and Company is not terribly important."

"Oh, I agree. It's amazing, isn't it, how prestigious the man has become, based entirely on his personal stature. I wonder, should it become known that a man of his reputation was brought down—well, would that precipitate a loss of confidence in the industry?"

"Why should that happen? Companies fail all the time."

"I was just thinking—this is such an unstable period in our history. So much of a negative nature has transpired—industry people disappearing, large parcels fail to arrive at their destinations, the robberies, murders, the roller-coaster prices, the recent difficulties with Zaire putting product into the market on their own..."

Sir John appraised Kinard soberly. "I took care of that matter, now I wish to deal with Maurice Foxman."

"Oh, I understand, sir. It's just that if a dealer of Foxman's reputation were to go under it might cause an economic catastrophe."

"For a man who doesn't mean to be argumentative, you certainly make a strong argument, Mr. Kinard. But your arguments have not moved me. Do this for me, Kinard, and I shall be in your debt. And I always repay my debts, one way or another."

The carrot and the stick, Kinard thought. Reward and the promise of punishment. If he couldn't have Sir John for a friend, he definitely didn't want him for an enemy. Still...

"Sir John, you must have your reasons for what you want me to do."

"Indeed."

"Whatever they may be, I can't see any justification for an action of this kind. Instead, I can perceive a number of practical reasons for acting otherwise."

"Such as, Mr. Kinard?"

"My obligation to my bank, for one thing. Foxman's debt has reached such a large amount that he exercises a certain control over us. If I closed him down, what would I gain? I'd be left with a nearly worthless firm and the bank would be out millions."

"I'll guarantee the debt and you'll gain my good will."

"Will you pay off the debt Sheryl & Sheryl owe?"

"What have they to do with this affair?"

"They owe my bank thirty million. Abrams, Selig and Anderson owe nearly twenty million. Other outstanding loans come to another hundred million. Even IMM can't pay them all."

"I'm concerned only with Foxman."

"Other banks are holding paper in large amounts, Sir John. Atlee Commercial in the Netherlands is owed sixty million by a single client. Paris International has seventy-five million outstanding to an individual borrower. All of us are in thrall and none have called in the debts for exactly the same reason— the debts are so large it would mean a complete write-off. The banks would have to *admit* a loss. For the same reason, the banks involved have not called in Brazil's debt, or Mexico's, or Poland's. In these precarious times, such an action would thrust a bank into technical insolvency and do tremendous damage to us all."

"Your logic is impeccable, Mr. Kinard."

"What is good for the industry is good for my bank, Sir John."

Sir John answered deliberately, his manner chilling. "Your reasoning is admirable. You've been of much assistance. I hope I have not inconvenienced you."

"I don't want you to think that I won't help if I can."

Sir John rose and Kinard did likewise. "I will not be prejudiced by this exchange, Mr. Kinard. I understand your point of view and admire you for daring to say so. Many men would not have done so." He guided Kinard to the door. "However, should you find yourself able, in some small way, to be of assistance in this matter, it would be sincerely appreciated."

"I'll give it my attention, Sir John."

"Yes, you do that. Thank you for coming."

"Thank you, sir."

Outside, in the warm London sunshine, Kinard began to shiver.

## chapter

# 25

KELLER RECEIVED THE NEWS while working out of his New York office. Five attacks on diamond employees in the city, four of whom had worked for Foxman and Company; three of the four had been robbed at gunpoint, the fourth had tried to flee and been beaten badly, requiring surgery. Nearly eight hundred thousand dollars in stones had been taken, wholesale prices given. The police were checking known fences; the insurance underwriters were conducting an investigation of their own, casual, superficial, and in the end they would pay off the policies, content to pass on the loans in higher premiums.

Keller alone seemed concerned. None of his informants, street people, pawnshop owners, fringe operators, were able to provide him with any hard information. The stolen gems had been swept out of sight and with each passing day were less likely to be found. After a week, they would be gone forever, the roughs cut; the finished stones recut by now and placed into settings by unscrupulous manufacturers and put up for sale in some of the town's most prestigious display cases. Keller wondered: The attacks on Foxman, could they have been merely coincidental?

Or was Maurice right and he was being singled out for punishment by the Syndicate, without Keller's knowing? Had he incurred so much of Sir John's wrath with this terrible result? If so, what was Keller to do? Never before had he come up against such a blatant conflict of loyalties: his obligation to the people who paid his salary, on the one hand; his commitment to learning the truth, on the other. He hoped he never would have to choose between them.

Then, providentially, the call came and he was able to put such distressing thoughts aside.

Detective Sergeant Sy Wechsler was a muscular man with tight, wiry hair turning gray. The job had put grooves in his face and pouches under his eyes but they were bright, alert eyes that were never still. He took Keller to see Georgy Tarassuk, who was lying under a sheet at the country morgue.

"That your man?"

"I never saw him, but he fits the description."

"Interpol IDs him as Georgy Tarassuk. Forty-three years old. A Soviet citizen by birth but he was carrying an American passport."

"Phony?"

"Looks like it. We're still checking."

"He came out when Moscow was still letting Jews emigrate, during détente."

"Brighton Beach is filled with them. Little Odessa, they call it. Lots of these people come from Odessa. Circumcised, only he doesn't look Jewish to me."

"Maybe not."

"His papers made him out to be a Jew and he was wearing a mezuzah on a gold chain around his neck. You said he was a Jew," Wechsler ended accusingly.

"I said he came out when the Russians were letting Jews out. Some people claim the Kremlin salted that bunch with its own people."

"Same as Castro did?"

"More or less."

"KGB, you think?"

"Not Georgy. He was a man who dabbled in this and that in Russia. Black market goods, anything to make a ruble. Stumbled into diamonds and decided the market was stronger in the West. Saw his chance to get out and he took it."

"A phony Jew?"

"Where was he found?"

"I'll show you, back to the beach."

Under the boardwalk, not far from the Aquarium, the sand taped off and marked "Crime Scene," guarded by a solitary bored patrolman.

"This is where they found him," Wechsler said. "Some kids, four of 'em, to be exact. They gave the precinct a call. Made it sound like a party, like they was having a really good time, you shoulda seen 'em."

"What did he have on him?"

"Not a thing. Cleaned out his wallet, no watch, no rings, just the mezuzah."

"Diamonds?"

"You kidding! Just a couple of twenty-two-caliber slugs in the brain and the IDs in his wallet, which is how I got to you. Charlie Hedden in Midtown South says you are the man when a diamond job comes along."

"Professional work," Keller said.

"Very neat."

"Nobody heard anything?"

"Nobody heard, nobody saw. It's like that, a lot of the time around here. Maybe it's the way it looks, just a killing of convenience during a robbery."

"Maybe."

"Only you don't think so?"

It was damp and dank under the boardwalk and Keller walked out into the morning sunlight and felt better at once. He brooded about the nasty way events were proceeding and when he spoke his voice was edged and edgy.

"What I know about Tarassuk, he was the kind who went in for lots of flash. Gold and diamonds, wherever he could wear them. One of those solid-gold Piaget watches that do everything but give a massage. Carried a bundle of cash on him all the time."

"That kind's ripe to be taken."

"Sure. Only now he's dead and picked clean."

"Those kids . . ."

"Sure. Wouldn't be the first time a bunch of kids stumble on a corpse and strip it before they call us in. It happens."

"Only you don't think so?"

"Lots of diamond people been getting knocked off lately, too many. In New York, in Europe, in Africa."

"Africa! You been to Africa?" Wechsler was impressed. "I always wanted to take one of them safaris. You ever taken a safari?"

Keller shook his head.

"What else have you got on this Tarassuk?"

"Somebody was mad at him. The way I figure it, Tarassuk was playing his own game and that somebody sent somebody else to straighten him out."

"Or finish him off."

"Yeah. Question: What in hell was he doing out here?"

"You kidding me. The ocean, the boardwalk, Coney Island. Lots of people come to the beach."

"Tarassuk lived the good life. Lots of money, lots of travel, lots of women. This guy went to the beach, he went to the French Riviera, to Sardinia, to Corfu. It doesn't figure, him hanging out with a bunch of Jewish émigrés."

Wechsler worked some sand into a mound with the blunt toe of his brown shoe. "What we have out here is what we call the Russian Mafia. If this character was hiding out and carrying gems and cash and so forth, there's plenty around here would hit up on him for the entire package." He shaped the sand into a neat pyramid, stole a glance at Keller. "Only you don't think so?"

"The kids didn't do it."

"I don't think so either."

"Could've been an accident."

"What kind of an accident?"

"A man needs some fresh air, takes a walk on the beach. It's safe late at night, he figures. Not likely he's going to be spotted by anybody who knows who he is. Maybe some wise guy looking for an easy mark spots him and takes him out when he fights back."

"Only there was no sign of a struggle. Just two in the head and down he went."

"Just running through the possibilities."

"Too damn many possibilities. The kids, a random job and

somebody on his tail who wanted him dead. Don't complicate my life, Keller."

"There's more."

Wechsler flattened the pyramid. "Hedden said that's the kind of guy you were, a thinker. Okay, lemme try one on you. What if you're wrong and he was KGB, into some of that spy stuff? Maybe his Russian friends decide he's been turned by our people. Hell, there must be five hundred KGB types working out of the Soviet Mission to the UN in the city. Tell me some of the people in Little Odessa are on Moscow's payroll and I won't be surprised, not me. How's that grab you?"

"Not bad."

"Only you don't think so?"

"I'll give you one. You heard of Russ Almaz? That's the outfit that does diamonds for Moscow and damned good at what they do. Hundreds of millions every year. Used to be all their stuff went through De Beers and IMM. Then they pulled a switch, began extending their reach. A certain amount of stones went out through private channels, meaning a higher markup for Russ Almaz and more control over the product."

"Shrewd operators."

"Whatever else they are, the Russians are sharp business-men. The point is, every once in a while some Soviet product gets itself misplaced."

"Misplaced?"

"Lost, stolen, slipped into the cracks of the system. Millions of carats go that route every year in every country, wherever the stuff is mined or cut or sold in quantity. Which just about covers the entire Western world. Agents everywhere are hus-tling for the almighty buck."

"Tarassuk among them?"

"The word I get is he moved a lot of stones for a lot of money."

"You saying he got greedy?"

"Maybe. If I were four kids cleaning out a stiff, I'd take it all and split, sort it out later. Not leave anything behind. Not a wallet with a bunch of cards and IDs in it. Not a mezuzah on a gold chain, not a bunch of kids."

"Same if you were working the beach and got lucky. Hit-

and-run guys don't get points for neatness."

"Exactly right."

"So where does that leave us?"

"My hunch is somebody was taking Tarassuk out for a reason and sending a message."

"What's the message?"

"Guys steal Russian diamonds, they don't live forever."

Keller spent the rest of the day wandering the streets of Brighton Beach, listening to the cacophony of Russian, English and Yiddish, inspecting the faces, the shops, trying to put the pieces of the puzzle together. A jeweler's window drew his attention, the proprietor getting ready to close for the night. Keller went inside.

"Too late," the man said. "Closing time. See, it begins to get dark outside."

Keller flashed his ID. "Just a couple of questions."

The man carried trays of rings to the safe at the back of the store. "A small dealer like me, what does the Syndicate want with me?"

"A man was killed last night." No answer came from the back room. "You hear me?"

"I hear."

"What do you know about it?"

"It's like a separate town out here. Apart from New York, apart even from the rest of Brooklyn. What happens in a town in Idaho or Michigan or upstate New York can happen here, too." He appeared in the doorway. "Am I making sense to you?'

"His name was Georgy Tarassuk. Did you know him?"

"I got nothing to do with people who get themselves shot."

"Did I say that, that he was shot?" Keller presented the man with his worst grin. "Tarassuk dealt in stones. He was a Russian."

"Never met the man." He emptied another display case and started for the back room again. "There's newspapers, you know. News gets around."

"The story hasn't broken yet."

The dealer went into the back room and returned almost at

once. "Maybe once somebody mentioned such a name like that to me. Maybe once."

"Tell me."

"What's to tell—a place like this, all kinds of people show up in Brighton Beach. Ordinary people, politicals some of them, avanturists."

"Adventurers," Keller translated.

"You're not Russian." It was said accusingly.

"Tell me about Tarassuk."

The proprietor pulled at his nose. "Somebody said Tarassuk was a man who enjoyed a good time. A man who liked to sit and drink and eat, a man who liked to be around women."

"Where would he do this?"

"In Bright Beach, there are clubs. The Metropole, the National, the Russian Garden. Most of them are open only on weekends."

"Which one is open during the week?"

"The Russian Garden. Yes, it is a very nice place. Ask for a man named Anatoli."

"A regular."

"The owner."

Anatoli was a well-fed man in his middle years with a veined neck and a barrel chest. He was the sort of man who functioned best on the far edge of whatever society he happened to find himself in. He greeted Keller warily.

"I have been a citizen of United States for three years already and a few months. Finally I pass all requirements, my English gets good enough. You can hear the improvement, no?" He laughed mockingly at himself.

"To live in such a wonderful country and not speak language is dumb, no? It is pleasure to live here. Free speech, free thinking, free movement. They are only things here that are free, no?" Again that pointed laughter.

Keller said, "You knew Tarassuk?"

"Oh, sure. I know Georgy. But he don't live in Brighton Beach, only comes to visit. Business takes him around."

"What business?"

"He buys, he sells. I don't know. Not my business, you know."

"You think he was into something?"

Anatoli fastened on a mote floating on the stale, still night-club air. Except for a man washing glasses behind the bar, the Russian Garden was empty, shabby in the harsh glare of a work lamp. Anatoli brought his attention to the coffee cup in front of Keller. "You like another cup?"

"Was Tarassuk bent?"

"What do I know?"

"Take a guess."

"Around here lots of people get bent. A man is a tailor, he has to drive a cab so he can feed his family. Another man waits tables and teaches English in his spare time. People work hard, steady people, dedicated to job and to family, to making future for themself and for children, okay. Only such a man looks around and what's he see? He sees man down street making up forged identifications for kids so they can buy liquor in bars and it pays good. He sees peasant women selling television sets for less than you can buy them for in stores. Nobody says to her where did you get the TV. Nobody tells on her to the police. Nobody cares. She gets rich and people get good television for less money. So after a while, people decide it is better to be a little bent and not work so hard. Always there is easier way, no? The American way, no?"

Keller decided not to address the moral question. "Tell me about Tarassuk and his women."

"All men like women. Tarassuk, he liked young women a lot." He shifted closer. "Don't tell my wife, I'll tell you, I like young women. But it don't do any good, not so anybody can notice." He grinned proudly. "America is a very sexy country, anybody will tell you. Very sexy."

"Was he with a woman last night?"

"In my place, you mean?"

"Yes."

"Do I remember such things! I don't remember."

"He was here last night?"

"Maybe. Maybe I noticed him on his way to men's room, maybe." He called to the man behind the bar. "Konstantin! Last night, Georgy Tarassuk, the fat guy who got himself blown away on the sand, was he with a lady last night?"

"Maybe. Yeah, maybe. I t'ink so."

"Who?" Keller said, restraining his impatience.

The barman stared at Anatoli, who nodded his approval. The barman smiled. "I t'ink so."

"For crying out loud," Anatoli shouted. "Tell the man."

"Sure. It was Tatiana."

"Ah," Anatoli said. "That is some woman, that Tatiana. Not a schoolgirl, but very fine merchandise anyway."

"Somebody he picked up at the bar?"

"Hey, what kind of place you think I run here? No pickups allowed. No singles at bar. No ladies alone at tables, either. No exceptions. They come with a date, okay. They come with friends, okay. No fooling around in my place, is decent place, Anyways, you see for yourself, bar is just service bar."

"He brought Tatiana?"

"Sure, that's it, he must've brought her."

"Where do I find her?"

"Is easy," Anatoli said. "We can find easy."

"How?"

"We look her up—in phone book."

Tatiana Petrov. The name was listed on the call bell in the outer lobby of the apartment house. A building like every other building on the street; faded red brick, a courtyard guarded by stone lions, the instituional green walls in need of a paint job. Working-class tenements erected around the turn of the century, designed to provide inexpensive apartments for family living. Keller had grown up in the Bronx in a building not very much different from this one. He remembered the bathroom most of all. A bathroom with a tub standing on claw feet and a sink with enough ledge space for soap and toothpaste, room enough for a water glass containing his father's false teeth at night.

The boy, Keller, loved the bathroom. It was a haven from the sound and fury of a family of six forced to live in four cramped rooms. Keller didn't have a room of his own until he was twenty-eight years old and he shared that one with his first wife. From family to Marine Corps and back to family, then marriage. Privacy was the most precious commodity he'd ever possessed.

That childhood bathroom. It boasted a lock that kept in- truders at bay so that Keller could spend time on the john or in the tub. He luxuriated in his occasional aloneness, mind drifting, dreaming great, farfetched dreams, or singing softly the songs of the day off nickel song sheets colored blue or pink or orange, or reading the novels of Thomas Wolfe or James T. Farrell or Fitzgerald or Hemingway. Keller didn't read much for pleasure anymore. There was never time for it. Not even on plane trips, when there was always paperwork to take care of, reports to write.

He pushed the bell button under Tatiana's name and a tinny, impatient voice came out over the intercom. "Yes, please, who is it?"

Keller identified himself. "Just a few minutes of your time, Miss Petrov."

"Who? What is it that you want? I am very busy at this moment."

"It's about Georgy Tarassuk."

He could almost hear her thinking it over, assessing the credits to be earned if she refused him entry against any debits that might accrue. She took her time, putting every detail into proper order, weighing her long-term interests. He wasn't sure, but he thought he heard her sigh.

"All right," she said. "Come on up."

The buzzer released the safety catch and he pushed the door open and walked inside. Her apartment was on the third floor, a climb up white marble steps, now worn and stained yellow in spots. The painted metal walls were flaking heavily.

Tatiana was waiting in her doorway, judging Keller before he got too close. He returned the compliment with professional interest. In her forties with flesh on her bones but in good proportion, she was a large woman, firm, her gaze level and steady. Her eyes were ice blue and her hair was blond, combed straight back and tied in an old-fashioned bun at the nape of her neck. She reminded Keller of a hundred women he had known in the old neighborhood: Swedes, Germans, Poles, Norwegians.

"What did you say your name was?" she said in greeting.

He eyed her gravely. She had regained her composure, was in full control now, determined to give nothing away.

"Keller," he said. "International Minerals and Mines security. I want to talk about Tarassuk."

"Who?" she said calmly.

"Georgy Tarassuk. You were with him last night."

She never blinked an eye. "Oh, yes. That one. We hardly knew each other."

"Invite me in," Keller said. "To sit down. Offer me a cup of coffee."

She shrugged and stood aside. He went past her into the living room. Neat, spotless; just this side of being shabby.

"You would like a cup of coffee?"

"No, thanks. Tell me about Tarassuk."

"You a friend of his? What?"

"Sometime last night, he was killed. Shot in the head a couple of times."

She squealed. A hand rose to her lips. Her eyes. A low, slow moan of grief. A nice performance, Keller thought. Disciplined, all emotions on tap.

"No, no, it cannot be."

"Some kids found him under the boardwalk."

"Poor Georgy. Why would anyone kill him?"

"I thought you might be able to tell me."

"Me! No. He was a man after a good time, that's all. We danced together, drank vodka and ate some blinis, altogether an unexceptional evening."

"Except that somebody took him out. Was he worried about anything?"

"Not that I noticed. He laughed a lot, joked a lot, said how much he enjoyed my company."

"How long have you known him?"

"Not long."

"How did you meet him?"

She brushed an unseen strand of hair off her cheek. "I cannot think straight. Someone must have introduced us."

"Where? Who?"

"I don't know. I can't remember. It isn't important."

Let me decide that, Keller thought, saying, "The Russian Garden maybe?"

"I think so. Yes, the Russian Garden."

"At the bar, I suppose?"

She accepted that. "He offered to buy me a drink. He seemed like a nice guy, so what was the harm?"

"Last night?"

"Yes. He had a few drinks and—poor Georgy."

"He brought you back here afterwards?"

"Oh, no. A man I hardly know, I would never invite him to my apartment. We said good night on the sidewalk outside the Russian Garden."

"I'll bet he put you in a cab, he was that kind of a guy."

"Yes, that was it. I left by myself in a taxi."

"And Tarassuk?"

"I never saw him again. So you see how little I know, how little I can tell you."

"About the Russian Garden, the bar is just a service bar, no drinks served directly to patrons."

Nothing fazed her. She delivered a sweet coquette's smile in Keller's direction. "You're right, of course. I was at a table, he came over. That was how it was."

"Let's see, I want to get it right. You were at a table by yourself—watching the floor show, right?" She nodded. "He looked like a reasonable guy, so you invited him to sit with you? Have I got it straight now, Tatiana?"

"Absolutely straight."

"I don't think so," he said coldly. "No pickups at the Garden. Anatoli doesn't permit unescorted women at the tables. No exceptions."

Again that coquette's smile. "A memory lapse. One forgets."

"A human failing. So you must have met Tarassuk elsewhere?"

"Of course, that was it. The Metropole. I was confused."

"The Metropole is open only on weekends. Another memory lapse, Tatiana?"

She took it head on, without apology. "I have a man friend," she said, rational in tone and manner. "He gets upset if I see another man. But I am a free woman, uncommitted, my life is my own. You are a cosmopolitan man, you understand."

"I still don't know where you met Georgy. Perhaps someone introduced you, a blind date."

She giggled, suddenly a young girl again, flirtatious and shy. What a beautiful woman she was, Keller thought. Overflowing with charm and sexual appeal, a loaded gun for a man with a taste for good-looking women.

"What difference does it make now? We met, we spent an evening together, and now he is gone. Poor Georgy. What a nice man he was and how sad that I shall never again see him. Am I to blame? Perhaps if I had been more giving, invited him back here, who knows, he might be alive today."

"You're terrific, Tatiana. Really very good. Quick on your feet, using the best of yourself. Only it won't work this time."

"I don't understand."

"I want a name, Tatiana, a name that satisfies me, that makes sense to me. Otherwise, I put in a call to Immigration."

She laughed. "Immigration! What for? I am quite legal, you see. My papers are in order, I have done nothing wrong. I am already a citizen for four years."

"And the FBI."

Her eyes seemed to freeze over, a thin skin of loathing. "You must leave, at once. Or I shall call the police. I will not be intimidated. I will not be threatened. I will not be harassed."

"Ask for Sergeant Wechsler, he's on the case. Go ahead, call." When she hesitated, he threw her a curve. "You're not Jewish, Tatiana. We both know that."

"What are you saying?"

"You lied to get into the country," he said, with much more certainty than he felt. He warned himself to go slowly, not to say more than he had to; one error and the game was over, she'd know he was bluffing. "That one lie should be enough to get you sent back. Which is it, Tatiana, Russ Almaz or KGB? Which one runs you?"

"This is insanity. I am what I say I am. A Jew from Odessa."

"Not that it matters," he went on aggressively. "By the time I'm done with you, you'll be worthless to your friends in Moscow. Without much trouble, I can get you sent up for three to five, and deportation afterwards, Tatiana. A woman with your looks, that won't be much fun. No men, no pretty clothes to wear, the end of the good life. A single phone call will set you up, Tatiana."

"I don't know what you're talking about."

"Try this, Tatiana. I let word out around Brighton Beach that you fingered Tarassuk for a KGB hit man. That will get a lot of people very uptight, angry, and wanting to take remedial action. Can you handle that, Tatiana?"

She embraced herself. "What is it you want of me?"

"A name. The one who sent Tarassuk to you in the first place?"

The name would mean nothing to him, she convinced herself. Geis was a cutout, a dead end for anyone digging too deeply. For Harry, Keller would be a minor annoyance, yes, but of no real consequence. It would stop with Harry, go no further, and Keller would get no information out of him. She needed the time to get out, to find a new base from which to operate, arrange a change of identity, create a new life. She could still be of immense value to those back home.

"I do not want to embarrass anyone," she said, summoning up that sweet smile again. "Harry introduced us. There, it is said. A man fixes up a man with a date, nothing more. You are making too much of this."

"What is Harry's name?"

"Geis. He told me Georgy was a man after a good time, that's all. A night on the town, that's all. A Russian émigré like me. So I agreed."

"Where do I find Geis?"

She gave him the Forty-seventh Street address, making a production of looking it up. Making it appear as if it was a number she was barely familiar with.

"He deals in diamonds?"

"In a small way."

Keller stood up. "You're in the wrong line of work, Tatiana, you lack the temperament. Better be on your way. It would be very uncomfortable for you to show up in my world again."

She waited until he was gone, waited for the trembling to stop, before she reached for the telephone.

## chapter 26

GEIS WAS IN HIS APARTMENT when the call came. He let out a cry of protest before she finished talking.

"How could you do this to me?"

"He backed me into a corner, Harry. I was scared. Everybody told me it was a safe job, impenetrable, that I'd never be found out. But he found me, Harry. How did he connect me to Tarassuk? How did he find out I wasn't a Jew, Harry? How did he find out I was an agent? Jesus, Harry, you think somebody's turned and is talking? What else can it be? Harry, I'm really scared."

"You should've kept me out of it."

"I got to run, Harry, get out of here."

Geis heard the panic rising in her voice and commanded himself to remain calm and in control, to marshal his thoughts. This Keller, a security cop for IMM, big deal. Nothing had happened yet that was worth worrying about. No way he, Geis, could be connected to Tarassuk's death. No way Keller could have found out about the scam. Everything was okay. Just as it was. A minor irritation, that's all, and it was up to him to scratch the itch.

"What else did you say to Keller?"

"Nothing, Harry, honest. You'll be all right, Harry. You're good at this work, you've been trained for it. But me..."

"Where will you go?"

"There's a number I'm supposed to call if something like this happens. The guy on the other end will have instructions for me. A couple of hours, I'll be out of town. New name, new identity, clean and starting all over."

"You'll be at the apartment for a couple of hours?" he said with disarming mildness.

That frightened her even more. "No!" she almost shrieked into the phone. "I'm leaving everything behind, everything. When I hang up, I'm gone. I'll make my call, Harry, and then nobody will ever find me again." Her voice went soft, pleading. "I did my best, Harry, I really did. It wasn't my fault. This Keller... watch out for Keller, Harry. He's tough and awful smart."

"He won't get anything, not from me."

"Yeah, that's right, Harry. He won't get anything, not from you. *Do svidanya*, Harry."

A fractured second passed before he translated the words for himself; English was native to him now, he had made a complete transition. He smiled into the phone.

*"Do svidanya*, Tatiana."

As soon as he hung up, Geis dialed Ralph Browning's number. There was no response. He tried again just before he went to bed that night and the first thing when he woke the next morning. Still no answer.

He opened his shop on schedule and tried the private line at Browning's office; no response. He dialed the bank's number and a secretary told him Browning was at a meeting, away from the bank.

Geis left his name. "It's important that I talk to him, soon as you hear from him." He busied himself filling the display case with his inventory. He was almost finished when Keller entered the shop.

Geis recognized him at once. The athletic set of his shoulders, the poised, alert way he held himself, the hooded expression on that bony face. No drop-in trade this one, no bargain hunter doing a little early-morning shopping. Keller wore no rings, no other jewelry, only a practical, unobtrusive watch on his wrist, a tool of the trade.

"Good morning," Geis said. "Can I help you?"

"Geis?"

"Yes."

"I'm Keller." He fixed Geis with those pale, sardonic eyes. "You got a call about me last night." Another man might have smiled to indicate that this was a game to be enjoyed, a game played by established rules that both of them were familiar with. Not Keller. Keller played by his own rules and he had no smile for Harry Geis.

"What call?" Geis said; Tatiana was right, he thought, Keller was tough and he was smart.

"Tatiana Petrov." Keller spoke the name in little more than a whisper, as if concerned lest it collapse on the air. And the delicacy of his manner made Geis uneasy. He had to shed any connection to Tatiana and had summoned up the nerve and strength it would take to do so when the telephone rang. It was Browning.

"You called me?"

"I'm busy right now. A man just came in off the street."

"Trouble?"

"You could say that."

"I had another call. I was informed that our friend in Brighton Beach had a visitor last night. Same one with you now?"

"You could say that."

"Deal with it, Harry. Tatiana panicked and she'll pay for it. Don't make the same mistake. Make sure it goes no further, whatever it takes. Protect the project, Harry. Protect Downes. Most of all protect me. Do I make myself clear?"

"Thank you, yes. I'll certainly call you back." He hung up and confronted Keller. "Okay, mister, now what in hell are you after?"

"Georgy Tarassuk."

"Who's that? Listen, I don't know what you think you're doing and I don't care. Why don't you just take your ass out of here!"

"You put Tarassuk in touch with Tatiana?"

About to deny it all, Geis realized the futility of it. Tell the truth, that was one of the maxims drummed into all new agents. When possible. Do not deny what is obviously true. Construct cover stories on the truth, altering it only to suit changing circumstances.

He manufactured a brief, embarrassed laugh. "What the hell, you got me. Yeah, Georgy and Tatiana. I was trying to be circumspect."

"Protect the lady's reputation, you mean?"

"Sure, that's it. Tatiana did call but I'd forgotten your name. Lady said you'd been around about Georgy. Poor Georgy. You're a cop working the case, right? I understand. Anything I can do to help, Officer. The city, it's a cesspool, crime everywhere."

"I'm IMM security," Keller said. "What's your connection to Tarassuk?"

Geis shrugged. "Hardly any. Once in a while, a little business. I can't remember the last time. Georgy free-lanced, y'know, bought where he could, sold where he could. Hell, the trade is lousy with guys like him."

"You set him up with Tatiana."

"I introduced them, that's all. The man was lonely. You know those Russian émigrés, they miss the Motherland. The old ways, the old language. Borscht and boiled potatoes. What the hell, no harm, no foul. A little hanky-panky is all. What's the big megillah, consenting adults and all that."

Nothing here now, Keller decided. Geis's guard was up, a shrewd little hustler who'd had time to prepare for this meeting. Keller's error; next time he'd dig into Geis's background, see what he could turn up. Not much, he was sure, men like Geis seldom left tracks. Still, the dots were being linked by a faint line and a vague profile was beginning to take shape. Keep pushing, he advised himself, and he was bound to make a breakthrough. He started for the door.

"Anything else you want to ask," Geis's mocking voice reached out, "just gimme a call. Always available to the Syndicate."

Keller turned back. "You'll be seeing me again, Geis, depend on it. It's all right now."

"What is?"

"For you to make that call."

Geis forced himself to wait a full five minutes before reaching for the phone. But when he spoke, there was still a tremor in his voice.

# chapter
## 27

DOWNES WAS ANNOYED and made no attempt to conceal it. "You could have chosen a better place for lunch."

Geis's mouth curled at the corners, lending a Mephistophelian cast to his squirrel face. He took a bite out of his sandwich, brown liquid tracing a path down his chin; roast beef and gravy on seeded rye and a cool beer. He spoke as he chewed. "Go ahead and eat. Food is okay here and it don't cost an arm and a leg."

"I avoid places like this."

They were in a shadowed booth at the rear of the Blarney Stone on Sixth Avenue, around the corner from Geis's shop. "Trouble is with you, Peter, you're a snob. Let's talk business."

Downes examined his sandwich gloomily, took a tentative taste. "I don't like the idea."

"Tough," Geis answered. "Because that's the way it's gonna be."

"It's too dangerous, I'm not going to do it and that's all there is to that."

A startled expression faded onto Geis's face; Downes's opposition was unexpected and intolerable, a cut at his authority. He shook a greasy finger in the other man's face.

"Listen, asshole, you do what I say you'll do. I say eat dog shit, you eat dog shit. Starting right now, we are gonna step up acquisition, and that's all there is to that. We go after fifty million and we do it in seven days, ten at the most. Boom-boom-boom, before anybody gets wise."

"We'll attract too much attention."

"You know what you are, I'll tell you what you are. A schmuck with earlaps is what you are. What do you think this is, some game you think you're playing! This is the real thing. We make the score, in and out, and nobody knows a goddamn fuckin' thing. We walk away rich. Both of us. You want to be rich, don't you?"

"I'm not so sure anymore."

Geis's face grew tight, jutting forward. "What in hell are you talking about! We're into it, dummy, and there's no way out. Just obey orders."

"What orders? We're supposed to be partners."

"Partners, hell! You work for me, you take orders."

"I've been wondering, who do you work for, Harry? Is Browning your boss? And if he is, who gives him orders? Is it Mafia? Or does the real power come from someone else? Come on, Harry, level with me."

"Level with you? Okay. For such a smart guy, Downes, you are really one dumb putz. You do like I say and you'll come out smelling like a rose. Otherwise . . ."

"You're threatening me." Downes seemed cheered by the notion. "I'm twice your size, Harry. I outweigh you by fifty pounds. I'm in fighting trim. What are you going to do, kick me in the shins?"

Geis stared in malevolent disbelief. "Scumbag, how about I get both your legs busted! Maybe an arm thrown in for free. How about somebody pumps a couple of slugs into that retard brain of yours. Maybe that'll put some smarts into you."

"That's not funny, Harry."

Geis stood up. "I ain't jokin'."

"That kind of talk—I guess that means Browning is Mafia."

"That's it, be scared, asshole. Be scared and be smart. You're not the kind to handle pain and blood, especially your own. So you do what you're supposed to do and you'll be okay."

Downes watched Geis leave in that quick, studied swagger of his, leaving him behind with a spreading fear and the check. The sandwich was tasteless, the beer was warm and his appetite had fled. He paid the check and walked out into the sunlight on the avenue, on his way to work. He never looked behind his back; if he had, he would have seen Keller keeping pace at a comfortable distance, blending into the shifting lunchtime crowd.

That night, in the bedroom of Downes's apartment, after making love efficiently but without passion or deep gratification, they lay next to each other in the semi-darkness and made all the obligatory declarations of fealty and love, all offered without force or feeling.

"Why didn't you tell me?" she said finally. "About your trip."

"How long have you known?"

"Everybody tries to keep secrets in this business, but it's next to impossible. We live in a fishbowl, most of us. Why didn't you tell me?" she said again.

Her voice had taken on a hard, resentful edge. "Maurice invited me only the other day," he answered quickly. "I wasn't sure . . ."

"Not sure whether you'd accompany him to London for his sight! That's hard to believe, Peter. It's an open announcement of how much he relies on you; that you're number two in the firm." She was out of bed, dressing swiftly. "Oh, I don't blame you. My uncle prefers a stranger in the company to his own flesh and blood. It's been obvious for some time, he's grooming you to take his place."

"Please, don't leave."

She paused, faced him, her cheeks flushed, her eyes blazing. "I should be the one he introduces at the London Sales Office. I should be the one he takes on this trip. I should be the one prepared to take over for him."

He sat up. "I don't want you to go, Ellie." He reached for her and she pulled back.

"No, don't touch me, Peter. Not now. I better leave, before I say something both of us will regret."

"I love you, Ellie."

He seemed like a stranger suddenly, a stunningly shaped and designed mannequin, with no substantial interior, another empty suit. His beauty left her unaffected, his declaration of love untouched, his words unmoved. She hurried to finish dressing.

"Perhaps I'm being childish," she said, without apology. "Foolish, even spiteful. But it's the way I feel and there's no reason to hide that side of me from you. Do us both a favor, Peter, don't crowd me. Not right now."

And for the first time, he perceived how deep her ambition ran. She loved the business with a passion at least equal to Maurice's, a reverence for diamonds that transcended her feeling for anything else. For anyone else.

Diamonds provided Downes with an opportunity to elevate himself in the world, to acquire wealth and respectability. For Ellie, that was only a small part of it; he'd watched her fondle a beautiful stone, watched while she studied it, assessed it with loving concern, seeking ways to enhance its natural beauty with an artistic cut, to bring it to a mystical plane of perfection.

He reached for his clothes. "I'll put you in a cab."

"No!" She almost shouted the word, one hand rising up as if to ward him off; then with restraint, a feeble smile. "I'll talk to you tomorrow."

The street outside was deserted. An empty cab came cruising along and kept going, the driver bent on other pursuits. She stamped her foot in frustration, angered at her own intemperate, impulsive actions. Exactly the sort of behavior that had plunged her into one personal and professional mess after another. She forced herself to slow down, to take a more deliberate stride. She began walking toward the avenue, where she might have a better chance to find a taxi.

None of this should have happened. None of it was Peter's fault. Nor was Maurice to blame. She couldn't blame him anymore. He was the unchangeable element in the blueprint, the foundation on which all their lives were being erected. Maurice had not messed up her life; she alone was responsible for that. There was no more time for rationalization or self-protective mewling. It was time to grow up, to become the

Ellie Foxman she was capable of being.

Ahead of her, just out of the cone of light from a streetlamp, a man appeared, turning to face her.

She stopped dead in her tracks; this was New York City at two o'clock in the morning, a street empty of pedestrians, of traffic, a street silent and suddenly ominous. What insanity had driven her to leave the relative safety of Peter's apartment by herself? She made ready to run when he spoke in a quiet, possessed voice.

"Miss Foxman."

She squinted into the night and, as if to make it easier for her, he stepped into the circle of amber light. It was Keller; after a suitable interlude, he advanced slowly.

"Didn't mean to frighten you."

You bastard, she wanted to say; you scared ten years off my life, she wanted to say. But she refused to give him that much. "I don't scare so easily, Keller," she said instead.

"Need a ride?" He indicated a gray Rabbit, battered and marked by the dents and scars of hard use.

"No, thanks. I'll catch a cab."

"I'm going your way."

Finally it struck her. "What the hell do you mean, going my way! What are you doing here! Why are you following me?"

"I want to talk to you."

"By what right do you put yourself in my life? Get out. Stay out. Stay away."

He opened the door of the Rabbit. "It's dangerous at night."

"You're not a cop, you have no authority." She scanned the street. Dark and still and studded with impenetrable doorways, dark alleys, threatening corners. Hiding places for muggers, murderers, rapists.

"Climb in," he said. "Door-to-door service. Safe, swift and the price is right."

"I don't want to talk to you."

"Don't talk, just ride. No obligations."

She measured him, checked the street again, and got in the car.

He drove with a confidence approaching arrogance, his strong hands relaxed on the wheel, shifting smoothly, the Rabbit responding at once to his touch. "Almost six years old." He tapped the dashboard. "A hundred and ten thousand miles and she purrs. Comes from tender loving care and regular checkups. You got to let a car know she's appreciated, wanted, loved. Just like a human being or a pet."

"No talking, you said."

"Just giving you a rundown on the accoutrements of my existence."

"Not interested," she said, staring straight ahead.

"Right. What shall we talk about?"

"I took you to be the strong, silent type."

"What about Peter Downes?"

She shifted around, her back against the door. "What about him?"

"Known him long?"

She examined Keller's battered profile in the changing light as they drove along. An odd face, a bleak landscape of colliding sadnesses.

"You want to know about Peter, ask him. Or don't you have the nerve to face up to him?" It was a challenge a bragging schoolgirl might have thrown down, empty, to no good end.

He considered his reply. He was beyond her antagonism, beyond being provoked. When he was ready to answer, there was music in his delivery, a low and mournful dirge.

"I've done some checking on Downes."

"How dare you!" Her indignation sounded fraudulent in her ears, a protest made out of form, not substance.

"Here's a brief bio," Keller said. "Downes peddled garbage stones to old folks on the hunt for a good investment. Diamond is forever, that was his pitch. Overpriced junk that could only go down in value. He also worked a boiler room out of Chicago, telephone sales, picking the pockets of the vulnerable. For twenty-nine ninety-five he'd send them a couple of glittery pieces of glass in a plastic container, telling them that if they ever opened the container the resale price would collapse. Poor suckers usually go for it, too, that's the amazing part. From Chicago to L.A., and a mail-order operation. That lasted six months; he grabbed the dough and never delivered the goods.

When the state attorney general got on his case, Downes headed cross-country, stopping now and then to fleece some lonely old lady. None of this was big, you understand. None of it anywhere as big as Foxman and Company."

"You don't expect me to believe any of this!"

"He's out to take your uncle. I don't know how yet, but that's the way it falls."

"That's a lie."

"Horses for courses, lady. If he runs true to form, this Downes, he'll take you, too."

"Keller, you have a warped mind."

"I'm telling you what I've found out so far."

"You're dangerous. Biased. Envious of your betters."

"Downes is up to something."

"You are the granddaddy of all bastards, Keller. Rotten in your heart."

"Downes is a crook."

"Damn you! What gives you the right to dirty up my life? Where's your evidence? Where are your witnesses? Stop the car, damnit, and let me out."

He kept on driving. "Once upon a time," he said matter-of-factly, "there was a Russian hustler named Georgy Tarassuk."

"You're certifiable, Keller. You should be put away."

"Georgy thought he had a good thing going. He picked up Russian gems from one place or another. Some of them were stolen, some of them were smuggled. That made certain people in the Soviet Union a little testy."

"So?"

"So Georgy woke up dead one morning with two bullets in his brain, twenty-two-caliber slugs. Same as your brother. Probably from the same gun. Robert was dealing in Soviet stones."

"No."

"Robert did business with Tarassuk."

"No."

"Tarassuk was connected to Harry Geis."

"Who is Harry Geis?"

"He's got a shop on the street. Hustles tourists, fences a

little, switches glass for the real thing when he gets the chance. Nothing big. Geis and Downes, they are in the something together."

She braced herself. "It's easy to accuse people, Keller. Show me some proof."

Keller shrugged, concentrated on his driving.

"Damn . . . Keller . . . by what right . . . who made you judge and jury?"

"Could be I made a mistake."

She took that to be a concession of failure, of weakness, a man who'd gambled and lost. "Peter Downes is a good man, better than you can imagine."

A quick look at her, then back to the road ahead. "I don't see you with him. Not seriously."

"Go to hell."

He pulled up in front of her apartment building, reaching for the door handle on her side, effectively locking her in place.

"You love him?" he said softly, eyes probing hers.

"Yes," she said, too quickly.

"I don't think so. Turned on, okay. Infatuated, as they used to say. But love, no. You and Downes, you don't go together. It won't wash. You like Japanese food?"

"Go to hell," she said again, made to feel inadequate, enfeebled, at a loss for words.

"I know the best joint in town. Over on Second Avenue, the best sashimi, we'll try it sometime."

"I can be had, Keller." Say it carefully, she admonished herself, don't give him the satisfaction of getting angry. "But not by you." She smiled demurely.

"Not even if I say please?"

"Not even if you say please."

He spoke slowly. "A Spanish poet said it best about a woman. 'Half full of cold, half full of fire.' That's you, Miss Foxman." He opened the car door. "I'll wait till you're safe inside."

"Why," she said, "are you doing this?"

"Somebody has to."

"Has to do what?"

"Put things right. Otherwise—disorder and chaos."

It took a very long time for her to fall asleep that night,

thoughts of Downes and Keller, her uncle and her father, fading in and out of her mind. He was an unsettling man, Keller, rawly honest, so much like Maurice, yet so different, without the protective coating of refinement and education and culture. An insurmountable wall distanced her from a man like Keller, kept her from knowing him, or understanding him. Or herself.

## chapter
# 28

MAURICE FOXMAN ARRIVED at the Connaught in good spirits. Being in the company of a younger man refreshed him, provided evidence that he was not alone in the business, that someone dependable and forthright stood with him. He judged Peter to be competent and thorough in the same way that he was. More and more Maurice had begun to think about the future, the fast-nearing time when he would no longer want to—nor be able to—conduct the business of Foxman and Company.

David was certainly not the man for the job. And Ellie lacked the steadiness required, the long-term commitment. He wondered if there was enough steel inside her. Still, they were both blood of his blood and eventually it would come down to them. Until then, someone had to run things or the firm would grow worthless. Downes might be that someone, the man who could save them all.

But he kept such thoughts to himself. That night over dinner in the hotel dining room, he confided to Peter his hope for a brighter future. "I've been giving a great deal of thought to these last bad sights. It occurs to me that in some way I may have wronged the Syndicate and Sir John. I can see where he might perceive some of my activities as being antithetical to

257

his interests. Certainly I never intended that. If I'm right, then I may have misjudged the man. After all, how different can he be from you or I, Peter? Let's concede, then, that I've offended him, given him cause to be angry. If so, he has delivered his message to me. He has inflicted his punishment, two poor sights in a row. Certainly that is sufficient. He must be satisfied, his ego salved, his anger assuaged. I am convinced that all that is behind us, a thing of the past."

"I still don't understand," Downes said. "A man of your standing, with your reputation for square dealing. How could it happen?"

Foxman provided an answer. "For a while, I allowed my own anger to rule my thinking. No longer. I'm convinced there is no vindictiveness in this affair. Matters got out of hand and I was not without guilt in that. Time settles all such things."

"Then you believe this sight will be normal?"

"I do, yes. If possible, we must make up for lost time, lost sales, and with that in mind I've put in a request for a larger buy than usual. Top-quality stones that will move quickly. If the response is appropriate, all will be as it was before."

Downes could see it; Maurice had been badly hurt, damaged in pride and pocketbook alike; and he was deeply afraid. And with cause.

That worried Downes. Company failures, when they came in the diamond world, came quickly, often with no warning. In a business constructed on daydreams and shifting values, disaster could set in without notice. Time might be running out on all of them. One way or another, he intended to get his rightful share.

In the morning, after breakfast, Downes escorted Maurice to the Rolls and watched him drive away. Then he returned to the suite and began making calls. He bought diamonds from half a dozen different sources, all supplied to him by Ralph Browning. Whatever amount he asked for he was granted, all purchases made on credit. He directed the purchases to be sent to a bank in Geneva, to be held there for subsequent reassignment. Delivery was to be immediate, payment within thirty days. All charged to P & D, Inc., Foxman and Company guarantor.

Midway through the morning, Downes began to experience

a new kind of fear, a cold, insistent fear that made him question himself and what he was doing. It was, he warned himself, almost too easy.

Mr. Severn, plump and pink as always, greeted Maurice Foxman outside the marble vault with his usual limp handshake before escorting him past the stone-faced guards into the room lined with stainless-steel vault boxes. Foxman seated himself at the long table covered with the soft black cloth.

"Foxman and Company," Severn announced, and one of the guards unlocked the appropriate vault and brought a carton no bigger than a shoe box to the table, setting it down in front of Foxman. The guard took up a position at one end of the table, Severn at the other.

For an extended moment the box shifted in and out of focus, as if seen through the wrong end of a telescope. Maurice felt apprehensive, as he had years before at his first sight; he remembered that fine short story by Stephen Vincent Benét and wondered which he was about to confront, the lady or the tiger.

His skull felt as if it were under continual assault, softening, swelling, his reactions slowed, his senses diffused. He braced himself against the pain and managed to open the box, the envelopes, scattering their contents on the black cloth.

A swift survey jolted him away from illusion, back to the new, harsh reality of his life. No more lies, no more deceptions; truth spread out before him in a glittering and virtually worthless array. The big stones were bad, the lesser ones worse; a collection that could not be marketed. Sir John had delivered the unmistakable message: the days of Foxman and Company as a force in the business were at an end. He was finished.

With trembling fingers, he returned each batch of stones to its envelopes, each envelope to the box. He fitted the cover onto the box and shoved himself erect, maneuvering himself in a series of short, jerky steps to face Severn. His voice sounded taut and thin in his ears.

"I wish to speak to Sir John."

Severn blinked once. "That will be impossible, Mr. Foxman. Sir John is unavailable."

"When will he be available?"

"One can never say."

"He's avoiding me. Why? What have I done?" Maurice became aware of the irregular beat of his heart and he felt weak, swaying slightly in place. "A man in my position, I don't deserve this sort of treatment."

"Are you feeling ill, Mr. Foxman?"

"The stones—these are trash. Useless and you know it. They can't be cut, they can't be sold. Useless, useless, useless."

"Would you like to rest?"

"An insult. An insult."

"Or a glass of water?"

The blood had drained from Foxman's face and his eyes became moist, unfocused. "You give me no choice."

"One always has a choice," Severn said. "To accept or not."

Maurice forced the words out from between gritted teeth. "I refuse the sight," and he staggered as though struck. One hand reached out for support, and he righted himself, held steady. "I shall not be treated in such a cavalier manner. I refuse the sight. I refuse."

"You have made your choice."

Maurice left, moving stiffly, struggling to maintain some semblance of dignity, Severn trailing him to the front door. Maurice turned to face him. "I have been in this business too long. Diamonds are my—I will not be dealt with as if I were some inferior creature. Tell Sir John . . ."

Severn interrupted with a sweeping gesture. "One does not tell Sir John anything. One consults Sir John. One offers suggestions. One informs him. Sir John tells the rest of us what we are to do. And he has ordered me to inform you, sir, that you and your company are suspended from the client list of the London Sales Office as of this date. Should you wish to make an appeal, a written application is in order. It will be passed up through the appropriate levels to Sir John's attention levels to Sir John's attention in good time. Good day to you, sir. Nice to see you again."

He stepped back inside and the doorkeeper closed the door, leaving Maurice Foxman alone and trembling on the street.

For Maurice, the flight back to New York was tedious and slow, an endless drain on his resources. He dozed occasionally, only to lurch into wakefulness, unable to locate himself in time or space. Memories darted through his mind, events and faces of his youth. Old dangers terrorized him once more and a cold sweat broke out on his brow. He felt weary, old, without energy or force. His body, and the life it had lived for so long, were burdens he no longer carried with ease or grace. A limousine was waiting at the airport and took him directly to his apartment.

A concerned Peter Downes turned Maurice over to his houseman and he helped Maurice into bed. Seconds later he fell into a deep sleep. When he awoke, dinner was waiting: broiled striped bass in lemon and butter sauce and asparagus, and a glass of Soave.

Afterward, he sat in a comfortable chair in the bedroom listening to a Rachmaninoff concerto on the stereo, his mind functioning with greater clarity now, seeing what had to be done. His processes had slowed and his body felt rested, if not relaxed. He considered every possibility open to him, measured each against the others, and when it all began to make sense, when he could find no flaws in his logic, he went back to sleep.

In the morning, he dressed himself. A dark gray suit with a shadow stripe, a white shirt, the collar smoothly starched and ironed, a pearl-gray silk tie. No sooner was he seated in his office behind his familiar walnut desk than his secretary entered carrying a mug of hot tea and a list of calls to be made.

He read over the names. "I'll call the Marquise from home this evening."

"I'll give you a note with her number before you leave."

"You do that."

"Mr. Kinard has called three times," she said.

Maurice tried the tea; it was much too hot. "Very well, shall we begin with Norman?"

She put the call through, handed him the phone and withdrew.

"Norman, good to hear your voice. I understand you've been trying to get me. I've been"—he hesitated—"abroad on business."

"Everything all right, Maurice?" The banker had a high-pitched voice with a faint vibrato, as if he'd once been an opera singer, now gone to age and a softening of the vocal cords.

Foxman pulled himself up straighter in his high leather chair.

There was a tired cast to his mouth and a pouchiness to his pale cheeks, loose folds of skin under his eyes. He worked the fingers of his hand in an effort to increase his circulation.

"Why not, Norman? Is everything all right with you?"

"Not exactly, Maurice."

"I'm sorry to hear that, Norman. How can I help?"

"There is a small problem, Maurice."

"Ah."

"The company's debt to the bank, Maurice. Some of my people are becoming nervous."

Foxman curled his fingers around the mug of tea. The warm ceramic was reassuring, making him feel the blood was running normally through his veins.

"Nervous, Norman? What are you saying to me?"

"I'm going to have to request some payment on the company's debt to the bank, Maurice. I'm sorry."

Foxman held himself in check. "Is there some difficulty at the bank?" Facts flashed onto the screen of his mind. Columns of numbers: credits, debits, income, overhead, profit if any. Numbers that were as much a part of him as his own name.

"A *substantial* payment, Maurice."

"Why suddenly at this time, Norman?"

"The debt, it's been climbing steadily."

An indication, Maurice told himself, of how effectively Peter had been doing his job. Thank God for that young man; his aggressiveness, his ability to go out in the marketplace and locate good stones would save them all. He started to reassure Kinard, explain what was happening, but the banker kept on talking.

"I've been hearing rumors, Maurice."

"About my company?"

"That your sights have been poor, three in a row, I've been told." More of Sir John's dirty work; twenty-four hours since the last offering and already the word was out. "Is it true, Maurice? Has the Syndicate cut you off?"

"A temporary misunderstanding, Norman. I intend to discuss this affair with Sir John in the next week or so, put it all right again."

"My people have done some checking, Maurice. Your expenditures are astronomical. I don't know how sales have been, but there is an abnormally inflated debt load."

"Twenty years, Norman. Surely you . . ."

"Maurice, please. Business is business."

"Have we ever had problems before?"

"Never. But I'm accountable to a board of directors, to the investors, to the examiners. There are procedures to follow."

"I need a little bit of time to take care of certain matters."

"I'm sorry. The bank is cutting back on your line of credit."

"How far back?"

"Fifty percent."

"That's outrageous, Norman."

"There's nothing I can do. If you fail to reduce the debt in the very near future, additional cuts will be made. Matters must not be permitted to get out of hand, Maurice."

"You understand this business, Norman. Is it the buys by P & D, Inc., that are troubling you and your people?"

"That's right, Maurice. You're the guarantor and . . ."

Maurice broke in. "Those buys are half in cash, half in thirty-day notes. As far as I know, all the notes were paid before the due dates."

"At first, yes. No longer. The size of individual buys has jumped upwards of half a million, one as high as a million. Totally on credit and with alarming frequency. I understand if you haven't been able to stay on top of this, Maurice. A man in your position has many responsibilities, many concerns and interests. It's understandable. But the game's a little too rich for my people, especially in light of the present condition of the market."

"Let me look into this."

"Good. You'll get back to me soon?"

"Within the week."

"Seventy-two hours, Maurice. That's all I can allow you."

"It's that serious?"

"I'm afraid so."

He put down the phone and rang for his secretary. "No disturbances, no calls, no interruptions of any kind. There's a great deal I have to think about, a very great deal."

During the next thirty-six hours, Foxman kept to himself. Except for a few overseas telephone calls, he saw no one, spoke to no one. He made notes, added up columns of figures, created financial projections for his company. Satisfied finally that he had reached a conclusion both workable and aesthetically gratifying, he repeated the process, making substitutions as he went along, testing one plan for another. Never finding the perfect solution to his problem, nor expecting to.

The hour-by-hour operation of the company went on without his supervision. Decisions requiring his attention went unmade. Auctions at which important collections of antique jewelry were put for sale went unattended.

David serviced showroom customers and Mattie managed the office, ordered supplies, put off paying bills for as long as she could. Peter tended the affairs of P & D, Inc., expanding his purchases to other names on Browning's list, piling up a substantial inventory and equally substantial debts.

On the morning of the second day after his return from London, Foxman summoned his sister-in-law to his office. She looked him over with frank concern.

"You don't look well, Maurice."

"Never mind me, Mattie. I'm fine."

"You're pale and drawn, you've lost weight. What's wrong?"

He waved the question aside. "When did I begin to need a keeper?"

"After all these years, I know when you're not feeling well, or if something's wrong."

"I'm a grown man, permit me to take care of myself."

She made a mocking sound. "You're more of a man than most. But you never did look after yourself the way you should."

He slumped back in the leather chair, gazing at her across the wide partners' desk. "It's been a long time, Mattie, for you and me, and still friends."

"Good friends."

"That's why I wanted to talk first to you."

"This affair with the Syndicate?"

"That, and the company debts."

"I've been concerned about that, too. You spoke to Kinard?"

"He's calling in some of the obligations, he's cutting short the credit line."

"You'll think of something."

He shook his head. "It gets harder and harder to fight. The

years, there's been so many of them. I'm too old to fight the battles, and I'm too tired."

"Old! Not you."

"Very tired, Mattie."

"Don't say that. You need a holiday. A checkup and a complete rest."

He told her what he knew; about the poor sights, the end of his relationship with IMM coupled with his inability to open up new sources, the rejection of his attempt to form a federation of dealers.

"That Downes," she muttered. "With his buying, he'll drive you into bankruptcy."

"You mustn't blame the boy. I thank God for Peter. What kind of inventory would we have without him? If he proceeds a little too quickly, well, he's young, impatient. Without his stones there would be no business for us to do."

"The only business I know about is the debts. I haven't seen much income."

"Peter knows what he's doing."

Does he? she wanted to say, and fought back the impulse. Where are the stones he's buying? Why isn't he selling them faster when he knows you need the income? But all she said was: "Talk to Peter, Maurice. The whole thing doesn't look right to me."

"I'll talk to him."

## chapter
# 29

THE LONG, LOW BUILDING sprawled over the flat landscape outside Johannesburg, stark white in the harsh sunlight, resembling a misplaced motel in need of a superhighway. This was the world headquarters of International Minerals and Mines, Ltd. Out of these offices were conducted the affairs of more than five hundred companies with a variety of public interests, but whose true—and often only—*raison d'étre* was the profit and well-being of the diamond operation.

Gold, platinum, silver and uranium were also mined by IMM companies. A consortium of transportation firms—ships, airlines, railroads—covered forty-three nations. Marketing, advertising, research; all commenced here. Factories and service organizations, retail stores, chemical plants, newspapers, magazines, an American movie company, two television networks; each an integral part of the global support system created by Sir John Messinger.

In air-conditioned chambers situated below ground level, security operations were conducted in spartan conditions. The floors were a shining black vinyl, the walls were painted a cool blue, the recessed lighting was bright but without glare. Tables and chairs were designed for practical uses and computer ter-

266

minals were attended by bright, intense young men and women.

From here orders were sent to black Africa, to England, France, Yugoslavia, the United States, Japan. Wherever diamonds were traded, IMM security was an active presence. Security agents traversed the world in behalf of the hydra-headed firm and Sir John, but few of them ever were summoned to the South African headquarters building. Even fewer of them ever met the man who commanded them. To most, he was a distant, shadowy figure whose name was spoken in hushed, reverent tones: Mr. Koenigsburg.

Born on a small farm near Capetown, Koenigsburg began his professional life as an armed guard at the Kimberley pipe, patrolling the rim of the great mine on the lookout for intruders. His orders: shoot to kill. Koenigsburg obeyed with rare zest: he killed five would-be poachers during his first year on the job, a record never equaled. His future was assured, and he advanced swiftly until he attained his current lofty position—Chief of Worldwide Security and Investigation, IMM, Ltd.

And now Keller had been called to meet Koenigsburg in a medium-sized room in one corner of the basement quarters, empty save for a small institutional table and chairs to match. The insistent hum of central air conditioning served as background for the occasion.

"Good trip, Keller?"

"The usual commercial flight, long and dull."

Koenigsburg, more than seventy years old, and still a towering figure, was heavy through the chest and shoulders, with long, bulging arms and hands scored with knobby veins. He inspected Keller with plain disapproval.

"No decent tailors in New York?"

Keller grinned appreciatively. "Pay being what it is in this outfit, I'm lucky to have a change of clothes."

"Are you applying for an increase in salary?"

"Why not?"

"Put it in writing and it will receive proper consideration."

Keller said nothing. Koenigsburg, he had learned, did things by indirection; he, Keller, had recently been awarded a raise in pay. Keller jerked his chin down in assent. It was all the thanks Koenigsburg expected or wanted.

"Sir John is unhappy," he said, in an almost unintelligible drawl. His accent had been twisted and altered by years spent living in such disparate locales as Chicago, Dublin, Monte Carlo, Lisbon. He was what he appeared to be, a professional policeman, humorless, suspicious, constantly on the lookout for trouble, convinced the next man he encountered might try to do him in. He was independent, tough and fair with the people who worked for him. He owned apartments in five countries and hotel suites were on permanent hire for his use in four others. He tried never to spend more than a few days in any one place and seldom announced in advance his travel plans. Work was all he cared about. He'd never married, never wanted to. He had no children, no living relatives. He missed nothing, he regretted nothing, he lacked nothing. He dealt with each day as it dawned and gave it very little consideration once it had passed.

"Yes," he said, "unhappy." He sought no response from Keller. He was merely providing information, preparing Keller for what lay ahead. "Trouble," he said. "Heads are going to roll. Sir John will kick arse, as you Yanks like to say." He didn't smile, he never smiled.

Keller waited; there was more to come.

"Folks around here are in a state, I tell you. Fact and rumor, bits and pieces of intelligence have put the big shots in a pretty snit. Which definitely includes the King of Diamonds. Himself flew in from London two days ago and has been raising the devil every since. All very proper and polite, he is, and whispery, but the populace is antsy and with good cause, I'd say. Which is why I sent for you, Keller, you get the picture?"

An answer was required. "What I've got are a few facts, a lot of talk and even more suspicions."

"Playin' it safe, ain't you? My number one genius investigator, turning bloody cautious on me, he 'as. Well, I say stuff it, mate. Caution ain't worth diddly-poo to me.

"Here it is, then. Smuggling's on the upside. Harm's being done to our people in increasin' amounts. Robberies, muggings, killings. Seven of our people have been hit on in the last six weeks. What the hell's goin' on? I say. What the hell's goin' on? Sir John says. Worst of all is that stones—rough and cut alike—have been oozing into the market in increasing numbers and we have not been able to track them down or put an end to the traffic. Don't like it a bit, Keller. Sir John don't like it a bit, also."

"Neither do I."

Koenigsburg glared and one lumpy hand curled up into an immense fist. "What're you doin' about it?"

"You flew me halfway around the world to ask me that?"

"Keller. Think of this as a war room. The enemy is out there. Attacking, always attacking. Getting stronger every day, you see. We are in a crisis situation, you and me. They are striking at the foundations of our lives. Crisis management, Keller, that's what we're about, Keller. Do you grasp the seriousness of what I am telling you?"

"Tell me you're not satisfied with my work. Tell me and I'll hand over my ID and my Air Travel Card. You want my job, you got it."

"I don't give raises to men I intend to fire. Anytime I want your job, I'll take it, all right. Remember that, Keller. The point is, from the information feeding into this office, I make the Foxman case to be at the center of our troubles."

Keller had come to the same conclusion. Which meant that Maurice Foxman, his reputation for lofty personal standards notwithstanding, was deeply involved. And Ellie, too.

"Sir John wants a firsthand report. Ever gone head to head with him before?"

"I met him two weeks after I was hired, that was all."

"That was ten years ago."

"Eight."

"Let's see now, you gave up on the New York cops. A homicide detective and you quit."

Quit; Keller hated the word. He had never quit on anything in his life. "I took an early pension."

"Any regrets, Keller?"

"Don't look over your shoulder, you once told me. There's nothing back there I want."

Koenigsburg checked his watch. "It's time. Be polite, Keller. Don't say more than you're asked for. I make myself clear?"

"I didn't miss a word you said."

Koenigsburg frowned as he led the way out. Keller had not agreed to his terms. As usual, the American was functioning on a long, loose rope of his own making. Always his own man. If he'd been any less of a man, Koenigsburg would have dumped him a long time ago.

## *chapter*
# 30

DAVID AND PETER met for drinks at Charley
O's. The lunch crowd had departed and the after-work drinkers
had yet to appear.

"What do you think?" Downes said, concerned about the
changing situation.

"About Maurice quitting? It was bound to happen, I suppose. My father is getting on in years."

Downes could not sort out his reactions to Foxman's announcement. Old ambitions played on his emotions and new
opportunities triggered a variety of future possibilities. He no
longer was sure of what he wanted.

"You'll be taking over," he said. It was meant more as a
provocation than a declaration of what he believed. What, he
wanted to know, was going on in David's mind? As Maurice's
son, was he privy to information Downes did not have?

"I don't think so."

"You're his only son."

"By birth, yes. But in no other way that matters. Business
is all Maurice ever cared about. He was always driven, always
working long hours, even on weekends. That may not all have
been his fault. My mother—what a beautiful woman she was,
gentle and refined, ephemeral. Looking back, I think she cared
for me more than she cared for Maurice, maybe that was the

root of the problem. And then she left him, taking me along. After that, I didn't see my father again for years. When we did get together, we were virtually strangers. Not that it matters much anymore, that's all part of the past. I'm glad he's getting out. It's time. The nature of the business has changed and Maurice has never been able to change with it, never able to keep up."

"You're young," Downes said. "You're more modern. You'll make the necessary changes when you move into his office."

David shook his head. "Even if Father offered it to me, I don't want the job. I'm not cut out for it. If Robert were still alive—but he's not. No, I was always a disappointment to Maurice and in many ways Robert was more Maurice's son than I could be."

"I can't believe that."

"It's true. I'm not saying Maurice stopped loving me. Just that he *appreciated* Robert much more."

"But you didn't appreciate Robert?"

"Robert had it all. He was a fine athlete, the great brain in school, and girls all flocked to him. He was good at everything he did and I was always less than I might have been."

"You underestimate yourself, David."

"Robert was very much like you, Peter."

"Are you saying you don't appreciate me, either?" It was offered lightly, with a brief, engaging laugh.

David took hold of the other man's arm. "You're my friend, you always will be. Although, who knows what might happen if you and Ellie get serious," he ended mischievously.

Downes decided to make things clear. "I'm serious now about Ellie. I want to marry her."

"Well. Congratulations."

"Not so fast. She keeps putting me off."

"She'll come around. No way she can do better."

"At least someone in the family thinks so."

David grinned. "She's quite a prize. Complicated, unpredictable, but a special case. Fiercely ambitious, isn't she? The woman doesn't know what it means to take a backward step."

"I think she's terrific."

"So do I. Better grab her off before someone else does."

"Oh, I intend to. Believe me."

\* \* \*

Peter and Ellie.

She lay still, commanding each set of muscles to go slack, caught up in a flood of contradictory emotions. She reached for the glass on the night table. The wine was no longer chilled and its bite was offensive to her tongue.

"I'm sorry," he said.

"It's all right." But it wasn't, not all right at all. He was an anxious lover, too desperate to please and too often unable to do so. Once it would have been enough to simply be with a man, to please him, to allow him free use of her body for his own pleasure, her reward coming out of that. No more. She needed something of substance. The words surprised her, made her conscious for the first time of the changes she was undergoing.

"Let me try again," he said with a petulant whine.

A small boy's annoyance, she noted, when things didn't go his way. She had changed, was changing; he was not. She had grown in the adversity she'd experienced, become more than she'd once been. All her life she had searched for the Truth; the ultimate experience, the purity of being. She had found instead the infinite ambiguities of life. The girl she had been was dead; long live the emerging woman.

"What's bothering you, Ellie?"

"I can't stop thinking about Maurice . . . Funny, but I'm no longer angry with him. I no longer resent the way he's treated me. My shortcomings, well, they're mine after all, aren't they? He gave me a number of opportunities to show what I could do and each time I failed. Every time he gave me the ball, I fumbled it. He was right to keep me at a distance. Has he told you yet?"

"Told me what?"

"That you'll be taking his place, of course. You are the logical choice."

It made so much sense to Downes that he'd been afraid to consider the possibility seriously. It had to be him, there was no one else. Not David, not Ellie. The invitation to rule would come soon enough and when it did it was vital that he be prepared. Once he took over, he would need all the help he could get. That's where David and Ellie came in. They could provide the glue that would hold his soon-to-be-acquired empire together. His marriage to Ellie, that would solidify his command even more. He reached for her.

She shivered and he mistook apprehension for desire. "You haven't answered my question."

"What question?"

"Has Maurice offered you the job?"

"Don't be ridiculous, Ellie. The job belongs to a Foxman. You or David."

She knew better. Peter was the anointed one, save only the announcement. A Gentile Moses would lead Foxman and Company out of the Wilderness to the Promised Land of solvency. And she, she would be just another anonymous member of the tribe, trailing in his glorious wake.

She sat up, the sheet falling away, making no attempt to conceal her nakedness. Her manner hardened and she spoke in a brisk, commanding voice.

"Peter, I fell in love with you, or at least I believed I did, which may amount to the same thing. You're marvelous-looking and you appeared to be kind and gentle, a compassionate man, which was a dramatic change for me. I made love to you because of the way you looked, Peter, as I am sure many other women have done. I felt affection and warmth toward you because of the way you acted, the kind of man you seemed to be. I appreciated you, Peter, and in some ways I still do. But I don't love you."

He flinched at her words. "But I want to marry you," he said, making it the ultimate argument in his favor.

She gazed gravely on him. "Maurice would approve of that. I'm convinced he's going to ask you to take over the company and run it and a marriage to me would certainly give the appearance of keeping it in the family."

"Then why not offer the job to you or David?"

"Maurice knows that David hasn't got what it takes and I, I have the ultimate failing, I am a woman."

"That's the feminist in you coming out."

"I'm a businesswoman. If I'm a feminist, it's in spite of myself. As for Maurice, he doesn't think I can cut it either. I know that I can and I know also that you cannot, Peter."

"Don't be too sure," he said without much force.

"Peter, I'm past the point of being kind for the sake of kindness. I won't indulge you. I won't cater to your major-league ego. There's something wrong with you."

That jarred him and he came up into a sitting position, face flushed, voice raised for the first time. "Wrong! There's nothing wrong with me."

She smiled wryly. "I'm afraid there is some weakness, a character flaw, something vital is missing, Peter. It shows up in bed, where you're all muscle and balls, all performance and not a drop of tenderness, no emotion. You say all the right words as if you've committed them to memory. But you feel nothing and everything I felt for you has been turned aside."

"I've never had any complaints before."

She laughed without humor. "Oh, you're good at what you do, Peter. But not because you feel anything, precisely the reverse—you feel nothing. And now neither do I. Making love with you is mechanical, technical—you do this, I'll do that, touch me here, I'll touch you there. It relieves the tension, Peter, but when it's over there are no residual good feelings, no emotions, no warmth.

"And it's not only in bed, Peter, that you fall short. The way you think, the way you talk, everything you do. Even that considerate manner of yours, as if you're trying too hard to make the right impression, to be good. I don't believe you, Peter. I doubt that I ever did."

He was afraid of where this was going, afraid that all his plans could be spoiled by this sudden display of strength and independence on her part. What if she undercut his position with Maurice? It might send everything down the drain, leave him without money, without a job, without a future. He wanted to fight back, to give the *appearance* of fighting back, but without offending her further.

"You're not being fair," he said.

"Listen to me, Peter, and listen good. Maurice likes you because you're a pal of David and because you agree with everything he says. You cater to his old-fashioned ideas about the diamond business and that reinforces his feeling that he's on the right track. Here you are, young enough to be his son, yet unlike me you don't insist on change, you don't make waves about women having a rightful place in the trade and Maurice thinks that's just terrific. He perceives you as a moral man functioning at the same high level that he does. But I know better, Peter, and if I were to tell Maurice that you're not much more than a hollow shell morally, that you're a cold and distant man going through the motions, that you're not much more than a mediocre fashion plate, you'd discover soon enough that blood is still thicker than water."

"You have no right to talk to me this way."

She ignored the protest and went on as if he hadn't spoken. "Let's assume Maurice is going to offer you the company, Peter. By now you must have realized that you're incapable of running it successfully by yourself. You'll need help."

"Yes, of course," he said quickly. "You. David. Whatever it takes."

"In this business you have to be smart, tough and ambitious to survive. You, Peter, are merely ambitious. You are after money and perhaps prestige, status. But for me, Peter, a company of my own, a sight of my own, are matters of life and death. I need to run my own business. I have to use my imagination, my intelligence, meet the challenges, exercise *power*. I want to go as far as my talent and my will and my courage will take me."

Breathing hard, the light playing on her bare breasts, she faced him. "Peter, you're not smart enough, not tough enough, you don't know enough. No way you can run the company without me."

He thought about Browning and Geis, about the scam, about all the things she didn't know. It was vital that he protect the scam, allow nothing to spoil that. She was right about the money; he craved money in large amounts more than anything else he could imagine, and he could imagine nothing he wouldn't do to get it.

"What do you want me to say?" he asked.

"Nothing, just listen. I'm going to offer you a deal."

He stared uncomprehendingly in her direction. What was going on behind that beautiful and suddenly impenetrable face? He had misjudged her totally, failed to recognize the steel core of the woman, failed to understand her determination, her resolute ambition. This new person—it frightened him.

"What deal?" he said simply.

"Here it is. Whatever equity Maurice gives you, you will turn over to me after an appropriate interval. I'll raise whatever cash is necessary to buy you out at a fair price/earnings ratio. When the time comes, you walk with a nice profit and you don't look back."

Downes thought it over. He was smarter than she gave him credit for, he told himself. His future with Foxman and Company was no longer at issue since the scam would leave the company firmly in his control.

He turned an injured, innocent visage toward Ellie. "I don't know why you're being so hard on me, darling. I have only had your best interests at heart. The bad feelings between you and Maurice, there's no reason for that to wedge us apart."

She quieted him with a gesture. "Make up your mind. Agree, and you're guaranteed a substantial amount of money. Refuse, and I'll make sure Maurice shuts the door behind you once and for all."

"I'm disturbed that you're acting this way. Whatever's bothering you, given enough time we can sort it out. The way I feel about you, Ellie, that's real, deep and real, sincere. Of course you're right, I could never run the company without you. Nor would I want to. So any arrangement you want to make is okay with me." A regretful smile curled his handsome mouth at the corners. "No need for you to threaten me, Ellie. No need for you to hurt me in order to achieve your ends."

She slid out of bed, turned toward him, hands on her hips. "Then it's settled."

"Except for one thing."

"And what's that?"

"Us, Ellie. What about us?"

That made her laugh. "You mean here, in bed?" She laughed again. "Well, Peter, you are a pretty thing and you do try so hard. With a little coaching, you may even improve your performance. I'm tempted . . ."

"You can depend on me," he said, reaching for her.

She stepped away, her expression implacable. "Not so fast. Tonight is over, right now there's nothing here I want."

## chapter
### 31

"FOXMAN! FOXMAN!" Sir John uttered the name at a high pitch and with considerable distaste. "Foxman and the others like him."

Unlike the rest of IMM headquarters, Sir John's office was neither spartan nor simple, designed instead to resemble a Victorian London sitting room. Gracefully hung draperies softened the harsh light streaming in through the narrow windows. Portraits of his ancestors decorated the walls, several in the muted style of an old Dutch master. A harpsichord occupied one corner of the room and leather-bound volumes filled the shelves along one wall. There was no desk, no file, no telephone in sight. A grouping of comfortable chairs surrounded a low, round fruitwood table on which stood sherry, hot coffee, tea and some small cakes. Koenigsburg and Keller declined the refreshments. Sir John, his back to the wall of books, spoke with controlled passion.

"Matters cannot continue as they are. Too much is at stake. Money aside, International Minerals and Mines employs thousands of men and women. People around the world look to us for their livelihoods, for guidance, for support. This company was organized by my grandfather and he bequeathed it to my father, who, in turn, taught me what diamonds could mean to this world. When the time is right, I shall deliver control to my sons. Until then, the legacy is mine, the obligation is mine, the power is mine to exercise as I see fit." His eyes raked the room as if daring anyone to disagree.

"I have been forced to cut him off, you see."

Keller understood; Foxman had been denied his regular sight. Sir John was going to drive the old man out of the business.

"Am I to assist this man in his revolutionary attempt to destroy what has been built so laboriously over so many years? Am I to cooperate in my own demise? Not a bit of it. Actually, Maurice is a charming fellow. Fine to look at, proud of bearing, and exceptionally intelligent, a lover of good music. They all are, though, isn't that the case? Intelligent, I mean, cultured, refined. Those Hebrews?

"But troublesome. Men like Foxman with their ingrained Old Testament notions of absolute right and absolute wrong. They cause too much trouble."

Keller found it hard to believe how anti-Semitic this Semite could be. A story going round for years insisted that during the Second World War Sir John had actually dealt face to face with the Nazi Goebbels. All for the survival and profit of the Syndicate. Listening to him now, Keller could almost believe the rumor.

Sir John swung Keller's way, a glint of amusement in his eyes, as if able to penetrate to the most secret portions of Keller's mind, as if able to read his thoughts. "They tell me you're a hard case, Keller. But smart, smarter than most. I've read some of your reports, masterpieces of reasoned knowledge. Each word deliberately chosen, omitting as much as you leave in. The work of a careful man. Tell me some of the things you've left out about Foxman."

Keller, a man seldom afraid, grew afraid. The man standing across the room teetered at the edge of megalomania, dangerous in the way that only a man who possessed limitless power could be dangerous, driven by demons and devils alien to most other human beings.

*What do you give to a man who has everything?*

*More.*

*More than ordinary men can imagine.*

"We are under attack. Rebellious men are in the field. Hostile, avaricious men, insidious schemers who would bring us all down, destroy the system. Diamonds are what they are after. Diamonds—the centerpiece of our firm.

"I am on to Foxman's devious ways. His subterfuges, his attempts at sabotage, his efforts to weaken my authority. He intends to make war on us. Recently he was in council with other dealers of a like mind—Halevi, Greenfield, Steinberg. Men of influence and considerable power and, by no coincidence, all are Jews. They plot against me, oh, yes. But I will not allow them to succeed."

Keller spoke without expression. "I submitted that report."

"So you did. A clever bit of detective work. Have you commended your man, Mr. Koenigsburg? I do it on your behalf."

"I said nothing about making a war," Keller said. "Nothing about a plot. Just a meeting of like-minded men, men of similar interests."

Sir John's face was tight, his eyes still, his mouth downturned. "What a nasty lot these people are, sneaking around the back alleys of our world to do their dirty deals. Foxman has been acquiring stones from a variety of sources worldwide. Peculiar sources. Dealers new to the scene. Men without credentials, men working out of their pockets. Did you know that, Keller? Apparently you did not. His purchases have gone steadily upwards."

Koenigsburg filled the ensuing silence. "From buys of a few thousand right up the line to a million per. The total at my last reading was sufficient to sell at retail at about thirty-five million dollars."

Sir John broke in harshly. "Thirty-five million, Keller. What are we to make of that?"

"All done," Koenigsburg went on, "through P & D, Inc., a subsidiary."

"In which," Sir John said, "son David Foxman is a partner with a certain Peter Downes."

"I know about Downes," Keller said.

"There's more," Koenigsburg said. "Foxman's nephew, the one who was shot, he was buying colored stones as well as diamonds out on the fringes of the trade."

"I know about that." Keller bit the words off. "It's no secret."

"Nevertheless," Sir John said, "an indication that Foxman has altered his normal way of doing business. Branching out, so to speak. Expanding beyond IMM control."

"The man is fighting to survive."

Koenigsburg scowled. "His niece is in the field. There's talk of creating a bourse of her own."

"Okay, Foxman's buying. Everybody supplements supplies and . . ."

Sir John cut him off. "An honest broker buys and he . . . *sells*. Buying *and* selling, that is our game. Foxman is not selling. Foxman hoards his purchases. Why?"

"Foxman is trying to force prices upward," Koenigsburg said. "Create a seller's market, to his own advantage."

"Is it possible?"

"If the numbers are right. Follow this scenario: Foxman drives prices up and at a certain point sells off his stock. If his inventory is large enough, the shock to the market is such that prices soon plummet, damaging everybody, small and large alike. Except those who got in and out at the right time, those in on the conspiracy. What a tricky affair, a well-conceived and malicious effort to undercut IMM's supremacy. I cannot allow that to happen."

Keller had hoped to keep his counsel until he could make a stronger case. The way things were going, he had no choice.

"Foxman is as much a victim as anybody."

Koenigsburg jumped in, voice loaded with threat. "Sir John spelled it out for you, Keller."

Sir John said tonelessly, "Go on."

"The possibilities you sketched out, you're right. Except for one key element, the danger doesn't come from Foxman."

"Who then, Keller?"

"Russ Almaz," Keller answered.

"Nonsense!" Koenigsburg burst out.

"Whoever killed Robert Foxman was after the diamonds he had bought."

"Nothing was taken. He was carrying when the police found him."

"Those stones came from a Lebanese trader, name of Kham-oury. All very legitimate. But in a hollow walking stick, there were Soviet stones, bought from a man named Tarassuk."

"I'm unfamiliar with that name," Sir John said.

Koenigsburg spoke out reluctantly. "A free-lancer who dealt in Russian goods, picking up whatever he could from the Soviet overflow . . . he was killed."

"Shot," Keller said, "with a twenty-two-caliber gun, the same gun that killed Robert Foxman. The description of the killer matches that of the man who tried to take me out in St. Tropez."

Koenigsburg swore. "Why wasn't I told?"

"I think the shooter is a Soviet hit man."

"Don't ask me to accept that soft premise, Keller. Why would Moscow turn on me? We have a deal."

"Unless," Keller offered, "it is in their self-interest to do so."

Sir John paced the room, circling like some voracious black bird in flight. He spun about, pointing accusingly at Keller.

"You tell me Moscow has gone rogue. I don't believe that. Smugglers have always existed. Thieves. Men on the fringes of our world. Russian stones are no different from any others, some always fall through the net and there are always men who live off the droppings."

Keller drew a verbal line connecting Vadim Lukas to Tarassuk, Tarassuk to Tatiana, Tatiana to Harry Geis.

"Geis!" Sir John exclaimed. "Another strange name."

"An insignificant operator on Forty-seventh Street. Some-how involved with the Russians. Somehow connected to Peter Downes."

"The same Downes that's in with Foxman?"

"The very same."

"Are you putting Foxman in league with the Russians?"

"No, sir. No one knows the Russians better than you, Sir John. You've dealt firsthand with them for years. You know how they think."

Koenigsburg watched and listened. Keller had usurped his role in all this and instead of resenting it, he was pleased, proud of his man.

Sir John sat down, crossing his legs, a precise, almost effete movement. "The Soviets are a strange people, capable of any action, no matter how extreme or outrageous. Treaties are devices to them, held to only as long as they are profitable. Contracts are to them without sanctity. I have never entirely dismissed Moscow as a threat to IMM, never. But why at this particular time should they move against me? What motivates them?"

"If the Russians choose, they can sabotage the industry, am I right?"

"Go on, Keller."

"Moscow possesses an unlimited number of diamonds. Stones out of Siberia, the new pipe in the Urals, the production of artificial product."

"Flood the market, you're saying?"

"Who can stop them? They, not Foxman, could drive prices down, destroy the foundation on which the industry stands."

"To what end?"

"Politics," Keller said, and, saying it, decided it was an inadequate answer.

"If you are right, if Moscow chose to, they could have dumped their own product at any time. Why not earlier?"

"Because they don't want to destroy the market. And that's why they need Foxman. They need to disguise the source of their stones. Ruin the market and they destroy the value of their own mines."

"You're suggesting there has been some change, some reason to make them act at this particular moment in history."

"The way I read it is this—the Russians don't want to surface behind a dumping movement, it would cause people to turn away from them. They have limited objectives and they mean to achieve them surreptitiously."

"How?" The word leaped out of Sir John's mouth, hard, stinging. When Keller could provide no sound answer, Sir John went on with renewed certainty. "I concede the point, the Russians could ruin IMM, if they chose to. But in so doing, as you pointed out, Keller, they would ruin their own industry. Diamonds bring increasingly large amounts of hard currency into the country, nearly a billion dollars a year at last count. The Russians, they are practical men. Hardheaded businessmen. They would make the world's best capitalists. They will do nothing to injure themselves. If I am to accept this theory of yours"—Keller opened his mouth to speak but Sir John gestured for him to be silent— "what motive do they have? Give me something that makes sense. What will it profit them, something that equals what they currently receive in money and other benefits? Can you do that, Keller?"

"Not yet."

"Until you can, I'll hold on my own point of view. Men like Maurice Foxman, double-dealing, hypocritical, there lies the cancerous growth eating away at the business. I intend to exorcise that evil once and for all."

"Give me a little more time," Keller said. "If I'm right— let me keep trying."

Sir John turned away. "Do as you must," he said, his voice heavy with despair. "As shall I."

## chapter
## *32*

HE SUMMONED HER INTO his office at the end of the workday. The lights were out and an eerie stillness permeated the place.

"I want to discuss my decision with you," he said, a note of apology in his voice she'd never before heard.

"You don't have to explain."

"Less an explanation than a catharsis, my dear, a cleansing of old guilts. As you know, I no longer have my London sight. Even more, stories about me and my business practices run wild up and down the street. Last night, at the Diamond Club, men I've known for years watched me out of the corner of their eyes, as if I were a thief. There are rumors that I was caught cheating the Syndicate—that I was selling off stones bought for manufacture in the boxes in which they came, all for a quick profit."

A quick stab of sympathy went through her. Maurice was a proud man: his business, his art collection, his widespread cultural interests, his chairty work; but his reputation was his most precious possession and he had protected it and enhanced it throughout his lifetime. That anyone could suspect him of underhanded behavior was indeed a torture.

"No one who knows you would believe that."

"If only that were true. For many people, it is easier to believe the worst of others, especially their friends. To discover the flaws in another man, the foibles and hypocrisies, can provide a great deal of pleasure, a larger sense of one's own moral superiority.

"I have been aware of some of the rumors for some time now. As you know, my sights have been primarily manufacturing sights. I buy mainly for manufacturing and for cutting. The whispers have gone around and nothing I said or did could kill them. A substantial number of my customers have taken their trade elsewhere and now Kinard has demanded payment on my debts. This morning he called in my line of credit entirely."

"After all these years!"

"My account with Morgan—most of their customers have to guarantee their debts with a lender. I have not had to do so for a very long time. Today they insisted that I personally guarantee every penny outstanding."

"That's unconscionable."

"Ellie, diamonds have made me a wealthy man. My personal fortune is slightly in excess of ten million dollars. But company debts amount to much more than that. Even if I were to put up my own money, it falls short of what's needed. In taking away my sight, Sir John has taken away my ability to function competitively. He has taken away my reputation as well.

"I have always stood up the way I believed a man should, done the best with what I had. Life for me has always been a never-ending war. And in the end, I've lost. There is no way I can continue. No reason for me to go on."

"I won't accept that," she said urgently, frightened by the dismal picture he was painting. "Let me help. We'll fight back. You and David and me. I promise you, one day we'll win."

A melancholy smile lifted his mouth at the corners. "I'm not leaving a thriving enterprise. I have dug a deep pit for us all and it is now up to you to find your own way out."

Her vision blurred and there was a distant ringing deep inside her head. "I don't understand."

"From this day forward, the affairs of Foxman and Company are in your hands, my dear. You are to be the new chief operating officer of the firm. You are going to take my place."

*chapter*
# 33

SHE WEPT.

And longed for him to cradle her in his arms and comfort her and allay her fears and the long-festering resentment she'd felt. But he made no move in her direction, offered no gentling words to bridge the gap between them. He waited and watched and when she ceased crying he spoke in a grave but gentle voice.

"You will want to know what brought me to this decision since for so long it appeared I meant to keep you away from the seat of power."

"Oh, yes," she said, regaining her composure. "Please."

"I recognized your ambitions a long time ago. You asked for this job. You argued for it. But you never truly worked for it. You insisted you had a right to authority but failed to prove that you could accept responsibility. You never earned it by your deeds, my dear.

"In a business like this, there is so much at stake. There is potential for immense profit, yes, and along with that potential goes an equally substantial responsibility for the lives and futures of the people who work for us. Managers of the shops, clerks, cutters, couriers, the people at the factories, the salesmen, bookkeepers, lawyers, stock boys, the people in the mail room. Foxman and *Company,* it exists because I willed it into being, a community of workers bound by a common need and a common goal. Call it an old man's ego, but I want it to continue after I leave, after I die.

"Shall I tell you when I began to change my mind about you?"

She nodded, unable to speak.

"When you left me, left the company, it was evident that you had made a gargantuan leap ahead in your personal development. You sailed out of the safe harbor on your own; you cut the cord finally. You chose to function as an independent person, no longer merely as Maurice Foxman's niece."

"I haven't accomplished very much, I'm afraid."

"You put yourself on the line. Took chances. When you failed to achieve the results you were after, you tried something new and different. You showed imagination, courage, persistence. You made a commitment when you opened your own office. And an even bigger commitment when you started up your own bourse."

"Only a very few dealers have expressed interest. No one's actually signed up."

"But what a daring concept. A woman operating a bourse for the first time. I imagine that created a great deal of talk at the London Sales Office. The bourse is real, it exists, because you willed it into existence. What excitement it is to nurture a dream and bring it to life. Nothing compares."

"I believe I can still make the bourse work. Not much next to the bigger exchanges, but a sound and solid operation."

"Given enough time, I'm sure you can. But you're going to have to choose, Foxman and Company or your own bourse. The choice is yours." She started to speak but he cut her off. "There's one more thing, the final and most important argument *you* made for following in my footsteps. The Chamblay choker."

"That was not one of my best moments."

"On the contrary. You made a mistake."

"Which was rectified, thanks to you."

"And then you pursued it to its logical end. You went back to Jeanette Manière, you convinced her against all odds to permit you to sell the Chamblay for her, and this time you completed the transaction properly. Jeanette was immensely

cheered by your competence—her words. She admires you
greatly and informs me that you are a young woman of many
positive gifts.''

"You spoke to her?"

"I did and agreed with her estimate of you. When I learned
what you had done, I realized that you had taken charge of
your own destiny, that you had turned a corner in your development, in your life."

"I owe a great deal to the Marquise."

"You've earned this chance. Now what do you say, will you
accept my offer?"

She tried to clarify her thoughts. ''There's David,'' she said
after a while.

"David may be resentful at first, although I doubt it. Eventually he will be grateful that his future will be assured under
your leadership."

She sat up straighter, used both hands to fluff the clouds of
shimmering hair. ''What about Peter? He certainly believed
you were going to name him as your successor.''

"In my judgment, he's a bit of a maverick. Best suited to
working on his own. Recently, I've begun to wonder—did I
let him stray too far? Early on his buys were well within company guidelines. I inspected the first two or three batches myself. The stones were well chosen. Since then, however, he
has stepped up his activities sharply, and in one sense that's
good. We needed the product. But he has contributed mightily
to our current debt problem. You will have to restrain Peter's
aggressiveness, harness his drive, curb his tendency to go too
far. You will have to develop your own manner of dealing with
him. With all the difficulties attached to the business."

She controlled her breathing, trying to slow her heartbeat,
remembering their last confrontation, and how unnecessary it
had been. At the same time, productive, she reminded herself,
reaffirming her belief in the soundness of her instincts and her
willingness to deal with problems as they arose.

"I will handle Peter."

He pressed the heel of his hand to his temple as if to counter
some deep pain. ''Life is seldom comprehensible and that may
be the greatest lesson of all. Understanding arrives reluctantly,
often out of anguish and disappointment. I've made too many

mistakes in my private life to attempt to give advice. You must make your own decisions. There is one thing you must do— you must sell the inventory Peter has created as soon as possible. Pay off the company debts and at least get even. Not even my personal fortune can accomplish that.

"Be cautious when you sell. Don't give an impression of panic. Go slow, steady, stretch out the sales. We would not want to flood the market or undermine the price structure. Once you've sold off, once you've gotten the company back on its feet, it will be up to you to carry on from there. Use your imagination, my dear, to put Foxman and Company back to the level it once enjoyed. With your intelligence and your flair for the dramatic, you may do much better than I ever did."

"I doubt that very much."

"Well, I no longer have any doubts, about you, that is. You have the ability to go as far as you wish in this business."

"I don't know, without a sight."

"Nothing I do will convince Sir John to relent. The Foxman sight is no more. One day you may be able to break through his pettiness and his biases, convince him to recognize your professional excellence. When that happens, who knows, you may yet become the first woman to win a sight. It's in your hands, Ellie. If you want the job, that is."

*chapter*
## 34

SHE REMAINED IN HER OFFICE late that night, going over everything that had taken place, struggling to make sense of it all. She understood as never before how Maurice had studied her activities from a distance, his guidance wise and subtle. He had exposed her to the diverse possibilities of the business, had allowed her to learn what worked for her and what didn't. All the contacts she had made, they were his contacts. All her skills were refinements of his. All her knowledge about diamonds had been passed along by Maurice, directly or indirectly. And when things had gone wrong, he had always been around to bail her out.

Without that familiar safety net, who would save her from future disasters? From now on, there would be only herself to depend on. It would have to be enough.

The minutes dissolved into hours, interrupted periodically by the sound of the telephone ringing. Darkness had settled over the city and still the phone rang every fifteen minutes or so. Peter, trying to reach her. Or her mother. Ellie wasn't prepared to talk to either one.

One more call and it sent her out into the street, walking east, turning uptown on Madison Avenue. Cutting across Fifty-sixth Street, she basked in her relative solitariness, the streets unusually quiet.

New York was a good place for her to be, her life privileged and generally rewarding. She dined in the best restaurants, enjoyed the theater, the opera, concerts, the long, slow Sunday afternoons wandering through museums. She traveled by taxi or rented limousine and understood that she was constantly shielded from the horrors of city life visited on those less fortunate. The city was her home and her workplace, her playground, and she enjoyed its kinetic rhythms, charged by its nervous vitality. She was of that class of people for whom New York was an ongoing party, quirky and expensive, a party only glimpsed at by the rest of the city.

Crossing Park Avenue, she realized she was hungry. At home, a refrigerator with some week-old yogurt, eggs, skimmed milk and peanut butter. That, and a long, lonely evening. She wasn't prepared for either.

Benihana ahead. Inside, a Japanese woman in a kimono escorted her to a seat at an empty hibachi. A waitress brought her a drink and took her order. She set herself against her hunger and willed the chef to appear and prepare her dinner.

A shadow materialized beside her, settling onto the closest chair. A low male voice ordered a scotch and water and declared that he was about to starve if not soon fed. Good, she thought, hoping that would bring on the chef. The voice was familiar.

New York men. The gravelly sound of them, city accents highlighted by a confidence that often slid over into arrogance. Live-wire types who existed on gall and guts and sometimes not much else.

The shadow raised his glass and drank. "Hits the spot! What's that you're drinking?"

Another lover, she remarked to herself, the voice insistent, penetrating, persisting in its familiarity. New York men.

"Vodka and tonic," she said. "And that ends the conversation."

His laugh was tinged with irony. "Must be the business. Diamonds do give a woman a cutting edge."

Keller; that voice, the distinctive cast to his eyes, to the set of his mouth, to the way he spoke. She was about to send him away when the Japanese chef appeared, a culinary samurai in white, cutting knives at the ready. He worked rapidly. Mushrooms and onions onto the already hot hibachi. To one side, a pile of shrimp, beginning to sizzle. The chef wielded his blade with speed and finesse; he sliced, he chopped, he lifted and turned, he speared.

"Wouldn't want to mess with this guy," Keller said.

"Leave me alone."

"No harm in a little friendly conversation."

"You're the enemy."

"You got me all wrong."

"Go away."

"What do you say to a truce? A break for rest and recreation."

"Unconditional surrender, those are my terms." She shifted around in a succession of herky-jerky movements. "Get your boss off my uncle's back."

"Lady, I am low man on the totem pole."

"Leave us alone."

"It isn't my intention to hurt you."

"You and your friends already have."

"You want to know who killed your brother? You want to know why?"

"My uncle knows, I know—the Syndicate."

Keller raised his glass. "Not so." He drank. "I'll give you this—Sir John's got it in for guys like Foxman. He makes them out to be too freewheeling, too independent, doing business however they want to. He doesn't like that, okay. But when it comes to knocking them off, that's not his style."

"My brother's dead and so are other good men."

"That doesn't mean the Syndicate's behind it."

"Who else?"

"A lot of things are happening."

"Such as?"

"I'm not prepared to say, not yet. Let's talk about something else."

"Okay. Why are you following me?" She went to work on the shrimp. They were hot, spicy and delicious. "Or are you going to claim this meeting is a coincidence?"

He watched her eat. She attacked the food with unabashed zest; he liked that. "If you wanted Japanese, you should've told me. I know a spot on Second Avenue, nothing better east of Tokyo."

"You were following me."

He killed off his drink and chewed on some shrimp, talking around them. "Following you is good work. I like the outfit. Flannel, is it?"

"*Silk* flannel."

"Nice shirt, too."

"A tunic blouse." The chef served the steak and vegetables. "You're not much on style, Keller. Maybe you're better at your job."

"A man does what he can."

She glanced quickly his way. The challenging tilt of his chin. He was having a good time at her expense. Peter would never have mocked her, it wasn't his way. He was polite, even courtly at times, anxious to please. Not Keller. The name fit; hard and unbending.

"Steak's okay," he said. "Onions are great."

He *was* mocking her; *bastard*.

"Take Chinese cuisine," he said.

"What about it?"

"Infinite variety. Subtle. Something for every taste. I prefer Japanese myself."

"What are you after, Keller?"

"A tranquil meal, that's all. Tasty, nourishing, along with some stimulating conversation."

"Is that what we're having, a conversation?"

"Two people talking to each other equals conversation. Speaking of two, everything going smoothly with you and Peter Downes?"

"Stay out of my private life, Keller."

"You've been on my mind lately."

"Save it, Keller."

"When we finish up here, let's take a walk."

"Too dangerous."

"When I was a kid I would walk everywhere at night. No sweat, never any trouble. I lived in the Bronx . . . ah, nothing stays the same. What about a movie?"

"You're wasting your time."

"Used to be fifteen cents for a double feature. Loew's 167th

Street, the Luxor, the Earl, Loew's Paradise, the Ascot. The Paradise had a sky for a ceiling complete with stars and clouds that moved."

"And you necked under the stars with your girlfriend."

"Never had a girlfriend, not then."

"I don't believe that, either."

"Cross my heart. Girls were too much for me. I felt uncomfortable around them. Scared."

"Scared, you!"

He grinned sheepishly. "So I grew up. I changed."

"I noticed."

"Getting to you, huh?"

"Forget it, you're still one of the bad guys."

"I've got a pretty good fix on who the real enemy is. He's my enemy, too."

"Even if you're right, what's that supposed to make us?"

"Allies. Pals. Good buddies."

Why was she feeding him straight lines? "No way I'm going to let you suck me in. Finish your steak and take off. There's nothing here for you, Keller."

"Walk you home?"

"Haven't you heard a word I said?"

"The city can be dangerous at night."

"I'll take my chances."

"Let's do it for the company. What've you got to lose?"

A great deal, she warned herself. "I'm not so sure I can trust you, Keller."

His smile was lazy and winning, the smile of a man about to get his own way. "Sure you can. As much as anybody you're likely to meet in a Japanese steak house this time of night."

*chapter*
# 35

SHE EXAMINED HER FEELINGS. Confusion, fright, titillation; what an odd man he was. At the entrance to her building he had stopped, turned her by the shoulders so that she faced him squarely. The act was so unexpected, so totally dominating, the controlled power in those big hands leaving her helpless in his grip. A fleeting softness faded into his eyes and he released her. He spoke in a low, caressing voice. "Good night, Ellie."

Not so much odd as different, she amended, thinking about him when she was alone in her apartment. Unlike any man she had ever known. She reached out for the young boy he once was, for the uncertain adolescent, afraid of girls. It was impossible to visualize him afraid of anything, he was so much a man who traveled without fear. Strength was his dominant feature, a strength that kept danger at a distance.

She wanted to know more about him, what had shaped him. What people were preeminent in his life? What events and influences had made him become the tough Keller she knew him to be, as well as the gentler, vulnerable man he had shown her tonight? She had found him to be a man of intelligence and wit, with a quietly ironic sense of humor, with an oddly sympathetic charm.

The telephone interrupted her ruminations; it was Mattie.

"Are you all right?" her mother began.

"Just got in."

"I can come over, if you like."

"No, thanks, I'm too tired."

"Have you reached a decision yet?"

"About Maurice's offer, you mean?"

Being with Keller had put it out of her mind. His presence had been overriding; she could feel it still. Suddenly he had become special: Why? Nothing he had said, surely. Nor done. What was it about him?

"Ellie!"

She brought herself back to the present. "I'll put up some tea, if you want to come over."

Mattie, anxious always to be involved in her daughter's life, said, "I'm on my way."

Mattie arrived fifteen minutes later. Long enough for Ellie to have showered and donned a long green Mandarin robe embroidered with gold and red dragons. Long enough for the tea to steep.

They sat at opposite ends of the long couch in the living room and Mattie inspected her daughter with a practiced eye. "They say the only thing worse than not getting what you want is getting what you want."

Since Robert's death, Mattie had existed in the grip of a pervasive and unrelenting guilt, convinced that in some unidentifiable way she had been responsible for his murder. Some forgotten failure as a mother, a failure of nerve on her part while raising him that caused him to take unnecessary risks with his life, some genetic disorder that she had passed on to him, leaving Robert weak and susceptible to assault. Now, in whatever way possible, she intended to shield her daughter from danger.

Ellie stared without expression at her mother.

"Well," Mattie said. "Isn't this what you wanted? A company of your own?"

A vision of Keller's bony face came drifting into Ellie's view, strangely appealing and mocking. What right had he to intrude on her life? How dare he question her about Peter? She hoped he was wrong about Peter, but she feared that he wasn't.

"Damn!" she said aloud, and the image of Keller fragmented and was gone.

"What is bothering you, Ellie?"

"Nothing is simple."

"A discovery that ranks with Marco Polo's discovery of noodles in China."

Ellie smiled grimly. "I had dinner with a man this evening, not Peter."

"Everyone has to eat."

"Don't you understand? Peter and I are *involved*."

"Involved? It means so much more today, so different than when I was your age. Does he want to marry you?"

"I don't want to marry him."

"Still, you're *involved*? Involved, what a complicated word. Oh, dear, I am so old-fashioned. So, tell me about your dinner companion. Are you also involved with him?"

"I barely know him."

"That, I'm guessing, is relatively unimportant. Whoever he is, he's made an impression on you. What is the phrase people use now—he's gotten to you."

"Yes, I suppose he has," Ellie said. "He's a strange man."

"How is he strange?"

"Keller is unlike any man I've ever met."

"Does he have a first name, this Keller?"

"He's never told me, he must have."

"But you don't know it. *That* is strange."

"I suppose it is."

"Tell me about Keller."

"He's a rough-cut, the edges left unfinished. Full of contradictions. There's a concealed part of him, something he always keeps to himself."

"A very private person."

"Yes, but you can also see to the center of him, to where his strength comes from. There's a tightness about Keller, explosive, ready to go off at any minute."

"Sounds like a dangerous man to have for any enemy."

"I think you're right."

"But good for a friend, from what you say."

"Yes. I believe he would be a very good friend."

"Is that what you want from him—friendship?"

"I don't know. Anyway, there's Peter."

"Are you in love with Peter."

"Love! Lately I've begun to believe I've never had a truly loving relationship with a man. Passion, yes. But love—I don't know."

"This Keller, he has got you upset."

"I feel . . . traitorous, as if I'd betrayed Peter by talking to Keller. You don't approve, do you? You don't even understand."

"For heaven's sake, Ellie, give me a little credit. I'm not a complete wimp. There have been complications in my life."

"Not like this."

"You think you're the first woman ever to get caught between two men?"

"You?"

"You're too old to be surprised that your mother is also a woman. I haven't always been an old lady with bleached hair and a map of wrinkles. Because of all the horrors, I've tried to put my youth behind me. But you can't deny the past forever."

"Mother, you surprise me."

"I have come to understand a great many things recently. You saw Maurice as your father's enemy, didn't you? Certainly that is the picture Emil painted."

"Not so much an enemy anymore. More of an obstacle. He clings to notions and ways that are out of sync with life the way it is lived today, with my needs, my desires."

"And me, did you see me, also, as an enemy?" When Ellie hesitated, Mattie went on. "I understand, if you did. I always defended Maurice and stood against your father. That must have seemed like a terrible betrayal to you."

"And to Daddy," Ellie added quietly.

Mattie sighed and nodded heavily. "I know that now."

"In his lofty way Maurice cloaked his real intentions toward you, and later toward me, which was to use us in subservient positions in the business and in the family, to keep us in our places, as he saw it."

"I know that now."

"You do?"

"Even a mother learns," Mattie said ruefully. "Oh, yes,

Maurice took care of us, all of us, and at the same time imposed his will on us, his power. For so very long I was threatened by your father's ideas, and yours. I had experienced enough danger, taken enough risks. I resented his efforts to change things, I wanted to remain in a safe berth in Maurice's harbor. Yes, I betrayed your father, not by making love to his brother, but by sharing his attitudes, his beliefs, and by rejecting everything Emil valued. And when your father was demeaned and frustrated because he was forced to work for Maurice, he received no comfort from me, only more criticism, more opposition." She snuffled and looked away. "I've made an awful botch of things, haven't I?"

Ellie responded brightly. "You've come a long way. We both have."

She embraced her mother and they laughed together and soon they were weeping, arms about each other. Presently they separated and Ellie sat back and drank some tea.

"This is a momentous occasion," she said. "My feelings toward Maurice, my anger—there's no way I can reconcile the way I feel with what he wants of me."

"Are you sure you want to do this?"

"Considering what you've just told me, I thought you'd be pleased."

"Why?"

"Why? The reason is obvious. Maurice has used me as he used you. Now, when he needs me—well, I don't need him."

"Ah, revenge is what you're after."

Ellie thought of her conversation with Peter, of the arrangement she'd forced on him. Yes, revenge had been part of it, the desire to take over the company despite Maurice's best efforts to keep her outside. But when he offered her the job he had subverted her plan and now she intended to pay him back.

"Is that so bad? He's hurt me, hurt all of us for a very long time.'

"Your uncle is not an evil man, simply a misguided one. He understands that he's made mistakes and he's trying to rectify them, as best he can. Take that away from him, Ellie, and you'll damage yourself at the same time."

"You're telling me to accept the job?"

"I'm telling you to do what's in your best interests and in the best interests of the family. No one else can do the job the way you'll do it. Not David, not your friend Peter, no one Maurice can bring from the outside. If Robert were still here, he could not do it as well as you. Yes, I'm telling you to take the job. You're the best of us all, Ellie, the one we can all depend on."

A nagging thought ricocheted around the inside of Ellie's skull: to accept Mattie's advice would be to somehow betray the memory of her father.

## chapter
## 36

"WE DID IT!" Peter Downes cried exultantly. "Fifty million dollars!"

"Mazeltov, Peter." Geis arranged a taunting expression on his pinched face. "Today you are a man."

Downes sobered instantly. Harry's sarcasm, his mocking tone, his blatant insults were all a prod under Downes's skin. There were times he longed to pick Harry up and shake him, prove to him once and for all the limits of his freedom. But there was something about Geis that inhibited Downes, caused him to hesitate and be afraid.

Ralph Browning's honeyed voice summoned him back to the present. They were in the banker's office—late at night, to ensure privacy—and the stillness imposed a fraternal intimacy to the meeting. Downes felt as if he—they—were members of an exclusive secret society.

"Admit it, Peter, it was easier than you first believed."

"Yes, it was, Ralph. But I'm glad it's over, done with."

"Not yet, lover boy," Geis said in a peevish, irritating voice. "Not until we get rid of the stones and have all that hot cash in our little hands."

"And," Browning said, "let us not forget about Foxman and Company."

"When do we do it?" Downes said. "The longer we wait, the more vulnerable we become."

Geis cackled with delight. He enjoyed every moment of it. The intricacies of design, the subtle secrets that belonged to him alone, the succession of triumphs great and small that made the game worth playing. One or two more steps and it would be over, all trails leading to them, to *himself*, obliterated. Nobody would be able to lay a hand on him: not the cops, not the Feds, not even the Syndicate. That security guy, Keller— at first Geis had been scared. But it was just a shot in the dark; Keller had nothing to go on, no place to go. Let him nose around, he'd come up empty. Soon this campaign would be completed and he would rack up another notch in his belt. He could almost taste the juices of his victory.

"Maybe we don't," he said to Downes.

"Be quiet, Harry!" Browning said, in a rare display of emotion. "I'll say what has to be said."

Geis glared at the banker. He had never cared for Browning, found him too sleek and smooth, too far removed from Geis's grimy existence. Still, Geis accepted the rebuke without comment; his time would come.

Browning addressed Peter Downes. "Raising our sights from twenty million to fifty million proved to be a simple matter, as I said it would be, Peter. We merely stepped up the size and tempo of your purchases. The larger debt was still carried by Foxman."

"Which could turn out to be a problem," Downes said. "I told you, Maurice is stepping down. He's named Ellie to take his place."

"It should've been you, schmuck," Geis said, a touch of gloat in his metallic voice. "You screwed up."

Without thinking, Downes struck back. "If you don't like the way I handle things, you can . . ."

Browning spoke firmly. "No more of this. We are a team, a three-headed organism. Each of us is equally involved, equally entitled to credit or blame. No more squabbling."

"Ellie is good," Downes said, his loyalties divided. "Better than I am, better than any of us."

"Her?"

"Enough, Harry." Then, to Downes: "What are you concerned about, Peter?"

"The debt level. Foxman's bankers are on his back. They're demanding payment, cutting back on his credit line."

"As was inevitable," Browning said.

"Suppose they close him down?" Downes said.

"Can they do that?" Geis sounded worried for the first time. Without Foxman and Company, all that planning, all that work would be lost; they would have to begin over again.

Browning was also concerned but he refused to let it show. "What do you suggest, Peter?"

"If we could sell off some of the inventory."

"It's still in Switzerland," Geis said.

"We could bring it over here in twenty-four hours, if we had to, couldn't we, Ralph?" Browning nodded slowly. "That way Foxman would be able to pay off some of his debts and maintain his credit. When we take over we'd be taking over a company that was still functioning."

"When shall I start selling?"

"First thing," Geis shot back.

Browning was less impulsive. "I don't think so," he said slowly. "Hold back, Peter, let the pressure on Foxman build. When he broaches the subject again, as he certainly will, bring up the conditions of the market, stress your desire to obtain the most advantageous profit position for the company. You will be gracious but reluctant, with utmost concern for the maintenance of the market price per carat. Of course you will sell, in order to keep the company going, but you will do so in small lots only. Remember this, Peter, we *need* Foxman and Company as a going concern."

"I understand."

"At some time, when the moment is right and when the company's debt level is so huge that not only its future is in doubt but also the future of its major clients, at that moment I shall step in and volunteer to salvage the situation. Or rather, my bank shall. The bank will buy up the debt load, thus keeping Foxman from the stain of bankruptcy and in so doing take over active control. When that happens, Peter, you will become chief executive officer of Foxman and Company. You will run things,

Peter. With my advice and consent, of course."

"I appreciate your confidence," Downes said, wondering why he felt so uneasy, as if his worst fears were about to come true.

"Then it's agreed," Geis said.

"I'm to gather all the stones in one place and wait."

"Sure, Peter, wait," Geis said, adding with a tight triumphant grin: "And while you're waiting, you keep on buying."

"Keep buying!" Downes was confused. "We've got fifty million. Let's make our move, take the money and run."

"We got a good thing here, Peter." Geis issued the words with unaccustomed gentleness in his voice, eyes searching Downes's face for a reaction. "No point in letting it get away too fast."

"The plan was . . ."

"We know what the plan was," Browning said. "And a very good plan it was, too. So easy, so correct, so businesslike. Consider this, Peter. What if we enlarged our operation? Double it, perhaps, triple it?"

"Or go after ten times as much." Geis's face squeezed together eagerly, his voice thin and rising.

Downes's eyes skittered from side to side, unable to come to rest on either man. "That's crazy!"

"Eminently sane," Browning said. "Give it the benefit of your best thinking, Peter. Is it really so outrageous? Is it really beyond our capabilities?"

Downes struggled against his fear, tried to clear his head. When he finally responded, it was in a deceptively calm voice, his words measured. "The concept is certainly sound enough. We've proved that. Theoretically."

"Let me repeat myself," Browning said. "By selling off a portion of Foxman's debt, we can reinforce our buying position, Peter. *Your* buying position. If the debtors are happy, if their fears are allayed, no one will bother about future purchases, no matter how large they are, until it is too late to do anything about it."

"The credit?" Downes said, desperate for a way out.

"The residue of the fifty million in stones," Browning answered in that calm, measured way of his. "That will be your collateral. And remember, Foxman is *still* the guarantor of record. None of us will have any financial or legal responsibility."

Downes decided to proceed slowly, feeling his way. "It's an intriguing idea."

"It can be much more than that, an extremely rewarding one."

"It would be a challenge, an imaginative exercise."

"Then you agree that it can be done?"

"It's a board game." Downes laughed to show he wasn't taking it seriously. "You throw the dice and move the pieces, a game of chance."

"Much more than a game," Browning said.

"All those variables," Downes answered. "Let one of the sellers become suspicious..."

"That won't happen."

"If one of them demands that we step up payments..."

"That won't happen."

"If one of them were to go past me to Foxman..."

"Foxman's out," Geis reminded him, stealing a triumphant glance at Browning.

"To Ellie, then. That would be worse, much worse."

"The dame is hot for you, Peter," Geis said, the words washing across his lips with tactile pleasure. "Give her another good schtupping and you're home free."

Downes felt squeezed, diminished. "Why? Fifty million split three ways, that's enough to last each of us for a lifetime. It's enough for me."

"Old American saying," Geis said cheerfully. "You can't be too rich or too thin."

"Follow the logic," Browning said. "Anyone controlling that many good stones could in fact control the market."

"The Syndicate would never stand for it. They'd step in and..."

"Consider this: a challenge to the Syndicate's virtual exclusivity of supply. Consider: a major attack on the Syndicate's sources, its prices and its sales."

Warning signals went off along the network of nerves in Downes's body. Sweat broke out on the palms of his hands and a great, wrenching shudder gripped his spine.

"Can't be done."

"Tell me why not."

Downes tasted his own fetid fear. The threat went beyond the Syndicate's wrath—and that danger could be terminal—but there were Geis and Browning to contend with. The magnitude of their ambition was overwhelming and stretched far beyond his capability or his willingness to take chances.

"Can't be done," he repeated, shaking his head.

"I disagree, Peter. Look at your Miss Foxman. I'm told she had already laid down a pipeline into the Muslim world. Surely you could tap into that line, if it becomes necessary. Perhaps even take it over exclusively. But more importantly, I can guarantee sources that will supply you with precisely the number of stones you'll need, stones of the desired size and quality."

"I still don't like it. What's the purpose?"

"None of your fucking business!" Geis burst out.

Browning raised a quieting hand. "Now, Harry, Peter is entitled to know what I have in mind. As a matter of fact, that's a very good question." A benign expression shaded Browning's face. His hands came up to form a steeple and he nodded once or twice, as if bestowing holy blessings. "With that much in diamonds stored away, I intend to contact John Messinger directly and demand of that gentleman that he grant us certain concessions or else I . . ."

"You expect me to go up against the Syndicate!" Downes was horrified. One leg began to quiver and he made a concerted effort to hold it steady. "Forget it!"

"Just do your part," Browning said. "Leave Sir John to me. I want to look that eminent personage right in the eye when I make my demands, see the expression on that supercilious face. I want to see his reaction when I tell him I intend to drop half a billion dollars in gems into the market."

"You'll destroy us all! Drive prices down! Put everybody out of business!"

"Unless Sir John cooperates."

"That's blackmail. He'll never give in. Why would you want to destroy IMM?"

"That's precisely what I don't want to do, Peter. And neither does Sir John. He won't let it go that far. When he is faced with the possibility that his precious cartel is about to be brought down, his monopoly ended, he will opt for survival. He will give in."

Downes's brain functioned clumsily. "I don't get it, what are you after?"

"Everything," Geis said.

And Browning added solemnly, "I intend to *control* the Syndicate."

Downes's breathing was labored. "It can't be done."

"But you're wrong. Consider: Sir John will eventually want to know what my price is for *not* dumping my diamonds. Very simple. I'll tell him—you, Peter, and Harry and I, must be appointed members of the IMM board of directors. Three other people, whom I will designate, must also be appointed to the board. With those six votes in hand, and with that half billion in stones in reserve, we will direct policy of the Syndicate. We will be able to dictate operating decisions. We will control and shape all the details of a multibillion-dollar global enterprise with considerable influence in a score of countries around the world."

"Ralph, you're scaring me."

"As I shall scare Sir John."

"This is more than I bargained for."

"Of course it is. But *always* it was what I had in mind. This is no impulse notion, Peter, but the result of considerable planning and research. It can be done, it will be done."

"What if something goes wrong?"

"You think my reach exceeds my grasp? Not at all. This is a reasonable concept. Not so much different from what we've done up till now. Simply a matter of execution. And with your help, Peter, it shall come to pass."

Downes began to tremble, and he set himself to keep control of his body, of his emotions. His sphincter tightened and he pressed his thighs together. This insane grab for power and riches, there was no way he could handle something this far-reaching, this massive, anything so dangerous. All he had ever wanted was to make money and move on, secure in the belief that his victims would never seek him out, that they would accept their losses in embarrassed silence. This was different. This was the major leagues, and though the rewards were almost incalculable, so, too, were the risks, along with the promise of a swift and terrible retribution.

None of this was for Peter Hilary Downes. Reject it out of hand, he commanded himself. Say no to Browning and Geis and their wild scheme. Let them keep the entire fifty million. Even without his share, his future was assured; he still had Ellie. He loved her, he wanted her, he would make her happy. They would marry and spend the rest of their lives conducting the affairs of Foxman and Company. He would work hard, be honest, a faithful partner, a faithful husband. They would have a family, become pillars of society with an apartment in New York, a house in Woodstock, a condo in Vail. Why take chances when it wasn't necessary? To hell with this garbage, he was getting out.

"Any questions?" Browning said.

Peter hesitated. Why not go along for a while, see how things worked out? He had always fantasized about being rich and powerful and Browning was offering him that chance. Face it, he reminded himself, nobody deserved it more than he did.

"Conditions are favorable," Browning was saying. "We have a rising market, substantial inventories in the vaults of the dealers. They are all looking to sell at the crest. Hoarding has begun and for a certain interval our operation will not attract excessive attention."

"What if the Syndicate refuses to bargain?"

"That isn't going to happen. Sir John cannot withstand the threat. In a collapsing market, he'd lose the big merchants, the important buyers, his most strategic outlets. Not even IMM can afford that for very long. His own stockholders would eventually turn on him. With us selling cheap, he'll have to compete and that will send prices on a downward slide that once begun will be impossible to stop. He'll recognize that. We, along with market forces, will allow him no room to maneuver, no choice except to meet our terms."

Downes considered it from every angle. Despite his fear, despite the reservation and doubts he entertained, it was certainly no more improbable than what they had accomplished so far. Just keep going, straight ahead. Once Sir John succumbed, his position as operating chief of IMM would become vulnerable, his tenure limited. Sooner or later, he would be forced to resign. Someone else would take his place. And that someone? Certainly not Harry Geis, wrong on so many counts. Not Ralph Browning, a man with a genetic predisposition for functioning in the shadows. That left only Peter Downes. God in heaven! He would be the most powerful man in the diamond industry, one of the most important businessmen in the world.

"The stones," he said, his mind ranging ahead. "Where are we going to get the stones we'll need?"

"Leave that to me."

"Where will they come from?" he insisted. Without a sound answer, he understood, the entire scheme would crumple. "From where?"

Browning displayed that superior benevolent expression once more. He spoke with quiet confidence. "From the Soviet Union, of course."

## chapter
# *37*

THE CALL FROM BAKSHIR KHAMOURY came at ten minutes after three in the morning, New York time. Ellie woke with a start. She had been dreaming and for a long, terrifying moment wasn't sure where reality began and fantasy left off. She switched on the night light and read the green digits on the clock. She swore silently and reached for the phone.

"Yes . . . ?"

An overseas operator asked her to hold on and someone said her name, and repeated it, a faintly accented voice with a cheerfulness that was appalling at that hour.

"I am Bakshir, my beautiful American friend, Miss Foxman. Oh, how fine it is to speak with you again. I, Bakshir, am your devoted admirer. I hope this finds you well and in good health, dear lady."

"Bakshir, it is the middle of the night in New York."

"I have been trying to make a connection for many days. The telephone system is impossible here. Not the worst in Africa, but certainly far from the best. Do I find you happy, dear Miss Foxman? Your image dances before me night and day, provoking lovely and marvelous dreams in my mind. Have you favorably considered my proposal further, dearest one?

**312**

Become my wife and make me the happiest of men."

"Bakshir, I cannot believe you called at this ungodly hour to propose to me. Where are you anyway?"

"Sierra Leone, my pet. In my rooms at the Mammy Yoko. You may not know it, of course. A reasonable lodging but nothing more. Outside it rains perpetually and one dares not venture forth without mackintosh and bumbershoot at the ready. I despair of ever being dry again. Last evening I attended the National Dance Troupe at the Cape Sierra Hotel. Riveting every one of them, they cause the heart to pound and the blood to rush. I await breathlessly the day we may enjoy them together."

"Why are you calling me, Bakshir?"

"I have traveled all over this country. Up and down the rivers—the Mano, the Maro. Wherever one goes the word is the same. A disastrous decline in production of diamonds exists all over."

Awake now, she swung her feet to the carpeted floor. "What are you trying to tell me, Bakshir?"

"The future is uncertain, my dear, dark even. Shipments cannot be guaranteed."

"But there will be some shipments?"

"As you know, at heart I am an optimist. However, the picture is gloomy."

"You're able to get hold of some stones?"

"Not if I am to supply you."

"I think you'd better explain that to me."

"I am made desolate, but destiny is destiny."

"Come on, Bakshir. Level with me. What is going on?"

He uttered a small cry of regret. He moaned. He invoked the grace and kindness of Allah. "Life is cruel. Men are wicked. Only Allah is good and constant. I am no longer master of my fate, no longer able to maintain our previous business arrangement."

"I was depending on you, Bakshir. You are my primary source." She needed to make sense out of what was happening. "Without you, I may be out of business."

"Miss Foxman, my love. My most precious one. My true and only love. You cannot know what happens out in the real world. Pressures build."

"Pressure from whom?"

"Who can say for certain? My suppliers receive warnings that to deal with me should I continue to deal with you means the termination of their economic well-being."

"Who gives these warnings?"

"Unnamed government officials. Men unimportant enough themselves to be intimidated. Important enough to understand that they are at the mercy of those in the highest spheres. Private parties who send underlings with thick necks and dull eyes, men who owe allegiance to whoever pays them. Twice my workers have been robbed, the poor men beaten badly. Thousands of carats of exemplary stones have been lost to me forever. Poor me! Poor me! Such episodes are devastating. I am left weak and fearful. Oh, yes, I am a coward, I admit it, a weakling and a coward. Forgive me, forgive me. It is not that I love you less, dear Miss Foxman, but I love life and solvency more. What is one to do?"

"Hold out, Bakshir. Fight back."

"My dearest love." A muffled sound came over the wire, a cross between a sob and choked-off laughter. "Such a suggestion is unworthy of you. It is utterly without merit, it pains me to say. Destructive to us both. Stupid, if you don't mind my saying so. Does one fight against the rain? Or the wind? Or the sun when it bakes the land? No, no. One can only preserve one's flesh and spirit and what assets exist until the danger is past. Men have been assaulted, other men have been killed. Someone in my position, can I afford to be killed? Two wives, all those children. Grandchildren yet to come who depend on me. Oh, no, you cannot know how overburdened with responsibilities I am."

She allowed her eyes to close and went over it all again. It really wasn't a surprise. It was in keeping with everything else going on; that morning she had received notification from the Browning Bank that her loan application had been turned down. No reason given. Now this.

"Bakshir, what if I closed down my bourse?"

"An excellent idea, lady. This is no time for the launching of new experiments."

"What if I went to work for my uncle?" How long would that last? she wondered idly. The company was in serious trou-

ble. Large debts, diminished income, all departments showing
less and less activity. How then did P & D, Inc., continue to
function so well? Why was Peter able to buy when no one else
could? She would have to ask him; there were so many questions which needed answers.

"Your uncle will welcome you with the proverbial open
arms, I am sure. However..."

"However?"

"Nothing will suffice, I fear. Word flies as if on the wind
that to do business with any Foxman is to incur wrath at the
highest places and court disaster, personal and professional.
Poor me, poor me."

She tried to make him change his mind but nothing she said
had any effect. He had been threatened, brought to heel.

"Tell me, Bakshir. Who is behind this?"

"One can only guess."

"Let me guess—the Syndicate?"

"In our trade, dearest lady, who else is there?"

A conclusive answer. IMM was intensifying the war against
her uncle and since she bore the name she, too, would pay the
price. This was Sir John's final push to drive Maurice to the
wall, to destroy the man and his company.

Oh, it might be possible to hold on to some insignificant
place in the business, to cling to the edges, but the days of
glory were over. Wiped out in a ruthless economic vendetta.

She made one last try. "Won't you help me fight back,
Bakshir?"

Her voice, shaky and without force, betrayed her. Bakshir
had no trouble making up his mind. "One cannot fight against
a mountain. One cannot hold back the sea. One cannot prevail
over the forces of Allah when they are unloosed."

There was nothing more to say. By selling the inventory
acquired by P & D they could restore their solvency, but there
was no longer a future. Foxman and Company was finished,
she was finished.

No more sleep that night. She lay uneasily in bed until she
could tolerate it no longer. Daylight had begun to seep in around
the edges of the drapes in her bedroom when she showered and
made ready for the day ahead. She put on a purple cashmere
tunic over a white silk blouse with a floppy collar and rolled-

back cuffs. Except for the solid-gold watch from Cartier, she wore no jewelry. By the time she left the apartment, Ellie knew exactly what she had to do.

Maurice, behind the big partners' desk, contemplated his niece. His decision to invite her to be his successor had been made only after a great deal of consideration, a great deal of soul-searching; her decision, he was sure, had been arrived at with no less difficulty.

"It will not be easy," he said. "But I'm pleased. I allowed the business to drift into a kind of economic limbo. Perhaps it was my age, perhaps I waited too late to retire, perhaps I clung to the traditional ways instead of changing with the changing times.

"Without making an excuse, Robert's death was a tremendous shock to my system, I see that now. Foxman and Company has been a ship without a rudder since then. The authority and leadership I should have provided was absent. Look at the ledgers, my dear. Our debts are great, our income is minimal and our obligations have continued without letup.

"Perhaps I placed too much faith in the old ways. The Foxman sight was the source of so much good for the firm and I acted as though it would go on forever. I should have diversified our sources, as well as our markets. Expanded the entire operation. For years I tried to contain the firm, careful not to become too big. I wanted it to remain manageable. I see now that it might have been my ego at work and what I wanted was to keep personal control over the entire business. I should have encouraged you young people more, turned over more important tasks to you, allowed you to grow and build the company. That's the way your father saw things. He addressed the future in terms of the new generation, as he used to put it. I suppose he was right—I'm even convinced he was right, now. But I was not prepared to surrender my hold on things. What I believed had served me well. Perhaps I—both of us—were victimized still by the horrors of Europe and the Nazis. Emil wanted to change everything and very quickly. I clung to what I knew and felt safe with. Was I so wrong?"

Ellie had no answer. All her conviction washed away, all her resentment. She saw Maurice for what he had become, a man aging and losing his grip on a world he had created, *his* world, life slipping out of his grasp. Had he been so wrong? And if so, was she prepared to tell him so? The answer came slowly.

"You did what you thought was right, Uncle."

"Perhaps," he said. He straightened up in his chair. "You will have to exercise a firm discipline. Some of our people may have to be let go. Our procedures should be brought up to date. And you must make sure that Peter begins selling off the stock he's accumulated, you will need the flow of funds. It will take time, but if anyone can reverse the negative direction I've allowed us to take, you are the one."

"I'll do my best."

"And that will be good enough, I have no doubt."

"If you have any specific suggestions . . . ?"

He folded his hands. "I think not. There can be only one captain on a ship and from this day forward you are the captain. No, it won't be easy, but I have faith in your ability and your courage."

She longed to embrace him but could not bring herself to do it; she clung to the last traces of her father's memory. The final vestige of immaturity kept her in her chair. Her voice was gentle with affection. "I'll try not to disappoint you."

Maurice smiled gratefully. "I'm sure you won't."

She wasted no time. First, a visit to Mattie.

"I'll need a lot of help. Will you stand by me, Mother?"

"I'm sure you'll get help from all of us." She clapped her hands once. "Now, to business. What can I do for you, boss?"

Ellie grinned before she answered. "I can use my own office for the present, but once Maurice has moved out I'll take over the larger space, I'll need it. I'll also need a secretary, preferably someone with a diamond background. Someone who knows enough to keep her mouth shut."

Mattie made notes, saying nothing.

"I've been thinking about installing computers. That should allow us to keep a closer watch on purchases, sales and current stocks. It will also expedite and simplify our bookkeeping procedures. Make some calls for me, set up interviews with half a dozen of the top companies. Let's shop before we buy and let's find out if it's more economical to rent."

"Anything else?"

"I'm closing down my own company. There are some calls to make, one or two arrangements to settle, a number of letters to write."

"Do it out of this office. I'll assign a temporary to you. When do you want to begin?"

A big, pleased smile spread across Ellie's face. "Why, Mother, can't you tell? I already have."

An hour later, she presented herself to David. "Got a minute for your only girl cousin?"

He was on his feet, welcoming her, getting her into his most comfortable chair. "Nothing too good for the new boss."

"You heard?"

"Smoke signals went up first thing this morning. By now it's common knowledge over bagels and cream cheese at the sandwich shop in the lobby."

She laughed briefly and sobered quickly. "How do you feel about it, David?"

He rolled his massive shoulders. "A dollop of envy when I heard, but it's gone. The job's not for me nor me for it. I'm happy to go along with things as they were."

"There'll be changes, David."

"I suppose that's inevitable. Well, just give me the word and I'll adapt. That's my biggest talent, keeping a low profile and getting along."

"It's going to be a tough pull for a while," she told him.

"Is Foxman going to survive?"

"That's the big question. I'll do what I can."

"Anything you want from me, just say so, Ellie. You can count on my support. Have you discussed this with Peter yet?"

"That's next."

Downes was on the phone. Making what appeared to be a substantial buy. She listened attentively; he was good, understood the market and held to the price he was willing to pay. He stated his terms, insisted on prompt delivery and dictated the method of payment. He was strong, knowledgeable and confident. Everything he should be.

"Assemble the package," he said in closing, "and let me

know when you're prepared to ship. I'll provide date and destination at that time." He hung up and came out from behind his desk, taking her hands in his, drawing her to her feet. He kissed her on the mouth. "I'm so glad for you."

He seemed to be sincere, yet she knew he had expected the top job for himself. Certainly he must have been resentful, experienced some pangs of jealousy. Anything else would have been less than human. No matter; he would have to learn to live with his loss; she was in charge now. She disengaged and sat back down. "Let's talk business, Peter."

"Your way of telling me to keep business apart from pleasure? Absolutely right. Okay, boss lady, what's on your mind?"

She wanted to get it out in the open, but decided to let it slide. She spoke in a crisp, cool voice. "You know that we've been cut off from our regular sights? Maurice never developed other sources and neither have I. You, on the other hand, you've been buying regularly and in substantial amounts."

"Unfortunately at steeper prices. The profit margin is considerably lower since we have to compete with Syndicate stones."

"But P & D's overhead has been absorbed by Foxman."

"A negligible figure. The expenditures continue to be high."

"Exorbitant. I've been looking at the records. Frankly, they leave a lot to be desired. Names of buyers, complete records of sales including dates of delivery, storage..."

"Neither David nor I ever claimed to be good at paperwork." He delivered his best smile in her direction. Her aloof manner, the distance she put between them so quickly, caused his guts to constrict.

"Tell me about that call, Peter. Sounded like a substantial purchase."

"It was." He hesitated, decided to go on. "One point three million worth of stones."

"I'm impressed. And the seller?"

He answered reluctantly. "Hamid el-Sheikama."

"I'm not familiar with the name."

"A free-lancer, working out of Tunis. Reliable, according to the information I've received."

She leaned back and looked away. "I thought I'd touched all bases but that's a new one to me. What's your secret, Peter?"

Again the knot formed up in his middle. She had no way

of knowing that his sources were conduits set up by Browning to handle Russian stones. Again the fear that he was in over his head. He ducked his head. "Let's face it, darling. Maurice has offended a great many people. There's been severe pressure to keep people from dealing with him. Besides, he worked one side of the street and I work another. He based his entire business on goods bought at discount, either refusing or unable to afford the higher markups."

"I suppose you're right. I'd be interested in seeing that shipment when it comes in."

He set himself firmly in place. "Whatever you say."

"Also your other sources. Get up a list of the names for me. All of them, please. Where the stones are coming from. All the numbers: weights, ratings, so on. Sometime tomorrow, okay?"

He swallowed a protest. This was no time to go head to head with Ellie. It would do no harm for her to know with whom he was doing business; not anymore. He brought a sheet of paper out of his desk drawer, handed it over. There were fourteen names on it, along with addresses and telephone numbers.

"These are my people," he said, with forced casualness. "I'll have to work up the rest of it."

"I don't know any of these outfits."

"Believe me, I had to really scratch to find these people." Or at least Ralph Browning did, he thought. These were the banker's men, obscure Muslim dealers who appeared to have unlimited supplies of stones for sale. "The usual routes are closed tight to anyone connected with Foxman and Company."

That accounted for it, she remarked to herself. Aloud, she said, "Your success is admirable. However, it's placed us all in a peculiar bind."

"I don't understand."

"Your buys are vital to us, to the future. The problem they've made, however, is immediate. They have created a monumental debt for us. The banks are closing in, our credit standing is in jeopardy. We've got to stop the outflow and start bringing money in. I want you to start moving your stock."

"Selling off, you mean?"

"As soon as possible."

"That's not a wise move, Ellie."

"Okay, you've got something to say, say it, Peter."

"First of all the market's on the rise. To sell at this time means the eventual loss of substantial profits."

"The market may peak in a week or a month or a year. We can't wait."

"I want to go on record as being against..."

"Objection noted," she said brusquely. She was annoyed, an unfocused sense of something not in place, as if they were pulling in opposite directions, at the same time giving lip service only to having the same goals. He seemed to be holding something from her, information, tactics, always agreeable, but never quite agreeing with her.

"A little patience, Ellie. Sure, I'll start selling. But at a deliberate pace. Why screw up the market?"

She was suddenly wary, warier than she had been of him. For the first time, the chemical jolt his presence provided was absent.

"I'm beginning to get unhappy, Peter."

"Have it your way. Say the word and I'll sell off all the stock, but a few more weeks..." He left it at that, letting her think about it while he considered Geis and Browning and what their reaction would be should he be forced to unload the entire inventory. Every muscle in his body tensed against the realization that everything was about to go down the drain. Somehow he had to stop her. "Tell you what, Ellie, it's clear you don't have the faith in me Maurice does. Under these conditions, I can't do my best work. Let's just put an end to this. I'll stop buying for P & D. David can dump our holdings and I'll resign from the company, as of right now."

Guilt ran through her like a furry creature, darting and uncatchable. She was ashamed, suborned by his frankness and willingness to give up everything for the good of the company. Is this what it meant to be number one: to live in a state of constant conflict, personalities clashing over every decision, over every policy handed down from the top? She came out of her chair.

"When I want your resignation, I'll ask for it."

"I'm beginning to think you don't trust me, Ellie."

Was that it? she asked herself. Was it a lack of trust on her part or simply an executive decision made to ensure the future financial health of the company? The job was hers but her confidence in her ability to do what had to be done was shaky.

"I have only the best interests of the company in mind, Peter."

"Am I to think you believe I don't? It looks to me as if we've got a clash of egos here—"

Ego? Was she simply attempting to exercise her superior position at his expense, to make herself feel better? She refused to believe that.

"Here is the way I want it, Peter." Her voice sounded unsteady in her ears, hesitant and a little shrill, girlish. She cleared her throat and began again. "This is the way I want you to handle things. About the market, we don't want to do anything that might shock it. No surprises. The price must be maintained. But in order to keep Foxman and Company functioning I must have cash. The only way to get that cash is to sell off some of the stones you've accumulated."

"I agree. A judicious sale here and there, a few hundred thousand at a time."

She made a quick, violent gesture, as if to stem the flow of words. "The debt must be serviced so as to keep our credit, that's vital. And I must have cash on hand to keep operating."

"I understand. What I had in mind—"

She cut him off again. "Here's what you'll do—make up a package of good stones. One carat or heavier, D-flawless, all good product, and arrange for their sale."

"How large a package?"

"No less than nine million dollars."

The cold finger of dread marched along his spine. "Won't that defeat your purpose? Won't—"

Again that quick gesture. "It has to be done, Peter. Please, do it." It was an order, not a request.

"It will take time."

"How much time?"

"The stones are in various locations. A selection will have to be made and transportation arranged."

"Do it."

"Where shall I conduct the sale?"

"Why not here, in New York?"

He hesitated. "Geneva might be better. I've made some good contacts in Europe. I know a buyer who might snap up the entire lot at top prices." He looked into her eyes. "As long as you're convinced this is the way to go, Ellie."

"It's the only way," she answered without hesitation. "Or else we'll all go under."

Downes made the call as soon as he was alone.

"We're running out of time, Harry! Ellie insists that I sell off nine million in a single package."

"Damn! You've got to stall her, move it in smaller amounts."

"I tried that. It didn't work."

"Then buy faster. This thing should be completed in a week at the most. In and out, that's the way to go."

"That's crazy! I've been in touch with every name on Ralph's list. Nobody is geared up to move that fast. They haven't got the stock."

Geis grew thoughtful. "Let me talk to Browning. I'm sure he'll take care of it. The man has connections."

"Harry, I don't mind telling you, I'm getting scared. Ellie's going to be all over things. You'll see, nothing will get past her. She asks the right questions, she'll insist on answers."

"Shit in your blood, that's your trouble. Nothing's changed. You buy faster is all, you buy bigger."

"What if she changes her mind, Harry? What if she decides to unload the entire stock?"

"Just like that?"

"Yeah, bang, bang, bang."

Geis felt his muscles contract, his resolve harden. "That dame is in the way."

"What do I do then, Harry? What do I do?"

"I'll take care of it."

"Something could go wrong and I'm out here in front. I'm not about to spend ten years in the slammer. If she calls for an accounting, insists on seeing the goods now, what do I do then?"

"No balls, Peter, that's you. Just suck it up, man, and keep your mouth shut. Nothing's going to happen."

"She won't sit still, Harry, not and watch the company go under. She'll do something about it. That's her nature. She's smart and she's tough and she won't stay outside for very long."

Geis wanted to scream at Downes but thought better of it; they still needed him.

"Trust me, Peter."

"We're running out of time."

"Leave it to me, Peter. I know what has to be done, I'll do it."

Geis considered.

The hell with Browning. Too often he'd found the banker soft, ready to make compromises, willing to turn away from the more efficient, if sometimes deadlier, forms of persuasion. The less Browning knew about this, the better. He reached for the phone and dialed a number. He let it ring twice and hung up. Without waiting, he called again. Three rings this time, before he hung up. He sat back to wait.

Nearly twenty minutes later his phone rang. "Geis speaking."

"You recognize my voice?" It was flat, faintly accented and toneless, all emotion squeezed out of it. The voice went with the man; a perfect match.

"Never miss with you, Lenny."

"How many times you got to be told, no names. How do you know your line isn't being listened to?"

"It's clean. I sweep it twice a week. Anyway, who's gonna bug a small-timer like me? I got a job for you."

"I already got a job."

"The security man?"

"You called to ask me questions, is that why you called?"

"Maybe you can't handle the work load." Geis laughed to show he was only kidding. The man on the other end of the wire did not laugh. Some time elapsed before he answered.

"Who is this person?"

"Ellie Foxman."

"Has this been approved by the Rezident?"

"The Rezident has no authority in this. You've been informed by the degree of sanction on this assignment." And then, slowly and forcefully: "It is not your place to question my judgment."

And, quietly, the reply: "Where do I find the Foxman woman?"

"Jesus! Do I have to wipe your ass for you, too? You know where she works, track her down. And make it look good. An accident, a robbery, whatever."

"Yes, yes."

"Do it fast, Lenny. Right away. The success of the project calls for it."

"I'll take care of it."

"Be gezunt."

"What's that mean?"

"Yiddish for 'be well.'"

*chapter*
## 38

PUBLICITY RELEASES WENT OUT to the dailies and the trades announcing her appointment. According to the public relations office that handled the Foxman account, Ellie was the youngest person ever to take charge of a major diamond firm and the only woman. "A FIRST!" blared the release in oversized red type. Interviews were scheduled with a writer from the *Times* business section, *The Wall Street Journal* and, naturally, *Women's Wear Daily*. She appeared on the cover of *Savvy*, on *Live at Five* on NBC-TV, with David Hartman, and she flew out to Chicago to do *The Phil Donahue Show*. The topic of discussion: "The Role of the Woman Executive in Business, Her Present and Her Future."

Back in New York, she attempted to assimilate in the shortest time possible the million and one details of running a large company. She knew diamonds, but realized quickly how little she knew about other important aspects of the business. She could have used some time in a business school, she reminded herself. There were the buyers who suddenly recognized her existence and would deal with no one else; and the talented cutter who threw temper tantrums at the slightest hint of criticism and another cutter who went into a deep depression if he was ignored. Always it was Ellie who had to rebuild shattered egos, tranquilize jangled nerves, vow that conditions in the workplace would soon improve. There were prices to set, shipping dates to be met, the complex operations of the different departments to be kept running smoothly.

There were assignments to hand out; she discovered that she was strong in administrative work and in personnel, weak with the numbers and even less current with the legal ramifications of the business. She did what she could on her own, and when she needed help, she asked for it. A year before, she would have considered that a sign of weakness.

One day flowed into another without notice until one morning she woke up on her side, hugging her knees, and she began to weep. And couldn't stop. She did not want to burden Maurice with what were now her problems. Mattie wouldn't do, nor would Peter. She needed a hard head to provide straight answers, a strong shoulder on which to lean. She called Keller.

An uninterested secretary said he was out and would she care to leave her name. The secretary didn't know when Keller was likely to return. She didn't know where he could be reached and would Ellie care to leave her name.

Ellie left her name.

Two days later her phone rang a few minutes before midnight, just as she was drifting off to sleep. That now familiar serrated voice jarred her back to full wakefulness.

"Where have you been!" she cried. "I called two days ago."

"The job calls for a lot of travel. What is it?"

"I have to talk to you."

"I just landed at Kennedy. The answering service told me you called. I need some sleep. I'll buy you lunch tomorrow."

"That won't do. I need your help, Keller, and I need it soon."

"Okay," he said. "Got any scotch?"

She greeted him at the door, a drink in hand. He took a long pull and arranged himself comfortably on the sofa. She brought out a platter of small sandwiches and a pot of coffee.

"Go ahead," he said, applying Russian dressing liberally to a sandwich. "Talk."

"I've taken over for my uncle."

He took a bite of the sandwich, washed it down with the remainder of the scotch. "I heard. Congratulations."

"I'm scared, Keller."

"Everyone is, of something. It's what you wanted."

"It's a beginning."

"Bite off more than you can swallow, you may choke on it."

"Spare me the philosophy, Keller."

He put the sandwich aside and drank some coffee. "Lady, I am tired and I am dirty. I have been on the go for seventy-two hours, getting nowhere. If what I've got to give doesn't suit you, I'll be on my way."

"I'm sorry." She refilled his cup with hot coffee. "I don't know what it is about you, something gets my back up."

"My Bronx charm, gets 'em every time. Tell me your trouble."

She tucked her feet under her and said, "I'm concerned about Peter."

"Downes? You insisted he was your—hope for the future."

"I changed my mind."

He finished off his sandwich. "It sure took you long enough."

"Don't get tough with me, Keller."

He warned himself to back off. The lady had a lot of spine, no matter what was troubling her. "All right, let's have it about Downes."

"He's been buying."

"I told you that."

"In greater amounts than ever. I talked to him about it and he just got defensive. Too defensive, it seemed to me."

"And he's not selling," Keller tacked on.

"I told him to sell off about nine million."

"Is he going to do it?"

The question surprised her, made her think. "I don't believe Peter dares oppose me directly. I ordered him to assemble the package, to arrange the sale."

"That should help you."

"Yes." She grew pensive. "Peter argued against it, but I finally convinced him."

"Good."

"He kept talking about the rising market. He'd prefer to hold on to inventory until prices peak out."

"That makes sense."

"Yes, but our credit standing. It's bad and getting worse. Never hold product, that was a basic principle with my uncle. Keep the cash flowing. He never tried to squeeze every cent out of a deal. He felt . . ."

Keller interrupted. "The stones Downes has been buying, when it comes to size and quality, what's your professional opinion?"

She shuddered, struck by a sudden chill. She raged at herself for being sloppy, for letting this slide, for lack of judgment. Then a quick flash of hope.

"Maurice saw them."

"You're sure of that?"

"Yes. 'Nice stones,' he said. Yes, he looked at them."

"When?"

Another chill; she embraced herself. "Some time ago. At the start. When Peter first began to buy."

"But not recently? No one's seen the stuff lately, least of all you?"

"No."

"And the purchase orders?"

"My mother would know about that. She handles that sort of thing."

"Have they been checked against the inventory?"

"I don't know."

"Oh, great. Your uncle was zeroed in on the Syndicate for a very long time. He saw Syndicate ghosts in every corner. He trusted Downes, obviously, and gave him a free hand. An old man trying to fight an old enemy, an enemy he thought he understood, and refusing to consider any other explanation. Purchases of such magnitude. Christ!"

"Maurice has never been the same since Robert was killed, since that first poor sight."

"Okay," Keller said, helping himself to another scotch. "Where are they?"

"The stones? In the company vaults, I assume. In our banks."

"Where? In New York?"

She shuddered. "In different places at different times. Depends on where sales could be arranged."

"Where, damnit?"

"New York," she answered softly, "and London. Tel Aviv,

Brussels. Foxman has outlets in every major city in the world."

He stared stonily into middle space. "What else?"

"I don't know what you mean?"

"What else did you want to talk about?"

"Everything seems to be falling apart. My primary source went sour. He admitted to governmental pressure on his contacts, to threats of violence and in some cases actual violence."

"You think IMM is behind that?"

"Who else is there? Isn't there some talk, rumors?"

"I'm security, not sales." He heaved himself erect. "More and more diamonds are being taken out of the normal ebb and flow. And not coming back in again after the usual lead time. Good stones, too. One carat or more. Somebody's holding."

"Peter?"

"Somebody is."

"Besides Peter?"

"Looks like it to me."

"But why?"

"So many questions, very few good answers." He took a step toward the door and she felt panic rise up in her. She came to her feet, moving toward him.

"What happens now, Keller? What are you going to do?"

"You are going to do it."

"What?"

"Set up a meeting for me with your uncle. Tomorrow at ten o'clock will be okay. For privacy, his home would be best."

He left her standing there, legs trembling, afraid to be alone, aware that in some way she'd been chastised, scolded, left to stew in her own simmering juice. It took her a very long time to fall asleep that night.

*chapter*
# 39

THE HOUSE WAS ON a quiet tree-lined street between Madison Avenue and Fifth. Faced with granite, it was wider than any of its neighbors and one floor higher. A few steps led up to a glass door protected by a latticework of black iron. A man in a white jacket and white gloves admitted Keller to an elliptical reception hall with a floor made of pink Italian marble, polished to a high gloss. On the walls, a Matisse, a Monet, a Van Gogh, two Cézannes and a Picasso from his blue period. Keller, seldom impressed, was acutely impressed, and he went from picture to picture, lingering over each.

The man in the white jacket and white gloves became impatient. "This way, sir."

Keller pointed to the Matisse. "Look at this," he murmured.

The man in the white jacket and white gloves sniffed. "I work here, sir, I live in. Now, if you will step this way, Mr. Foxman is waiting. Miss Foxman is waiting."

Keller bared his teeth, the beginning of his fright mask. "Lead on, pal."

Maurice Foxman's study was a book-lined room with dark polished woods and leather furniture showing the signs of much wear and an equal amount of care. An antique French table at the far end of the room served as a desk; it was swept clean save for a bronze bust which Keller thought might be by Epstein. Foxman, in a dark green velvet smoking jacket, a silk square at his neck, offered his hand.

"Good of you to come, Keller."

"Thanks for seeing me."

Foxman indicated Ellie, seated in a club chair to one side. She wore a high-collared Cossack blouse of white cotton with intricate lace insets and a long flowing mauve skirt over sleek mauve leather boots. To Keller, she was more beautiful than ever, possessed of a secret, mystical quality that defied understanding. A rough stone with the dark promise of a deeper beauty, pure and lasting.

"Good morning," he said.

"Good morning."

"Have you had breakfast?" Foxman said.

"Nothing for me, thanks."

Foxman nodded and the man in the white jacket withdrew. Foxman sat down behind the French table, hands flat on the smooth clean surface. "Ellie tells me you have doubts. Questions. Suspicions."

"All of that, and more."

"The nature of your trade. It must make the normal exchanges of an ordinary life difficult." Foxman smiled, as if to take the edge off his words.

Keller smiled back. How seldom he smiled, and almost never laughed, Ellie noted. But now—for a split second that hard face had opened, providing a hint of what he must have looked like as a boy, vulnerable and spontaneous, full of optimism. The mood was quickly spent, the face clenched up again, alert to the myriad of dangers surrounding him.

"Very difficult," he said, no self-pity in his voice.

"For example?" Foxman said.

"Two marriages," he said, not addressing Ellie. "Two divorces. If they offered marriage insurance, I'd be in the assigned-risk group."

"I see what you mean," Foxman said. "Life seldom permits us to go our own ways unimpeded. Fate has a way of pushing or pulling, maneuvering us to its own veiled purposes. Two marriages. You're an optimist, Keller, a man willing to take another chance, seeking an answer to the mystery."

What mystery? Keller almost said aloud but didn't; he was sure he knew.

"I suspect you're a romantic, Keller."

"Or a realist."

Foxman smiled ruefully. "For some men, romance is like a vestigial religion they can't shake off. Romance is the meat on which they feed their souls."

"Is that you, Keller?" There was a taunting echo in Ellie's voice.

Before he could answer, Foxman spoke. "Now to business. Your business, Keller."

Keller thought he detected a slackness to Foxman's jaw he had never noticed before, gone the finely drawn line of his masculine handsomeness, absent the courageous look that had given form and substance to his fine profile. His eyes were moist and sad, as if he had pulled back into some remote corner of his own psyche, his power and drive diminished.

"I got into this when Robert was killed. Check it out, come to a logical conclusion, help the law get onto the killer, that was my assignment. Routine, simple. Only it didn't turn out that way. There have been other killings along the way."

"Related to Robert's death?" Foxman said.

Keller cautioned himself; the old man might be fading but traces of his former sharpness were in plain view.

"One in particular, Mr. Foxman. Georgy Tarassuk, taken out recently."

"Should I know the name?"

"I mentioned him to you in Rome."

"Oh, yes."

"He's the one who dealt in Soviet stones. Part of Russ Almaz's artery to the West."

"The Soviets . . . what connection is there between them and Robert?"

"I believe Tarassuk went into business for himself, without informing his masters in Moscow. Knocking off a shipment of Russian stones when he could, smuggling when he could, selling where he could."

"To Robert?"

"The evidence supports that contention."

"Poor Robert. He was smart, but not smart enough to deal

in smuggled goods. But it fits the facts, doesn't it? I'm afraid I have to believe you, Keller."

Ellie nodded a sad assent.

Keller hated to see how much they hurt, and he'd inflicted it. He said, "Let's talk about IMM—anyone trading in stones makes certain assumptions, buyer and seller alike. That prices will remain stable, that supplies will not be dramatically increased or decreased without warning."

"Correct. That's the sole reason the Syndicate has been able to function and maintain itself for all these years. We have all been silent conspirators in this international monopoly, all of us willing subscribers to Sir John's policies, the good and the evil. I am ashamed of the role I played in this, ashamed." He was breathing hard when he stopped.

Keller spat it out. "IMM buys up every stone it can in order to keep economic conditions on an even keel."

"Yes, yes. Diamonds are released according to projections of future sales, no more, no less."

"Get on with it, Keller." Ellie's voice was quiet but commanding. "We all know how Sir John functions—the marketing reports, the research, the dealer surveys."

"And so determines almost to the carat how many stones will sell in any given year. What if all that were suddenly changed? What if a huge supply was secretly assembled? First-rate stones. What if, at a predetermined point in time, word was let out that the hoarded diamonds were about to be dumped willy-nilly on the market . . . ?"

"Nonsense!" Foxman said hotly. "Nobody would . . . nobody could . . . everybody knows the consequences. Nonsense! Nonsense!"

"Just playing What If. Indulge me, Mr. Foxman. What if someone did dump an infinite number of stones? What then?"

"Ruinous. Simply ruinous. Prices would plummet. Stocks would become worthless." Foxman blinked and his eyes filled with tears, his voice broke. He massaged his left wrist. "The market would go crazy. People trying to unload all their holdings before it hit bottom."

Keller leaned forward for emphasis. "Just the threat might be enough."

"Maybe not," Ellie said, without conviction. "If we all remain calm, consider the alternatives."

"No, no," Foxman said, almost to himself. "No dealer would be able to hold fast in the face of such an attack. The market swamped, depressed, quality stones available for fifty dollars a carat. Thirty. Ten. Merchants, manufacturers, dealers, we'd all go under."

"IMM could ride it out," Ellie said. "Sir John would support the price structure and . . ."

"No," Keller said. "Even the Syndicate would fall."

"Keller," Foxman called in a tremulous voice. "You truly believe such a monstrous plot is in force?"

"I do."

"But who? And how?"

"I've worked up a scenario. We start with your nephew, Robert, and work our way back. He bought stones stolen from the Russians and smuggled into Africa and was killed for them. Tarassuk, who sold him those stones, was killed by the same gunman, a Soviet pro, the same man who tried to shoot me. Tarassuk knew a woman named Tatiana, who, I believe, is part of a Soviet network in the New York area. At least she was. She has links to Harry Geis, a dealer on Forty-seventh Street. And this is where it's going to hurt, Mr. Foxman. David . . ."

"My David!" Foxman held tightly to his wrist and his eyes closed. "Not David."

"David and Peter Downes."

"Of course," Foxman said, with obvious relief. "We all know about Peter."

"Downes and Geis are connected."

"I won't believe that," Ellie said, believing it, however, only because Keller said it was so.

"How?" Foxman said.

"I followed Geis," Keller said without inflection. "I had him watched, I had Peter watched. Downes was too smooth, too good to be true; his present didn't match up with his history." Keller continued, apparently oblivious of the pained expression on Ellie's face. "Geis is tight with Ralph Browning, and so, of course, is Downes. He brought you to Browning, Ellie."

"That doesn't prove anything," she snapped.

"Browning the banker?" Foxman said, struggling to regain his composure.

"My hunch is that Geis and Browning are tied in to Russ Almaz."

"Why?" Ellie said. "Why is this happening to us?"

It was Foxman who responded in a slow, heavy voice. "Keller, you do not believe that this is exclusively directed against Foxman and Company." Keller nodded. "You believe Russ Almaz has unloosed a massive attack on our industry—but to what end?"

Keller filled his lungs with air. "I believe the Russians hope to drive IMM to its knees and so take over at the highest levels."

"That doesn't make sense," Ellie said.

"Nor to me," Foxman said. "The Syndicate is the prototypical capitalist enterprise. Why would the Kremlin get involved?"

"For exactly that reason. Moscow has never been averse to making a buck. There's more: IMM shades every aspect of the national life of South Africa. It exerts influence over economic policies though it has continued to remain apart from politics. Under Soviet rule, that would change. Suddenly the people at the top of IMM would call for a softening of racial policies. Nothing too abrupt, just a gradual modification. At the same time, word would be spread unofficially throughout black Africa and other Third World countries that the Russians are behind it—Soviet influence in those nations would rise. Step by step, the Russians could begin to squeeze the diamond producers, quid pro quo. Business alliances would be formed, political alliances reflected in votes at the United Nations, treaties signed, military bases established. All of Africa would go East, and eventually all of the Muslim world, led by Libya and Syria. Eventually Iran would become totally isolated and fall under Soviet influence. And how long would Israel be able to hold out against the kind of pressure that would now be generated? And all this time the Russians would be collecting increasing amounts of hard currency with which to buy the grain they need from the U.S., from Canada, from Argentina. And the technology."

"Beautiful."

"If true," Ellie said, without much force.

Foxman came to his feet unsteadily, bracing himself on the desk, head swiveling as if unable to focus. All color drained out of his face and drool formed in the corner of his mouth.

"First Sir John and his thugs, now the Soviets. The new Nazis. They imprison our people, they kill them, they mock the rights of free men everywhere."

"Uncle!" Ellie cried. "Please, sit down. You're exciting yourself too much."

Foxman circled the French table and staggered, one fist raised in a feeble gesture of defiance. "I fought them, the Nazis. I will fight the Soviets, too. They must not be allowed to do this awful thing, they must not. We must oppose them. Fight . . ." He coughed and lurched against the side of the table, mouth gaping as if about to scream; instead, a trailing moan issued and he pitched face down into the lush Bokhara on the library floor. And lay without moving.

## *chapter*
# *40*

      DAVID AND MATTIE JOINED THEM outside the cardiac unit of Lenox Hill Hospital and they kept vigil until Maurice's physician appeared.

"How is my uncle?" Ellie said.

The doctor addressed Keller, assuming him to be the dominant male in the family. "Mr. Foxman is in critical condition, I'm afraid. He suffered a massive coronary infarction, and considering his age, I cannot be optimistic." The physician kept talking but Ellie tuned him out. Her uncle had absorbed too much punishment over his lifetime. The Russian conspiracy was the final straw. He had finally been beaten.

"There's no reason for you to remain here," the doctor was saying. "There's nothing you can do and you won't be able to see Maurice. Go home, get a good night's sleep and trust us to do our best for him."

"I will stay," Mattie said softly.

"So will I," David said.

"And me," Ellie said.

"No," Keller said firmly. "This may go on for some time and you have a company to run. You need your rest. I'll take you home."

"If there's any need, I'll call you," the doctor said.

Ellie protested but Keller insisted and in the end she gave in. Outside, Keller flagged a cab and gave him Ellie's address. As soon as they were under way, she began to weep. "For so long, I resented my uncle. I was angry with him."

"He didn't seem to mind."

"I never told him why, never gave him the chance to tell his side of the story."

"Very little got past that man. Whatever your reasons, he understood."

She put her face against his shoulder. "I feel ashamed, Keller. I've acted like a spoiled child."

He held her until she stopped crying, said nothing while she dried her eyes. When they arrived at her apartment house, Keller paid the cabbie and helped her onto the sidewalk. He wanted to comfort her, to reassure her; it was a reaction he was not entirely comfortable with.

"I like your uncle. In my world, he comes close to being unique. He's smarter than most, and he stands up for what he believes. I like that."

Not far behind them, a car door closed, guided almost silently into position, a disquieting deviation amidst the harsh discordance of city noises. Keller glanced over his shoulder. A man was coming their way without haste, hands plunged deeply into the pockets of his Burberry.

Ellie was speaking and he turned back to her. "It took me a long time to recognize Maurice for what he is."

"He's a winner," Keller answered. "He'll come through this time, too."

The sky was clear, speckled, with no threat of rain. The air was still and humid, much too warm for a coat.

"Do you really think so?" she said.

A vexing image surfaced in Keller's brain. Something vague and shadowy nibbled at the edges of his consciousness. Something vital that should have been identified and named. Deliberately he came around, positioning himself in front of Ellie. The man in the Burberry was no more than thirty yards away, on a street otherwise empty of human traffic. A slight man under a coat much too big for him. A faint lift to his mouth as if he derived some secret satisfaction from the moment. He came forward more quickly, a small man, deceptively fragile, with the taut, muscular swagger of a jockey . . . Leonid!

Keller shoved Ellie hard, sending her stumbling backwards between two parked cars. She gave a cry of protest, of anger; he didn't hear, already sprinting toward the low stone wall that surrounded the garden in front of the building. Without looking, he knew that Leonid had yanked his weapon from a side pocket, was tracking him. As he dived over the wall, he heard the pop-pop of a silenced .22 caliber. The bullets smashed off the sidewalk, chips of concrete flaring out in all directions.

Keller rolled, reaching for the .38 S & W holstered at the small of his back. He got one quick shot off, meant only to interrupt Leonid's concentration, to buy a second or two. It worked; Leonid went down on one knee, steadying his gun hand, trying to make sure this time. Keller sent another shot his way, coming closer than the Russian appreciated. Leonid had come to do a job, clean, simple and at minimal personal risk; he wasn't looking for a Wild West shootout. He turned and ran, Keller after him.

Keller kept pace. Behind by no more than fifty feet, he tried to close the distance before they reached the avenue. Suddenly Leonid ducked behind a parked car and began shooting.

Keller hit the pavement. His pistol, jarred loose, skidded a dozen feet away. He scrambled after it on hands and knees. A shot bit into the concrete to one side, sending a blossom of sparks into the night. In a prone position, Keller returned fire. Abruptly, as if by common consent, the shooting stopped.

Keller rolled, taking up a new position behind a red Datsun 280Z. He couldn't see Leonid but knew the Russian was nearby, plotting his next move. It would come with deadly suddenness, from an unexpected direction. Leonid had been trained to kill, to locate his victims and finish them off without a struggle. This was not his preferred way of doing his job.

Keller squinted into the darkness. No sign of Leonid on the sidewalk, no sign of him in the street. The shots had disturbed the neighborhood and lights were coming on and here and there a window opened, a ringside seat at a live-action drama. By now someone would have called for the police, that was what

Leonid would think. Time was running out for the Russian; he had to fight or run. Keller wasn't so sure; people didn't like to get involved.

Out of nowhere—Leonid. No more than ten feet away. He had squirmed forward under the line of parked cars and now sent shot after shot toward Keller. Keller dived, putting the Z between himself and Leonid. He bounced off the ground running, cutting back, snapping off two quick shots at the man on the sidewalk.

The first slug caught Leonid on the right hip, spinning him, causing his return shot to go high. The second bullet ripped into Leonid's breastbone, slicing upward into his heart and exiting behind the Russian's left shoulder.

One look told Keller that the little man was dead and of no further use; Leonid would be unable to answer any of his questions.

Keller shoved the .38 into his belt and went back to where he'd left Ellie. She was trembling, but dry-eyed, clearly relieved at the sight of him.

"Let's go," he said, steering her for the nearest corner.

"The police . . . ?"

"I want to get out of here before they come. It's been a hell of a day, I need some sleep."

"Those people . . ." She indicated the open windows. "They'll recognize you, us."

"Forget it. Just another shooting on the streets, even on your own block. I'll make a phone call and IMM will clean it up. We're good for twenty seconds on the six o'clock news, that's all. Come on, I don't want you involved."

They walked rapidly and after a couple of blocks he ushered her into a bar. A waiter brought two scotches to their booth and went away, never looking at them.

"He was waiting for you, Keller," she said. "How could he know you'd be there? How could he know that you'd be with me?"

He grimaced. "It was you he was after. When he spotted me, it was a two-for-one bargain day."

"I was so afraid. I'm still afraid."

"Anybody with any sense would be."

"You weren't."

"The hell you say." He stared into his drink and discovered nothing there that was going to help. "Do you believe me now, about Peter Downes?"

She turned away. "Whatever he is, Peter would never let them kill me. He wants to marry me."

"I wonder if he's thought through the paradox. Those friends of his, Browning and Geis. To them you're just an itch to be scratched. The guilt would appear to point to IMM. With you out of the picture, Downes gets control. At worst, he controls David."

She looked into Keller's rugged face; it was all there, the life he led, the beliefs he held fast to, the quiet certainty and courage of the man. It was not a pretty face, but it was the face of a man who had lived life according to his own dictates, never squandering his moral currency. Of all the men she'd known, he reminded her most of Maurice.

"What happens now?" she said.

"First, we finish our drinks. Second, it's back to my place. Don't argue, the Russian may have a backup. In the morning, well, we'll both go back to our jobs."

In his apartment, he made up the sofa in the living room, insisting that Ellie use the bed. It was a large bed, surface hard, with a musky male aroma that made her want him next to her. The idea startled her and she allowed herself to wonder briefly what sort of a lover Keller would be.

She became aware of him, watching her from the doorway.

"I owe you," she said.

"For almost getting you wasted? Not yet, you don't. Sleep well, I'll see you in the morning."

"Damn, Keller. Must you always be so tough? Come over here." And when he failed to respond: "Please."

He went to her side of the bed and she raised up, one arm circling his neck, drawing him down. His lips were surprisingly soft, gentle and affectionate. She was stunned by the outrageous visceral message her nerve ends sent spinning off to her brain. She shuddered and clung tightly to him.

He unloosened himself and stepped away.

"Oh, don't go, not yet." It was spoken as a childish plea

and she disliked herself for being weak, for wanting him more than he wanted her.

"I'm a romantic—at least your uncle seems to think so. Anyway, it's been a bad night. Getting shot at may turn on some guys—not me. Go to sleep, both of us need the rest. There's a lot to do and a lot more like Leonid still out there."

## chapter
# *41*

WHEN ELLIE WOKE the next morning, Keller was gone. A note was propped up on the kitchen table.

*Instant coffee only. Eggs, butter, etc. in fridge. Help self. Call if you need to, I'll be close. You sleep great, a solid gold medal winner. You're welcome.*

*Keller*

She read the note twice, folded it carefully and placed it in her purse. It was, she decided, a love letter, the best Keller could manage. The best she'd ever received.

She showered and dressed and drank some instant coffee; it was stale and tasted bitter. She poured most of it into the sink, leaving the ceramic mug sitting where he was bound to see it, to let him know she appreciated his hospitality.

At Lenox Hill, Mattie was still waiting. Her eyes were swollen and she looked as if she hadn't slept all night.

"How is he?"

"Not good. Not strong."

"Have you spoken to the doctor?"

"He's not encouraging, it was a massive attack."

"Can Maurice have visitors?"

"He'll want to see you. But only for a few minutes. Don't get him excited."

The blinds were closed and in the dimness Maurice appeared shrunken in the bed, the once handsome, dominant figure no longer in view. Tubes and wires connected him to monitors and oxygen and an IV. Faint blue traces were visible under his translucent skin. When she touched his hand, he reached for her reflexively, his grasp feeble but determined. His eyes fluttered open and he spoke her name in a voice no longer recognizable.

"Are you all right, my dear?"

"The question is, are you all right?"

He managed a weak, sly smile. "How can I be all right, when I'm still alive?" He attempted to laugh at his little joke but the laugh turned into a racking cough. A nurse materialized to give him water through a bent plastic straw. She fussed over the pillows, checked the connections on the tubes and wires and cautioned Ellie not to stay too long.

"I love you, my dear. You were the daughter I never had. Was I too hard on you? Perhaps I was. Perhaps I could never bestow affection as freely as I would have liked. But the love was always present, the respect, and despite . . ."

"Despite?"

"Despite what you thought of me."

There was no point in denying the obvious. "The bad feeling between you and Daddy."

"Ah, Ellie, there was so much anger, so much suspicion and resentment. We were of one blood, all that remained of our family. It should not have been the way it was."

She bent and placed her cheek against his. His skin was icy and the scent of death clung to him.

"Soon you'll feel better, Uncle."

"Yes, soon." And it was clear that he would not deceive himself, especially not at the end of his life; he was dying and he knew it.

"Oh, Maurice. Forgive me for being a fool, so harsh, so stupid."

He made no answer; he was dead.

* * *

Services were held in Temple Emanu-El. The synagogue was crowded with friends, colleagues from around the world, business acquaintances who knew Maurice Foxman by reputation only and cherished what he stood for.

The cortege was long and made its way slowly through Manhattan to the Holland Tunnel and out to the cemetery in New Jersey where Emil had been buried.

At the graveside, no more tears; Ellie, Mattie, David. They were dry and empty, made less by Maurice's passing. And the ride back to the city was still, hardly any words spoken; there was nothing more to be said.

The limousine delivered David and Mattie to her apartment, Peter and Ellie remaining in the car.

"You'd probably like to be alone," Peter said as they got under way.

"We have some serious talking to do, Peter. Today. You come with me."

In her apartment, she left Downes in the living room while she showered and changed into a skirt and blouse. Her hair was pulled back, held in place by a rubber band. When she appeared again, she found Downes with a drink in his hand.

"I needed this," he declared, half in apology. "Poor Maurice, he meant a great deal to me. Fix you one?"

"Spare me, Peter. This is no time for sham and hypocrisy. It wasn't Maurice's way, it isn't mine."

He recognized the hostility in her manner and turned away, taking a seat across the room. "What's wrong, Ellie? Maurice was the most important man in my life. I would have done anything for him."

"Perhaps you should say you would have done anything *to* him."

A flush came onto Peter's swarthy cheeks. "What do you mean by that? Maurice befriended me, he took me in, he..."

"Yes, and you have almost ruined his business."

"I would never do anything to hurt that man."

"You have been steadily driving Foxman and Company toward bankruptcy. This wild buying of yours."

"That's my job. Maurice commissioned me to build up company stocks. Those bad sights, he couldn't get stones. You couldn't. I had to make sure we had something to sell. *You* told me to buy . . . Maurice had no other sources."

"And it was you who got him in the end. Your schemes and scams."

"I don't have to listen to this!" He shoved himself erect.

"Sit down, Peter." She breathed deeply, seeking to control her anger. "Have you assembled the sales package?"

"Nine million—that's a lot of diamonds to pull together. I—"

"Then you haven't done it yet?"

He flexed his fingers and avoided her eyes. "I'm working on it."

"I want it done at once, do you understand?"

"It's almost finished," he said without much force.

"And the buyer?"

"I've lined one up—he may take the entire lot."

"When will you know?"

"This afternoon, possibly. Tomorrow at the latest."

"Then all parts will be in place tomorrow?"

"Yes. I'm sure of it, yes."

"Good. I'm flying over to London. Contact me at the Connaught when you're ready to go."

"You'll come to Geneva?"

"A sale of this magnitude, of course. At the bank, I assume."

"Yes, at the bank."

"I'll be there."


Ellie spent the next two hours alone, reviewing the events of the last few weeks. When her mind was made up, she put a call through to Sir John Messinger in London. She was told he was not available, would not be available for some considerable period of time. This done, she left to see Mattie and David.

They sat around a glass-and-stainless-steel coffee table in Mattie's living room. Ellie repeated Keller's suspicions, brought them up to date on her meeting with Downes and listed the dangers facing each of them as a member of the firm. She ended by telling them of the attack on her and Keller by Leonid.

"I read the story in the *Daily News*," David said. "The police identified the man as Leonid Ostroikov, a Soviet national. The Russian ambassador has made a protest, calling it an act of aggression against the Soviet Union. He blamed the Jewish Defense League and said it was all part of an international Zionist plot."

"If not for Keller, I'd be dead. Keller is convinced Leonid shot Robert, and others as well."

"Oh, my God," Mattie said. "It's the Nazi business all over again. Kill the Jews, for one reason or another. Your uncle was right about it. The business, it's just too dangerous. Give it up. We've enough money, you don't have to work."

"I'm not going to surrender. Not to the Soviets, not to the Syndicate."

"What choice do you have? We can't stand up to all of them."

Mattie began to snuffle, dabbing at her eyes with a handkerchief. David stared motionlessly into space. Each was waiting for the other to take charge, for life to exercise its will on them. To Ellie, the difference between herself and her mother and cousin was clearly defined. They were motes on the wind, drifting with the current.

Maurice had been a man who created his own existence, his own persona. Through struggle and determination, he had achieved his ends, turned himself into the man he had always wanted to he. Ellie would be no different. She would never give up.

"I can," she answered Mattie. "I will."

"I don't want you to be hurt."

"If I surrender, if I run away, I'll be hurting myself."

"You're only one human being, you can't make war on the Soviet Union."

"If what Keller says is so," David added, "they'll send others to take Leonid's place."

Ellie looked from one to the other and back again. She loved them both and needed them in her life. But they needed her even more. To lead, to give support, to take care of them in the same way that Maurice had always taken care of them.

"I will fight," she said.

"Alone . . . ?" There was terror in Mattie's voice.

"I won't be alone," was all Ellie said.

She called Keller.

The same uninterested voice informed her Keller was out of town, out of reach.

"Tell him Ellie Foxman called. Tell him I need to talk to him at once. Today. Right now. Tell him I'm on my way to London on the next flight out. If I don't hear from him in the next two hours, tell him not to bother."

She readied herself for the journey, letting it all percolate in her head, ceasing to think about it only when convinced she was as prepared as she was likely to be. If necessary, she would make this critical assault on the enemy stronghold by herself; she hoped it wouldn't be necessary. The house intercom buzzed; the doorman announced her limousine had arrived for the trip to Kennedy.

"Five minutes," she said, and closed her bags. Keller, damnit! When she needed him most, where the hell was he?

She slung an in-flight bag over one shoulder, another in hand, and made one last quick survey of the apartment. She was halfway out the door when the phone rang. It was Keller.

"I gave up on you."

"What is it?"

"That damned secretary, she's a robot."

"Shirley's been there before, she doesn't get worked up. Okay, talk."

That was Keller, blunt, to the point, with no time to waste. Her faith in him returned; his powers loomed large once more. Her personal superhero.

"Maurice died."

"I heard."

"You weren't at the funeral."

"I had something to do. Why did you call?"

"Where are you, Keller?"

"Venice."

"Why are you in Venice when I need you here?"

"Is something wrong?"

"I'm on my way to London. I tried phoning Sir John, he refused to answer."

"That figures; you're a Foxman."

"Set it up for me, Keller."

"A meeting with Sir John? I don't know about that."

"Then I'll do it without you. Goodbye, Keller."

"Hold it! Don't hang up." The long wire crackled and Keller sounded uncharacteristically weary when he spoke again. "I'll give it a shot. I'll get back to you."

"At the Connaught tomorrow. If you can't pull it off, I'll find a way to do it myself. Goodbye, Keller. I'm running out of time."

"Wait!" she heard him say, but she hung up and left. She'd waited too long already.

# chapter
## 42

AT ABOUT THE SAME TIME that Ellie was landing at Heathrow in England, Peter Downes entered Ralph Browning's hotel suite in Geneva. Harry Geis was with the banker.

"All that's necessary," Browning began, "is for Miss Foxman to appear at the bank at the time of the proposed sale. I assume you've taken care of that?" he said to Downes.

Downes was reluctant to tell his partners about the downward turn in his relationship with Ellie. He perceived himself walking the razor's edge between her and them and struggled painfully to maintain his position. "She's in England."

"But you can get in touch with her?"

"Is it absolutely necessary that she be here?"

"Hell, yes!" Geis snapped out. "You know how this job works."

Browning, in a tranquil voice designed to be soothing, said, "Something of this magnitude, the chief executive of the selling company must be in attendance. Is there some difficulty you haven't mentioned? Please, Peter, no surprises at this late stage."

"No," Peter said. "As soon as we're finished here, I'll contact her. She can make it over without any trouble. The stones are in the vault and the buyer is in place."

"Excellent," Browning said. "This should allay Miss Foxman's anxieties regarding the company's fiscal status and reassure her about your sincere good efforts on her behalf. Above all, Peter, we wish your relationship with the lady to continue and to grow. Thus will you be able to go on buying on our behalf without any substantial interference. I congratulate you, Peter."

When the others had left, Browning poured some twenty-year-old scotch into a glass and sat down to savor his success. Project Flawless was the culmination of his long career. He had worked hard for the Cause, as he liked to think of it. He had followed orders, laid the groundwork for this one big sting. Big enough, he mused with satisfaction, actually to undermine the capitalist economy. All his labors, all his planning, all the time away from home and his family were worth it. He was about to execute the greatest and most dramatic success of any sleeper who had ever served the Soviet Union. The future glowed with promise. Certainly he would be awarded the Order of Lenin and all the material rewards that went with it. He would return to Mother Russia, live openly again as a Russian citizen. All the benefits of the good life in Moscow would be his.

A persistent knocking at the door drew him back to the present. Who could it be? He was expecting no one. Perhaps Geis, returning to check some insignificant detail, or Downes, requiring additional reassurance. He smiled patronizingly and opened the door.

A dapper man with an unyielding expression on his cultivated face stared up at Browning out of still, dark eyes.

"You shouldn't be here," Browning said, without thinking.

The dapper man went past Browning, examining the suite with considerable distaste.

"You live very well, comrade," he said.

Browning shrugged and sipped some scotch. "I live as my public position dictates. I am a banker and bankers do live well."

"A capitalist," the dapper man said. "Tell me, comrade, you enjoy being a capitalist?"

"Can I get you a drink, Andrei?"

"You have vodka?"

"Scotch only, I'm afraid."

"In my house, there is always vodka."

Browning ignored the criticism. Whatever the reason for this unexpected visit, it could mean only additional complications and that made him nervous.

"Why are you here, Andrei? Rezident of the KGB Geneva meeting privately with an American banker. It can hardly advance our cause and is unlikely to go unnoticed."

"I have my orders."

"And my orders were to remain independent of contact with people in your position."

Andrei smiled a thin, mirthless smile. "Do I frighten you, comrade? Do you have something to be afraid of, something to hide?"

"This meeting puts me in jeopardy, Andrei, and that means the operation is in jeopardy. That is all I fear, nothing else."

"Your sincerity is reassuring. Be at ease, my friend, this is just a friendly little visit, nothing more."

"What do you want?"

"For myself, nothing. For the Motherland, everything. In this matter, I am only a messenger. I am instructed to inquire—this operation of yours, when does it culminate?"

"One other party must arrive in Geneva. Tomorrow at the latest, I'm sure. Why do you want to know?"

"And then?"

"And then I shall be one step closer to taking absolute control of a major American diamond company. From that base, Project Flawless will be able to proceed to its natural and inevitable conclusion, the takeover of International Minerals and Mines."

"I'm afraid that's not possible, comrade."

Browning felt his extremities turn icy and numb. He held himself stiffly. "I don't understand."

"Project Flawless is over, finished, terminated, by command of Moscow."

"But we are so close."

"It is over, comrade. Tatiana was uncovered and she put a security man from IMM onto Geis."

"That can't be true! I'd have known. I . . ."

"It is true. Tatiana was brought out; she is now back in the Soviet Union being thoroughly debriefed. Geis's cover is blown, which means you are vulnerable. Leonid is dead, as you know. A certain Vadim Lukas, a conduit for stones in Paris, has disappeared. Three of our people in Europe have gone to ground and two others in the United States have been pulled out. Project Flawless had gone as far as it can go, Comrade Browning."

"I can still make it work. Even without Geis. All I need is Downes and he's in position."

"Downes is worthless to you. This security man—his name is Keller—certainly he will bring the FBI, possibly the CIA. Who knows where a thing like this might lead? Moscow must not be further embarrassed. Definitely not in public. Nor do we wish to lose any more of our people. No, my friend, somewhere you committed a massive blunder. A miscalculation. All this time lost, all this work. But nothing more must be lost. Certainly not the diamonds. Where are they now?"

Browning stopped listening. Had he in fact committed some egregious error? Had someone higher in Russ Almaz grown disenchanted with his efforts? Or envious of his achievements? Did this mean demotion? Punishment of some kind? Was he to be locked forever into some dull and menial job in Moscow or some lesser city?

The vagaries of political life in the Soviet Union had become remote concerns during his years in America; he had forgotten the constant suspicions that permeated the bureaucracy, the ruthless displays of ambition that often cost men their careers, their freedom and sometimes their lives. What awful fate awaited him at home?

Andrei, as if reading from notes, said, "Possibly you are about to receive some high award, comrade. Who knows, the Stalin Prize itself might be forthcoming. A fine dacha outside of Moscow. A position of respect and importance. The Party takes care of those who serve it faithfully. The stones, comrade, where are they?"

Reluctantly Browning brought himself back to the present. His options were limited; whatever future remained to him would be at home among his own people, whatever life he had would be lived out as a Russian. Anything else was unthinkable; though he had passed himself off as an American for so long, in his heart he had always remained Russian, would continue to live as a Russian and die a Russian. He straightened up in his chair and smiled graciously.

"In New York, comrade. The bulk of them are in New York."

"The *bulk* of them? And the remainder?"

"Here in Geneva. In the Foxman vault. Circumstances forced us to sell nine million and—"

Andrei cut him off. "Can you retrieve them?"

"Only Downes and the Foxman woman would have access to the vault. I suppose Downes could be sent after them."

"I don't think so. Downes would question any abrupt change in plans and, as you've made clear, he is an emotionally unreliable man, not one of us." Andrei considered the situation. "Very well, the nine million must be sacrificed, a regrettable loss but under the circumstances acceptable. Very well. Now to proceed. You, Browning, will leave at once for New York City and take possession of the stones and carry them back to the Soviet Union."

Browning slumped back. His fate, whatever it was to be, would be decided by men more powerful than himself. His destiny, for the foreseeable future, was merely to obey orders.

"There is still Harry Geis," he said.

"Yes," Andrei drawled. "In my opinion, he has transformed himself into a petty hoodlum and a capitalist. No longer is he a man to be trusted. You will say to him nothing of our conversation, comrade. I do not doubt that should he discover that Project Flawless has been terminated, Geis would attempt to get his hands on the diamonds for his own profit. His greed would blind him to the fact that he could not last long once it was known to us that he had taken them, a fact which I am certain is equally clear to you."

"You need have no concern over where my loyalties lie, comrade."

"Good. As for Geis, I'll direct his destiny myself."

"That's it, then?"

"You have your orders, you have only to carry them out. One day we shall meet again in Moscow, comrade, and drink a toast to our adventures in good Russian vodka."

"Yes," Browning said, remembering the well-stocked bar in his lush New York apartment. "In vodka, comrade."

## chapter
# 43

SHE ADMITTED KELLER to her rooms at the Connaught. He looked grim, the bony face lined with weariness. There was nothing pretty about that face, nothing sweet or endearing, a face that had never been handsome; but there was a determination to him, a manliness, the kind of face that continually revealed fresh facets, the kind of face you would never tire of looking at.

She came up behind him. "I knew you'd be around."

He turned her way. "This thing is coming to a head."

"Peter called me an hour ago. From Geneva. Nine million dollars' worth of good stones are in the vault and a buyer is lined up and waiting."

"Oh, they are good, very good. They intend to make certain Foxman and Company remains in business, allowing them to pile up a mountain of first-rate diamonds. You're going, of course."

"As soon as I finish with Sir John."

"Did it ever occur to you I might not be able to arrange it?"

"Frankly, no. My faith in you is boundless, Keller."

He made a face and muttered. "Don't push your luck. Most of my leverage went out on this one, so give it your best shot. Whatever you've got in mind, it better be good." He looked her over. In a pale gray worsted suit with a chalk stripe, tailored with a soft hand, over a taupe blouse with a floppy bow at the throat, she looked more beautiful than ever, elegant and at the same time casual. Her hair was luminous, flaring out from her head in delicate clouds. When he spoke, the voice had lost its edge. "The old man's a hard case. He's smart and he's dangerous. Watch yourself, lady."

"I'll do my best."

"I'll say this, he's never seen anything as good to look at before."

Her grin was spontaneous. "What a nice compliment."

"Don't be too sure," he drawled, a down and dirty turn to his mouth.

"I'll take it as one, the first you've ever paid me." She sat down and motioned him to the chair opposite. She spoke in a girlish voice. "Am I going to pull it off, Keller?"

"I'm betting on you."

She nodded once and her manner was quickly transformed, as if in his faith in her she found added confidence. She took on some of the same graceful authority Maurice had possessed. "All right, Keller. Tell me everything you know about Sir John."

"Tough as you'll ever meet. Born to wealth and power, he has tightened his hold on both. He controls men and corporations, presidents and kings; he manipulates dictators and rebels alike. He maintains open lines to the top echelons of every government in the West and the ones that matter behind the Curtain.

"If he wants something done, it usually gets done. He is strong. He is shrewd. He is ruthless. He can spot the flaw in a diamond quicker than anyone I've ever known. In a diamond *or* in a man."

"What about a woman?"

"Make a mistake and he'll eat you alive. I've never heard of him doing anything to hurt himself. Nobody forces him to do anything not in his own best interests. Nobody."

"You talked him into seeing me."

"I presented some facts to him, he made up his own mind."

"What kind of facts?"

"Sir John has a certain appreciation for beautiful women."

"That's twice in one conversation, Keller, you've said something nice to me. I'm getting to you, huh?" She produced a wide, lingering smile.

He managed a dark scowl and ignored the question. "Don't come on to him."

"What about to you?"

"Just make sense. He'll spot a phony argument as quick as he spots a phony diamond. He's got no use for either one."

"You give good advice, Keller."

"This is your only chance with him, make the most of it."

"When do I get to see the man?"

"Now," he said, standing. "Let's go."

## chapter
# *44*

ROSEWOOD PANELING covered the walls of
the long room, which was dominated by a coffin-shaped con-
ference table. Sir John was waiting when they were ushered
in. He delivered a formal bow of welcome in Ellie's direction,
waited for her to be seated and sat down himself. His mouth
was severe, his eyes flat and unblinking, his stance proud and
inflexible. He had approached this meeting as he approached
every other event in his life, viewing it as another opportunity
to be exploited for gain, for pleasure, for power.

"Keller spoke very highly of you, Miss Foxman," he began,
giving away nothing.

"He spoke highly of you, too, sir."

He studied her. And liked what he saw. There was a boldness
in those sea-green eyes, a stubborn tilt to her chin, a fierceness
of tone and manner that informed him she would not give
herself over easily to another's wishes. He conjured up an old
memory of Maurice Foxman; culture, delicacy and a refined
intelligence marked the man. His niece radiated a well-fash-
ioned toughness, a hardened pragmatism the uncle had often
lacked. He decided to waste no time on preliminaries.

"What is it you come for, Miss Foxman?"

He was forcing the issue, taking the high ground before she
could establish her own position. She replied in kind.

359

"To save Foxman and Company from disaster, Sir John."

"And how do you hope to accomplish that, may I ask?"

"Two ways. First, I want you to restore to the company the sight you took from my uncle."

"Done, let me remind you, only after Foxman refused the last offering."

She recognized her mistake; Keller was right, Sir John was no ordinary man. His was a dominating personality, quick, intense, and always dangerous.

"Only after you deprived him of the high-quality merchandise to which he was entitled. You made a concerted effort to damage his position in the market."

"The man decided to turn against me, become my enemy, the enemy of International Minerals and Mines. He began buying from other sources, he moved into colored stones without informing us of his intentions; he tried to enlist other dealers into a union aligned against me; he was buying immense amounts of diamonds from underground sources, hoarding them, planning some insidious strike against me and mine. And lastly, Miss Foxman, he was smuggling diamonds."

She shook her head from side to side. "No," she said forcefully. "No, not my uncle. My brother bought smuggled stones. I concede that. I regret it as my uncle must have regretted it. But Foxman and Company was not involved, had nothing to do with it." She was breathing hard and struggled for control, exhaling deliberately. "Now, sir, may we discuss the current situation?"

Sir John stared at her, giving nothing away. He replied as if she hadn't spoken. "Another man would have been less tolerant of your uncle's assaults on my operation than I have been. And you, a member of his family, you have altered nothing of your company's activities. You still acquire large numbers of stones."

Keller decided to step in. "Not exactly," he said. "It was Downes, in alliance with Geis and Browning. Downes does the buying."

"The same thing."

"Not for Foxman and Company. Downes buys as part of a massive swindle directed first at Ellie's company, Sir John, and eventually at IMM itself."

"Nonsense, Keller. I expect better of you."

Keller went on without pause. "Downes buys Russian stones from fronts, buyers who appear to be operating in the traditional framework, but actually are Soviet outlets. He buys with Foxman's credit. When the scam is completed, the Soviets will be able to control the market.

"You've worked it all out, Keller."

"It's logical."

"Is it? This obsession of yours with the Russians—give it up, Keller."

"I can't do that, sir."

Sir John swung back to Ellie. "For the moment, Miss Foxman, you continue to function in ways antithetical to the well-being of our industry. Your efforts to open up supply lines in black Africa, to create your own bourse, to force yourself upon us and so make us alter our traditional way of doing things. In what way are you so different from your uncle?"

"I run Foxman and Company now. If I am less the gentleman than my uncle was—well, put it down to my unwillingness to be pushed around. By anybody."

Sir John allowed nothing to show on his face. "My grandfather was a man without education, without breeding or background, a salesman for a small Austrian toolmaker. On a selling trip to South Africa in the last year of the last century, he perceived the possibilities of that land and he stayed on. He soon recognized the unlimited mineral wealth present in the country.

"He passed his vision on to his son, my father, and it was he who developed the diamond mines that were to become central to IMM. My father was a man of limitless ambition, a daring man, afraid of nothing. He took the family into zinc and copper, into natural gas, into platinum and uranium and gold and vanadium and coal and steel and more.

"But it was my grandfather who saw diamonds as the locus of our interests, and passed this love of gems to my father and eventually to me. I care about diamonds, Miss Foxman, about how they are mined and cut and used and sold. Diamonds provide livelihoods for people all over the world, shape their lives, provide good fortune to them and good years and give considerable joy to millions of other people.

"My grandfather, my father, myself, we have raised IMM out of personal creativity and intelligence and perseverance. One does not run such a complex of enterprises without making enemies. When it came time for a fight, each of us fought. And always won. No one has ever prevailed over IMM, Miss Foxman. No one ever will."

"It is not my intention to damage IMM, Sir John." There was no retreat in her tone, no indication that she was intimidated. "I know better than that." Conciliation was what she offered, not concession. "However, I can become sufficiently irritating to that Chinese puzzle you head up to make you pay attention."

"I am paying attention, young woman. Or haven't you noticed? It would be a grievous error to lose sight of who your enemy may be in this world."

"Locate your enemy and destroy him, is that it?"

"Those I can crush, I crush. Those I can frighten, I frighten. Those I can buy, I buy. Does that answer your question?"

"What if you can accomplish none of them?"

"Chinese puzzle, you said. A good description of my organization. When compromises are in order, I make them. As a result, I have partners, alliances, agreements. Some companies I own outright, others I influence; still others look to me for protection. Do whatever is necessary, that is the abiding dictum of my life, with one simple goal in mind—the ultimate supremacy of International Minerals and Mines, Limited. One way or another, I get my way. That is a fact, Miss Foxman."

"Things may be different this time." It was Keller who had spoken, his voice tinged with irony. "The usual methods may not work. Not against an enemy much more powerful, with too many troops."

"Still the Russians?" Sir John said.

"Still the Russians, Sir John."

"And you, Miss Foxman, are you here to ally yourself with me in this great war against the Russian bear?"

"We may be able to help each other."

"Let me make my position crystal clear. At first, I could not accept your premise concerning the Soviets, Keller. I saw it as self-limiting for them, in the long run self-defeating. Since then, however, I have accumulated additional information. Keller, it seems I may have been mistaken.

"It appears the Soviets suffer from an acute case of tunnel vision. Always fearful of outsiders, they perceive threats when only rewards are offered. They count up disasters when profits are within reach. Imprisoned by pious political and economic principles, Moscow is psychologically unable, in the long term, to act in its best interests."

"Then you agree with Keller," Ellie said eagerly, "that the Russians are plotting against the Syndicate?"

Sir John grimaced. "The term offends me. IMM is a community of like-minded enterprises, each functioning according to the laws and limitations of the various nations in which they operate."

He pulled at his lower lip, lost in thought. "I have come around to your position, Keller, yes. I concede certain difficulties in our business. Too many diamonds are loose in the marketplace, diamonds not under our authority. Should they suddenly be made available, the carat price would plummet. For a long time I believed that Maurice Foxman and his friends were trying to do just that. Seems I was wrong. My intelligence people confirm Keller's reports."

He nodded approvingly at Keller. "I resisted your earlier attempts to bring the truth to me. I rejected the additional information I was privy to. I withstood the internal logic of what I was told; something I seldom do. I based too much on my agreement with the Russians. My deal with the Kremlin, it was favorable to both sides, and I saw no reason why it should not go on forever. I know better now.

"With the Soviets for an enemy, I began to feel as your uncle must have felt about me, Miss Foxman. Outmanned, brutalized at every turn. I have been trying desperately to avoid the confrontation with Moscow, to no avail."

"I still find it difficult to understand," Ellie said. "What do they stand to gain?"

Keller answered. "It's all part of a grand strategy, Soviet global ambition. It works this way: They aim to infiltrate deeper into South Africa's black revolutionary movement, turn it more and more until it coincides with the Kremlin's ambitions.

Once Moscow controls IMM, it will be able to influence and even direct the South African government's racial policies and military positions."

"Policies," Sir John said, "that I have never supported."

"Next," Keller said, "By taking over a major capitalist industry the Russians establish powerful lines into the banking and credit markets."

"Very good, Keller," Sir John said. "It was that fact which convinced me. I'm rather impressed that you understand such esoteric economic ramifications."

Keller ignored the remark. "Last, they will guarantee a continuous flow of hard currency into the Soviet Union by controlling the sale of and the prices of diamonds, many of which they produce themselves. In that way, Russ Almaz will preserve its own diamond wealth, while gradually enhancing its worth, until their producing mines become the primary source of gems for the West."

"A nice touch," Sir John commented. "The bastion of socialism enmeshed in a crass effort to exploit the free competitive marketplace for its own materialistic gains. All done with the covert support of imperialistic IMM."

Ellie stared at him without flinching. "What are you going to do about it?"

"Is that why you came, to ask me that?"

"I came to demand that you relent in your attacks on Foxman and Company. That you reinstate our regular sight."

"No woman has ever had her own sight."

"Then it's time one did. I'm here to claim it."

"I am not prepared to discuss that with you, Miss Foxman. As for your previous question—yes, we will fight. And frankly, the outcome is in doubt. Not even International Minerals and Mines can withstand an ongoing assault from a major world power. Not even I have that kind of force on call."

"For the first time we agree," Ellie said. "No way you can take on Moscow and win."

"What are you saying!" Keller snapped. "You'd let it all go? Your company, Ellie? IMM? All of it, without a struggle? What in hell is wrong with you people!"

"Listen to me, Keller. Neither Sir John nor I can stand up

to the Russians. Not head to head, certainly. But we do have some substantial advantages."

"Such as?"

"Let's face it, the people in the Kremlin do not want their participation in this sleazy affair made public. Duplicity, thievery, smuggling, murder; and all in order to make *money*. They don't want their socialist purity called into question around the world. No way. Or their honor as a sovereign nation. Think of the headlines—Soviets connive with IMM and South African racist regime. Can't you see it, Keller? The plot they've cooked up is the strongest weapon we have against it."

Sir John shook his head. "Still, if we do not fight the Russians, who do we fight?"

"Their agents."

"Browning and Geis," Keller said.

"And through them, Moscow. But never directly. We can stop them cold, if we're smart enough and tough enough.

"That brings us to my second reason for being here," Ellie said, surprised at how calm she was, how firmly in command of herself. "The Soviet scheme to take over my company. They cannot be permitted to do that. I intend to stop them."

"How?" Sir John said.

"I will attack them at their weakest point," Ellie said flatly.

"I'm afraid I don't understand."

"Peter Downes," she went on. "He bought up sixty million dollars' worth of gems, thanks to the reputation of the company my uncle created, thanks to Foxman credit. Downes knows where those stones are, he knows what plans have been made for their disposition. He knows what Browning and Geis intend to do next. He must be made to confess his part in the plot, to implicate the others, to let the Soviets know that they cannot take us over with impunity."

"A laudable concept, Miss Foxman. But why should this Downes fellow talk?"

Ellie hoped her confidence wasn't outstripping her grasp of the situation. "I had Downes sell off some nine million dollars' worth of stones. Those stones are waiting in a Geneva bank for transfer to a buyer Peter has lined up."

"They won't be there," Keller said, with all the pessimistic authority of a professional policeman. "The vault will be empty, or loaded with glass. They intend to break your company."

"For a while I believed that, too," Ellie said. "But breaking us would not make any sense. They intend to use us. They need Foxman in order to establish their seemingly legitimate credit rating, a base from which to continue buying and hoarding stones until they are strong enough to attack the Syndicate itself, Sir John. First Foxman, then IMM."

"Given the logic of your case," Sir John said thoughtfully, "I must ask again, how do you plan to stop them?"

"By getting to the vault before the scheduled sale. By removing those stones."

"And then?" Keller said.

"Let Downes confront an empty box at the time of the sale."

"I still don't get it."

"But I do, Keller," Sir John said. "Downes expects the stones to be in the vault, he put them there, they *must* be there in order to keep Foxman and Company solvent, for the plot to go forward. Isn't that your thinking, Miss Foxman?"

"Yes, sir. Once Peter discovers the stones are missing, he will understand the Russian scheme has been broken. He'll believe Browning and Geis took them. His life will be a ruin. Certainly he will suffer a jail term, and the Soviets being what they are, he may even be at mortal risk. I know Peter, that empty box will unnerve him so that he'll panic, spill everything he knows about the scam and direct us to the rest of the stones."

"Do you read Mr. Downes similarly, Keller?" Sir John said.

"It makes sense. He's not a strong man. Your presence on the scene, Sir John, might have a powerful impact on the situation."

"Very well, we'll go to Geneva together, all three of us."

"Can you get into the vault?" Keller said to Ellie.

"As chief executive officer, my signature is on the bank card, along with Peter's. The only question is, can we get to Geneva quickly enough?"

"Oh, I'm sure we can," Sir John said. "One of our company planes should do the trick. After all, we don't want to miss delivering a very substantial kick in the teeth to our Russian friends . . ."

## chapter
# *45*

THE BANK WAS LOCATED in a stately private building with an unobstructed view of the lake. A large man with a distinctive bulge under his arm admitted them, checked their identification and directed them to a small elevator made of wood, glass and polished brass. It carried them smoothly and quietly to the third floor. Waiting for them in the ample reception hall, a cadaverous man. Without a word, he led them into a meeting room where two other men, in somber suits and exquisitely shined black shoes, greeted them. The shorter of the pair was Leon Böhle, vice-chairman of the First International Swiss Bank of Geneva & Lugano. His manner told all; here was a man cognizant of the seriousness of life and all its transactions.

"Allow me to introduce you to Mr. Nicholas Yankelevich. Mr. Yankelevich is the buyer of your stones."

Yankelevich was medium in all his proportions, designed by a considerate Nature to fade into whatever environment he found himself. Camouflaged in ordinariness, he found in that ordinariness his strength and his salvation. He clicked his heels and bowed over Ellie's hand. "My pleasure, my pleasure."

"Your name is unknown to me, Mr. Yankelevich. Are you new to the business?"

He took one step backward. "My offices are in Hong Kong, in Tokyo and elsewhere." He looked over at Leon Böhle expectantly.

The banker indicated the long, narrow table against the near wall. On it sat a metal box about the size of a large milk carton, dark gray in color with handles at either end. It was sealed with red wax, sealed for a second time, Ellie knew, less than an hour ago.

"This container was removed from the vault only minutes ago, lady and gentlemen," Böhle said smoothly. "Brought to this room under guard and since then under my personal surveillance." He spoke with a sober sense of pride; the box, the vault, Böhle himself, were equivalent elements in the bank's vaunted security system.

Yankelevich tapped his breast. "In my pocket I have a check in the amount agreed upon." He directed a benevolent glance in Downes's direction. "Certified, naturally. Nine million one hundred and twenty thousand dollars American."

Downes cleared his throat. He was aware of his heart racing and wished Browning had come along to supervise the exchange. Browning had the style and the confidence, the experience in such matters. He could deal with the unexpected. Not that Downes anticipated any trouble; it had all been carefully plotted, every detail, every step, even to the questions that might be asked, the objections raised. The check in Yankelevich's pocket, for example; the total amount was on deposit in support of the check, in case someone had investigated.

His glance went to Keller. Who was he? Ellie had described him as a friend, an adviser. "A diamond maven," she had joked, using the Yiddish expression for expert. There was something about Keller that bothered Downes; he was too alert, too physical, not the kind of man who searched for bubbles, clouds and feathers. Why was he here?

"Let's get on with it," Ellie said.

"Yes," Downes said, putting on a confident smile. "It isn't every day I consummate this large a sale."

Böhle maneuvered them into position around the table. "I am removing the seal," he declared, suiting action to word. "I am opening the box." He stepped back, allowing the others to examine its contents.

"Empty!" Yankelevich cried. "What does this mean? I am not amused."

Downes peered into the box, inspecting the shadowed, shallow corners, seeking evidence of some trick, a trapdoor, a magician's sleight of hand. He found nothing.

"This can't be," he muttered. "Nine million dollars of—I saw to their delivery myself. I—" His mind flashed backwards and forwards in time, straining to find the key to this stunning conundrum, dimly aware of the awful consequences about to befall him. Panic stirred his bowels and the compulsion to run, to hide, to be alone in some distant dark and safe place was almost overwhelming.

His head swiveled, eyes leaping from face to blank face, finding understanding nowhere. He was without friends, without allies, left only with critics and enemies, each one intending to do him harm. "How?" he asked, as much to himself as to any of them.

Ellie answered in a voice toneless, cold, without hope. "The stones are in a safe place, Peter, safe from you, safe from Browning, safe from Harry Geis."

Looking at her now was as if he were seeing her for the first time. An impenetrable polished veneer masked her, her skin taut, her eyes still and bright, her voice edged with an unshakable authority he had never before noticed. She was a stranger, this Ellie Foxman. He could recall nothing of the way she was, not the warmth of her flesh, nor the softness of her fingers, nor the thick musky smell of her body beneath the covers. This Ellie Foxman was distanced from him by forces he could not fathom, transformed forever and outside his reach.

"Why?" he said plaintively.

Yankelevich glared at Downes, spoke in a clearly angry voice. "I am entitled to an explanation. What is happening here?"

Downes began to stammer. "A-a-a mistake. Y-y-yes..."

Ellie broke in. "You're wasting your time, Mr. Yankelevich. Your time and the time of your backers in Moscow."

"I beg your pardon." Yankelevich blanched and took a backward step, his mouth flattening out into a thin, disapproving line. "What has Moscow to do with this?"

Ellie smothered a smile. "You may inform your people that

they have failed, they have been defeated by Foxman and Company." She swept the room in a swift haughty sense of command. "Defeated by Ellie Foxman, sir. Tell them that. Now, it's time for us to leave," she announced to Downes and Keller.

Downes protested but made no effort to keep Keller from guiding him out of the room.

"Thank you, Mr. Böhle," Ellie said, going after them.

"Everything was correct?" Böhle said.

"Oh, yes, quite correct, thank you."

## chapter
# 46

ANDREI SAT IN THE LOBBY of the hotel until Geis appeared. When Geis entered the elevator, Andrei went after him. Geis got off at the sixth floor, Andrei at the seventh. He located the fire stairs and walked down one flight, went directly to Geis's room. The door was ajar and he entered.

"You were not supposed to contact me," Geis complained at once. "You're risking my cover."

Andrei showed no concern. He sat down and spread his legs comfortably, hands folded across his round belly. "Comrade Browning is nowhere to be found."

"You checked his room?"

"Naturally. Where is he?"

"How would I know? Having a cup of coffee. Buying a Swiss watch. Getting his pipes cleaned. Whatsa difference?"

"The comrade has been ordered to return to Moscow with the diamonds."

Geis was unable to conceal his surprise. "How come?"

"At once."

"Some kind of trouble?"

"I obey orders, not question them. You would do well to do the same."

"Back off, Andrei. I been doing my job for a long time and

there's been no complaints. Stay off my back, okay. Anyway, we're talking about Browning."

"Exactly. Since last night I am looking and cannot find him. All night he was not in his room. All night I was telephoning. Where is he all night?"

"Shacking up with a cute little Swiss cheese, maybe. Don't get your water hot, he'll show."

"You trust him?"

"Trust him? Why shouldn't I trust him?"

"I know he is wanted back in Moscow. I know he received his orders, since I delivered them myself. And suddenly he is out of touch for too long. That is all I know."

"You said he was supposed to take the diamonds to Moscow?"

"They were to go by diplomatic pouch, he was to go by commercial flight."

Geis laughed. "Well, you can bet he ain't carrying all them stones around in his pocket. He must've went after them."

"Where are they?"

"For a while they were held in certain banks, here in Geneva. But then it got time to put them where we could get our hands on them when the time came."

"That was your idea?"

"Well, no. Browning suggested it."

Andrei frowned. "And where is that place?"

"In New York, of course."

Andrei picked up the phone and called the front desk, asked for Browning. He listened and then hung up. "Browning checked out this morning, about four a.m. He has gone after the diamonds."

"Sure he has."

"Without telling you? Without telling me?"

Geis began to grow uneasy. "Just obeying orders is all."

"I think not. The man was too soft, too much the capitalist, too accustomed to Western ways of doing things. I believe he is after the stones for himself."

"Not Browning. All these years he was working on this job. All these years he planned."

"Precisely. He had a long time to plan this betrayal of his

country. When I gave him his orders, he simply accelerated his schedule."

"If you're right . . ."

"I am right. You said the diamonds were in New York? You know the exact location?"

"Bet your ass I do."

"Then it is up to you to get to them first, prevent Browning from stealing what belongs rightfully to the Motherland."

"And after?"

"Once you recover the stones, you will contact the Rezident at the UN and arrange for their return to Moscow. These orders come from the highest levels."

"I'll take care of it. And what about Browning?"

"When you find him," Andrei said matter-of-factly, "kill him."

Later, in his office at the Soviet Embassy, Andrei went over it all in his mind. There could be no doubt, it would all work out according to plan, his plan. Should either Browning or Geis betray his sacred trust to the Motherland, a hard and just punishment would be swiftly meted out.

## chapter
# 47

IN THE HOTEL LOBBY, Downes hesitated. "I have some business to take care of."

"We have a great deal of serious talking to do, Peter," Ellie said.

"Give me fifteen minutes."

"Now," she said. She nodded to Keller, who took hold of Downes's elbow, his grip powerful and painful.

"The lady said now. Let's go."

Hang loose, Downes warned himself. Go along; they had no evidence against him, could prove no criminal act on his part.

"Suit yourself," he said.

In Ellie's suite, Keller put Downes into a chair, seating himself opposite, eyes glittering, an awful expression on his bony face.

It was Ellie who spoke first. "The game is over, Peter. For Browning, for Geis, especially for you, Peter."

Downes's brain pitched and yawed and for a fragmented moment he felt as though he were going to lose control of his sphincter. He braced himself. "I'm sorry, those names you mentioned, who are those people?"

"Stop it!" she commanded. "Understand me, Peter, it's fin-

ished. You're finished. You're going to do some hard time and
that's not something you can handle very well."

"What's going on? What's this all about?"

"A lovely scam," Keller put in, a terrible grin revealing his
clenched teeth. "No telling how far it might have gone, if you
pulled it off. But in this league almost is nothing. Drive Foxman
and Company to the wall, that was the plan, and you very
nearly did it. You could smell the millions, right, Downes?
You figured to come out the other side rich and sassy. Too bad
you came up empty instead. No money. No diamonds. Nothing."

"Face it, Peter," Ellie said. "You never had a chance."

Keller said, "If we didn't get you, Browning and Geis would
have."

"No," Peter said, eyes flashing to Ellie. "You can't believe
I'd do anything to hurt you."

She answered in a low, insistent voice, clearly in command.
"Time's running out. Browning and Geis are on the move, after
the remainder of the sixty million, Peter. You, they left you
behind to take the heat by yourself."

"You're going up, man," Keller reminded him. "Make your
peace with that. How much time you put in, that's still open.
That's up to you."

"Browning," Ellie said, demanding Downes's attention. "He
was the brains. The organization, the money, that was his work.
Geis, he was your connection. He seduced you in the scam,
Peter. Who gave Browning his orders, Peter?"

Downes made an effort to tough it out. "I don't know what
you're talking about."

"Cut your losses while you can," Keller said.

"That's good advice, Peter," Ellie added. "If this isn't turned
around, Foxman and Company will go under. You know that.
Without the sixty million in diamonds I can't cover our debts.
I don't intend to allow that to happen. The New York district
attorney would love to get in on a massive fraud like this. If
you help me, Peter, I may be able to help you."

Downes blinked; there was no compassion in Ellie's face
and he saw Keller as a loaded gun aimed at his heart. In prison
all the faces would be hard, all the hearts without sympathy,
without understanding, no one on his side.

He shuddered. "I don't want to go to jail."

"Browning and Geis," Ellie said. "They're Soviet agents."

Downes reached back. "Where will the diamonds come from?" he had once asked Browning. "From the Soviet Union," was the answer. Downes hadn't wanted to think about that.

"You were a fool," Ellie was saying. "They let you believe you were using me and my uncle while they were using you. Whatever you were promised, you'd never have gotten it."

"They killed more than once," Keller said.

"They murdered my brother. They won't hesitate to murder you. Look at me, Peter, listen to me. I am your last chance. Your only chance."

The last of Downes's strength drained away, the last of his courage. "Oh, my God."

"First Foxman and then the Syndicate. That was the plan, wasn't it?"

Downes put his face in his hands, began to sob. "I'm so afraid, so afraid."

She measured Downes dispassionately and saw him for the weak and indecisive man he was, far out of his element and lost and frightened; how had she ever loved him? The intimacies exchanged, it was unimaginable now. But then she was no longer the same woman, no longer angry and submissive, and resentful of that submissiveness. A fresh surge of confidence, of strength, made her understand that the reins of power were in her hands now, securely held. She was in charge of Foxman and Company, responsible for its welfare and the welfare of its employees and its clients, in charge for the first time of her own destiny. In control of every aspect of her life.

"Downes," she said coldly. "I am your last hope. Without me, you have no one." She gestured and Keller opened the door leading to the adjoining room. Sir John stepped into view, advancing on Downes.

"Act like a man, sir," Sir John said crisply. "You got yourself into this, get yourself out as best you can. Look up, man. Lift your head."

Downes obeyed, his smooth cheeks streaked with tears.

"Meet Sir John Messinger," Ellie said. "He is with us, Peter. The Syndicate is with us. Against you, Peter, all of you. So you see, it is hopeless, it is over."

The sight of the legendary chief of International Minerals and Mines sapped the last of Downes's resistance. Sir John was larger than life and much more terrifying. Downes began to tremble.

"Here it is," Keller said. "Either we get those stones back or you're just another battle casualty in this war."

Downes's eyes remained riveted on Sir John, unable to free himself from that ascetic visage, those unforgiving eyes. In them he saw a bleak, painful future for himself, a future without hope, without friends, and no escape.

As if reading his mind, Sir John spoke again. "No one cares about you, Downes. No one."

"Browning," Downes said to Ellie, looking for support. "Maybe he took them to Russia by now . . ."

Sir John turned to Keller. "Do you think so?"

Keller shook his head. "The stones are no longer in Geneva, haven't been for some time, that much is clear. No, Browning and Geis were here to stand at Downes's back, to make sure he didn't chicken out. Something got in the way. Something changed their minds. Maybe one of them panicked, decided to cut and run. Maybe their bosses back home got cold feet and called them back in. Maybe there's a double cross going down that we don't know about. What I do know is that Browning split and Geis left a few hours after meeting with the KGB Rezident out of the local embassy. They could have sniffed us out, figured it was all going sour. Maybe Browning's trying to save himself, I just don't know."

"Save himself from what?" Ellie said.

"What's your best bet?" Keller said to Downes, who shook his head more in regret than in refusal. "Where are the stones?" Keller persisted.

"I don't know. They never told me."

"Maybe not in so many words," Ellie said. "Maybe you're not consciously aware of it, but you know where they are. Think about it, where did you make the buys?"

"Browning put me onto various dealers. Istanbul, Venice, Cyprus, Marrakesh, all over."

"You had the stones shipped to different Foxman branches?" Ellie said.

"Yes."

She fell silent, running it through her mind. "They've gathered them up in one place," she said, with a great deal of certainty. "Some place where they could get their hands on them, if necessary."

"And it became necessary," Keller said.

"They're in New York," Ellie said flatly.

"And Browning's gone after them," Keller said. "Browning's bank, that's the logical place."

"Sounds reasonable," Sir John put in.

Ellie gave it some consideration. "No. Browning isn't the type to put himself unnecessarily at risk. He wouldn't want the evidence too close. A safe spot and accessible to him." She broke off and looked around. "Who else was involved, Peter?"

"Nobody. Just the three of us."

"Geis," she said after a moment. "It has to be Geis."

Keller agreed. "Something set Browning off and he's gone after the cache."

"And this Geis after him?" Sir John said.

"Exactly," Ellie answered.

"But the stones could be anywhere," Sir John said. "New York is an extremely large city."

"There can be only one place," Ellie said. "Secure and easily accessible. Geis's shop on Forty-seventh Street. Every merchant on the street has a safe, a substantial box that would hold all those stones."

Keller said, "That's it. But Browning's long gone. We'll never catch up with him."

"Perhaps I can help," Sir John said. He went to the telephone and made a call. "Willy," he said. "John Messinger here. . . . Quite well, old boy. . . . Glad to hear it. Willy, I have a bit of a problem. I'm in Geneva with some young friends of mine and they need a fast flight to New York. Can you arrange it? . . . Oh, that's good! Ever grateful, old man." He hung up. "A plane's waiting at the airport to take you to Paris. At Orly they'll hold the Concorde for you."

"Let's go," Keller said.

"Without me," Ellie said. "I've got some business to wind up."

"As do I," Sir John said. "Must be back in London today.

Stay in touch, Keller. This is all quite interesting."

"What about me?" Downes said nervously.

"You," Keller answered. "You go where I go."

## chapter
# 48

THEY WERE ONLY A FEW MINUTES out of New York when Downes said what had been on his mind all along.

"What's going to happen to me?"

Keller felt neither pity nor sympathy. Downes had been brought down by an ambition that far exceeded his talent, his imagination and his courage.

"Depends," he answered absently.

"Ellie won't let them put me away. She won't press charges, you'll see."

Keller gazed out of the window. Manhattan, its night lights glittering, passing below, a magical spread at this distance.

"We land in a few minutes."

The Concorde put down at Kennedy and a company limousine was waiting. Grand Central Parkway was alive with outgoing traffic, the usual flow of commuters heading for home. Inbound, there were no delays.

"Where are you taking me?" Downes said.

"Geis's store."

"He'll be gone by now." Downes knew that his only chance lay in recovering the diamonds. But they were easy to transport, weighing no more than forty pounds, easy to conceal, easy to ship.

"We made up a lot of time on Geis."

The limousine rolled along Forty-seventh Street and coasted to a stop across the street from Geis's shop. Keller glanced up and down the street. A tall man with hunched shoulders hurried toward Fifth Avenue. A pair of Hasidim in dark suits and tieless white shirts moved in the opposite direction, in animated conversation, beards bobbing, hands waving. They disappeared into the subway kiosk.

"They give you something for me at the office?" he said to the driver.

Without a word, the man passed over a brown paper bag. Keller brought out a .38-caliber police special and a handful of ammunition. He loaded the cylinder, six shots.

Downes, eyes on the weapon, drew back. "You want me to go in there with you?"

A vision of Ned Creer flashed up onto the screen of Keller's mind, the remembered volley of gunfire that had greeted them years ago. That was never going to happen again; the job was his, the responsibility was his alone. All the risks were his.

Keller climbed out of the limousine. "Stay in the car," he said.

Relief in his voice, Downes slumped back. "Whatever you say."

Keller turned away and crossed the street. The interior of the store was dark, apparently deserted. A brief flicker of light caught his eye. Someone was in the back room, using a flashlight sparingly. Keller tried the door; it was locked.

He moved quickly to the main entrance of the building. The heavy brass and glass doors were unlocked. A desk in front of the elevator bank should have been attended by a security man; it was deserted. A door in the opposite wall had Geis's name on it.

Keller looked inside. The shop was long and narrow, barely illuminated by light from the streetlamp out front. To his right, a display case. To his left, the watchmaker's workbench and beyond that the back room. Another flash of light froze Keller in place. A few seconds and the light went out. Whoever was in there knew his way around. Browning? Not likely; the banker had too much of a start. Geis, then. A good catch, packed solid with vital information, if he could be made to talk.

Keller glanced back over his shoulder. The damned security man, where was he? Having a smoke in the john. Or grabbing a drink on the fire stairs. Maybe nodding off in an empty office. There was no time to look for him. Keller made up his mind.

He raised his right leg and struck with as much force as he could muster. The glass door panel exploded noisily, shards splintering all over the floor. Keller charged through the gaping space, bent low, gun ready.

In the darkness, Keller's feet landed on some glass and he went skidding, falling heavily on his back. He heard an oath from the back room and then a shot rang out. And another. He rolled to his right, feeling his way, seeking cover. He heard footsteps.

"That you, Geis? Keller here. Give it up. It all ends here."

In answer, a shot went whirring overhead. Keller fired at the flash. Another shot came his way and this time Keller braced his gun hand before squeezing off three well-spaced rounds. A soft grunt followed and the sound of something metallic hitting the floor. And finally a body falling over.

Keller made his way to the wall, feeling for a light switch. A bulb went on and he stepped into the back room. Harry Geis lay on his back, air bubbling out of the bloody mess that used to be his chest. Keller knelt at his side.

"It's over, Geis. Where are the stones?"

Geis coughed. "Bastard . . . Browning . . . he got here first."

"Tell me where he went, Geis. He cut you out, I'll get him for you." Another cough, a spasm, and Geis was dead. Keller looked around. The safe was ajar and, except for some odd pieces of jewelry, it was empty. He had expected nothing more. Holding the .38 at his side, he went back outside to where Downes and the driver were waiting in the limousine.

"Anything I can do for you, sir?" the driver said.

"Got a phone in there?"

"Yes, sir."

"Call IMM headquarters. Tell 'em there's been a shooting. Geis is dead. The diamonds are gone. Tell 'em to send some people along to clean up the mess I made. Tell 'em I'm gonna call the cops from the store phone. Can you get that right?"

"I think so."

"Good. Be the only thing that went right here tonight."

*chapter*
# 49

THREE DAYS LATER, Ellie flew Swissair out of Geneva, nonstop for Kennedy. As they passed over the English Channel the captain announced they would be putting down at Heathrow Airport.

"Only a brief stop, ladies and gentlemen," he intoned in that dispassionate voice all commercial pilots affect. "There is no problem with the aircraft but some administrative questions have to be resolved. As soon as that is settled, we'll be on our way."

The plane came to a stop at the terminal and moments later Ellie spotted her luggage being transported toward the unloading dock.

"My bags," she protested to a stewardess, "they've taken them off."

"Miss Foxman, is it? Yes. Will you follow me, please?"

Outside the first-class exit door, a man with the hauteur of a Coldstream Guard presented himself.

"Miss Foxman." He inclined his head slightly. "My name is McKinley Waugh. I'm to be your escort, miss."

"I'm not going anywhere. Except to New York. Aboard this flight. Are you the one responsible for removing my luggage from the plane?"

"I did make the arrangements."

"Well, you can just unmake them. Put my bags back aboard at once."

"I can't do that, miss."

"Why not?"

"Sir John would disapprove."

"What's he got to do with this?"

"Everything, miss. Sir John wishes to speak with you. I have a car waiting."

Sir John greeted her formally, an impenetrable mask drawn down over his eyes. "So good of you to see me," he said, as if she'd been given a choice. "I've reserved rooms for you at Claridge's. Or elsewhere, if you prefer. If you'd like to attend the theater this evening one of my people will make the arrangements. Whatever your taste."

She decided to go along with the game. "Claridge's will be fine."

"Excellent." He seated himself behind his desk. "By now you know what has transpired?"

"Harry Geis, you mean. Yes."

Sir John worked himself deeper into his chair, his expression aloof. "General belief to the contrary, my people avoid violence whenever possible. This unfortunate incident—if Keller killed, it was because his own life was at stake. Keller defended himself, I want to make that clear."

"Knowing Keller, I have no doubt about it."

He sniffed dryly, marking the subject closed. "Unhappily, Keller arrived too late at Geis's shop to retrieve the diamonds."

"Yes, that news reached me, too."

"Have you thought about how you're going to handle the problem?"

"I've thought about very little else since. Some assets remain—a comparatively small inventory, the New York factory and the one in Puerto Rico and the hotel shops. During these last few days in Europe, I've been negotiating for the sale of the shops and I may have a buyer for the Puerto Rican operation. It's all simply a stopgap, of course."

"I agree."

"Seems to me I've been chosen to oversee the dismantling of Maurice Foxman's empire, not exactly what I hoped for.

Bankruptcy is inevitable, the only way to buy enough time. If I ever can do so, I intend to pay off the remainder of the debt. But for now, it's goodbye to Foxman and Company."

"I should prefer otherwise." He looked at her with a long, grieved expression. "Your uncle, others in the trade, have seen me as an evil presence. A rogue Jew, they say. They repeat false tales about me, turning into an anti-Semite. They say I dealt with the Nazis for personal gain."

"And did you?"

"Oh, yes, I was in contact with certain high-ranking Germans. Goebbels, to be exact. What a loathsome creature he was; his brilliance warped by hatred. Vicious and greedy and it was that greed that I was able to exploit. I traded diamonds out of the company vaults in return for safe passage for Jews to freedom. All told I was able to win the release of eleven thousand four hundred and twenty-eight people. Not nearly enough."

"I've never heard anyone speak of . . ."

"No one knew. Publicity was anathema to Goebbels. Can you imagine, that Jew-hating murderer *selling* Jews for profit! One word in the press and he would have canceled the deal."

"I wish my uncle had known about this."

"I told no one. Only one person worked closely with me on this, a man named Koenigsburg, and he will go to his grave without speaking of such matters. It had to be done, it was done. That's all there was to it."

"The more I see of you, Sir John, the more you surprise me. The more I appreciate you."

"No more than I appreciate you, my dear. And because I do appreciate you so much, I would like you to remain active in the diamond trade."

"When all this is settled, I should be able to find a job somewhere."

"Not what I had in mind. I would prefer your company to continue as if your uncle were still alive."

"But Maurice is dead and the company will soon join him, I'm afraid."

Sir John stood up and Ellie, taking it as a gesture of dismissal, did likewise. "Sit down, please," he said. "As you know, there has been no public announcement of the recent unpleasantness perpetrated by Downes, Geis and Browning. At least not yet."

"I wondered about that. A sixty-million-dollar sting and not a word in the papers or on TV. At least four men are dead and nobody's made the connection. Surely some elements of the media function outside of IMM influence?"

For the first time, he smiled. "So many companies go into making up IMM. So much money is spent on advertising and publicity. Our connections are vast, our interests interrelated. Executives are in constant communication. Favors are asked for and granted, debts incurred. At IMM, we try to create a climate favorable to ourselves. We would rather men owe us than we owe them. I called in a few chits, that's all. Yet that all may change."

"I'm impressed."

"Consider this: should it become widely known that such a sting could be effectively pursued, it would give other unsavory types inspiration. None of us want that."

"What about Moscow? Won't they come up with another Geis one day, another Browning, put the whole sordid business into motion again?"

"Quite possible. But not in the near future. The Kremlin has no desire to destroy the market; that would not be in their own self-interest. The Russian can be daring when he perceives opportunity with an attendant low risk factor. But he is not self-destructive, I assure you.

"Were this affair to come to public attention, the Soviets would lose many of their friends and supporters. Murder, fraud, deceptive business practices; oh, no, the Russian wants none of that known, despite the fact that all of us know it. Odd. Even more, such information if it became the stuff of headlines could cause a panic and turn people away from diamonds, send prices downward. Moscow wants to avoid that, too."

"So the Russians get off scot-free."

"No, the Russians will not get off scot-free. And, neither will IMM. The Russians must be taught a lesson. Yet, so must the customers of IMM. The cornerstone of IMM policy has always been that on certain occasions a money loss is necessary in order to maintain the long-range general welfare.

"I shall make it known to the Russians that IMM is willing

to publicize this whole affair. That we shall drag their name through the mud; accuse them of capitalistic venality and international thuggery. Such an announcement would make any of our traditional diamond contacts thoroughly convinced of our determination to stop their trading with the Russians.

"Operation Flawless was not an attempt to make money from selling diamonds; it was a way of gaining access to our system of distribution. The Russians have no internal mechanism for such capitalistic merchandising. And no way of stepping into the chaos if their continual flooding of diamond markets were to destroy IMM. Now that Operation Flawless is destroyed, the Russians will continue their thievery, but at a volume that keeps the traditional system intact, and IMM's weapons holstered, at least part way. Some people will always be willing to do business with the devil, Miss Foxman. Many more will not. No dealer of merit and substance would, upon reflection choose to depend on the Russians. And I assure you, if he did, the wrath of IMM would inconvenience him mightily.

"It is nice irony, don't you think, that for the Russians to continue their thievery, they must keep intact the integrity of the capitalist distribution and pricing structure.

"Miss Foxman, we need stability in the market. We need to reinforce the old traditions of integrity and belief in controlled market conditions. I say with deep personal sadness that these are the standards in which Maurice Foxman believed and by which he was judged, by most everyone except me. As much as he needed IMM's best sights, IMM needed and still needs his kind of integrity—requires his kind of example in the circle of his peers.

"Miss Foxman, the mantle of Maurice Foxman has fallen on your shoulders. And I for one am happy that it has. IMM needs you to keep his spirit alive, to maintain the old virtues among the circle of diamond merchants whose adherence to tradition and market coherence makes the life of IMM endure."

He brought a folded piece of paper out of his pocket, offered it to Ellie.

"What is this?"

"A bank draft in the full amount of the debts incurred by Mr. Downes during his tenure with Foxman and Company. It is neither in my interests nor in the interests of the industry to see Maurice Foxman's company fail. Integrity and honor are too hard to come by. This will buy the time you need to rejuvenate the firm, to bring it back to its once lofty status."

"This is for fifty-five million dollars!"

"It should cover all immediate eventualities."

Sir John had saved her fortune; insured her dignity, and, undoubtedly caused the humiliation and death of her uncle. It was a concatenation of emotions, which left her stunned, half victim of the past, half chevalier of the future.

Tears filled her eyes and Sir John took a backward step, one hand raised. "Please, Miss Foxman, none of that. Consider this as an investment on my part to maintain the equilibrium of our industry. I have made such investments in the past, when necessary." He cleared his throat. "We shall all be better off for having you with us."

"It's too bad Maurice can't be here to see this."

"I misjudged your uncle and I regret that. Hardly my first mistake and not likely to be my last," he said as he guided her to the door. "Ah, one more thing—I have issued instructions that you be granted a regular manufacturer's sight of your own, that you receive preferred treatment. Whatever the size of your purchases, I assure you the stones will be of the finest quality."

He shook her hand, releasing it quickly. "How kind of you to drop in and talk, Miss Foxman."

*chapter*
## 50

THE FLIGHT BACK to New York seemed endless, no sense of progress being made. For Ellie, it was a time of confusion about the past and considerable trepidation about the future. A jumble of emotions and clashing memories competed for her attention and she began to wonder if she would ever be able to clear them away, attend fully to the present.

Why no surge of elation? No profound joy? Where was the visceral excitement that went with winning? With getting everything you ever wanted?

The first woman to be granted a sight.

President of her own company.

She scarcely dwelt on her victories. She thought ahead. The Bombay connection would have to be reinstituted and another factory might be in order. Perhaps in Tel Aviv. Or Amsterdam. Operations across the board would have to be expanded. With a steady supply of excellent product coming from the Syndicate, the sales force would have to be enlarged. And the shops; why limit them to hotels? New ones could be placed in strategic locations around the United States for starters. The most prestigious department stores, for example: Bergdorf's, Neiman's, Bloomie's, Sakowitz—in the grandest shopping malls.

The New York operation would have to be brought up to

date. The jewelry design section refined, manufacturing increased, but always maintaining quality. Nothing stood between her and the fulfillment of her wildest fantasies. Thanks to Maurice, thanks to Sir John, whatever she wanted was within reach.

Why then this lingering melancholy, this vague sense of loss?

Bereavement over the death of her brother and her uncle, yes. And the humiliation and imprisonment of Peter Downes. How naïve she had been, how self-righteous, how indulgent. How easily she had separated the world into good and evil, how readily she had located herself on the side of the angels. She had been wrong about Maurice, wrong about her father, equally wrong about Peter. Had she ever loved him? Or had he been just one more in a long line of beautiful men whom she had used and who had used her, in the end giving so very little to each other? No easy answer offered itself, none ever would, she decided. Of one thing she was convinced, there was no room in her life anymore for men like Peter Downes; she wanted more than he had to give, was entitled to more, would demand more.

Coming out of customs at Kennedy, she searched for a familiar face and saw nobody she knew. Disappointment took hold. Why wasn't David here to meet her? Or Mattie? Someone from the office to escort her into town? After all, she was the president of the company, returning with great good news.

As she headed for the taxi stand she heard her name called in a low, distinctive voice. Keller! All this time she had managed to exclude him from her thoughts, to distance herself from him, to keep her emotions cool and objective. She came around with a toss of her head, aware of the excitement that suffused her.

He stood ten feet away without moving. The slight list to port, the compact frame, the vaguely sardonic turn of mouth.

"Looking good," he said.

She resisted the urge to rush at him, to fling her arms around him, to kiss him lovingly. She held her position, faintly annoyed, as if by appearing he had usurped some personal right inherently her own.

"What are you doing here, Keller?"

"I've got my car." He picked up her bags. "Let's go."

"You failed," she said.

"At what?"

"To get the diamonds back."

"They're far beyond my reach."

His smile was slow, confident; smug, she thought.

"I'll take you back to your apartment. You'll want to clean up, rest, get ready."

"Wipe that smile off your face."

"I thought we could have dinner at Orsini's and afterward I have tickets for Avery Fisher Hall."

"Are you giving me orders, Keller, or asking me out?" There was a dancing light in his pale eyes she'd never before noticed and a softness at the corners of his mouth. "Damnit, Keller, I don't even know your first name."

"Joseph. Joseph P., for Patrick," he said with a characteristic shrug. "Okay with you?"

"I'll stick with Keller."

"Fair enough." He hesitated, then kissed her lightly on the lips, lightly but at length and with considerable feeling.

"You kiss nice, Keller."

"So do you."

"I should've known. After all, you warned me you were a romantic." Laughing, she took his arm and allowed him to lead her to the gray Rabbit for the slow drive home. No need to hurry, there was time now for everything.

# Bestselling Books for Today's Reader

___ **EIGHT MILLION WAYS TO DIE**     08090-X/$2.95
Lawrence Block
___ **LIVE FOR LOVE**     07385-7/$3.95
Shana Carrol
___ **THE DAY THEY STOLE THE QUEEN MARY**     07640-6/$3.50
Terence Hughes
___ **STRANGERS BY DAY**     06402-5/$3.50
Vicki Malone
___ **TWICE LOVED**     07622-8/$3.50
LaVyrle Spencer
___ **DOWN AMONG THE DEAD MEN**     07638-4/$3.50
Michael Hartland
___ **SEA STAR**     07729-1/$3.95
Pamela Jekel
___ **BRASS KNUCKLES**     07730-5/$3.50
Ben Mochan
___ **BRIDE OF THE WIND**     07874-3/$3.95
Stephanie Blake
___ **THE THESEUS CODE**     07744-5/$3.50
Marc Hammond

Prices may be slightly higher in Canada.

---

*Available at your local bookstore or return this form to:*

 **JOVE**
*Book Mailing Service*
*P.O. Box 690, Rockville Centre, NY 11571*

Please send me the titles checked above. I enclose _____ Include 75¢ for postage and handling if one book is ordered; 25¢ per book for two or more not to exceed $1.75. California, Illinois, New York and Tennessee residents please add sales tax.

NAME_____

ADDRESS_____

CITY_____STATE/ZIP_____

(allow six weeks for delivery)             **SK23**

# Bestselling Books
# from Berkley